THE SPRING OF VALOR

**Center Point
Large Print**

**This Large Print Book carries the
Seal of Approval of N.A.V.H.**

THE SPRING OF VALOR

An Historical Story

FRED· GROVE

CENTER POINT LARGE PRINT
THORNDIKE, MAINE

This Center Point Large Print edition is
published in the year 2011 by arrangement with
Golden West Literary Agency.

The text of this Large Print edition is unabridged.
In other aspects, this book may vary
from the original edition.
Printed in the United States of America.
Set in 16-point Times New Roman type.

ISBN: 978-1-60285-942-5

Library of Congress Cataloging-in-Publication Data

Grove, Fred.
  The spring of valor / Fred Grove.
    p. cm.
  ISBN 978-1-60285-942-5 (library binding : alk. paper)
  1. Missouri—History—Civil War, 1861–1865—Fiction.
    2. Large type books. I. Title.
  PS3557.R7S67 2010
  813′.54—dc22
                                              2010029541

THE SPRING OF VALOR

Chapter One

Missouri, 1860

Daniel Wade heard the first muffled *r-r-rump* of drumbeats across the still October afternoon as he stopped the wagon on the long, wooded slope north of town. The thumping faded, ceased altogether, and abruptly struck up again, an intrusion upon the serene scene of Foley's Prairie spread out beyond the flicking ears of his brown mules, Zeke and Babe.

Down there, among the tall ranks of nodding scarlet maples, neat frame houses slumbered behind white-washed palings, their cool porches laced with morning-glories and honeysuckle vine. But it was the rust-colored road, serpentine, winding southward toward the powerful Missouri River, miles away, that held his eye. Always it seemed to point and beckon to far-yonder places he was going to see someday.

He drove ahead, the empty wagon bed chattering over the ruts, and presently passed along a broad, shaded street. By this time he had located the source of the drumming as coming from the east side of town.

In the vicinity of Rookwood's General Store, he

wound around wagons and buggies, and tied his mules, noting families in from Coon Creek and his own Indian Mound district. A little later, having called at the post office for his father's copy of the out-of-town weekly *Democrat* and filled a list of frugal supplies at Rookwood's, he was idling beside his wagon when he heard the choppy drum again.

Its rolling *vroom, vroom* rising, then falling, relayed a holiday mood, like the 4th of July, or the olden days his father often recalled, before the Mexican War, when Missouri had the Militia Law and all able-bodied men between eighteen and forty-five drilled in companies and there were good times at the musters.

Marching figures in uneven fours entered the dusty street and an erect, stiff-legged shape shouted—"Com-pan-nay left . . . harch!"—louder than necessary, it seemed to Daniel, and the marchers turned, clumsily bumping. They were determined, nevertheless. "Hup-hup." Some had old rifles; some carried staves.

"Don't keep step any better'n last time," Daniel heard a quavery voice remark.

Now, behind the clomping company, he saw two riders following—a young man and a young woman—and he recognized the trim, booted figure of Justin Vandiver. He did not know the girl in the dark green riding habit. The broad brim of her feathered hat shadowed her face, yet revealed enough of her pale features to stir his memory without conclusion.

At another overly harsh command he turned his attention again to the marchers. Twice a month, on Saturday afternoon, the local Home Guard drilled to the enthusiastic drubbing of a boy drummer and the stentorian commands of Stark Chittenden Hooper, who alone had the makings of a complete uniform: black campaign hat, dark blue trousers, and marching blouse. Generous coils of gold braid swirled down each sleeve. A body could see that he was kind of proud of his get-up and, some said, of himself.

It was customary at the drill's climax for Hooper—elected drillmaster, it was said, because he had the strongest lungs and had picked up a scattering of military rudiments and because no one else coveted the post—to march his twenty-odd lads down Main Street and dismiss them in front of Rookwood's store. This was the afternoon's highlight. And thus they moved now, toward the invariable audience of farm families, townsmen, giggling girls who kept glancing and not glancing at the young citizen soldiers, and a sprinkling of ancient veterans who liked to drop droll observations on the company's awkwardness.

Precisely in front of the store, Hooper stiffened and shouted—"Fours left . . . harch!"—and the eager company, bumping, tramping, brogans lifted high, jostled into a ragged line. "Halt! Order arms!"

That executed, Hooper called for the first sergeant to dismiss the company.

Jesse Nance, shy and raw-boned, stepped forward, his rifle at a self-conscious droop. A girl tittered; her father glared her to silence. Nance halted, flustered before the gawking crowd. He started to shift the rifle to his left shoulder in order to salute Hooper with his right hand, thought better of it, and hesitated. The girl tittered again.

A curl of intolerance squeezed into Hooper's lips.

Nance's face flooded a dismayed crimson. He returned the weapon in haste to his right shoulder and brought his left hand to the hammer and away. Hooper's arm, elbow stiff, snapped up and down. Nance about-faced and sheepishly dismissed his comrades, his strained voice almost inaudible.

After the company broke up, Hooper strolled toward the store. His carriage remained erect. He waved to Justin Vandiver and his pretty companion, paused on the other side of the street. He nodded here and there and touched the brim of his new hat to the women and girls.

Daniel reckoned Stark Hooper knew most everybody in the county. Whenever he met a newcomer, it was said, he put down the man's name in a little black notebook, so he could speak it out first thing when they met again. Such horse sense was to be expected of the only young man from Foley's Prairie, and some distance around, to attend the state university at Columbia. That distinction alone set him apart. It didn't matter so much that he had returned home several months later—expelled, folks said—displaying worldly manners and dandyish clothes. Set to reading law in the office of his father, the judge, he would enter Missouri politics within a few years.

"Wisht you wouldn't holler so blamed loud, Stark," a farmer piped. "Scares my mules."

Laughter followed, and Hooper sent back his satisfaction, showing white, even teeth. "Now that makes me feel better," he said in mock gravity. "For a while there I was afraid the boys couldn't hear me." He was strolling on, nodding left and right, overlooking no one.

Daniel sensed what was coming when he saw Hooper slow step and settle his inquiry on him, from head to foot. "We can still use another good man, Daniel."

"No war yet, is there?" Daniel said, feeling the sting of heat on his face. Why'd Hooper have to ask him again in front of folks? Why did Hooper, without actually saying as much, make it seem just a mite peculiar that he didn't join? Furthermore, had Hooper organized the Union

11

company to defend the county in event of trouble, or was it to set himself up in the public's eye? Fact was, he had first tried to form a local club of Republican Wide-Awakes, now going strong down river in St. Louis among the Dutch, but Foley's Prairie favored Stephen A. Douglas, the Little Giant. That was plain. Too, Daniel couldn't see just what there was to guard against yet.

"Well, if war comes and we're faced with a common foe, I say we all want to be prepared," Stark Hooper replied, laying a patriotic stress on the words that brought nods and "you betchas" from the old men humped on the store's benches and boxes.

With an all but imperceptible motion, he flicked lint from his left sleeve and stepped on, carrying an air of able importance, at ease. He was squarely built, blue-eyed, several years older than Daniel. A full, tawny mustache adorned his upper lip; the clipped hedge of his goatee was trimmed to a stylish point.

"Mark my words, folks," his assured voice resumed near the porch. "If Lincoln's elected, we'll see a power of change in Missouri."

To Daniel's thinking a mighty general statement, calculated not to ruffle local political fur.

" 'Cept Abe Lincoln won't carry Miz-zoo-ree," a querulous voice replied. "Not by a damn' sight."

Hooper, skirting a direct stand, said: "Be a

12

horse race, Uncle John. You betcha. Douglas is strong. So is Bell. I don't know about Breckenridge."

Daniel lost interest. He heard the same querying conversation at home from his father, a staunch Jacksonian Democrat, heard it over and over, and from the neighbors, and there was little else in the newspapers.

Around him the families were starting home. The backing and hawing and the calling of farewells made a pleasant mingling of sounds. Beyond, he could see the two riders stopped beside the buggy of Judge Hooper. In no hurry to go, Daniel wondered how many Saturdays had passed since his father had come to town. More, he realized, than he could remember.

A feeling grew in him after a bit. The commotion of wagons and teams was slacking. Neighbors were staring behind him, their expressions watchful, waiting. He half turned, thinking of his mules, and drew slowly still.

Just beyond stood a knot of Coon Creekers. In front, Andy Green, short-necked, stout as a keg. Beside him towered Tim Forehand, Coon Creek's spitter—champion everything. Green's round, friendly face, a warm spark among these dark scowls, yielded an uneasy protest when Forehand, hands on hips, blurted: "Well, perfessor. You Injun Mound boys still afraid to join up?"

"Didn't Jesse Nance?" Daniel said.

13

"Him, sure. But you . . . you afraid?"

"I don't hear any guns going off around here."

Andy Green's placating voice thrust between them, meant for Forehand: "I'd say Dan don't have much time to march, way he works. And hirin' out when he can."

Forehand wasn't swayed. "I's still askin'," he said.

A wildness flew up within Daniel. He stood his ground, conscious of all voices shutting down on the porch and all movement ceasing in the street.

"I'll decide for myself," Daniel told him.

"If you ain't for us Union boys, you're against us," Forehand said, and made a stir of going forward.

Daniel, stiff, waiting, wasn't expecting Andy Green to shrug it off and say—"Come on, Tim."— and throw an arm around Forehand's shoulders. He did so in one smooth motion, and, when Forehand balked just enough for the crowd's benefit, it seemed, Green locked his arm tighter and turned Forehand toward the tavern across the street.

Several grudging steps and suddenly Forehand whirled to glare at Daniel, as if daring him to follow. Green got him headed around again. It all made Forehand look very dangerous, yet amenable to persuasion and reason.

Their movements away tugged on the other Coon Creek boys. One followed, one more, until all were trailing after. Voices on the porch resumed, a disappointment in their tone. Drivers sent teams jangling down the street. The two riders went off rapidly.

Daniel's rankling bit as he untied and climbed to the seat and backed out his team. Although a rivalry had existed for years between the two districts, it had little to do with the fact that a majority of Coon Creek's families were Northerners; that Southern people, like Daniel's, prevailed in numbers around Indian Mound. No, he thought, loyalty to the Union wasn't the cause. Rather, he was merely one of the few whom Tim Forehand hadn't bullied into a brawl to be stomped and beaten.

He drove slowly homeward through the cool afternoon. Half an hour later he saw the vast home of Major Vandiver looming past the end of the lane, sheltered by giant maples and sycamores and elms. The gabled windows put Daniel in mind of veiled green eyes, a hint of secrecy behind them as they gazed out on a common world of toil and sweat, ignorance and suffering. He'd never been inside. Now that would be something!

For a space he let his imagination contemplate a dazzling scene of rich carpets, tapestries, numerous paintings, soft chairs, delicately carved divans, glittering silver pieces, and bowing darkies. The great house's seclusion enhanced its distant impression of elegance and dignity, totally lacking in the few large country homes that Daniel had seen. At least he preferred to think so, because the Vandivers were held in respectful esteem.

The major, a come-here Tennessean of a dozen years ago, had served with distinction in the war with Mexico. He looked like a soldier, standing some six feet, four inches, and his beard hung like a snowdrift down his broad chest. It was characteristic of the Vandivers that they did not lord themselves above their less fortunate neighbors. Breeding, manners, looks, education, generosity—these gifts seemed inherent to them and not to be abused. They had yet to engage in cuss-outs over loose hogs and stray cows, disputed property lines and stud fees, although the major was said to have killed a man in a duel at Franklin, Tennessee.

Daniel left behind the majestic house and the cavernous wooden barn and the scatter of neat outbuildings, and was about two miles beyond when he saw the dust of two riders on the road. They halted and appeared to be waiting for him. Nearer, he saw Justin Vandiver wave, and he waved back. Meantime, the pale, even features of the girl, growing more distinct, kept striking through to him; in a rush he recognized her. He could only stare in surprised silence.

"Don't you know her?" Vandiver said, his

smile amused as Daniel reined up. Vandiver shook hands.

"I remember Miss Laurel," Daniel said, and took off his hat. "She looks mighty fine."

Vandiver leaned back in protest. "Don't say that. You'll spoil her even more than they did in Saint Louis, if that's possible."

"A most ungallant remark, Brother. And I remember Daniel Wade. I knew him the moment he spoke up back there in town." Looking squarely at Daniel, she said: "I'm glad you showed spine. They had no right to force you before a crowd."

Her voice! *Why*, Daniel thought, *it didn't sound like Foley's Prairie a-tall.* It was cultivated and light, warm and musical to the ear. He said: "That's not the end of it," and saw their expressions change.

The moment passed quickly. "We're in somewhat of a quandary, Daniel," Vandiver said. "I thought I remembered some persimmon trees nearby. Somehow I can't seem to find them."

"What he doesn't want to admit," his sister interposed, "is that he's lost this close to home."

"Believe you missed them about a mile back," Daniel said. "There's a grove on the turn-off to Swink's Spring. It's right on my way. I'll show you."

"I trust this will not delay you," Vandiver said. His clean-shaven face had a questioning look, unmistakably sincere. His features, like his sister's, were well formed but not so finely shaped, and his eyes were a deep blue. He had a horseman's leanness, a quickness. But Daniel's strongest impression was of an enveloping earnestness flowing from Justin Vandiver, of a person touched by humanity and selflessness, while blind that he possessed such power.

"No trouble," Daniel said.

"My father says there is no more obliging family in the county than yours."

Daniel made an uncertain movement of his hand and slapped the reins over the mules' rumps, thinking a sad truth. Why his father had never accumulated much. What he did not give away, he let his neighbors borrow, and of what he did not lend, there was scant left sometimes. Frequently his giving bordered on the foolish—a sudden, unthinking notion, as a poor man might who wished to make himself seem bigger than he was to his neighbors or ever would be. Thinking that, Daniel felt a stab of shame. All said, there was no denying his father's honesty and sincere intent to help others; he just gave too much.

They moved briskly along the road, the blooded Vandiver horses head tossing, bit fighting, eager to run. Daniel guessed Miss Laurel's habit to be velvet. He could call to mind nothing of comparable elegance, unless it was

18

silk, which obviously it wasn't. Her jacket came in at the smallest waist he had ever seen, and her skirt fell in voluminous folds over her mount's shining flanks. As she and Justin rode in advance of the wagon, bits of their bantering remarks drifted back to Daniel. Having no brothers or sisters, he found the teasing a new experience. He envied them a little, and was glad they rode ahead. Otherwise, he'd be staring at her.

When a low, wooded ridge humped beyond a rail fence, Daniel called and pointed: "Over yonder's the grove!" The Vandivers turned their horses, halting, and Daniel flapped the reins to continue on his way. He wasn't expecting Miss Laurel's invitation.

"Won't you come with us? I declare I don't believe Justin knows a persimmon from a crab apple."

An old habit jogged him. He eyed the slipping sun and thought of the chores awaiting him.

Vandiver added his cheerful invitation. "We can't tarry long either, Daniel."

Daniel was studying the ridge. "It is down a piece. Reckon I'd better show you." He stepped down and tied the mules to a tree off the road, expecting to see the Vandivers preparing to jump their splendid horses over the fence. Instead, they were tying up to the rails. An eddy of feeling warmed him. They were going to walk when they could as well ride.

Miss Laurel went to the fence and paused, glancing back. Her brother, smiling faintly, pretended to have discovered a distant object of extraordinary interest.

By then Daniel was there. He stiffened, uncertain, and held out his hand. She took it, her gloved hand astonishingly small in his. He saw now that her large eyes were also a deep blue, and he made a swift correction: no, they were violet. Waves of light brown hair curled beneath her feathered hat.

At the instant of her touch Daniel became conscious of his rough clothing, of his square, knuckled hands and blunt-toed brogans. One thought bolstered him. He had kept up his reading. Maybe he could halfway converse with her.

Her expression reassured him as she sat a moment on the top rail, then swung lightly down.

They started walking across the browning pasture grasses. Vandiver followed more slowly. Daniel tried to think of something suitable to say. Nothing came, not a word. He walked on, his mind stuck. In no time at all they seemed to reach the wooded rise. He turned down it to the laden persimmon trees. Vandiver caught up, and they ate the sweet, plum-like fruit and, like all persimmon eaters, soon had enough. Vandiver strolled away, gazing about at the woods and off toward the pasture. His hurry spoken of at the fence wasn't evident.

"You can surely see how the country rolls from here," Miss Laurel said, delighted.

"You bet," Daniel agreed, but could say no more. What ailed him? He couldn't talk at all the way he wished, in adroit, clever phrases, despite seeing that she was trying to put him at ease.

"I like Foley's Prairie much better than Saint Louis."

With an immense relief, he saw the opening and seized his opportunity. "I reckon you've been going to school there, Miss Laurel?"

"Miss Perdreauville's Young Ladies' Academy," she supplied with an accent that seemed to tinkle in his ears and which he sensed must be exactly correct, although free from any affectation. She displayed a tiny grimace of disregard. "I wish Justin and I had gone to school here. So we'd know more young people. Before we went away, you know, we had tutors."

He marveled a little. He hadn't known about the tutors. That explained further why he had seldom seen her before she grew up. Just glimpses of a small, pale face as the family carriage passed on the road to town. She was, he figured, about seventeen.

"Justin didn't like military school in Kentucky any more than I liked being gone," she went on conversationally. "Still, he made the honor list and was chosen cadet major."

"You got better schooling by going away . . .

21

beats Foley's Prairie," he pointed out, and a thought, which he had bared to no one, escaped him. "Next year," he began, only to amend, ". . . sometime . . . I'm going to the state university. That's the closest place I know where there's all the books in the world a body would want to read." Thus he had hoped last year and thus probably he would hope again next year, and the next, and on, until he became another illiterate Tim Forehand almost, too ashamed to go because of his age. His words flailed back. Suddenly he wished to recall them, as if they had a boastful ring.

"I hope you can go," he heard her reply, sounding pleased, he thought, and perhaps impressed. "As for books, we have a library at home . . . a fairly large one. You're welcome to read anything in it you'd like. Even"—a jesting smile shaped in one corner of her pretty mouth— "UNCLE TOM'S CABIN."

He questioned her face while his heart pumped faster. Did she mean that? Only sons and daughters of slave owners mixed with the young people of other slaveholders. An exception was Stark Hooper, whose father was a man of public standing, a somebody, a judge.

"I've read it," he said. "Can't see how it fits us much around here. Guess New Englanders think it does, however. We don't have slave gangs. We don't make a business of selling slaves down the river. I've never seen one whipped."

"Yet slave auctions *are* held in Saint Louis," she said, frowning. "I've seen the place. It's at the east door of the courthouse. Buyers ship downriver to Memphis and on to Louisiana. Justin's seen whole gangs of darkies, handcuffed together, shuffling through the streets." As if the drift of their conversation displeased her, she sat on a log and spread her skirts.

There was ample room beside her, and perhaps he read an invitation to sit, he wasn't sure, but he continued to stand. He gripped his hat; he couldn't remember removing it.

"Mister Wade," she said, "do you like poetry? . . . Keats? Yes?"

Something within him fluttered up, released. He heard himself saying, " 'A thing of beauty is a joy forever,' " and, a sudden excitement suffusing her face, she exclaimed: "Why, that's from 'Endymion' . . . 'It's loveliness increases.' " As she paused, he led on: " 'It will never pass into nothingness.' "

And then, together, they said: ". . . 'but still will keep a bower quiet for us . . . and a sleep full of sweet dreams . . . and health . . . and quiet breathing. . . .' "

They ceased in unison, their gazes meeting. She clapped her hands in the delight of discovery, and a powerful sensation spread all

23

through him. A question stood in her eyes.

"That's the only part I remember," he admitted.

"You recited it well, and you must read *all* of Keats," she insisted. "I've a volume of his work at home. You're welcome. . . ."

Justin Vandiver returned at that moment, bringing Daniel to realize the afternoon was fleeing in runaway strides.

He was the first to start back. By no means would he impose himself on their pleasant company. Already he could feel a late chill taking over the dull prairie. Walking, listening to their entertaining banter, he kept silent and, coming to the fence, held up so that Vandiver assisted his sister.

In moments they were mounted. They called out thanks to him again and waved as their restless, long-limbed mounts, copper coats shining, took them swiftly down the road.

Daniel, driving on, followed them in thought long after the rapid race of hoofs had ceased behind him. He had the strange feeling that Justin and Laurel Vandiver did not actually exist. That, through illusory clouds, he had chanced to see two fanciful beings rushing away on winged horses. They were, he thought, as rays of light that had penetrated the murky corners of his hardscrabble existence.

Dusk hazed the stubbled fields when Daniel drove across the branch and entered the narrow lane, squeezed between crooked files of snake-rail fencing. The mules moved nimbly now. Fleetingly he saw only the mass of oaks, scarlet against the last of the sun, before the house revealed its crotchety shape—the slanting lean-to, the wide front from which small windows peered in guarded caution, the weathered shaft of the stone-cut chimney. Built of hewn logs that his father had covered with clapboards, the house could claim birth back to troubled times, when the Sac and Fox harried the settlers—that accounted for the undersized windows, which in springtime blazed up with flames of red geranium blossoms from the hand of his mother. In the front yard rose her brave hosts of hollyhocks, marigolds, and touch-me-nots.

A yellow-haired dog ran out barking, but quit when Daniel called: "Shep . . . Shep . . . !" Rattling up to the house, he made out the pale-clothed figure of his mother watching from the door. He waved and drove on to the well, scaring up a flock of red chickens. There he unhitched and drew fresh water for the team. In the log barn he unharnessed and pegged the gear; from the corncrib he took four ears apiece for Zeke and Babe, and climbed to the loft and forked down hay into the mangers.

Over by the cowshed, he could see his father on a three-legged stool, head braced against the flank of a brindle cow while he milked. Shaking his head, Daniel went out and across, dropping the bar of the pen just as his father stood and turned with a gallon pail of sudsy milk.

It cut into Daniel how often he saw his father in that attitude—thin body bent, one burdened shoulder lower than the other, pain clouding his flint-blue eyes under shaggy brows. Sam Wade carried a bullet from Doniphan's expedition into Mexico, and one piece of lead had changed his life, left him unable to do a full day's work, which stubbornly he did just the same, and often turned him bitter and querulous over the state of the nation's government. *Doniphan was a great American. Greater even than Thomas Hart Benton. Almost as great as Andy Jackson.* Retold until Daniel knew its details by heart, Doniphan's campaign had been the peak of his father's life. Nothing of note had happened since.

"I'm late," Daniel said.

"Man goes to town he's got to visit a little. See his neighbors. Can't sweat all the time."

"I'll take the pail, Papa."

A look sparked Sam Wade's tired eyes. He straightened his crooked shape. "You and your mother. You'd think I was helpless. I can still do my share. When the time comes I can't, I'll say so." He went tramping away, swaying with the bucket, a doggedness to his walk, an independence, too. All good, Daniel was aware, except when his father overdid himself. Following to the wagon, Daniel gathered up his purchases.

As he entered the warm house and smelled the mingling of wood smoke, cornbread, coffee, and prairie chicken roasting in the Dutch oven, his mother looked up from setting the table, and he saw the full attention of her eyes. A look that said she was proud of him. A telling she was careful not to disclose around others, ever; most times noticeable when he'd been gone a while, to town or off working for a neighbor. When busy around home, he seldom saw it. Still, it was a wonderful thing to know in a secret way.

Emily Wade, dark of eye and hair, looked tall alongside his slope-shouldered father. Practical and neat, seldom given to lengthy utterances, she smiled a good deal and made the best of a sparse life. To Daniel, her capable hands were never idle. Varicolored quilts covered the beds. Clean white curtains hung at the windows. The floor of split hickory logs was always swept clean. She had only one vanity, her long hair, kept parted in the middle and coiled in long braids low on the back of her head; combed out, it fell in a glistening cascade below her waist. Emily Wade's face, wide across the cheek bones, was remarkably smooth and dispelled her age. Folks said Daniel favored his mother.

During supper, his father ate steadily before he spoke—for food came before talk.

"Any news from town?"

"Same talk . . . about the election," Daniel said, and wondered whether he should tell him.

"Did the company march?"

Daniel, nodding, caught his mother's eye. She knew what was coming.

"Did they ask you to join 'em?"

"Stark Hooper did. I refused again." He wouldn't mention the row with Tim Forehand.

"Give your reason?" His father didn't sound angry.

"There's no war. That's what I told him. Besides, I don't have time on Saturday to go marching around."

"No sign there won't be a fight," Sam Wade said, and continued his supper. His swept-back, ash-gray hair and thin beard accented his lean face, giving him a hawk's alertness, and Daniel had wondered if that alone wasn't what had pulled him through the long marches and battles with Doniphan's men. Then his father said: "Just remember a state's got some rights, too."

Daniel, seeking to frame his answer with care, said: "I know. Same time Missouri's got tol'able Union folks," and realized he was merely drifting toward an argument he wished to avoid.

His mother selected that moment to begin clearing the table. Sam Wade finished his coffee and pushed up. Seated in a cane-bottomed chair before the fireplace and its bed of cherry-red hickory coals, he drew on his spectacles and commenced reading the front page of the *Democrat*, frowning all the while. When he spoke, he picked up the conversation precisely where they had left it.

"Dan, you say Missouri's Union. I reckon it is, an' then some. It's Union and it's slave . . . in the same churn. Take our own family. Haven't I told you?" Indeed he had, many times. Daniel settled back to listen once more. Sam Wade said: "Your grandfather Wade lived in Virginia. He owned slaves before his creditors skinned him, before he moved out to Ohio an' the land speculators skinned him again . . . . Take your mother's people . . . the Lesters, in North Carolina. They had niggers, too."

"It wasn't right, Sam," Emily Wade said firmly, speaking for the first time since supper. She rocked back and forth, knitting without pause, her cheeks smooth, her position between them not unlike an arbiter. "I'd druther be like we are."

"I don't say it's right, Em. I'm just sayin' how it was and how it still is. Dan, you've seen free niggers. How do they strike you?"

"Kind of uppity," Daniel admitted.

"That they are. A sore trouble, and a-stirrin' up the other niggers. I want them kept in their place. Not set loose amongst us."

"Papa, can we blame free niggers for showing off a little, for having pride? They've done

29

something . . . they're free! A white man would do the same." Several times in recent months he and his father had talked along these lines, and always the results came out the same, unsolved, unchanged, a feeling that no common ground lay between them any more.

"Why, a white man'd be worse . . . only white men ain't the slaves. That's the way it is." Sam Wade jerked his jaw up and down in anger. "Abolitionists have moved in north of us. A Southern man's barn was burned two weeks ago in Shelby County." He shook the *Democrat* for authority. "We can't put up with the work of Black Republicans. No respect for authority. Forces folks to take the other side."

Daniel said nothing. You did not interrupt Sam Wade at this stage of a discussion. His father had been through one hard war and still suffered from it. He understood the temper of men, the trend of violence and the rough-and-ready politics of his state. Despite his prejudices, there was much to what he said. *If,* Daniel thought, *he would only hold on to his temper.*

"It's worse," Sam Wade said, "over in Bates and Vernon counties. Jayhawkers slip in, free the niggers . . . then, if a Missouri man gets caught going after his property in Kansas, he's hung."

"That's not right, either," Daniel said.

"No . . . it ain't right!" Sam Wade declared, and lurched to his feet. "Dan, you need to make up your mind about these things. Take a stand. You're gonna have to. Astraddle a fence is the poorest place in the world in a dirty fight. Both sides will gun you. You won't have a friend." He ceased. His stubbled face, grayish, the pain lurking there in shadow, held a look of prophecy and sadness. "If Lincoln's elected, Confederate companies will be formin' up. You better think about that, too. You're twenty years old."

Daniel saw another feeling enter the gaunt face, a kind of condoning which he remembered back as a boy. He saw the desire to express something and he saw it pass, elusive, unspoken, as his father limped off to bed.

Daniel sat still, watching the fire, listening to the steady creaking of his mother's rocker. The wordy editors of the *Democrat* might write about the "winds of partisan interests blowing stronger", of the "moving tide" and of a "threatened Union". But his father, uneducated but wise, a poor man who had never owned a single black man or hired slaves from their owners, had summed up matters the clearest of all: neighbors were taking sides. More would. Nobody could stand aloof. Nobody. A vast, dark cloud seemed to be moving across the sky.

Chapter Two
A PROPER LETTER

On a blustery Sunday morning after the election, Daniel hitched up and drove his parents along the road angling north toward the New Hope Church. After four miles, they came to a line of twisted cedars that stood like wary sentinels around the old cemetery. Whenever they drew near, about when Daniel smelled the first pungency of the gnarled trees, Sam Wade would turn his hard brooding that way and, after long moments, sit back facing the road, silent and unconsoled. He did so now, his intensity identical for as many years as Daniel could remember. His mother, always calmer, lifted her head higher when she gazed off, a soft smile for this quietest of places.

No one spoke. Daniel knew that his father had yet to accept what had happened a year before Daniel was born—the death of his brother James, when a baby.

Onward a short distance, Emily Wade said: "We're having a mighty pretty fall, Sam. Did you ever see so many bright colors?"

His reply was a negative shake of his head.

Daniel was glad when the church appeared in the distance. Constructed of hewn logs, and the mortar white-washed with lime, it looked neat and sturdy. There his father would begin his gradual return to the present. By the end of the sermon he would be himself again, ready to exchange comments with his neighbors on corn fodder, mules, chicken hawks, cows, weather, and to contribute pertinent observations on state and national politics.

Daniel noticed more wagons, buggies, and saddle horses than usual, and he wondered if Lincoln's election wasn't bringing out more folks. If a man hadn't got his fill of politics in town last Saturday, he would after church today. For the Little Giant had gone under.

"We're late," Sam Wade snapped. "I don't like bein' late."

"Brother Winn will have ample time left to preach on when we get inside," Emily Wade prophesied.

They found seats on the back slab bench just after Brother Levi Winn, a great rake handle of a man whose uncut hair dropped away in an orange-reddish mane down his elongated turkey neck, had finished praying. Whereupon he opened in customary manner, nodding to one and all, his crooked nose seeming to peck at the congregation for its many sins, and began speaking of the fruitful earth and the labors of the husbandman and the coming of Thanksgiving.

For long minutes the nasal voice droned over the crowded room. Daniel, trailing his eyes about, noticed Tim Forehand sitting with his family, and Andy Green and Jesse Nance among theirs. Daniel felt himself grinning. Of the three, just Jesse was following the sermon. Andy dozed. Tim was contemplating the wealth of yellow hair belonging to Mattie Hull, seated in front of him.

Suddenly Daniel heard a *thump* from the pulpit. Brother Winn was waving his arms, and now and again he stomped the floor and tiny geysers of dust spurted up, and his voice cracked and his black stock turned askew. He talked about backsliders and the "harvest of corruption" and denounced gatherings where fiddlers played "devil's music" and people danced and "they was flesh against flesh" and hankering for things of the world. He slapped his pigeon-breasted chest and stomped again, shaking his head till his red hair danced a-dangling. He stopped as suddenly, his mouth snapping shut like a trunk lid, one bony-knuckled hand raised and his long forefinger pointing as a schoolmaster would a hickory rod.

There was still a greater corruption a-going on, he said, across the South, across Missouri, and even around Foley's Prairie, where men held other men in bondage, paid them no wages, and sometimes sold them as you would cattle or mules or hogs.

From the corner of his eye Daniel saw his father growing tense, saw him lean back and stiffen there, set, arms folded. His mother did not move. Once Daniel had believed all preachments. When the Great Comet appeared like a flaming sign across the northwestern sky early in the fall of 1858, emblazoned there for about a week or more, and farmers stood in their yards at twilight, awed, apprehensive, watching the fiery tail, Brother Winn had flung down a portent of war, which was reasonable to accept in view of the troubles along the Kansas-Missouri border between proslavery and free-state men.

In addition, all calamities and disasters, including the drought of 1854, when the crops failed in northern Missouri, and the thunderstorms that smote the countryside in spring and summer, and the outbreaks of smallpox and cholera—those mostly in the olden days—were construed from the hardwood pulpit as indications of divine wrath, sent to punish people for their misdeeds. As for the mighty flood on the Missouri of 1844, when folks said a body looking across saw only water and treetops, and whole log houses drifting, sometimes a chicken roosting on top, and hills of driftwood and fence rails, and now and then an unlucky farm animal, and a body could hear the roaring for miles—Daniel could never determine what particular sin was responsible. Brother Winn seemed to settle on the safe ground of mankind's general cussedness, which he said was sufficient, and which he liked to abuse often and roundly, notwithstanding accounts Daniel had read that attributed the deluge to the melting of unusually heavy snows in the Rocky Mountains that June.

So Daniel had believed until he began to perceive that Brother Winn, a plain, natural, well-meaning man who walked everywhere on his calls, wasn't "well read" and spoke chiefly from the shallow well of his superstitious frontier interpretation of doctrine. Still, now two years later, who could deny that his forewarning of war wasn't about to come true?

Daniel was expecting, almost hoping, Brother Winn to ease off presently, to run out of steam. No slave owners attended the New Hope Church, its congregation being too poor to buy darkies. Nevertheless, men like Daniel's father, and the Sampsons and the Russells, had Southern roots and defended the old traditions whether they followed them or not. Too, if Brother Winn kept on, he was certain to lose some regular invitations to Sunday chicken dinners.

Instead, Brother Winn continued to bull right in, and a new respect for him took hold inside Daniel. He listened, in admiration and a little fear, while the parson wheeled up his mightiest ammunition yet, the Scriptures. First, he hurled Galatians 3:28, thundering each word as a separate shot: *There is neither Jew nor Greek . . . there is neither bond nor free . . . there is neither male nor female: for ye are all one in Christ Jesus.*

Daniel liked that; it made a crib full of horse sense. Good for Old Levi for reading up.

Wherefore, Brother Winn, his eyes as burning as fireballs, his face as awash had he sweated in a summer hayfield, fetched up an argument that gathered in the Jews and Gentiles, and loosed more bull's-eyes from Ephesians 2:11 and on to Ephesians 3. Furthermore, he thundered, anybody who questioned the Bible was an infidel doomed to burn in everlasting hell.

Sam Wade squirmed, a hint he ached to answer.

About then Daniel sensed the closing. The harsh voice changed and fell away, lodged on a neighborly note. Brother Winn, sopping a blue bandanna over his streaming face, spoke of "heavenly places" and the "slain enmity" and how strangers and aliens, everybody in fact, could meet as fellow citizens in the household of the Lord.

When the last hymn was sung, Daniel got up feeling a warm elation, a comfort, tempered by concern when he saw his father's face.

Sam Wade's expression was so much rock.

And when their turn came to file through the doorway where Brother Winn stood, pumping hands, he held back. He said distinctly: "Levi, I reckon you got the right to preach what you believe about this nigger trouble, an' the Union, an' you can be a Lincoln man if you like. But I don't have to agree just because you say it. . . . Another thing. Why'nt you just render unto Cæsar them things that are his'n, an' let this outside business about fiddle music and dancin' alone? If President Andy Jackson and our own Colonel Doniphan eased their minds of care by listening to the fiddle, I reckon it won't hurt the ordinary likes of us."

Finished, Sam Wade limped out, his bent body more upright than usual. Daniel, following behind his mother, who walked with eyes downcast, was conscious of an acute silence and Levi Winn's hurt face.

By custom, after church, the families lingered to visit, the men and women separating. Today, however, Sam Wade marched straight to his wagon, untied the team, and would have climbed up at once to leave had not his wife spoken, her calm voice more reminding than differing.

"I didn't ask about Patty Russell's new baby boy. He's been poorly of late."

Sam Wade appeared to catch himself. "All right, Em. Plenty of time for *that*," he said, and retied the team.

As she left, the men and boys gathered in a slack clump near the Wade wagon. Plug tobacco and corncob pipes came out. Until today Daniel had always looked ahead to this friendly session.

Reuben Nance, Jesse's father, was talking. "A good sermon. A mighty good sermon. Didn't know Levi had it in him, did you, boys?" he said, a general remark.

"Depends on how a man thinks," Sam Wade took it up, and Daniel felt a familiar weariness. "Me . . . I didn't like it one little whit. Too one-sided. A preacher ought to keep his nose out of politics."

"I didn't agree with him about fiddle music and dances . . . young folks need that," Nance replied, and a thoughtfulness appeared in his lank face and settled in his mild blue eyes. "Have to say I did about the other part"—he seemed disinclined to name it—"about slavery and such."

Sam Wade's voice cut. "That neither. I could quote him just as much Scripture from the other side. There's Genesis nine, twenty-five . . . Leviticus twenty-five, forty-five . . . Joel three, eight. It's just as strong the other way, maybe stronger. Levi didn't give both sides."

Reuben Nance cut off a chew and brought blade and tobacco to his mouth, a deliberate gesture. All the Nances had the mark of woodsmen: far-eyed, quiet-moving, not a grain of extra

39

tallow on their tough bodies, slow of talk and slow to rile, thrifty, devout, and yet a limit to their humility.

"If the Bible says slavery's right," he said, "then the Bible's wrong." His voice had an edge.

"Well, it's there," Sam Wade said, as blunt as a mule's kick.

All at once, in shame, Daniel wanted to lead his father away, and dared not try. Catching the embarrassment in young Jesse's light eyes, Daniel realized suddenly that they felt alike, and he understood a further truth: the difference lay not between them, the boys, never would, but between their fathers, brought up on old ways.

"Guess it is, Sam," Nance said, slow-paced. "There for both sides. I read in the paper where some Jayhawkers hung a Missouri man. Claimed he'd kidnapped a darky. Claimed they did it according to a law found in the Bible. . . . Quoted Exodus twenty-one, sixteen. Something about 'he that stealeth a man and selleth his . . . he shall surely be put to death.' "

"That's twisting it around," Sam Wade protested.

"I'd say so myself," Nance said, considering. "A poor excuse for murder." His mild gaze seemed to dismiss the argument and to say they were long-standing neighbors. He traveled his eyes about, his slow smile forming. "Be a husking-bee at our place Saturday after next.

You-all come." His clear invitation included everyone. "I imagine there'll be a bite or two to eat, along with the dance."

Everyone nodded or murmured acceptance save Sam Wade, when all the time Daniel was hoping his father would show a neighborliness equal to Mr. Nance's. His father's manner was more civil by now, but he did not nod or speak. Nance turned away, and so did the others.

Brother Winn, black hat on, emerged from the church and stopped to visit with the first family he met, sweeping off his hat and pumping hands all around again.

The Wades were driving off when Daniel's mother touched a finger to her lips in alarm. "Why, Sam, it's our turn to have Brother Winn to dinner!"

Daniel halted the team. They all looked back. Brother Winn and the Nances were visiting now; apparently he was being asked to dinner. Daniel saw his up-and-down head motion, his half bow. There was no doubt when Brother Winn climbed aboard the wagon.

Daniel slapped the reins and drove ahead. His mother and father were silent; they didn't have to say it. He could trace their thinking by his own. Living in a district where people prided themselves on generosity and friendliness, Sam Wade today, through stubborn anger, had forgotten his manners. It left something akin to shame.

They covered some distance before Emily Wade, her voice groping, said: "We can ask him for next Sunday, Sam."

The light-legged mules pulled them over the next wooded rise. They were that far when Sam Wade let out his answer. "I won't go again to a church where any Black Republican preaches half truths."

After dinner, Daniel strayed to his room. Here as a boy he had played hours with the fanciful James, or he had taken his brother out to run on the sunlit cow pasture, or to wander in the cool woods, or to follow the dimly winding path along the little creek. But gradually the make-believe game dulled, abandoned when Daniel grew older because he couldn't lure James back to live with them, hard as he tried in the belief he might and thereby make his parents happy, especially his dour father, and also relieve his own loneliness. By the time Daniel was ten, James had passed on a soft summer cloud to a world of golden sunshine that never changed, and there he stayed. A face forever fair and congenial, eternally distant. A small face whose features, he remembered his mother saying, had been just like his father's. In time Daniel almost doubted that James had existed at all.

Here as well were Daniel's few books. On gloomy winter evenings they became candles glowing steadily in the dark and drafty room. Among them the work of Missouri's own Thomas Hart Benton, Old Bullion, his THIRTY YEARS' VIEW, and IVANHOE and ROBINSON CRUSOE, and a volume of Bancroft's rhetorical HISTORY OF THE UNITED STATES FROM THE DISCOVERY OF THE AMERICAN CONTINENT, Prescott's CONQUEST OF MEXICO, Townsend's SPELLER AND DEFINER, THE SCARLET LETTER, Tennyson's POEMS, biographies of Washington and Jackson, the last a cherished gift from his father. Old Hickory's familiar features—lean and taut as a good drum, his shock of straight, white hair, the mark of the struggling frontier always about him—were those of a trusted friend. A staunch Union man, too, by his record.

Daniel stretched his long length back flat on the checkered quilt covering his bed, cupped hands behind his head, and his mind, as by signal, called up Miss Laurel's face. Truth be he could and he couldn't remember how she looked. Her riding habit, the perfect lineaments of her face—everything got mixed up in a fine haze. And then the persistent thought, a rat's gnaw in his mind since that afternoon, returned to nag him. Would it be proper to write her, to ask— maybe *inquire* was the correct word—if he might borrow the book? That tantalizing possibility loosed his visualization again of the Vandiver library and more books than he had seen in all his lifetime, and Miss Laurel looking very much a part of such a grand place. Would a letter be presuming on mere mannerly words? Would it? He knew what his father would say: "Stick to your own kind." Same as keep to your place. Same as any nigger. By dogs, he'd say nothing to his father.

Once more he drew the nub of the problem back and forth through his mind, sizing it up and down and across, swinging from difficult decision to easy uncertainty. His resolution tired after a while, wandered, and he closed his eyes, dozing.

The sun outside the room's single window had slipped a notch when he stirred again. But his head was clear. He sat up and slipped to the hardwood table where his books stood, and sat down, his big right hand taking up the goose quill pen. He commenced to write, his scrawling labored. He wrote and scratched out, wrote and scratched again and again. His self-disgust rose. Clever phrases eluded him, even the bare, correct ones. He couldn't budge beyond—**Dear Miss Laurel**—and he thought: *I'm a tongue-tied country jake*. An angry impatience seized; he continued. And at length a sentence formed. Another. He forced himself to persevere. He'd lick no man's boots. His father was wrong to hold that a body couldn't try to better himself.

When Daniel looked down at the finished page, his words struck him as awkward in expression and miserably lacking the lofty tone he intended to convey. Could he say it better? He knew he couldn't now. Was his grammar correct? He thought so, hoped so. An intuitive voice said he was wise to hold his message brief and to the point. He read the letter through again:

Dear Miss Laurel,

I have thought about your neighborly offer to let me borrow your volume of poems by John Keats. If such is still to your convenience, and you are not studying the volume at present, or don't aim to soon, or aim to lend it to another friend, say I call for it at your home? I would take mighty good care of such a fine piece of work and return it to you as soon as I have read it through in a few days.

I trust I am not presuming upon your kind nature, knowing as I well do how one good book far outshines a few of our puckery Missouri persimmons.

Sincerely, your friend,
Daniel Wade

His hands were moist with sweat as he finished.

His courage deserted him completely, and he got to his feet as though he had committed a wrong. He strode to the window and back, and stopped, dead still, possessed by a headlong excitement that hurled the blood hot and plunging to his face.

In moments he was striding down the lane, bound for the post office at Foley's Prairie.

Chapter Three

INDIAN MOUND VERSUS COON CREEK

Sam Wade raised no protest when Daniel prepared to leave for the husking-bee at Reuben Nance's farm. It was his mother who looked up. Just for an instant he saw her longing revealed, no longer. Her smooth face settled in the calm order so familiar to him, content again, and he went out.

He pondered his father's stand while he stripped off the corn shucks, readying the bright yellow ears for hauling to the wooden cribs. Always before the two had worked side-by-side, his father doing more than need be, for helping your neighbor was a feverish duty to Sam Wade, and he less than able to render a full day's labor.

In the distance Daniel could hear laughter and

the pleasing hum of women's voices from the long log house, and the clatter of preparations for the big supper to follow the shucking.

Later, he walked to the well and drew a bucket of water. As he drank from the dipper, he saw Mattie Hull leave the kitchen. She swung a wooden pail. She stopped and gazed in his direction, a hesitation too deliberate to miss. He continued to drink, pretending not to see her. Within moments she was idling toward him. Her approach was part stroll, part saunter, a slow, rhythmic switching of generous hips.

When he could ignore her no further, he hung the dipper back on its peg and turned to take her bucket.

"Why, thank you, Dan'l," she said in a feigned surprise that fooled him not a whit.

"I'll get you some fresh," he said, and emptied into the stock trough and let the well bucket splash and sink on the heavy rope. He started drawing up, his movements strong and even, making the pulley squeal complaint.

"Dan . . . l," she pursued, "we could be partners tonight."

Mattie, who came from a hard-pressed Coon Creek family, had a purring way of stressing a boy's name, he remembered, a kind of dwelling on and drawing out the last part, an overdoing, speaking as she fluttered long lashes and gazed out of bold hazel eyes. She was about his age, therefore high time she was finding herself a husband; yet she seemed older than he. Amplebodied, with a wealth of yellow hair that never quite stayed up, Mattie was turning into a heavy young woman. Buxom and handsome now, she would eventually take on a coarseness. She liked to roll her eyes and twist her rich, curving lips to speak in slurred innuendoes. Daniel guessed himself somewhat wary of her and the superior knowledge he sensed she owned; strangely he felt more at ease around Miss Laurel.

"I'm a poor dancer," he said in truth, and filled her bucket. "You'll have more fun with somebody else."

"Fun?" She cocked an insinuating eye. "What sorta fun, Dan'l?"

"What I said. Fun with a good dancer."

"You . . . mean somebody like Tim Forehand?"

"Plenty of good dancers," he said, refusing to speculate on Forehand's ability and thereby encourage her to hint around some more, which he saw she intended.

She looked him up and down, and, when she smiled, he saw the even line of her strong, white teeth. "You'll never learn if you hold back from things, Dan'l. How d'you know you can't dance if you've never tried?"

"Oh, I've tried," he said. "That's how I know." He cut short by taking up the bucket and walking toward the house, his abruptness leaving her trailing him a step. Inside, he could see a crowd of women and girls passing back and forth to a long table, and he smelled ham and bread and pie baking. He set the bucket down on the step and turned, only to find Mattie right behind him. She made no effort to move aside. He couldn't avoid bumping her, a light brushing, during which he felt the unyielding pressure of her soft body. She laughed as he stepped out of the way, and he knew his anger showed.

Her slurring voice followed him away. "Dan'l, I'll save the first set for you."

Soon after supper the house was cleared for dancing. Reuben Nance sprinkled cornmeal on the puncheon floor and hung lanterns on wall pegs. About dark, Uncle Asa Christian took his chair on a plank platform supported on barrels, and commenced tuning up. At the first high-pitched shrieks of the fiddle strings, eager faces appeared in the doorways. A wonderful air of expectancy fastened upon the watchers. Not one to spoil the spell he was slowly creating, Uncle Asa turned the fiddle pegs again and again; now and then he plucked the finger board and drew the bow tentatively, his expression engrossed; it seemed to remind him that he alone possessed the secret of enticing music from the sensitive, difficult instrument in his rough hands. No one spoke a hurrying word to him. He continued the ritual while the weary matrons, faces flushed from the kitchen's heat, trailed in to sit on slab benches around the walls, and the children ran here and there, in and out, and the stir of restless feet became steadily audible. Uncle Asa seemed not to notice. The shrieking and sawing persisted, more teasing than ever, vexing, harassing, because everyone knew the fiddle was tuned and ready.

Just when the fretful waiting reached an unbearable strain, Uncle Asa tapped his limber foot, tossed back his long black hair with a twist of his head, rested his chin, and, his whiskered face resolute, ripped into "Billy in the Low Ground".

Somebody whooped. Somebody stomped.

Reuben Nance, dressed in Sunday blue suit, white shirt, and black stock, gained the platform in rapid strides. He called: "Grab your partners!"

The night, warm for November, and the pulsing music fired a feeling all through Daniel. He stood hesitantly in the yellow lantern light outside the front doorway, watching the eager couples rush past him. Andy Green and his girl dashed by. Farther out in the yard, where the Swink boys, Amos and Obadiah, had a jug of home-made whiskey cached under a wagon quilt, Daniel heard Tim Forehand's iron voice lift in the long-drawn squall of a river bottom panther.

"Dan'l, you waitin' on me?"

Mattie Hull stood beside him. She swayed closer, touching him. He got the warm scent of her, the heavy-sweet heat of her vitality.

"Better find yourself a *good* dancer," he said. He was evading, and he sensed she knew it.

She said: "Maybe I think you're good enough."

"I don't think so."

"You won't dance with me?"

"I told you why."

"Well . . . ." A tiny muscle quivered tautly in her broad face. A baffled anger took root in her voice. "You always did have different notions, Daniel Wade. With school and books and such."

"What's wrong with school?"

"Well, what's schoolin' but airs?"

Heads were turning. He would have left her had that not looked like retreating. "I'm doing your feet a favor, Mattie," he said as calmly as he could muster.

A growing pressure piled up around the doorway. More couples crowded through, laughing, talking, arms locked, and the scents of soap-scrubbed girls and doused violet toilet water, and the sweat of brawny young men and the straight whiskey they had drunk, traced an agreeable whetting across the night.

Tim Forehand towered in the midst of them, his rugged face a-glitter. Sweat dappled his forehead. His rollicking expression dampened when he spied Daniel.

"Tim," Mattie said, placing a firm grasp on his arm, "let's dance."

He grinned his ready acceptance. "You bet, Mattie," he said, and started on, then paused, discovering a belated amusement in her offer. "What's the matter? Won't the perfessor here shake a leg with you? An' him the smartest feller I know?"

"Oh, come on," Mattie said, impatient.

"Wait a minute. I get it now. You want t'dance with a Coon Creek man . . . a real man. That it?"

Daniel stiffened. Before the big man could say more, Mattie's stout arms yanked him toward the door. Forehand didn't resist. He went in with a whoop.

Daniel attached himself to the shifting clump of men and boys. Both Coon Creek and Indian Mound families were well represented here tonight. There'd be a fight or two before the dance was over; it was a little early yet. Feeling a tug on his britches, he turned and heard Amos Swink whisper: "Your turn to visit the jug." They slipped away from the light and the older eyes, and presently drifted back, Daniel's insides warm and his pulse quickening. The Swinks were as proud of their limestone-water whiskey as other farmers were of stout mules. Around Daniel the talk criss-crossed from crops and weather to foot racing and wrestling and fighting, and to who was the best man in the district with a flail. Inside, Uncle Asa was taking after "The Mississippi Sawyer", that fast jig tune. The whooping and stomping mounted higher.

An older man spoke, his voice somehow matter-of-fact and careful. "You boys been readin' about Fort Sumter?"

"Well . . . some," Sim Russell said vaguely. "Just about where is that?"

"In the Carolinas."

"An' what's the news about it?"

"'Pears like Abe Lincoln aims to keep a-holt of it, an' the folks down there, they aim to take it."

"By jinks," young Sim exclaimed, "I'd hate to see the country take a set at each other over such a far-off place! Money's got to be the reason. You can size up Yankees right off . . . money. That's all they're after . . . that an' tellin' folks what to do about their niggers . . . . I reckon the Dirty Dutch in Saint Louis will side right along with 'em, too."

"Everything'd be just dandy if Stephen A. Douglas won," a disappointed voice said. "He carried Missouri, he did."

"But Lincoln beat him."

Daniel was listening more to the music and fun-making. The Russells, he recalled, were much like the Wades: they owned no slaves and worked none. Now the Swink boys' father was calling the dance with the vigor of a muleskinner bellowing his team up a steep grade. A quick-silver moon bathed the yard. Such a night wasn't right for serious politics and war talk, or neighborhood rows, for that matter. Nonetheless, his common sense kept raking up Tim Forehand and the fight building between them, and, when Amos Swink murmured another invitation to the wagon, Daniel declined. A chill had invaded the evening. He decided against going inside to watch the dancing. If it was coming, he'd wait here. He was still there when a horse *clopped* up and the rider dismounted.

Everyone turned as the erect figure of Stark Hooper strode into the mellow light, eyes drawn to his stylish derby, tight-fitting blue broadcloth coat and trousers, and a speckled waistcoat across which looped a heavy gold watch chain.

Hooper paused to acknowledge, to sweep his eyes around, to shake hands. He called names without faltering. He seemed to know every man's, every boy's.

"On the look-out for volunteers?" Obadiah Swink inquired, coming in from the wagon. His voice was beginning to blur.

"Might say I just believe in being prepared," Hooper said, and jogged his goateed chin at Swink. He tilted his head and seemed to peer off through the vast starlit night and search for mysterious revelations, perhaps to find them because of superior insights into the future. The last impression was a mere hint of manner, held only a moment, but there. He said—"I'm afraid it's coming, boys."—and stuck out his hand to Sim Russell, who leaned back.

"I won't shake with a Black Republican. Damned if I will."

"And I'll defend your right to make that free choice any day of the week," Hooper replied serenely.

It was a clever, disarming remark, and young Russell could only gape, too startled to reply. Hooper pressed on, trailing the strong aroma of bay rum. When he saw Daniel, he thrust out a hand. "I'm still counting on you, Dan."

Daniel shook on impulse, half-heartedly. As he withdrew, he had the prickly sensation of being tricked. Taking Hooper's hand here tonight just about marked you as a Union man, when, in the country, at least, handshakes were reserved for friendship, for special patriotic observances like the 4th of July, long absences from home, or when a neighbor had been poorly a long time. Not for a man who circulated as often as Stark Hooper.

"Don't ask me again . . . I'll let you know if I decide." Daniel's voice jumped out, flat and sharp. But Hooper was moving on to the house; it was nigh impossible to offend him.

"When's somebody goin' to organize a Confed'rate company around here?" Sim Russell complained. "Justin Vandiver could. I'd like to see him do it. He's been trained at soldierin'. Folks like him."

Daniel, unmoving, could feel a pull this way and a tug that way within himself. What did he think! Sim Russell's stand about secession and slavery, ignorant though he might be of the latest newspaper reports from Charleston harbor, was far clearer than his own. Certainly he gave honest voice to old prejudices.

Not long after, Daniel saw a buggy shape through the gloom of the lane, circle as if hesitating and start back. No one had to say to whom it belonged, being the only one of its kind in the county and therefore an oddity. A slender, single-seated two-wheeler, English style, a perky conveyance that sported a curved dashboard and leather top, and storm-proof windows when needed, having slits for the reins and isinglass panes. Only the Vandivers could drive that downright frivolous rig and give it an air of usefulness.

Jesse Nance went forth and waved. The buggy stopped. For the first time the music had ceased, therefore Daniel caught Nance's shy but courteous greeting: " 'Evening, Justin. Reckon you come to see Father about the corn?"

"Yes . . . but we'll go on." Vandiver sounded apologetic. "Didn't know you were entertaining. We won't intrude."

"You're not. You and Miss Laurel wait. I'll fetch Father."

Not waiting for a reply, Nance legged for the house. In moments Reuben Nance appeared, long-striding to the buggy. The voices there joined, then lost distinctness when the music struck up again. Justin Vandiver got out and assisted his sister down.

He turned to her. "Isn't that some music!"

"Come in and dance," the elder Nance invited. "You're mighty welcome."

"Like to, Laurel?" her brother asked. "For just a minute?"

"Yes, I would!"

He laughed, and they all strayed toward the house.

Seeing her again, Daniel felt the blood rushing to his face. She wore a light-blue shawl about her shoulders and a white, long-sleeved dress; although possibly plain and simple in her eyes, to him she lent it a reserved refinement and taste. She didn't see him, and he did not press forward. For the sight of her reminded him of his letter, posted two weeks ago and not answered. He could draw but one conclusion. He had presumed; he would not act again.

He watched Justin and Laurel enter and pause, framed in the blaze of light. He saw them whirl out of sight, leaving Reuben Vance nodding approval.

A powerful feeling pulled Daniel after. He advanced to the doorway, slipped through, and halted, left stiff by the onrush of music and light, the chorus of many voices, clumping brogans, and the hot excitement the dancers imparted.

Unforeseen, as was his teasing way, Uncle Asa sawed his bow to a still wilder frenzy and, as suddenly, dropped his arm, snapping off the last of "Leather Breeches". Noisy applause followed. Uncle Asa beamed and indicated a brief delay while he mopped his face.

Seeing the Vandivers leave the floor and turn his way, Daniel froze and remembered the presumptuous letter. What should he say if anything? His uncertainty fled upon their immediate recognition of him.

"Daniel," Justin Vandiver said, "will you look after Laurel for me while I talk corn and mules to Mister Nance?"

Daniel inclined his head. "Glad to."

"Good evening, Mister Wade," Miss Laurel said.

"'Evening." For him the easiest response in the world was to return her smile—speech, something suitable to the occasion, was another matter. He could only stand there and continue to regard her. Around him all eyes seemed to be watching his awkwardness. As he faltered, he saw her expression change and her lips form to speak a moment before Stark Hooper cut rapidly through to them. Rather, to her. Laurel turned.

"It would be most considerate of you, indeed, to honor me with the next dance, Miss Laurel," Hooper broke in, and bowed. The words rolled from his mouth, as easily summoned as a country boy's hound whistle. His assurance before her was complete. He showed no awareness of Daniel.

Her violet eyes moved from Hooper to Daniel and back. "You are the one who's considerate," she said, and hesitated. "Except Daniel just asked me."

Hooper's naked surprise stabbed through. He controlled it; he stood a mite straighter. "After that?"

"We can't stay," she said in all graciousness. "Justin will be ready in a minute."

Uncle Asa tapped his slab-like foot, skidded his agile bow, and sailed into "The Goose Hangs High".

Hooper's back arched, more erect than before. His attention switched to Daniel for the first time, then he bowed himself away.

Daniel, still doubting his ears, saw Miss Laurel extend a hand, and he took it, and they moved out on the floor to the forming circle and became part of it, like pegs suddenly fitting into place. They whirled in and out, slowly to begin, Daniel aware that she was guiding him expertly while not seeming to. His broganed feet were stumps that he had to lift by conscious effort, one by one. He stumbled and caused a racket. Heads turned. His rigid body refused to obey him. He set his mouth, grimly determined to follow the calls and keep up. Everyone must be watching.

Miss Laurel took no notice that he could see of his awkward floundering. Of all the faces whirling and cavorting about him only hers wasn't blurred, only hers retained a constant clarity.

Gradually a slow confidence found root within him. Somehow he was executing the figures, weaving, wheeling, swinging to the roared calls, even though late most times. After a bit, he began to anticipate the maneuvers. His body loosened, his footing became surer. Miss Laurel felt light as a leaf as the circle changed, and alternately he let her go and caught her again. Each time her hand met his securely and imparted assurance. A vast sense of enjoyment filled him.

Suddenly his brogans were clumping the hardwood floor. He checked up, at last aware that the wild music had ceased and he was still dancing. He released Laurel's hand. His face flamed. The other dancers laughed. She laughed, also, so to help him see the humor of it, and quickly he did. He heard his own laughter, and through it he discovered a fresh feeling.

Uncle Asa was leaving the platform.

Looking for Vandiver, Daniel ran into Mattie

Hull's indignant gaze across the room. She threw him a remembering disdain and swept outside on Tim Forehand's brawny arm.

"Miss Laurel," Daniel said, turning back, "you're a mighty fine dancer. I can't say as much for myself."

She stood a head shorter than he. She was smiling up at him, her fair complexion flushed. "I enjoyed it. Every step." Her tone was convincing. So had it been, he remembered, about the book.

If his face told him, he didn't know. But again he noted that expression of hers to speak, and again Stark Hooper materialized before another word could be said.

"Miss Laurel . . . Miss Laurel." Hooper was almost reciting her name, suggesting that he liked the resonance of his own voice. "It takes you to show us how to dance."

"Oh, I don't think so," she said. "Didn't Daniel do fine?"

Hooper ignored that. His intention became clear to Daniel—Hooper was going to cut in and escort her away.

Firmly Daniel gripped her elbow and guided her toward her brother and Reuben Nance. Hooper swung to the other side, unabashed. Arrived, Daniel recalled his manners, said—"Thank you, Miss Laurel."—and left them. Going off, he had the dim intuition of something left unfinished.

Outside, the milling couples blocked his way. He turned aside, confused. If he'd never sent that foolish letter! It rose in monstrous proportions, reminding him once more of his infernal awkwardness and meager store of social graces. He smelled whiskey before, unprepared, he heard Tim Forehand's rough voice.

"See you run with quality folks, perfessor. What's it like 'way up yonder?"

Mattie hung on Forehand's arm. Resentment, discontent, raw anger—they swelled her mouth. Daniel read a glittery accusation of himself in her eyes.

He said—"Tim, you've made too many trips to the wagon."—and stepped to go.

Instantly an arm as hard as an oak limb grabbed him, spun him. Daniel broke the hold. In the following instant the two stood clear, eyes locked. To Daniel's utter astonishment Mattie screamed, and in the doorway's light he saw a joyous expectancy replace her sullen expression.

"Tim . . . he's throwin' you around!"

Her goading wasn't needed, for Forehand, bristling, was closing in. This time, abruptly, Daniel shoved on Forehand's chest and the big man fell against Mattie, who screamed even louder.

Out of the house bounded long Reuben Nance. All at once the jostling crowd stilled. He sized up the situation with a glance.

"All right, boys. Be no fighting around the house. Settle it away from here."

Nance's voice and his steady manner ruled the hushed watchers. He waited, banked in him the understanding of a man once a rough-and-ready country fighter himself.

One couple drifted out, and another; presently everyone was in motion, the younger boys running ahead. Forehand and Mattie went eagerly.

As yet, Daniel wasn't mad enough to fight. Events had happened too fast. He moved with the crowd, swept along. It wasn't unlike log riding when Coon Creek sang bank-full in the spring.

As the lights in the house fell behind, the excitement whipped up and a high-pitched voice raised the call and cried it back: "Fight! Fight!" Somebody yelled—"Come on . . . behind the barn!"—and there followed a pushing and rushing to arrive first.

Daniel paced on. Faces kept bobbing up to peer into his, seeming to look for some hint of the fear he should have. He said nothing.

A strong hand seized his arm. "This won't do," Andy Green argued. "I'll try to talk him out of it."

"Let him be . . . it's been coming," Daniel said, still walking. What Andy Green meant to convey without saying the words was that he was over-matched. "He'll dog me hereon if I don't."

Toward the low silhouette of the barn the dancers pressed, Daniel in their center, Andy Green flanking him, past it, and around behind to an open place where the pasture began. There they formed a loose circle. In no time at all Daniel found himself opposite Forehand and Mattie.

Forehand, his humor raspy, said: "Git out of the way, Mattie."

She obeyed, slowly measuring Daniel a relishing look as she switched over to take position behind her champion.

"Maybe you'd druther kite back to the house, perfessor," Forehand said, his drawling voice simulating concern. "Dance with them quality folks . . . the Vandivers. 'Cause there's gonna be blood let here if you stay."

Daniel's breathing shortened. He stood motionless. Everything—starting with the dance—now Forehand, the hissing crowd, Mattie's venom, the pale night—had an unreal quality.

"It's your craw that's full," he said. "Not mine. No call for you to run down the Vandivers."

"Git ready," Forehand growled.

For reply, Daniel removed his coat and skinned his shirt over his head, and, as he pitched them to the nearest hands, he heard the bet-making going: drinks, four-bits, six-bits, tobacco plugs, and stake-holders being decided, the odds favoring Forehand. He thought: *Indian Mound against Coon Creek.* He'd wrestled, jumped, foot raced, and swum with other boys, and fought a little, but never against an opponent the likes of quarrelsome Tim Forehand. Who, it was said, had licked all the lads along Coon Creek, sometimes two at once. Who, further said, had thrashed a bear of a river roustabout outside the tavern in Foley's Prairie, rendering the man senseless, to be carried off, and who, Daniel had witnessed for himself one Saturday in town, could jerk a mule to its knees.

Across from him, Forehand was leisurely finishing preparations. He held shirt and coat out to Mattie, waggled his shaggy head, and assumed a high, mimicking tone. "I dasn't risk gittin' 'em soiled, y'know, because of the dance. Be just a bit, Mattie."

He squared around suddenly, and Daniel received the impression of a raw-boned, rock-hard body that glistened menacingly under the pallor of the crisp moon. Ready, now, Daniel reacted mechanically. He raised fists and stepped forward, his stance straight. A chill breeze touched his face; inside him a fire was racing.

Forehand advanced in a confident crouch, the thick trunks of his arms lifting. Suddenly he lowered his long-haired head and charged like an angry bull. Daniel twisted to avoid the rush, late. Something rammed his left side, and he felt himself flung off balance into the crowd. He heard a chorus of savage yelling, and realized hands were righting him and pushing him back into the ring.

Forehand waited on the far side, hands on hips. He seemed to be grinning as Daniel stepped forth again to meet him. He loafed out unhurriedly entering the crouch. Of an instant his brogans beat the packed earth. He lunged forward, low, fast, and feinted from his right to left, and Daniel was caught flat-footed. Pain crashed through his right ribs and chest.

The night spun, the wild yelling soared, and he landed on his buttocks, hands braced. He pushed up in haste, a hot shame upon him.

"This time's for keeps," he heard Forehand taunt him. "Me and Mattie, we aim to dance the next set."

In the distance, faintly, Daniel could hear Uncle Asa's fiddle resuming, sending bitter-sweet music across the night, calling the dancers back.

Daniel came ready again. He saw the old maneuver commence once more, as though each had rehearsed his part. Except Forehand, first, cut a little ridiculing jig, and the crowd laughed, after which he got down to taw.

An instant flailed Daniel as keenly as his shame and his hurting. Instead of going in straight up, he hurled himself before Forehand could crouch, and drove the point of one shoulder into Forehand's chest. His attack drew a surprised grunt of pain.

"Perfessor . . . you're plumb mad."

Daniel kept crowding him. He slugged Forehand's face, Forehand's belly, and smashed him backward, vaguely aware of taking as much in return. He tasted the brine of his own blood. His head was humming. His face and chest relayed a strange numbness. But he felt no real pain. A wild elation blazed: he could stand up to Tim Forehand. By dogs, he could!

Even as he knew, he could feel Forehand's wrath erupting and the blows striking faster and harder.

"Hit 'im, Tim! Hit 'im!" Mattie's voice.

They thudded together like young bulls in an April pasture, grunting and hacking for breath, disdaining any fancy footing. Getting the taint of sour whiskey, Daniel battered the wide beltline. Forehand gave a pinch of grudging ground, a little more. He bent and covered up and lashed back wildly with haymakers, grunting each time he swung. Now Daniel had to back up and use his long arms to beat Forehand away from his body. As he did, the hissing rose louder. *By dogs, let 'em!*

They slugged, pawed, wrestled, mauled, tugged, clutched, fighting across the circle and back. When Forehand sought to ram him, Daniel, instead of retreating, clamped both arms around

Forehand's bulky shoulders and threw him to the ground.

Forehand seemed startled; he lay there an instant. No more. He leaped up before Daniel could spring upon him.

A mutual pause now as both dug for wind. Daniel dragged a hand across his bleeding mouth. Forehand stood all humped up, glaring, heaving. This time he waited for the attack.

Wary, Daniel circled around him and, rushing in, aimed for Forehand's middle; he couldn't take it there. Forehand surrendered footing, and Daniel drove after him, swinging, surprised when Forehand dodged sideways and stuck out a foot. Daniel tripped, sprawled. He rolled over on his back and reared up to see Forehand, bulging with murder, pounding in to stomp him.

There was time only for Daniel to glimpse the dark wedge of Forehand's broad brogan descending. He groped, grabbed, caught, held. With both hands he twisted savagely. Forehand's sharp outcry broke. Daniel, on one knee, shoved the foot higher; suddenly he twisted and jerked backward.

Forehand fell on his back. He made a ponderous flapping, his breath knocked out from him. Daniel pounced across and thrust Forehand's shoulders down, all his strength behind the hold. He held there. Under him, Forehand seemed dazed, inert. A moment and Daniel lurched to his feet. It was over by the rules, if there were any rules tonight.

Jesse Nance stepped between them. "That settles it. Mighty nigh a draw, I reckon . . . but Dan pinned both Tim's shoulders. You all saw that. . . . Now let's get back to the house 'fore my father takes a piss-elm club to the pair of you for spoilin' the dance."

Forehand was dragging up. His head hung. He didn't look Daniel's way as he took a tentative step on his right foot.

As the crowd dissolved, Daniel felt his coat and shirt laid across his arm. Merely holding them was an effort. Hands slapped his back. Voices spoke to him. He didn't look, he didn't care. When he got himself together to go, it seemed that the whole bruising punishment he had taken returned at once. Spring thunder rolled inside his head. His stomach kept hitching up and down. His lungs burned. He wobbled off.

He had no idea how much time had passed before he reached the well, where the nonsense with Mattie had sprouted that afternoon. It occurred to him that he didn't remember seeing her around after the fight; fact was he remembered no one much except Andy and Jesse. The brawl seemed unimportant now . . . everything.

He drew a bucket and gulped dippers of cold water, and, when he had enough, he doused the stinging trough water over his face, chest, and arms. Wincing, scrubbing away the stink, dirt, and blood, he discovered damage unfelt before.

He was pulling on the coat when he heard foot-steps plodding around the barn. Tim Forehand limped out of the shadows. Still naked to the waist, he carried his clothes like so many rags, wadded in one big fist. He trudged straight to the partially filled bucket Daniel had left, clamped hands to it, and drank like a work horse, letting the water slosh over his bare chest.

He banged down the bucket, and Daniel, in weary acceptance, prepared for more trouble. *This time, by dogs. . . .*

Forehand did not wheel about as Daniel expected. He did not cry out in shamed fury. For a long breath he stood still, watching the night.

"That Mattie," he muttered, picking up an angry bewilderment. "That cussed Mattie . . . she went off with Sim Russell." He hurled that out of him, and tore away to cross Reuben Nance's cornfield.

Recalling his own long walk, Daniel put him-self in motion toward home. He was relieved, skirting the house, to find the two-seater gone and everybody inside taking refreshments. He hurried on, knowing he wasn't a fit sight.

Chapter Four

THE GREAT HOUSE

In the timber's speckled shade, Daniel Wade cut and sawed, split, gathered, and loaded armfuls of firewood into the wagon. On this second day after the fight, he still winced from the numerous dents Tim Forehand's fists had made. Yesterday he had held back from church-going. If his neighbors expected him to strut, and mistook his absence for victor's stratagem calculated to cause further awe of the only conqueror of Coon Creek's mighty champion, they were dead wrong. All of him above the waist felt bruised, and he wondered if Tim's face bore as many marks as his own.

None of the Wades had attended church. His father would not again as long as Levi Winn preached Union.

So today it was good to sweat, to move without thinking. Fetching another load to the wagon by the timber's edge, he noticed a horseman cantering across the cow pasture. He knew the high-stepping copper gelding almost at once, as he had the English two-seater Saturday evening.

Justin Vandiver waved. Out of apparent heed

for the nervous brown mules, he reined down to a running walk. He called out a greeting and just before he halted and dismounted, for a fleetness, Daniel got a striking effect of flawless rider and mount. It was like a scene in a print—an heroic pose in the Andy Jackson book. Why, Daniel couldn't understand. Unless—unless it was the way the dazzling sunlight happened to fall on face and figure, on polished leather and coppery flanks, but he knew that wasn't why. It was something he felt.

Vandiver swung down, and Daniel saw the blue gaze go over him, a pointed scrutiny that questioned. Vandiver's manner was strangely one of embarrassment.

"Daniel," he said, "I think I owe you an apology."

"Don't see how."

"Didn't you get in a fight at the dance . . . with Tim Forehand over something he said about my family?"

"Tim was looking for a reason. He found it."

"But it was a reference, wasn't it"—his expression was amused—"about us *quality* Vandivers?"

"Tim was half drunk," Daniel said. For no reason at all he was defending Forehand, and it puzzled him.

"Just the same, I'm sorry you had trouble on our account."

Daniel added no more. How could he explain how it happened?

Vandiver shook his head, a trifle bewildered. "Here you whip the big buck of the lick and you don't want to talk about it, believe I'd brag. . . . Too, I've a message from my sister. No chance for her to tell you at the dance. She wants you to come over Sunday afternoon. She said something about some books."

Daniel's mouth fell ajar. His heart seemed to leave off, to start up again. He tried to cover his amazement and knew he hadn't.

"She didn't get your letter until she came home Friday after visiting some of our quality kin in Columbia." Again his amusement showed. "Two o'clock be suitable? I told her perhaps that wouldn't be. Your work?"

"I'll be there," Daniel said.

With incredible slowness the days dragged past until Sunday afternoon. Did, until the moment he turned off the road to stride down the lane leading to the massive house. His assurance evaporated and he felt an actual dread of rushing forward too fast, of being ill-prepared.

His appearance fretted him most. He wore his father's black stock, which was too small for the strong column of his throat; a white shirt and his own brown coat, outgrown, several inches short for his long arms, a well-brushed brown hat of chimney-pot shape, and brown-yellow nankeen trousers—all usually reserved for Sunday and special occasions. His mother's knowledgeable washing of the durable trousers in warm water and Irish potato scrapings had finally removed vestiges of the fight. But, to Daniel's dismay, at the price of shrinking up around his ankles. Also, he had chosen to walk instead of ride a mule, which, obviously, wouldn't be proper. Walking, however, laid a film of dust over his greased brogans, and his only alternative was a sly swipe or two before Miss Laurel noticed.

He went on doggedly. He reached the dusty lane's end and passed through the open gate of a black iron ornamental fence. His heavy brogans clumped on red bricks that he knew came from Major Vandiver's kiln, no less, laid in a pretty drive curving up past a mounting block to the front door. Neat brick walls led away and behind the house. Beyond, he noted a sturdy wooden building that he took for the ice house he'd heard about—folks said the Vandivers had watermelon on Christmas day—and the latticed face of a summer house. Off yonder, he saw the wilted countenance of a vast flower garden, which somehow retained a suggestion of faded spring and summer glory.

These were mere glimpses, mere impressions. For it was the house that gripped his attention, as it had since he could remember passing on the road to town. Up close it loomed much larger, a grand white cloud resting among the giant trees.

His brogans thumped across the wide verandah to the door. He delayed, took charge of himself, and worked the brass knocker three times, the harsh metallic raps grating on his ears. A pause, the rustle of footsteps, and a Negro woman opened the door. Her pleasant eyes beheld him curiously.

"I'm Daniel Wade . . . ."

"Come in, Mistuh Wade," she said in the softest voice of his recollection, before he could finish his rehearsed speech. "Miz' Laurel is expectin' you."

As she took his hat and showed him toward the parlor, he felt his brogans sink into a moss of carpeting. To his left climbed the arching spine of a polished mahogany staircase. When he turned his head, the Negro woman wasn't in sight. One thing he'd noticed right away: she didn't have the servility of a slave. She didn't even act like one. Neither did she flaunt the brass of a free nigger.

He posted himself on the edge of a carved divan and gazed around, conscious of his long-conjectured picture changing. There was a simple, refined elegance here, not exaggerated, not over-indulged. He gazed at the piano. At the stately clock ticking on the mantel over the brick fireplace where a cheerful fire burned. At lamps, at tables with arched legs.

His trailing eyes paused, fixed on the painted portrait of a woman whose life-like resemblance to Miss Laurel startled him. He rose to stand nearer the wall, drawn by the unusual warmth that seemed to live still in the depths of the violet eyes. His mind swept back.

"Do you remember her, Mister Wade?"

He started and turned at Laurel's voice. She came to him in greeting, offering her hand. And in the little while that he held it, he felt again her hidden strength that he had discovered during the dance.

He nodded, flashing back, seeing a buggy and two children near his own age and an extremely pretty woman driving a fine team.

"Do you remember the time you were walking along the road, and my mother wanted you to ride with us and you wouldn't get in?"

"My shoes were muddy," Daniel said.

"But a thunder storm was coming up. She worried about you all the way home."

Shoes! He'd forgotten to clean his while he waited. "Your mother," he said, hesitating, "was the finest-looking lady a body could hope to see anywhere."

Her face grew quietly composed. "Thank you for saying so, Mister Wade."

Before long he was seated on the divan. She

occupied the chair across from him, enveloped in the rustling waves of many petticoats and the long skirt of her green dress, held out with hoops. If she noticed the marks on his face or his dusty shoes or his high-water trousers, he couldn't tell by her expression.

He became lost for words. His throat felt dry. He observed her more closely. Her features weren't so perfect as her dead mother's, although he supposed artists painted people more exactly than they looked in real life. Her mouth curved up just a trifle in one corner when she smiled. Her nose tilted ever so little at the end. To him those minute exceptions in an otherwise patrician face only made her more real, less remote. He was staring. Realizing, he focused his gaze on the carpet.

"How did you get home that day?" she asked.

"I cut across the fields. When the storm came, I hid in a cave near the old Indian mound."

"A mound . . . an Indian mound?" she said, intrigued.

"You've never been there?"

"Oh, no. Nor even heard of it."

It gave him a pleasant feeling to fill that gap in her knowledge. "It's down a way from the persimmon grove."

"It must be very interesting. I'd like to go there sometime." She seemed sincere; she just wasn't making parlor chatter.

He began talking. For the next several minutes he described the place and his findings there, arrowheads, a stone hatchet head. A sobering thought weakened his enthusiasm. He had no horse, no buggy, no way of taking her to the mound. And would she go if *he* asked her?

"Would you like to see the library, Mister Wade?"

She seemed to speak just when he ran out of something more to say, standing as he rose and leading away across the plain of velvety carpet to a corner of the house. There, sunbeams played over the room through windows on two sides.

He caught his breath over the books. They sprang in tiers toward the high ceiling, clad in magnificent mahogany cases. He forgot her, he forgot his surroundings as he swept his hungry gaze over the brown and black volumes, some embellished with gold lettering. These books were as new friends, ready to welcome him and to share their secrets with him. He stepped across, his eyes gulping the titles—Irving, Hawthorne, Shakespeare, Scott, Byron, Carlyle, and more, more! Their mere numbers overwhelmed him, turned him both humble and elated.

Miss Laurel chose a small book from its case. "Here are the poems by Keats," she said.

He took the book reverently, his brown fingers opening and closing around it. "I'll take mighty good care of Mister Keats," he swore.

"You may have more than one book," she said, smiling at his earnestness. "Why don't you take several at least?"

"I'd rather borrow one at a time." He was tempted by his hunger. But what if something happened to a single one of these treasures? How would he repair it or replace it?

"Father says not enough of them get read."

"You must have read a good many fine books at the academy."

She contorted her face, wryly engaging. "Some . . . when we weren't learning about manners and the arts and such accomplishments as grotto-work and gilding on wood." She curtsied and assumed an elegant pose of extreme high dignity and superior breeding. Her violet eyes acquired an indifferent expression. "Mister Wade," she breathed, aloof, "you must be aware that our Conservatory of Music is unexcelled anywhere. . . . That our Expression Department has no rival within the spacious borders of all Missouri . . . even America . . . and, dare I say, Europe itself. . . . Our moral life here at the academy is beyond the teeniest hint of reproach, sir. . . . Indeed, only high-born young ladies may attend our noble institution . . . ."

For another moment she continued to regard him from that detached attitude, and then, unforeseen, they were laughing together.

"That's why I liked your letter, Daniel," she

79

went on. "There was heart in it. Sincerity. It was even a little funny, for truly I detest persimmons."

She did beat all! He was discovering that sometimes she called him Mr. Wade, which made him uncomfortable, and sometimes Daniel, which he liked.

"I didn't know what you'd think," he said.

"Think!" She held her chin high, her affront instantaneous, and a bit lofty, he thought. "Did you think I would show the discourtesy of not replying?"

"Well, I didn't know. You see there's a heap of difference, Miss Laurel. You're a young lady and all, the daughter of . . . ." He stumbled, suddenly over his head. And with a teasing smile, she supplied for him: " . . . of a slave owner. Though we don't call them slaves. We call them by their first names, or refer to them as darkies or our black folks."

He sighed his relief. "There was no call for me to feel bad if you didn't answer. Maybe you figured I was presuming, and now I know I was."

Her laughter tinkled as little bells. "Daniel Wade, you *are* an honest boy."

Her eyes, he'd learned after this time, were not only warm and kind but humorously discerning. He stood rather close to her, and he wondered when that had happened. The sunlight found flecks of red and gold in her light brown hair, worn in curls over her forehead. Her way of pinning it up well back drew attention to the slender shaft of her white throat, which pulsed when she laughed. She had the sheer breasts of a budding young girl. Her waist was no larger than a sapling.

He got the faintness of a wonderful sweet mist about her face and hair. Its exact essence escaped him. Whatever, it was beyond his limited experience. The closest he could judge was peach blossoms. He'd never known another girl quite like her. She seemed, like Justin, to belong elsewhere than among the prosaic, mule-and-fodder surroundings of Foley's Prairie.

He saw her searching his face. "I know it's not mannerly of me to ask," she said, her voice grave. "But what in the world happened to you?"

He touched his face involuntarily. While spellbound over the books, he had forgotten his scarred features. And the perception gathered that the paths of their conversation had been leading to this question. Why not tell her he'd whipped Tim Forehand? Impress her? These thoughts raced as he scanned the bookshelves again.

"Nothing happened," he said, an answer, he realized at once, that wasn't an answer. Movement took his eye. He turned.

Major Vandiver stood in the library entrance, elderly, massive, dignified, snow-white beard banked down the broad grade of his chest.

Laurel was a moment speaking. "Father . . . this is Daniel Wade."

"Indeed . . . indeed!" He had a cavernous voice. "We need no introductions."

Having never met the major, having never been nearer him than about the distance from the porch of Rookwood's store to the post office, Daniel was taken aback by such heartiness. The major advanced in measured step, impressive in black swallowtail, broadcloth coat, set off by gray pantaloons, austere satin vest, and low shoes and white stockings. His presence dominated the room.

Daniel waited for him to speak again.

"Good afternoon, young man."

"Good afternoon, sir."

Major Vandiver's handshake was precise, formal, and brief.

A pause fell, and stayed, and all at once the afternoon changed for Daniel. A cloud seemed to pass over the sunlit room. His stiff awkwardness recurred. He saw inquiring gray eyes peruse his face, dwell there, appraising, and slide over his clothing and drop, last, to the book he held. He had a nettling sensation, as though from under the cliff-like brows the major was sizing him up and down and around and under as a buyer might look for blemishes on a mule. Yet Daniel saw no actual surface rudeness, for the major was too much a gentleman, but the questioning was real, a disapproval Daniel sensed more than he saw.

Then, in a voice that seemed to come to his defense, Miss Laurel said: "I've invited Mister Wade to borrow some books. Heaven knows they get little use, as you say."

"By all means." Into the strong, fleshy features there crept a new contemplation, akin to surprise. "You read much, young man?"

"Whatever I can find."

Major Vandiver gestured Daniel to a chair and slowly, likewise, lowered his dignified self. Laurel became a part of the background.

"You sound ambitious," he said. "But perhaps you ought to be more selective for the sake of your mind."

"There's not much choice, sir . . . wasn't until Miss Laurel kindly showed me your fine library."

"What do you make of UNCLE TOM'S CABIN?"

"It's not a true picture. Not in Missouri."

The massive white head nodded, approving. "True or not, it's got the North stirred up. You would be better informed to read the newspapers."

"It seems to me, sir, the papers are one-sided, too. I was hoping you had a book they say is far more truthful than UNCLE TOM'S CABIN."

"What is it?"

"THE IMPENDING CRISIS OF THE SOUTH. By a man named Helper. A Southerner."

Major Vandiver's eyes cut. "You won't find it in my library, young man. I consider it dangerous to the South . . . and, well, to the Union as well. Incendiary. Inflammatory. Seditious. South Carolina has banned it."

Daniel, while reared to respect his elders, couldn't hold back. "Maybe they banned it because it's true. Because slavery does hurt the poor whites." There! He'd said too much. He could tell by the major's firming jaw and by Miss Laurel's apprehensive face.

"Young man, if I were you, I'd read the book before I referred to it."

Daniel nodded agreement. "I just read an account in the Missouri *Republican*. It said that, although the South claims otherwise, the North produces more farm products. That the North's hay crop is about twice the value of the South's cotton crop. That only in Indian corn and beans and peas are the slave states really ahead. That free labor is more profitable than slave labor. That. . . ."

Major Vandiver towered up from his chair, all his dignity summoned. The pouches under his straight, hard eyes looked ashy pale. In that instant Daniel thought of his father's inflexible face at the church. The major said: "Take some advice. For the sake of yourself and your parents, and in view of the feelings around here about the Union and secession, I suggest you watch your tongue. Weigh every word before you utter it."

Daniel was stunned into silence.

After a little, the major's rigid expression abated. A part of his former cordiality reappeared, yet just a part. "You understand, young man. Of course, you do. I favor keeping the Union together along with its old traditions." Fixing Laurel a look, he left the room on measured steps.

Daniel faced her, an apology rushing to his lips. Both hands were pressed to her cheeks. He saw concern and perhaps he saw fear. He said: "I didn't mean . . . ."

She shook her head. "It wasn't your fault. Father can't talk about things any more without losing his temper."

"I'd better not borrow this, after all," he decided, and handed the book across.

"No!" She pushed the book away. "You must read it!"

For a pause they held that deadlock, her warm hands resisting against his. She was determined. She meant for him to take the book home. He saw that truth, and he drew back. He said again —"I'll take mighty good care of it."—and saw her lips form humorously to his seriousness. So in that brief time she had regained her self-control.

Walking down the lane, the book tucked under

one arm, he considered the major and discovered a keen disappointment. The major talked Union and slavery together, when they couldn't be patched up any more, and he held himself powerful high, although he could have reasons.

A horseman turned off the road and entered the lane. It was Stark Hooper, who spied Daniel at the same time. As Hooper rode toward him, Daniel saw the astonished fall of his mouth.

Hooper pulled up. His eyes clawed over the meaning of the book; they said Daniel had no right here. "I hear you whipped Tim Forehand," Hooper said, and, when Daniel didn't answer, he added curiously: "It's hard to believe, looking at your face."

A white heat plunged through Daniel. He managed to say: "Didn't you see it? You were there."

"I was escorting Miss Laurel to her carriage. As a rule, I avoid country brawls."

"I reckon shaking hands is more your style than fighting."

Hooper flushed. He set spurs, his mount bounding ahead, and Daniel walked on. Yet he was seeing Stark Hooper's new suit and vest and hat, and he almost envied Hooper then.

His consciousness of that handicap never entirely left him, even when he called a third time, not long before Christmas, to return

Carlyle's FRENCH REVOLUTION. He wore the same tight-fitting coat and trousers, the same hat and heavy brogans. At least, knowing what to expect by now, he had achieved a moderate self-confidence. First, a chat in the parlor with Laurel, an interval in the library to choose another book, then departure.

He lifted the brass knocker, rapped discreetly, and waited, hat in hand. There wasn't time for the just-audible rustle of footsteps. Instantly the door opened, and he looked into the level stare of Major Vandiver.

Daniel, surprised, delayed for him to speak first. He received no more than a bare inquiring: "Yes?"

"I've . . . I've come to see Miss Laurel, sir," Daniel said, thinking the book he held was explicit enough. Always before the soft-voiced Negro woman had seemed to anticipate his calling.

Still, Major Vandiver did not step back in invitation. The trap of his mouth opened a crack and clamped shut. Daniel saw the shadow of reluctance; it began to fade, then vanished, swept aside by the decision settling over the proud face.

"Young man, I regret to inform you of this. But my daughter is not at home to you."

Daniel stood motionless, stupefied. The major's next words struck about his ears like hail: "Perhaps I do not make myself clear. Miss Laurel does not wish to see you today and will not at anytime in the future."

Daniel's voice had fled, deserting his throat to hide in the wall of his chest.

"You understand, young man?"

There crashed upon him unbearable shock and hurt, and last of all a futile anger that paralyzed his throat and tangled him deeper in shameful muteness. Everything he felt Daniel knew must be written across his numb face and staring eyes, because he saw the major give a tiny wince and he heard him murmur, yet firmly— "I'm sorry, my boy."—just before he closed the great door.

Daniel remembered nothing more except the clump of his brogans falling as stones on the wide verandah. Not until he turned out on the road did he, with a start, discover the book still in his hand. He looked at it, sickened anew. Just its touch burned his flesh. He jerked to rush back, but realized he was too late. His vision was blurred. Objects had a hazy look. He brushed a hand across his cheek; it came away damp. He walked head down, his angry shame unreceding.

He slept that night uneasily, sick anger rising to his brain, as strong as before, his first thought when he woke in the black of early morning to the sound of wind and rain flailing and shaking the old house. He listened a while, his senses telling him the rumbling storm was wearing itself out. A pit of rain stung his face. He lay still, blinking, thinking. Suddenly, in panic, he threw back the covers and stumbled across the wet floor to the chair by the open window. He groped and touched the chair seat and swayed away, too sick at heart to pick up the ruin of Carlyle's water-soaked masterpiece.

Chapter Five

THE COON CREEK BOYS

Muffled against a cold February wind, Daniel was in a relaxed mood as he sent his mules jingling toward Foley's Prairie. Late as he'd been about it, he could mark off an achievement at last. Save for scant wood chopping and corn husking now and then, there was no hiring on neighboring farms during the winter. In his bitter determination he had become quite a searcher, sometimes striding fifteen miles for half a day's work, once seeking as far north as Monroe County, only to return without fortune and part of his savings spent. But today he had enough chore money to send off for a new copy of the FRENCH REVOLUTION, an amount learned through correspondence with a Boston publishing house.

Passing the persimmon grove reminded him with wounding clarity of his brief experience with nonsense last autumn. Off there, the leafless trees and the dead-grassed hills looked bare and ugly. He felt the hold of a mirthless self-derision. Why, the major had done him a favor! By relaying Miss Laurel's wish, the major had saved him a harsher lesson later on. What an ignorant fool he'd been to think she might see something in a country jake whose clothes fit like a scarecrow's, whose manners were crude, whose—he stopped in disgust.

Yet when he started along the stretch where the Vandiver house loomed, starkly white among the naked trees, all his feelings sprang up to torture him again, and he knew an actual pain of body and mind. He fought the impulse not to whip the mules faster.

When he drove in from the north, an unusual racket of drumming was *r-r-rumping* up from the east and west sides of town. There was no let-up to the swelling beats; the sounds rode hard on the gusty wind, as though two companies marched, instead of one.

Some distance along the broad street, he looked west and saw Stark Hooper's unmistakable figure erect alongside the Union company. Daniel pulled up to watch them turn by him. At Hooper's hoarse shout they swung onto Main, brogans tramping a steady rhythm. Daniel noticed the difference. They marched straighter today; they kept their ranks more even and in better time. Less bumping now on the turn. Perched on the high wagon seat, he saw Coon Creek faces casting him looks as they filed past. Hooper paid him not the slightest recognition.

Daniel was ready to follow in the company's wake when the coming of the second drum caused him to look curiously around. The second company came on in a manner equally as steady as the Union boys, and the trim figure in command marched as Daniel pictured an experienced officer—none of Hooper's exaggerated strut. Some young men wore red shirts that peeked beneath the collars of their heavy coats and black trousers. A few carried rifles, most nothing at all. The blur of approaching faces cleared, materialized to familiar shapes. Sim Russell, intent, proud, cheeks pinked by the cold, marched in the leading line of fours.

Daniel turned his closer attention to the trim officer, clad in gray hat, gray frock coat, and blue trousers, and felt no surprise when he found it was Justin Vandiver.

Vandiver's voice, distinct and calm, ordered the turn. His men drew about. They went *hup-hup* down the street, bound for the center of town where Hooper was lining up his company for dismissal in front of Rookwood's.

A realization overspread Daniel. The gap of

two months suddenly closed. He sat hunched and stiff. In the Confederate company, formed since his last trip to town after Christmas, and in Hooper's were just about all his friends. While he watched, they seemed to be marching away from him, and he was separated from them forever.

Afterward he did a thing he had never done before. He drove behind the store and tied his team. Slipping quietly through the Saturday crowd, he made his way around to the street. The Unionists had broken up. He saw Andy Green and Tim Forehand going across to the tavern. Other Coon Creekers watched while Vandiver prepared to dismiss the Confederates. The Coon Creek boys laughed and called out good-naturedly to Sim Russell, and mocked his stand at attention—chins high, mouths pulled grimly down, lower lips protruding, chests arched, arms sprung back.

Their laughter pinched off when Daniel stopped to watch. No one spoke to him. He went on to the post office. Coming out minutes later, he noticed they hadn't moved. No laughter relaxed their faces now. He saw an elbow dig, and he heard a muttering pass. They all turned to watch him.

A cool ripple started creeping up Daniel's back. His heart was hammering. He took slow steps toward them, expecting a quarrelsome remark. To his surprise they said not a word, although their eyes were hostile and their mouths ridiculing. By then he was past them, aware that no one had moved. But when he came to the store's corner and turned, he heard their heavy steps pick up on the plank walk and follow him.

He kept his pace deliberate. He reached the alley's entrance and paused, so they could see he wasn't hurrying. He turned into the alley, covered several rods, and came to a flat-footed stop. His team and wagon were gone.

He stared blankly, until the gnaw of a savage comprehension broke through. He wheeled and saw them watching him, and, if he hadn't known before, their malicious expressions told him beyond any doubt.

A taunting shaped across their fixed faces, a wild violence.

There was a heaving pressure in Daniel's stomach, a swelling thick in his throat. He took one backward step and stopped, forcing himself to hold his place.

Without a word they rushed him.

He struck the nearest face and saw it keel away. But before he could land another blow a crush of muscular bodies slammed into him. He felt a volley of fists and kicks upon his flesh. His hat toppled, was stomped under. His head buzzed. His heavy coat hindered him. He wrenched loose, and they surged after him like a pack of farm dogs, their throat-torn voices rising around him.

He smashed another face. He used his knee when somebody rammed him—a blow that straightened up the Coon Creek boy, as the fight became a welter of flying arms and legs and heaving bodies, as they beat him backward. Suddenly they had him ringed in, and he couldn't stand off so many. His back jarred hard against the wall of a wooden shed. Its jolt gave him a flash of strength. He swung fiercely, clearing a space, and braced himself, hacking for wind: "Come on . . . one at a time."

They formed a half-circle close about him, their eyes glittering. One fighter groped for him, and another. Daniel, swinging, tried to ward them off singly. He was punching and wrenching from side to side to keep the wall at his back, when two figures ran down the alley.

The next he knew someone was roaring—"Let 'im be!"—and pawing his attackers, shedding them with each powerful hand swipe. Two men burst through the pack.

The first and biggest was Tim Forehand, the other Andy Green. They squared around and seemed to post themselves beside Daniel, and Forehand raked his voice over the Coon Creekers: "I say let 'im be. He whipped me fair an' square. I'll bust the first man that jumps him."

Daniel was as dumbfounded as the Coon Creekers. They exchanged astonished looks and fixed open-mouthed stares on Forehand.

"Maybe so," a winded voice spoke up finally. "But why'n't he join up?"

Forehand's ruddy features spewed scorn. "You just been in a month yourself, Seth. When'd you git so almighty right like a preacher?"

Seth Coots's homely face went blank. He shook his head as a man dazed. "But you. . . ."

"Never mind what I said before," Forehand anticipated him. "Ain't a body got a choice? Why, you aimed to join the Confederates once."

"I reckon a body has," Coots begrudged. "Except. . . ."

"Except, hell! An' where's his team and wagon?"

The Coon Creekers stirred guiltily.

"Well . . . go git 'em!" Forehand roared, and they started off.

Daniel, astonishment still upon him, picked up his wadded hat and began slapping out the dirt and reshaping the crown. He said: "I'm obliged. School was just about out for me."

"I ain't one to hold a grudge," Forehand said, and thrust out his thick right hand. Daniel took it.

Andy Green said: "Dan, you been mule-headed for a good spell. Join up. Now. That is, if you want to."

Daniel continued to knead his hat.

"You can't put it off much longer," Green said.

"Looks like I will, Andy."

95

"But why? Why?"

They didn't understand, and he didn't either, precisely. Except that, when he spoke, he seemed to find the very kernel of the thing he sought: "Because I can't see myself killing Sim Russell or Justin Vandiver. Nor you or Tim or Jesse . . . if I was on the other side."

As the words fell and he finished, they left a vague sense within Daniel of having compounded a riddle that none of them could quite fathom, simply because they had not experienced enough.

"I see," Andy Green said, but his voice trailed off. He continued to watch Daniel, but his glance was sidelong.

Such gravity was too much for Tim Forehand. "Perfessor, you're the only lad that ever bested me man to man. So they must be something to what you're sayin'," and he whacked Daniel across the back.

Chapter Six

BROTHER WINN'S PROPHECY

To Daniel, winter's last harsh days hung on with defiant surliness and delayed the plowing, the oat sowing, and early corn planting. When weeks passed and the book did not arrive, he questioned his decision. Now the Vandivers would think he intended to keep the original volume, better had he returned it ruined. He paid less heed than usual to the papers, to the news of seceding Southern states seizing one federal arsenal after another. It seemed long ago, yet only February, when Missouri had voted against secession.

Thus, on a Monday in middle April, after dinner, when Reuben Nance came saddling up to the house, he supposed the call was to fill some neighborly need.

Daniel's father went to the door and raised a greeting, but Nance didn't dismount. He rode up closer and said solemnly—"Heard the news, Sam?"—and before Sam Wade could ask what, Nance said: "Fort Sumter fell yesterday . . . surrendered. Word came in over the telegraph in town."

Emily Wade hurried to the doorway, her dark eyes narrowing. "Reuben, you mean the war's started?"

"Ain't shootin' war?" Sam Wade answered for him. "Get ready, Em. We're goin' into town."

At two-thirty that afternoon Foley's Prairie appeared to be celebrating the 4th of July. Over the wide porch of Rookwood's store the flag whipped in silky furls. From the middle of the broad street bandsmen tooted a ragged, but spirited, rendition of "Yankee Doodle". Families crowded the walks, stood in the streets and around wagons and buggies, and Daniel saw more people swarming in from the country, afoot, driving, horseback. A sign sprouted up above the milling throng: SONS OF THE SOUTH. The tavern was doing a steady business.

But the thickest mass was outside the office of the weekly *Citizen*, an old-line Whig paper turned Republican and, accordingly, forever banned in the Sam Wade household. Men kept going up and scanning sheets of paper posted on the message board by the office door, then turning away to gesture and talk some more. While Daniel watched, a stooped man, haggard, distraught, shirt sleeves rolled up, eyeglasses perched low on the long prong of his nose, appeared with a bundle of newspapers, a signal that brought the crowd surging about him.

Going across with his father, Daniel felt a swell of pride. No man was any calmer, and many were not so calm. Despite his limp, Sam Wade carried himself with soldierly possession, and Daniel saw respect in the eyes of men returning his father's nod.

A wedge of men and boys blocked them off before they reached the newspaper office. His father borrowed a copy of the *Citizen* and started reading. He read in rapid jumps, his flint-blue eyes flicking over the columns. Without a word he passed the paper to Daniel. It was full of the siege and surrender, about Major Anderson and General Beauregard, and President Lincoln's appeal for volunteers. Daniel's eyes caught on an advertisement near the bottom of the front page. A slave buyer wished to purchase "one-hundred likely young Negroes from 10-25 years of age. I will pay the *Highest Cash Prices. . . .*"

After a bit the Wades rejoined Emily at the wagon, and presently Daniel heard a distant stir, a murmur of approval and expectancy, and hand clapping, and he saw a stout box being fetched from Rookwood's and placed under the flag. And over the heads of the watchers the high hat of a man started passing through the crowd like a length of upright stovepipe. Gradually the figure of the wearer became discernible, a broad, dignified man, and Daniel saw Major Vandiver ascend the box.

Just seeing the major again hurled the heat of hurt anger through Daniel. He watched the major raise his right hand and deliberately remove his enormous hat, the practiced movement of a speaker to command attention before he spoke.

"Friends . . . fellow Missourians . . . ," the major began, his voice as resonant as a bugle call. Another wave of applause drowned out his following words.

Daniel was absorbed, listening, straining to hear above the noise, when his eyes found Miss Laurel's face in the crowd on the store's bunting-draped porch. A paralyzing ache overcame him. A saucy, flowered hat crowned her brown curls. Now and again she moved her graceful shoulders and twirled her pretty blue parasol. She looked proud and self-possessed, a part of the excited throng. Justin stood with her. In contrast to the other agitated young men, he seemed almost indifferent.

Fragments of the major's speech lodged in Daniel's mind: " . . . .no state has labored more faithfully than Missouri. . . . We have but one course to pursue . . . honor and responsibility. . . . Our sisters of the South. . . ."

He looked at her again, then turned to listen. The major was calling for calm, for preservation of the Union, for protection of property. And property, Daniel well knew, meant slaves. The major wanted no change, when change was already here.

When Daniel let his eyes stray again, Justin had gone. Stark Hooper stood beside Laurel. His gold-braided uniform gave him a resolute air. People kept glancing his way. When Hooper's eyes weren't on the major, he was bending to murmur to Miss Laurel or brushing lint off the spotless sleeve of his uniform. Her thoughts, it was evident, weren't entirely on her father. Or Hooper. She would look close about and off and around. Yet always, when Hooper spoke, her searching had stopped.

Daniel saw her gaze travel past him and hesitate, suddenly to swing back. He saw her discover him, and he experienced a wonderful longing. She showed a faint start of recognition, but then, as he stood transfixed, too frozen to do other than stare back, she tilted her chin and appeared not to see him at all. A coolness transformed her lively face. She said something to Hooper, who launched into an attentive comment.

For the life of him, Daniel couldn't bring his mind to bear fully on the gist of the speech. All he could make out, between listening and watching Laurel, was that the major, although opposed to secession, was equally against the use of arms to compel the South to stay in the Union. By then the major was stepping down to moderate applause while the band played the new Southern song, "My Bonnie Blue Flag", and, when Daniel looked for her once more, Hooper was escorting Laurel through the crowd to her father.

Judge Hooper took the box next. A tall, stately, side-whiskered man with sad gray eyes, pleasant but unsmiling, he spoke in lofty-sounding tones of the Constitution and the Declaration of Independence. Secession wasn't right; it wasn't legal. Missouri must not allow the impulsive actions of other states to sway her toward violence.

"Missouri is not South, it is not North," he

concluded gravely. "It is both. We are one."

About then Daniel located Laurel and her father across the street. Her attention no longer wandered. She held her gaze straight on the judge, who was receiving respectful applause and a round of "Yankee Doodle". The crowd, Daniel sensed, wanted one side or the other, not fence-straddling compromise.

Daniel heard a commotion, sudden movements, shouts, and he saw old Tobe Russell mount the box. Russell snatched off his hat and swayed, his quick old eyes glittery and wild and a little drunken. Here was a later image of young Sim Russell: vindictive, independent, hot-headed, rough-talking, tobacco juice staining gray chin whiskers, but, also, loyal and generous and God-fearing, a product of the old Missouri frontier.

He swung his arms and said: "With all due respect to the major an' the judge, I can't agree with 'em a-tall." A good many laughed and clapped. "I say no state's got call on another'n. An' I won't put up with no Black Republican or no cowardly Abolitionist . . . the kind that sneaks up and sets fire to a man's barn in the dead of night . . . a-comin' in here tryin' to tell us how to run our affairs. By jinks, no!"

"You tell 'em, Tobe!"

"Hangin's too good for Abolitionists!"

Daniel's father was grimly nodding, affirming.

"An' they's the foreigners . . . the Dirty Dutch

that's come into our grand old state," Tobe Russell stormed on. "They aim to set the niggers free amongst us, they do. Stir up trouble for peaceful folks." His raspy voice arched higher. He was shaking with self-righteous fury. "Why is it the Yankees treat their help worse'n the sorriest nigger ever was? Tell me! An' if a state's got to be hog-tied to the Union against its will, then I say the Union's no good, nohow. An' if the Union states aim to try it on us, I say let's settle this thing once and for all!" He slapped his hat against his lean thigh, uttered a piercing hunter's yell, and, stepping down unsteadily, flung a last greeting to the crowd, a wave that struck Daniel as somehow pathetic.

Old Tobe received considerable applause, and the band played "Dixie", but it wasn't an ovation. There were a good many Union families turned out today, Southern folks among them.

"Somebody speak for the Union!" a man shouted. Other voices took up the cry.

Already a rake-handle shape, in shabby hat and coat, was going forward, and when Brother Levi Winn stood up on the box, Daniel's first thought was of a gaunt scarecrow looking down over dense ranks of waving corn. The crowd fell oddly silent, perhaps dreading the voice of its own conscience, and Daniel heard his father mutter and saw him grow stiff and forbidding.

Brother Winn, hat in hand, considered his

listeners much as he would his little New Hope congregation. Except he seemed different some ways. His uncut reddish hair looked longer and more unkempt, and in the cave-like sockets of his eyes there burned a weary reproach. He prayed, even here, and so long the crowd became restless. At last, when he touched forth on Galatians and Ephesians again, treading softly, Daniel saw the prelude to another thundering sermon, such as the one that had caused his father to depart the church. But Brother Winn continued the same softly inquiring tone: "Why should any man ask more rights and privileges for himself than he's willin' to give all others? Your first allegiance ain't to the state of Missouri, generous as it is, or to the old Union or the new Confederacy . . . it's to God Almighty, an' He says let the oppressed go free. Treat all men as brothers. Gentile or Jew . . . black or white."

An angry shout tore: "This ain't Sunday, Levi!"

"I know it," Brother Winn rebuked, unperturbed. "An' I ain't through."

Daniel prepared for the familiar foot stomping and arm waving, the head shaking and the chest pounding. He waited, but those gestures didn't come.

"What's happened, folks, is this," Brother Winn said. "The Lord brought us into a plentiful land to eat the fruit and the goodness thereof. And what did we do? We dee-filed the land, we polluted it . . . the gift. Done it with human bondage. . . . Old Jeremiah he said . . . 'Thine wickedness shall correct thee.' And old St. Paul he said . . . 'He that doeth wrong shall receive for the wrong that he hath done' . . . an' they's no respect of persons."

Brother Winn seemed to grow taller and his voice softer, yet still distinct, his mournful eyes more brooding, and of a sudden to Daniel it was as if a page turned and Brother Winn, the long scythe of his bony right arm outstretched, stood above them wearing Biblical camel's hair and a leathern girdle.

"I'm goin' to make a prophecy," he said, and was silent. He ran his eyes about. An unwillingness poured into his drawn face. "An unquenchable fire is comin'. A mighty wrath. We can't run now. There's hardly a family around Foley's Prairie that won't suffer, I'm sorry to say."

The stillness of the crowd was also Daniel's, and shortly he heard a muttering commence and come as a rising wind along the packed street, in it a protest likewise his own, an intolerable objection.

A shred of time passed. It took another moment for Daniel to understand. That was all of the prophecy. As Brother Winn stepped down, a spasm of movement jerked the watchers nearest Daniel. His father started off, his face a pale mask. Emily Wade's intuitive hand reached out and settled over his arm. Sam Wade held up.

Daniel was aware of anger-flushed faces wheeling for Brother Winn, now passing through the throng. He heard resentful voices and he experienced the sweep of an erupting excitement. Just a scattering of these men owned or hired darkies. Still, some mysterious identification seemed to connect them, to muddy their reason and control. Against them, as a slow-forming tide, he could see small drifts of Union men arraying themselves to protest Brother Winn. One shoving and shouting match started.

A rapid *r-r-rump r-r-rump* broke out from up the street. It was thumping steadily before Daniel grasped a sudden change: the jostling had ceased almost as it began. Men were turning to the sounds, the dark contortions on their faces dissolving. He saw relief as well. A shamefacedness, too, as neighbor drew away from neighbor to clear the street, for the Unionists were *hupping* forward, and the band, after a silence, was tooting "Yankee Doodle" again.

Stark Chittenden Hooper was outdoing himself, stiff-legged, erect as a flagpole, while the company, every man toting an old rifle or shotgun, determined, marched eyes front, brogans clomping. They tramped to hurrahs and cheers and hand clapping, past Rookwood's and the main body of the crowd. Whereupon Hooper bellowed them about, and they halted, arms grounded, facing back the way they had come.

A waiting—and more drumming kicked up and the Confederate company turned onto Main. The band, struggling, left "Yankee Doodle" and switched to "The Bonnie Blue Flag". All the marchers wore red shirts and blue trousers. Their stride was clumsy yet jaunty. Their self-conscious faces glowed. They carried an assortment of arms. Seeing Justin Vandiver, Daniel thought: *There's a soldier*.

When the Confederates drew abreast of Rookwood's, where the crowd was thickest, the cheering and clapping swelled. "Hurrah for Jeff Davis! Hurrah for South Carolina!" Onward, Vandiver maneuvered his column around and halted even with Hooper's. Each commander dressed ranks. Now, in unison, side-by-side, they marched away.

Caught unawares, the bandsmen struck up a tactful "The Arkansas Traveler". Two weaving figures struggled to mount the speaker's box at the same time. Both lost balance and fell. Everyone laughed. Finally Daniel saw it was a holiday.

When the companies reached the center of town, a deepening convulsion of emotion seized the crowd. The tumult rose to an uproar. Girls trailed beside the tramping columns, calling boys' names and waving. An old man hobbled out and touched Justin Vandiver's arm.

Two blocks farther the companies executed turns and marched back to Rookwood's, formed a solid front, and halted.

Right after dismissal an acuteness awoke in Daniel. Few young men other than those in the companies were on the street. People were staring at him. He could feel their eyes singling him out. They seemed to ask: *Why are you standing there with your family? Why aren't you in a company?* His face grew warm. Girls threw him inquiring looks as they strolled by on the arm of a carefree Unionist or Confederate. He saw a flicker strike across his father's lean face.

Nothing was said then.

Sam Wade, who was driving the mules, spoke when Foley's Prairie was a distant hum behind him. "I never thought a Wade wouldn't fight," he said; still, the tone of his voice left a hopeful waiting.

But Daniel, searching his own silence, couldn't find the meaning he thought his father would understand, and he said nothing back.

Chapter Seven

THE APPARITION

All at once Sam Wade began going into town every day for war news or over to the farms of his Southern neighbors, especially the Sampsons and the Russells, leaving early and often returning after dark. He looked grim and preoccupied, impelled by an urgent purpose. He muttered a good deal and brooded about raising troops and the fate of the federal arsenal in St. Louis, which side would seize it, and how he hankered to carry a rifle again as he had with Doniphan's men.

"You went once," Emily said. Although practical and patient, she was wise enough not to say her husband was too old for another war. "You did more than most, Sam."

"Leastwise," he said, for Daniel to hear, "I won't stand back if they's a fight . . . if I'm needed again, if the barn-burnin' Abolitionists invade Missouri."

"It's not them that worry me," she said thoughtfully. "It's our hot-headed Missouri folks. What they'll do."

"They'll fight!"

"I mean neighbor against neighbor, Sam. That's worse."

A week after Fort Sumter's fall Sam Wade came home in late afternoon to hand Daniel a brown package from Boston. His father lingered, the cant of his head inquiring.

"It's a book," Daniel said, hoping to end the questioning there.

"You have books."

"Not like this, Papa," Daniel said, and floundered. He had to explain, and he feared what would happen when he tried. "I borrowed a book," he said, shunning mention of the Vandiver name as long as he could.

"Borrowed . . . where?" Borrowing, according to Sam Wade's strict code of conduct, wasn't far from stealing if not scrupulously limited.

Daniel lagged.

"*Where,* I said!"

"From the Vandivers' library."

Sam Wade was astounded. "Them!" His eyes probed; they demanded a complete explanation.

"Papa, I was invited. Miss Laurel . . . . But the book got rained on . . . ruined. I ordered a new one to take back. You understand? This is it, here. I bought it with the chore money."

By the bore of the cool blue eyes and the angle of the gaunt, stubbled jaws, Daniel knew he had changed nothing.

"Just goes to show you had no right there in the first place," Sam Wade said, concluding the longest conversation between them since the day the companies had marched together.

His father kept occupying his thoughts while he tramped through the redolent April twilight with the book under his arm. Daniel didn't know him these days; they were as strangers at the same board. There was a distance between them, a terrible distance. Like, he thought darkly, one of them was already dead to the other. What could he do to make his father as he used to be, when the Wades drove to town every Saturday and visited neighbors, and went to dances and corn huskings, before the talk about secession and free niggers and war became a kind of creeping sickness, a hatred spreading from farm to farm? Would it help if he joined the Confederate Army?

The suggestion seemed to sneak up, to pounce suddenly upon him. He'd never thought about it before. He walked on, troubled. He didn't know what to do.

Evening's dimness blurred the high bulk of the vast house when Daniel approached down the lane. Lights glowed on the first floor. Someone was playing the piano, music that drifted and hung, trembling on the evening, enabling the ear to catch each soft note. He wished to pause and listen, but drove himself ahead. If he stopped now, he might never go to the house at all. Listening, striding through the muted light, he could doubt ever having been inside that white world yonder, having seen its cheerful rooms and known its friendly books.

He erased that picture from his mind and passed through the open gate. His brogans thudded on the brick drive. He walked faster. He stepped across the verandah and rapped lightly with the knocker, half expecting the major's formidable shape again.

To his intense relief the Negro woman answered the door. Her forming smile dulled. Her dark eyes tried to mask surprise and hesitation.

He said at once—"Please give this to Miss Laurel."—and was conscious of how his voice carried. He turned without another moment's delay, and, as he moved across the verandah, he heard the music stop.

Along the road the night was warm and vaporous, gorged with the spongy, growing scents of spring, alive with the humming of insects. Misty streamers of white clouds and a first quarter moon shed an eerie glow over the still countryside.

Daniel scarcely noticed. He held a slack pace, reflecting on his bare note: The book I borrowed from you was damaged beyond return by my negligence. Here is a new one in its place. I hope it will do. Sincerely . . . . Distaste for himself thickened to gall. How simple he sounded!

His progress was aimless, without much conscious direction. He lost all sense of time, and hence felt a faint start after a while to find himself approaching the fork where the road to Swink's Spring branched east. The night was darker, more still, unknown, mysterious. That was when he heard it. A single hoarse cry running across the silence, so compelling and savage and wrong that he froze, every sense flung awake. He waited for the cry to repeat, possibly to be joined by the baying of hounds. When nothing came, he dismissed it and continued on, and then puzzled.

Before he could reach the fork a sound drew him motionless again. Not a shout this time. The noise was fainter. A murmuring and mingling of voices, a whole chorus of them. Everything was coming from the spring road, behind the dark wall of trees yonder. As yet he could see no movement.

A tramping and muttering grew out of the darkness, and then, swiftly, where the branch road curved, Daniel saw the bobbing flare of several torches and the shadowy forms of men afoot and of horsemen and a forbidding figure that was neither walking nor riding horseback.

He edged to the side of the main road and his staring dismay changed to fascinated horror, fastened on a specter astraddle a rail hoisted on the shoulders of masked men. Horsemen, swollen to distorted sizes in the shifting light and shadows, led the procession. Others rode the flanks and brought up the rear. If the front riders saw Daniel, they did not show it or else they scorned a single man's threat. For they rode straight down the middle of the road, forcing him to step quickly to the rail fence. When he twisted to look again, an overwhelming revulsion appalled him.

Slumped, ungainly, a long-shanked figure clutched with both hands the rail on which he was tied. A grotesque, pathetic figure that resembled some strange black animal, its ugly features just sprouting, its eyes two liquid holes. And Daniel knew: a man was stripped naked, smeared with hot pitch, and a pillowcase of goose down spilled over him. But why? And who could it be?

They were trooping by him when an amused voice called: "What was that there prophecy now? Mind sayin' it for us just once more?"

The suffering apparition on the rail said nothing.

Daniel's horror spread. He stifled a cry, his mind refusing to accept what his eyes and ears told him.

As the tail of the mob swept past, something in Daniel burst. A tide of anger, a hurt for the gentle person undergoing tortured humiliation. He started after them.

At once a horseman reined back to bar his way. The face under the black hat and mask was a dark blur. Daniel tried to dodge by. The rider cried out a warning and reined his dancing mount around. Daniel grabbed a booted leg, holding on fast. A whip lashed his head and shoulders and arms. He heard more riders pounding back, yelling as they came. They filled the road, and suddenly he was getting flogged from all sides. Savage slashes, that bit into his hide.

He lost the grip on the boot. He had to lift shielding arms above his face. They were beating him away, grunts and curses behind their blows. He made another lunge to break through, for his intolerable fury wouldn't let him quit. For that one moment he was free, until a rider swerved. He felt the solid crash of a horse's forequarters. Pain shattered his chest and shoulders, and he was going down.

He lay motionless in the damp grass beside the road, all breath and strength slammed out of him, his senses, too. His eyes, whether he opened or closed them, still saw the black horror of Brother Winn.

When he wobbled up, the riders were far down the dim road, and the last he saw of the rabble was the smoky wake of flaring torches turning off the road to Coon Creek.

115

Chapter Eight

AT THE INDIAN MOUND

The vividness of Brother Winn's humiliation haunted Daniel thereafter, never leaving his mind for long. Winn's masked tormentors had dumped their tarry victim near the Coon Creek community, evidently as a warning to Union families. On the same night two northern men were whipped. So the *Citizen* said.

Lost in his preoccupation, in his deep-seated loathing, Daniel was unaware of having come to the end of the row of stripling corn. His mules were idling close to the rail fence, waiting for him to turn them. He pulled them about, lifting the plow handles to free and turn the plow share, and started up another row.

True, the *Citizen*'s editor hadn't approved Brother Winn's persecution. He had even called the torture "regrettable". But neither had he outright condemned it. Daniel's bitterness smoldered. Now the *Citizen* urged calm and reason, careful not to take sides in a divided district. *Calm,* Daniel thought, *when a storm was breaking? When vigilance committees were forming in every township? When strangers and suspected*

116

persons were being expelled from the county and threatened with fifty lashes should they return?

Everyone seemed to be waiting for something. *You can feel it,* he thought. The best weather vane of any was his tight-lipped father.

At noon he watered Zeke and Babe at a branch, fed them corn in the wagon bed, and ate his dinner in the shade of an elm tree that over-hung the fence by the town road. Afterward, he leaned against the tree trunk and slipped his hat over his eyes. One moment he was conscious of the warm day's faint breeze and the smell of turned earth, and the next he dozed.

He woke to the tap of a single horse on the road. He stirred without turning his head. There was a cadence to the hoof beats, light, spirited, the gaited movement of a blooded animal. He settled back again, too drowsy to look.

When the horse was almost upon him, he opened his eyes, blinking and staring at Laurel Vandiver halting her mount.

"Good afternoon, Daniel."

He jerked off his hat and stood, speechless.

"You could ask me to get down out of the sun," she said, gazing off a little.

He came to his senses and clambered over the fence and down the bank to the road, and held himself stiffly silent as he handed her down and tied the gelding to the fence.

Laurel strolled to the shady bank and sat on the

117

grass and spread her long riding skirt about her, until only the toes of her small boots showed. Calmly she drew off her wide, single-feathered hat and shook out her light brown hair, fascinating motions that told him she was going to stay a while. He noticed furthermore that her blue riding habit gave her eyes a deeper and darker shading of violet.

A wariness locked him still. He had nothing to say. He stood away from her, his attention beyond her on a vague point across the road.

"You seem surprised to see me," she said.

"I reckon I am." Remembering, he felt his face grow hot.

She looked puzzled and turned her eyes downward to a blade of grass that she wound around her gloved fingers. "You sent such a fine new book," she said, after a wait.

"I hope it was good enough." His voice was curt. He could see no logical reason for her conversation, and again he saw her puzzled frown.

"You didn't have to send a new book . . . or anything at all." Her violet eyes, fully upon him, were bewildered and inquiring. "You didn't have to stay away because the book was damaged. Nor rush off when you brought the new one."

He tried to shake free of his confusion, unable to understand her. He said forthwith: "You forget what your father told me? Or is it easier to pretend you don't remember?"

An expression froze her eyes, left her mouth parted. "Told you . . . told you what?"

"Not to come to your home again. He said you didn't want to see me."

Her face went white with protest. "He told you *that?*"

Daniel, nodding, saw amazement and disbelieving anger pass successively across her face. "When?" she said.

"Just before Christmas."

"He didn't!" she said in defense. But her tone wasn't convincing, and she got up suddenly and averted her face. She stood like that several moments, her breathing rapid. When she faced around, he saw her anger was gone.

"Daniel, I didn't tell Father to say such a thing. Somehow . . . I guess . . . he took it upon himself." She faltered and looked down to her clasped hands. "Do you believe me?" she asked, looking up. "I can understand if you don't." Her gaze was unwavering, open and sincere.

After a time, he said: "I reckon I do, Miss Laurel."

She reached out impulsively and touched his arm. The momentary feel of her hand brought a tingling upon him, lingering even after she stepped back.

"Thank you, Daniel. I want you to." She was smiling, only to sober in another instant. "Now I see. Father did forbid me to see you again."

"Reckon I know why. I'm just a farmer. But I'm sure not ashamed of it."

"Oh, it's not because you aren't good . . . you are!"

"Good?" His hot resentment stung. "I don't know exactly what you mean by that."

"I mean . . . I mean," she said illogically, "I want to see you again, Daniel. I do. Why do you think I've been watching the road for you to pass?" She became accusing. "You never go to town any more. Today I was even going to ride as far as your house."

He took that in. Neither spoke for a bit. Could he believe her? Any Vandiver for that matter? But why would she ride so far if she wasn't telling the truth? Looking at her, he realized a striking revelation. In a short time she had changed his life and spurred his ambition. Most of all, she had made him feel like a man. It would be a terrible loss never to see her again.

He felt resolve tighten inside him. He stepped closer to her. "You say you want to see me again. Well, I say the same to you. I swear it. But how do I know you really mean it? Is it just quality-folks' talk to make me feel better?"

Her face tilted. Anger glinted in the violet pools. "I'm not in the habit of lying to you or anyone, Daniel Wade."

"Then meet me somewhere." He found her hand. He felt no answering pressure, but she

didn't draw her hand away. "Will you, Laurel?"
He studied her face for evasion and saw none.
His heart was hammering.

"Where?" she said at last, spots of color high on
each cheek.

A dumbness seemed to clutch them both. Not
far down the road a horse was coming.

Daniel ignored the intrusion. And without
thinking, the place leaped to his mind. "Indian
mound," he said. "Nobody goes there any more.
It's out of the way. You can ride across country.
Stay off the road . . . Sunday afternoon, Laurel?
Say, two o'clock?"

Her reply, if she spoke at all, was lost as she
jerked toward the cantering horse, and Daniel
dropped her hand, disappointed, his temper
swelling when he saw Stark Hooper.

Hooper reined up and his eyes appeared to
smother many things before he touched his hat
and smiled, his greeting for Laurel alone. "Did
you come over to help with the spring plowing?"

"Now that would be fun," she said, her reply
crisp. "And you, Stark. You disappoint me. Why,
you're following me around like some silly
schoolboy."

He sat more erect in the saddle, his usual composure dented. "Why should I deny it?" he said
boldly. "I am. Which is only what any devoted
admirer would do. Your father told me you'd

gone this way. Furthermore, he instructed me to escort you home." He dismounted and led his horse in, his gaze indifferently excluding Daniel, who eyed him with distrust and stepped in front of him.

"Maybe Miss Laurel isn't ready to go just yet."

"Never mind, Daniel," Laurel said. "My father has commanded. I know." Her angry hands were twisting reins free. "Stark, I am deeply moved by your devotion. For that, you may accompany me home . . . as far as the lane and no farther."

She led the gelding out, and Daniel, following, of a sudden came face to face with Hooper, also ready to assist her. Laurel's eyes moved from Hooper to Daniel, making no choice that Daniel detected. In the end each handed her to the side-saddle.

Hooper hesitated, his eyes hurling ridicule over Daniel's display of manners. Then he sprang up.

Laurel turned her horse and brushed Daniel a look he couldn't translate, and, as the horses swung away, he wondered again whether she had murmured a reply. Hooper had spoiled that, also.

On Sunday he left the house right after dinner. Would she be there? How could he be certain when she hadn't said? He left the road and took long, swishing strides across the pasture to the wooded rise and down it to the persimmon grove and beyond, careful to avoid patches of weeds for the appearance of his nankeen trousers. He wore neither hat nor stock, only a white shirt under the brown coat. Frequently he pressed his palms against his straight black hair, cut yesterday by his mother.

He stopped still when he saw the familiar rounded mound, shaggy with trees. It stood alone and away from the ridge and somewhat higher. A hushed silence pervaded here. Always he experienced an awed feeling when first coming upon it, and he did so now. For this was a lost place, in time and legend, forgotten save by old men and exploring boys now grown up, its secrets buried in the leafy mold beneath, guarding elms and oaks. With his friends he used to wage mock Indian fights around and upon the mound and drink from the nearby sweet limestone spring, and dig for Indian relics. Growing up, he had come to think of digging as sacrilege, a profanation, and had lost his taste for it.

He waited a long spell. Restless, he circled the mound and back, watching the southwest. When the sun read past two o'clock, his doubts pressed heavier and heavier and he braced his back against an oak on the ridge to wait out his thinning hopes.

He had about given up when he sighted the distant bobbing of horse and rider, yet too far away to recognize. They entered scattered green timber, disappeared, and emerged, the horse loping hard. He stood up, anticipation smashing through him, and rushed to the timber's rim and waved. The rider waved back.

Laurel rode in under the trees before she halted, breathless and somewhat disarrayed for her. She wore black slippers instead of boots, and a lock of wind-blown hair had strayed out under her hat. Her distress spilled into her voice: "I sort of had to slip away from company."

"Let me guess who."

She nodded. "But I don't think he followed me."

"He'd better not," he said, giving her a hand down. "Well, there's Indian mound, Laurel. How does it look to you?"

"A little scary."

"It's harmless. I'll show you."

She held back. "There's not much time, Daniel. I'll be missed pretty soon."

Letting her see his disappointment, he indicated a fallen tree where she could rest. He became sharply aware of her as he sat beside her, of her face like a pale flower framed under the hat. When she took it off, he noticed the gracefulness of her arm, now the delightful mist of her hair. And so they sat close to each other, not talking for a while.

"I reckon you think it's wrong to come here," he said presently, feeling it his duty to lead the conversation. Months ago, in her home, she had found ready topics when his store of words ran out. This afternoon talk seemed of no importance to her.

"Not wrong, except . . . ."

"Except your father wouldn't approve."

That obvious truth caused her to smile. Again the conversation dwindled, only this once Daniel felt no wish to revive it. The hot, early June air had a peculiar quality, a lassitude that lulled the senses. He gazed up through the green boughs at white clouds floating as loose cotton across the open blue sky. Later he thought to say: "Are you thirsty? There's a nice spring back around."

She stood so fast he was unprepared. Leaving his coat on the tree and keeping a step ahead, he led her around back of the limestone ridge to a clear spring. It formed a shallow little stream that broadened and meandered away, a streak of errant silver. Its sandy bottom glistened like gold, its round-washed pebbles like jewels.

Laurel cried out her delight. "Daniel," she continued, "I'm going barefoot! I'm going to wade. I haven't done this since I was a child."

She turned her back and bent down, and began taking off shoes and stockings. Daniel had a brief glimpse of slim, bare legs under her long skirt. Resolutely he unlaced his heavy brogans, pulled off his stockings, and rolled up his trousers. He was breathing very fast.

First, they waded across and back. In her face,

he saw a new and fascinating liveliness and pleasure. She held her skirt just above her slim ankles. Then, laughing and splashing, they went racing downstream. Laurel's skirt became soaked at once, and, looking at the ruin when they stopped, she laughed again. Panting, they knelt on the pebbled rim of the spring and gulped the cool water and let it course down their flushed cheeks.

"Reminds me," he said, out of breath, when they sat back, "of the story . . . about the two thirsty farmers on a hot summer day. Would you like to hear it?"

"Oh, yes."

"Seems these two farmers came to a water hole that stock had muddied up. Eli got down to drink and said . . . 'Hiram, why don't you come over here where the water's a little clearer?' And Hiram said . . . 'It doesn't matter a heck, Eli. I aim to drink it all anyway.'"

He watched her lips as she laughed, and her deep-violet eyes. Still barefoot, they rested in the dappled shade close by the cool pool, enveloped in the warm, moist breath of June. A strand of her brown hair kept falling down across her forehead, and she kept pushing it back. Now and again she said something, a word or two, a fragment of thought. His answers were sparse, or just a nod. Nothing mattered except to see her, to be here beside her, to watch the changing shape of her lovely mouth and the mystery of her eyes.

She half shut her eyes, gazing out from under long lashes. She leaned back on her hands and recited in a voice both light and grave: " 'A thing of beauty is a joy forever. Its loveliness increases. It will never pass into nothingness.' I wonder what all Keats meant by that, Daniel?"

He studied a moment. "I don't know. Maybe . . . he meant that beauty . . . I mean real beauty . . . is also of the spirit. So it can't die. Can't pass into nothingness. It will always be." Suddenly he said: "Guess that's not it."

"But yes . . . ." She favored him her open pleasure. "One of my teachers at the academy said almost the same thing. I remember, too, she said the deepest loneliness is to know love . . . then to lose it for all time, never to have again."

"Was she"—he smiled—"a maiden lady?"

"No, you ninny, she was not."

He kept watching her alternating expression, sober one instant, gay the next, and it reached him that being here was a completely different experience for her, something she had missed during her proper and protected life.

She traced a forefinger over the face of a white, round pebble. "I wonder . . . is it wrong to love so much?"

"I don't think so . . . no."

" 'A thing of beauty is a joy forever.' " Her voice had a sweet tone, and he thought her mouth, in forming the lines, gave them an added beauty, a compelling meaning.

"Daniel," she said, looking across at him, "would you mind showing me the mound, after all?"

He hadn't touched her since helping her dismount. When they started up the rounded, tree-grown slope, he took her hand. It tightened warmly against his rough, big hand.

Although the mound wasn't steep, Daniel's breathing was oddly labored. He guided her around a tree and stopped, and, as she came beside him, her face turned uphill, looking, he touched his lips to her smooth neck.

She slipped away and darted for the top, holding her skirts high, her slender legs flashing white. He sprang after her. For a few steps she outdistanced him, her bare feet sinking into the cushiony litter of grass and leaves, then, with quick, powerful strides, he overtook her and put his hand around her waist. Her body felt light and silky to his touch.

Onward the final ascent climbed, bough-shadowed and cool, speckled with sunlight, Elysian, mysterious. Some of that mystery affected them when, panting, they gained the top. Neither spoke. Laurel's hair was partly down. She brushed it back. It fell again. She let it stay.

They sat down on the yielding earth, and Daniel could feel the wind rising off the pasture below. It reminded him of a gentle green sea, rocking lazily under glass-bright heat waves.

She said: "I feel as though I'm sitting on top of somebody's house or cellar."

"I guess we are."

"Think how long ago the Indians built this! What ever happened to them? Where did they go?"

"Maybe game got scarce and they moved. Maybe another tribe wiped them out."

She trailed her wondering gaze around and sat up, considering the canopy of trees. "It's like a temple, almost. So still. I'd be afraid to come here alone."

"You're safer here than in Foley's Prairie, which is mighty safe."

"I feel safe with you, Daniel."

Her eyes were glistening pools, turned darker by her fair skin, and her lips were barely parted. He bent and touched his mouth to hers in an awkward and tentative way, unsure of himself. He could hardly believe when she did not evade or turn her head away. Her lips were full and responsively alive. He drew back, his head swimming, under the long lashes her eyes were all but shut, although intently watching his face. He felt her breath warm on his face. The misty fragrance of her hair and skin was all around him. He kissed her on the mouth. Her lips became incredibly sweet and giving; at last, he heard her say in his ear: "I was beginning to wonder if you cared enough to kiss me . . . even once."

"Care for you?" He placed his arm around her waist. "Reckon I was afraid to try."

"I knew something dreadful was wrong when you quit coming to the house. And after the way you left the book. I'm sorry . . . I thought you didn't want to see me again."

"And I thought you didn't want to see me."

"Do you still think so?" she said, and slid her warm arms around his neck.

Daniel was overwhelmed. Protectiveness consumed him. He laid his mouth on hers again and again. Afterward, they sat with their arms around each other, watching the woods and sky in silence, their heads touching.

But the afternoon was racing away. He started up. "It's late. You've got to go."

"I know."

He drew her up and kissed her once more. They strolled down the mound to the spring and put on their stockings and shoes. Laurel brushed at her hair and pinned it up. When she pulled on her hat, she didn't look so disheveled.

He kissed her, virtually lifted her to the saddle, and said: "Next Sunday, here?"

The shape of an uncertainty that he had been shutting out of his mind off and on all afternoon could not be found in her face.

"I'll try," she promised, and sent the gelding loping out of the timber.

Chapter Nine
DECISION

Daniel moved in a trance-like state of unbearable but rapturous ecstasy. He seemed to be floating, lifted to an overmastering height from which he could gaze beyond the range of ordinary human vision. He sensed her everywhere.

An inward joy shook him awake before each daylight, and at once her perfect image took over his mind. Time was a stubborn and tedious foe that mocked him by standing still over the tasseled regiments of young corn, and by dragging through the agonizing afternoon and dull evening, until last light faded from the blurred land. He was content to keep to himself. He ate like a hummingbird. He felt alternately weak and magnificently powerful, by turns given to despair and exaltation, as one who has come upon a rare discovery that he senses will not be repeated for him during his lifetime.

If his father wondered, he failed to remark or show by his manner, but then he wouldn't now. Not so Emily Wade. Daniel could feel her inquiring eyes following him across the room or observing him covertly at the table.

One day Sam Wade hadn't returned from the Russell farm when Daniel started the late chores. As the dog Shep heeled the brindle cow in from pasture for her evening feed of salted cornmeal and bran, Daniel saw the broken halter strap dangling. After milking time, he remembered and, leaving her tied, went to the lean-to shed where odds and ends seemed to collect.

Dim light leaked between the cracks. He looked for a strip of rawhide which he last recalled hanging on a peg near the door. It wasn't there. Searching the gloom, he found the strip farther back on the wall. He took it down; in doing so he noticed a garment hanging behind a stack of empty kegs, and recognized an old gray suit coat of his father's.

At the entrance, a contradiction caused him to stop and draw around. He didn't remember seeing the coat in here before, although he hadn't been inside the shed for several weeks. And, although the coat was an old one, it wasn't ragged and his father wasn't one to discard a usable garment. Curious, he stepped back and lifted it off the peg, became more curious when he saw it still had a respectable look. Walking outside, he started to lay it across his arm to take to the house when he discovered shiny smears of black splotching the breast and sleeves. He stared harder and touched one sleeve, at the same time not wanting to, and squeezed a sticky substance between his fingers.

He turned totally still, drawn up in revulsion and shock as his comprehension came full circle, on tramping feet and weird figures swaying out of the April darkness, and the acrid stink of torches and the helpless apparition gripping the rail.

A voice pierced his consciousness. His mother's clear voice calling him for supper.

He answered but did not go yet, incapable of movement. Across the twilight the tied cow was lowing at him. Almost by habit, then, he returned the coat to its place, untied the cow, turned her out, and walked toward the house. Through his hurt and shame he knew he couldn't stay here any longer.

He washed, combed his hair, and went to the table, where he bowed his head while his mother murmured the blessing, and ate his tasteless supper in silence, seldom raising his eyes.

"Something wrong, Son?" Emily Wade asked. He shook his head. She said: "You're not eating much lately. Tonight even less than usual."

"Not hungry. Been a hot day."

"Could be you drank too much water."

"I guess so," he said, relieved that his father was late. His supper lumped in his mouth and throat. He took a drink of water and dropped his hands to his lap, staring at his plate. The lumps became as rocks in his chest now.

"Daniel," she said sharply, "there is something wrong. What is it?"

"Nothing a-tall," he said, straining to sound at ease. One resolution saved his composure: he would never tell her what he had found. Not as long as he lived. He would bury the old coat tonight so she would never see its telltale smears. "Just reckon I've made up my mind, is all. Much as I can't stand the likes of Stark Hooper, I'm goin' in tomorrow . . . join the Union company."

"So you are?" She spoke as if she already knew. By her readiness he assumed she believed nothing else was behind his decision. Everyone knew the Union company was camped in Foley's Prairie, drilling and recruiting, as were the Confederates. When they would march away was anybody's guess. But the war in Missouri was coming closer. Not long ago General Lyon's German Home Guards, bedeviled while escorting surrendered Southern militiamen through St. Louis, had fired into a throng of civilians and killed a good many.

Now, however, seeing the wise eyes reading him, he wasn't so certain she took him at his word. He nodded, and saw the momentary stirring of fear beneath the calm front of her face.

At once Emily Wade displayed an unusual animation. Her face smoothed. Her capable hands fluttered. "I'll get your things ready. I reckon you're old enough to know what you have to do."

●●●

He wondered whether he really was, after all, following breakfast, while he delayed his leave-taking at the door. His big hands held a carpetbag and a sack of bacon and bread, and he wore his nankeen trousers, town coat, and a clean shirt and the chimney-pot hat. He was leaving without a weapon, for the Wades were too poor to own more than one old Hawken rifle, and it properly belonged to his father and might be needed at home. Daniel hadn't asked for it, and Sam Wade hadn't offered. That itself, Daniel sensed, was a bad sign.

He seemed to tower over his folks this Friday morning. Facing them, he felt a sharp concern. How old they looked! How worn by toil and making do with little! Now he was leaving them.

He set down his possessions and turned to his mother. At first she kissed him calmly; in another moment he felt her clutching his neck and shoulders and she kissed him hard, and the insight flashed through to him that in her profound faith she was striving to give him extra strength and protection.

When she took down her arms, he wouldn't look at her face, but he had felt its wetness. He turned to his father, for that moment forgetting, and uncertainly offered his right hand, "Well, Papa. . . ."

Sam Wade kept his hands stiffly down.

Somehow he managed to stand erect, so willed by extreme feeling. He said—"At least, you made your choice."—an acknowledgment—and then Daniel heard disdain, woven into bitterness: "But I can't see you fightin' your own kind. Sidin' in with barn-burnin' Abolitionists an' Saint Louis Hessians that shoot down unarmed people in the streets. No . . . by God!" His mouth was quivering, his thin chest working like a bellows. Bewilderment as stark as day lay across his accusing eyes. He began shaking with rage.

Daniel let his hand sag. He felt physically punished.

"Please . . . Sam," Emily Wade protested, a catch in her voice. She took an involuntary step between them.

There was, Daniel realized, nothing for him to say; it was too late for that. He picked up his things, and passed through the doorway.

Outside he hesitated, flagged down by a queer sensation which spoke to him, a twisting mixture of regret and dread. He couldn't go off this way. It was wrong. He stopped and looked back. His folks stood in the doorway now. A great wave of affection drenched him. He blinked to clear his vision.

It was past time to go. Yet he yearned to rush back to the ill, over-worked, stubborn old man there and throw his arms around him and try to tell him why he was leaving. As the impulse swelled to near bursting, it left him. No. His father wouldn't understand.

"They'll let you come home before you leave, won't they?" Emily asked plaintively, nodding yes before Daniel could reply.

"I reckon they will," he said. Once more he looked at his father, saying—"Everything's caught up pretty good around the place."—while he scanned the gray-stubbled face.

Sam Wade nodded to chores well done, no more. The hinges of his gaunt jaws worked, and the sternness in the blue eyes seemed to die down, to go out almost. But just as Daniel thought his father was going to speak or come across to him, Sam Wade's mouth stirred and settled, shut, fixed, and final. The blue eyes threw back an unrelenting expression, an almost stony indifference.

Daniel's gaze broke. He tipped his head to them and struck off down the lane, taking long, blind strides. A swift padding sounded beside him. A warm tongue licked his swinging right hand hard, and, when that happened, the lines of snake-rail fencing blurred before his eyes. Behind him he heard his father calling Shep back. Pacing on, the forbidding sensation piling up in him again, he could not but think that he had just told them good bye.

The sun showed late morning when he saw the dirty-white blooms of tents on the cow pasture

137

south of town, arranged so as to face across a company street. One shelter looked different from the A-shapes of the others. Its conical form suggested an Indian teepee. An unerring instinct informed Daniel that this shelter must be Stark Hooper's, because the flag flew there and because the tent stood apart from the rest of the camp and bore a lofty air of official importance.

His keen anticipation dissolved as he surveyed the camp. In place of marching men and drums and bugles sounding, he saw scattered stacks of rifles and shotguns and figures lolling in the tents, the sides of which were drawn up for coolness. After all the excited reports reaching Daniel in the country, the encampment looked runt-size.

He was close enough to hear voices when an indolent figure left the first tent and stopped to stare at him. It was Amos Swink, and he called: "Hey, it's him . . . Dan Wade's comin'!"

Every tent poured out shapes. They resembled pirates instead of soldiers as they streamed toward him, joking and grinning, knives at their belts, sporting loud-colored shirts. He knew them all.

"Come to join up, Dan'l? Sign the roll?"

"That's right," he said and stopped, sensing devilment.

Their faces acquired exaggerated scowls of ferocity. They kept walking, spreading out, and suddenly they ran up and surrounded him. Hands seized his carpetbag and food sack. Many arms took hold of him and lifted him, powerless, off the ground. He felt himself hoisted and thrown on a blanket and tossed like a wood chip. They kept flinging him into the spinning sky, again and again, until he lost all sense of direction.

When they let him down and he staggered up on swaying feet, someone jammed the chimney-pot hat down around his ears. Laughter rolled, and his own mingled with theirs as he set the hat right, and his shoulders were shaking with mirth. Last winter, he knew, he would have fought to the last drop of his strength.

After that, they fetched him off to the headquarters tent, trooping around him like chattering monkeys. Jesse Nance went in and saluted. Daniel did not. To his mind saluting wasn't necessary yet.

Stark Hooper, erect and dignified, sat behind a portable camp desk on which lay a sheaf of papers and pen and ink. Gold epaulettes with dangling fringe garnished the shoulder tips of his blue uniform, and it seemed to Daniel that additional gold braid had collected on Hooper's sleeves since April.

An expression started to form in Hooper's face. Daniel saw him take in the dilapidated carpetbag and the lumpy food sack. He saw Hooper's mouth curl under the mustache, a half amusement that vanished as Hooper jackknifed up and, pressing the handle of a long, curved sword against him, stepped around the table and offered his hand, his surprising behavior all cordial.

Daniel broke the handshake.

"Welcome, Daniel. Welcome. We're glad you're here. You can sign the roll now."

Daniel bent over the table and wrote his full name: Daniel Lester Wade. When he straightened, he saw again the new, unconvincing affability playing upon him.

"You came at the right time," Hooper said. "Our roster's shy of the men we need. Justin Vandiver's signing up as many as we are. I'm told some have already gone south to join General Price across the river."

"I'd say it's about even around here," Daniel said, unable to warm to Hooper's confidential manner. Now that he was in the company, he had no inclination to visit.

"He can bunk with Tim and Andy and me," Jesse said, and checked himself, as if he had overlooked Hooper's authority.

Hooper was magnanimous. "The thing to do. Be with your friends, Daniel."

The four of them were loafing on bunks in the tent when Daniel brought it up. "What's come over Hooper? I thought he'd shake my hand off."

"He's after a commission," Andy Green confided, looking wise. "Soon as the Army musters us in, we'll have to elect us a company captain."

Jesse agreed. "He could even make colonel if he signed up two or three companies. Not much chance of that around Foley's Prairie. Ain't enough boys. They say the woods northeast of town are full of Confederates."

"By jinks," Tim Forehand said, "I'd druther have me a Foley's Prairie man in charge any day than some fussy stranger. Leastwise, we know what to expect." He stretched out his powerful body and locked meaty hands behind his head. Contentment dulled his ruddy, uneven features. "This here's the life, perfessor. Wait till all the girls turn out to watch us march this evenin'."

"He means at retreat," Jesse explained. "That's when Tim shines."

There was afternoon marching, and early that evening, some time before the company formed for retreat, Daniel could see buggies stringing out on the road from town and groups of strollers, especially girls. After roll call and inspection, such as it was, Hooper paraded his forty-odd men up and down the cow pasture. High-lifting brogans clomped louder and raised the dust higher, and uneven ranks straightened noticeably when the company passed the feminine gallery.

At dismissal the company gravitated *en masse* toward the young ladies fluttering behind the rail fence. Seeing them, Daniel thought of Laurel. *Day after tomorrow*, he told himself, *I'll see her,* and the numbing weakness stole over his senses again.

By Saturday noon he understood the camp's character. Horseplay and careless tolerance of discipline marked the recruits' conduct. Only a few, like Jesse Nance, saluted Hooper, who stayed in his tent except when duties required his presence. With no bugler to sound reveille, Jesse had stood in the company street and hog-called the men to wakefulness. Some missed breakfast; others did not get up until morning drill. On a farm you rose before daybreak. Why not lie abed when there were no chores? And having no company cook, individuals of like tastes formed their own mess. Daniel ate with his tent mates.

Searching his carpetbag for clean socks, Daniel found a New Testament. Its crisp new smell and stiffness told him a great deal. His mother, who hadn't been to town since Fort Sumter's surrender, had purchased it long before he knew he was going to war, maybe as long ago as last fall.

About two o'clock, while most of the company loafed in the tents after mess, Daniel heard hoofs clattering. He looked out as two riders cantered up to camp. Their mounts looked worn down. Dust powdered their blue uniforms.

The lead rider spiked his stare over the lax encampment, a disparaging inspection. His mouth formed a taut line above the bib-like beard. His tired eyes kindled. "Who's in charge here?" he bellowed.

An angular Coon Creek youth, a walnut-size wad of tobacco bulging one cheek, his shirt tail flapping, ambled out while contentedly scratching his ribs and gestured as he might give obliging directions to a stranger asking which fork of the road to take. "Right down there, mister. That funny-lookin' tent. Stark Hooper's the drillmaster. I reckon he's in charge if anybody is."

A stony silence dropped. "Young man, do you know who I am?"

"Well, now, I can't say I recollect seein' your face around Foley's Prairie."

"Young man, I happen to be a captain in the regular United States Army." Iron clanged in the exasperated voice. "And when, in thunderation, are you going to learn to salute an officer?"

Glaring, the captain spurred on to Hooper's tent, dismounted, dropped reins for his companion, and blustered inside. Daniel decided the second man was an orderly. One thing sure, he wasn't any friendlier than the captain. He kept gazing off, chin elevated, back arched, ignoring the gawking volunteers trailing after.

After an interval, Hooper and the captain appeared. Hooper, wearing a subdued look, hurried forth, calling: "Fall in . . . fall in!"

They lined up double file between the tents,

after which the captain went along the front rank, inspecting the old rifles and shotguns, and eagle-eying every man from head to brogans. No one had a uniform except Hooper, and only one third of the company was armed.

His inspection completed, the captain faced them, saying: "You will remain in your quarters until further orders. Dismissed." He pulled on his beard and returned to headquarters with Hooper.

Not many minutes later Jesse Nance entered the tent. "Better get on your mules, boys."

"What's up?" Andy Green asked.

"We break camp soon as it's good dark," Jesse said, extremely thoughtful. "March clear to the Missouri. That sassy captain says General Lyon is steamin' up the river from Saint Louis. 'Pears like there's goin' to be a battle around Boonville. That's where General Price's Confederates are."

Andy and Tim jumped up, hooraying approval.

After dark? This evening? Daniel planted his big hands on his knees and glumly considered the bare dirt floor. The possibility hadn't occurred to him that he couldn't go home on Sunday, the day of rest. That he might not see Laurel before he left for the seat of war, when he hadn't even told her he loved her.

Chapter Ten
BOONVILLE, JUNE, 1861

As weary wraiths wandering the gray murk of early morning, the Union company boys struggled up the bank from the ferry and dropped to rest under trees on the south side of the broad river, hungry and footsore after the overnight tramp from Foley's Prairie.

Daniel heard an order—no cooking fires—and the ensuing grumbling. He took off his brogans and rubbed his feet, thinking ahead. Some miles up the river toward the town of Boonville the Missouri Confederates were waiting. Had Justin Vandiver's company learned of General Lyon's advance in time to leave? He decided not. He hoped not.

Around seven o'clock a puff of smoke blacked the sky downriver; inside minutes a covey of steamboats, masses of soldiers, horses, and cannon crowding the decks, churned in to the shore. The company got up as one to gawk. Deckhands flung out lines and tied up to trees, and, even as gangplanks dropped, troops began hurrying off to form ranks. Daniel heard guttural voices.

So here are the Dirty Dutch, he thought. "Hessians" his father also called them. Well, as far as he could tell, they didn't look any stranger than somebody from Foley's Prairie, although more were fair of face and hair.

Horses and cannon clattered off last, swelling the racket. A red-bearded officer reined back and forth astride a nervous black horse. He gestured, he snapped orders, never still. His voice crackled; men moved to it, hastened to him and away. Daniel picked him out as General Nathaniel Lyon, for the simple reason that no other officer behaved like a general.

The Coon Creek Company—that was how Daniel had begun to think of them—looked awed by the war-like scene. Stark Hooper watched off by himself. He would have presented a determined appearance, legs braced wide, arms folded, sword at his side, and his high-held face bordering on a lofty expression, had not the fringed epaulettes and the gold sleeve braid intruded a theatrical effect.

Daniel lined up to pass by opened wooden boxes where a soldier, his severe manner marking him a veteran, was issuing rifles, cartridges, and percussion-cap boxes. Daniel's arms sagged when he took the long-barreled weapon. It felt like a length of lead.

"Listen, you straw-foots!" the soldier raised his prodigious voice when the last man passed.

146

"There's just time to tell ye once how to load." He brought a rifle in front of his body. He bit the tail end off a paper cartridge, poured powder down the barrel, and dropped the bullet in after, then ramrodded it home, eared back the heavy hammer, and pressed a percussion cap on the nipple under the hammer. "There ye are," he said.

Obadiah Swink was puzzled. "What if it don't fire?"

A groan of shriveling disgust. "I knew it! Ye'd best be skinnin' mules . . . every mother's son. But Jefferson Barracks'll straighten ye out. Now git back to yer company."

When the Coon Creekers re-formed, self-consciously handling their new arms, the captain who had found them at Foley's Prairie dashed up, calling: "Mister Hooper . . . swing your company in column of fours at the rear . . . in reserve . . . !" Then he spurred away to catch the advance.

"Reserve?" Andy Green echoed. "We can fight as good as any damned Dutchman."

"It ain't just that," Jesse Nance qualified. "There some regular troops here. They know more'n we do."

"Supposed to, you mean."

While they waited, another company of smart-stepping infantry marched by, and a bantering voice spoke from the ranks: "Where you hayseeds from?"

Tim Forehand jerked. "Foley's Prairie . . . by jinks! Where else?"

A simultaneous roar of laugher swept the marchers, and the same distinct voice said: "We knew it wasn't Cincinnati."

"And," Tim jawed back, "I reckon you're from that little pea-piddlin' crawdad hole they call Saint Louis?"

The regulars were soon past, and before long the Coon Creek outfit hitched onto the tail of the bobbing column, the unmilitary shapes of clumsy country boys more used to straddling furrows.

Daniel forgot the heavy muzzleloader riding on his leather slings upon his shoulder, conscious only of the tense excitement pulsing along the column. Beyond the bottomland timber, as drawn on a page of *Harper's Weekly*, he could see the boats puffing smoke as they pulled out to stay even with the advance companies. Rising dust outlined the curving line of the march. Bits of sound flowed back to him through the steady tramping—coughs, mutters, chain clinks, caissons rumbling on the country road.

Even here, even now, his mind flicked to Laurel. Today he was supposed to meet her at the mound. What if he got killed? What if he never saw her again?

As the sun came hotter, beads of sweat dripped down his face. He squinched his mouth and nostrils against the thick pall of dust. Ahead and on the column's flanks skirmishers advanced, rifles ready.

When the first shot cracked in the woods, it was more like a distant pop than a musket going off. It didn't sound real. Further bangings dispelled that impression when he saw puffs of white smoke floating among the trees. From the marchers, two companies deployed right of the road and another hustled off left.

Just when Daniel thought the battle was commencing, however, all shooting ceased and the summertime woods fell drowsy-still again.

They seemed to march a considerable distance along the winding dusty road, into a deepening silence which he sensed was false. Objects grew in the distance, a brick farmhouse and figures scurrying about it and in the woods. A flag dangled there, a patch of white against the dark green forest.

Sudden cracklings of musketry ripped the stillness, and he saw blue skirmishers falling back, gesturing, shouting. The column stopped, and companies swung out to form a broad front. Smoke enveloped the line, and instantly Daniel, crouched with his company on the edge of a grove, heard the swelling splatter of rifle fire and smelled the stench of gunpowder.

Riders, whip arms flailing, hunched on lead horses, rushed artillery pieces and ammunition wagons to an open place. Quick hands freed the limbers, and the cannon dropped on their trails. Burdened men strained forward from caissons with red bags and round shot and fed them into the black muzzles. Cannoneers twirled ramrods, shoved the charges home. A moment. An eruption of red-yellow flashes and rumbling roars and the screeching hisses of hurtling shot as the gun carriages kicked backward. There was a gush of white in the woods.

Again and again the battery fired. Daniel saw shafts of flame fall short or find the distant trees. A bugle's feverish notes soared over the crouching, smoky lines. Men lurched forward with yells, flags tilted.

A hat-waving rider galloped over to the Coon Creek Company and shouted to Hooper. He, in turn, shouted something indistinct. The men near him stirred. Daniel felt a bumping and jostling forward. They formed a shuffling, ragged line, uncertain of themselves until Tim Forehand raised a screeching yell; others took up the familiar cry. Daniel's shouting supplied him sudden strength. Now they all walked faster and tramped out to open ground, merely pointing their weapons because of the blue ranks between them and the woods.

Menacing sounds, spiteful and whirring, bit into Daniel's ears. He ducked and halted from fear, aware of a like faltering around him. But no one fell or cried out. Milling, they started forward once more, partly shielded by the company ahead. He could see men stumbling and falling down, and he heard their screams. But oddly, as the line advanced faster, the bullet sounds slackened.

When the Coon Creekers reached the farmhouse, Daniel couldn't yet see the enemy. Most of the shooting seemed to be over, except for an occasional shot toward the river. In the woods several shapes lay among the broken branches. Some lay quite still. One was sobbing and moaning and clutching his stomach, his breath coming in soggy grabs, a mere boy whose new gray uniform was soiled with blood and dirt. A Dutchman bent over him, lifted his head, and gave him water from a canteen.

Daniel scanned the anguished, powder-blackened face. The wounded Confederate wasn't from Foley's Prairie, if that helped, and it did a little.

Affected by the suffering cries, Daniel, turning away, saw a like withdrawal on the faces of his friends. Instead of acting as soldiers, they shuffled and stared at the ground, behaving as neighbors gathered around a boy in agony after a mule's kick.

"All right, boys. Fall in. . . ."

On the instant, Stark Hooper was striding among them, brisk, efficient. Daniel stared at him dully. He had forgotten all about Hooper. Now, seeing him . . . .

There wasn't time to explore the thought further. He heard horses thudding up, and he saw General Lyon and two of his staff galloping by. Lyon's gaze took in the scene. His red beard bobbed; his voice was terse: "Your boys behaved very well, Mister Hooper."

Hooper saluted precisely. The officers galloped on toward the river. In that span Daniel found what he was trying to remember. He'd forgotten Hooper until now, mainly because he hadn't noticed him during the charge. And he forgot about that also as the command came to march after the regulars into Boonville.

The battle, if a body could call it that, was over. Two days later the Coon Creek Company boarded a steamboat for St. Louis.

Chapter Eleven

JEFFERSON BARRACKS

From afar the post reminded Daniel of a spacious village and the numerous barracks of long mule barns. There was bustling movement all about, and bugle calls and voices shouting commands, and soldiers pivoting and bumping on the dusty countenance of a parade ground so wide the shrunken figures there seemed miniatures.

An unconcerned sergeant took the recruits to a brick building, where belongings were left and weapons stacked, and then across to a smaller structure. Over the doorway black lettering on a board read: REGIMENTAL SURGEON.

"You go in here for physical examinations," the non-com said, and, when a boy balked in alarm, he shrugged. "Don't worry. It won't hurt a bit."

They formed a single file. After a short time, Daniel saw the line was shrinking fast. When his turn came, he faced a white-haired man whose round stomach stuck out like a large watermelon beneath his long, untidy surgeon's coat. Yellow stained his brushy beard. He was tipsily jovial, his bleary eyes struggling for focus. He reeked of whiskey, onions, and cigars, and his voice was blurred.

"Stan' right up, boy. Tha's' good." A grimy hand wavered up, forefinger pecking. Daniel felt a series of perfunctory taps on his chest. "See outta both eyes? . . . sure y'can. Open your mouth. Got'cher front teeth so's you can chaw cartridges?" A belching laugh. "Sure y'have. . . . Take a big breath. Ahhh . . . good! Turn aroun'." More superficial taps across his shoulders. "Ahh . . . good . . . good! Lift your knees now. Ahhh!. . . . Oh, you'll be fine, boy. You'll do fine. Fit as any man I ever examined. . . . Fine bunch o' recruits, Sergeant." The offensive figure swayed away. "Nex' man!"

Amos Swink, who was last, came outside shaking his head and muttering: "I just hope I never git sick."

From there they entered the quartermaster's and emerged like pack mules, arms stacked to their chins. In the barracks, they pulled on the strange, new uniforms. The sleeves of Andy Green's blue woolen blouse were too long for his short arms, and Daniel's too short, so they traded. There was a good deal of strutting, of suspender snapping, and jibing. For most of these boys, Daniel knew, including himself, the uniforms were the first matching suits of their lives, and few of the recruits had ever worn cotton flannel drawers before. Immediately the black brogans became "gunboats" or "boxcars", and the stiff leather cravats or stocks, which buckled around the neck, became "dog collars". Common sense dictated that seldom would the last be worn.

Daniel happened to look across and notice Stark Hooper. His uniform was as simple as the next man's, bare of adornment or rank. Sometime during the ride downriver from Boonville, Hooper had removed epaulettes, gold braid, and sword, and shaved off the stylish goatee and the tawny mustache. The nakedness around his mouth and chin complimented him. He looked younger, unaffected, and natural. Such modesty made Daniel wonder. *Did Hooper fear ridicule from the veterans?*

When the parading was over, Hooper went to a bunk and regarded the company tolerantly. "Boys, there's something we need to do," he said, speaking with a casual tone. "Not now . . . but tomorrow . . . we need to elect company officers and non-coms. Other men will join our company later today. We can't drill with our regiment until we're organized."

Once more he regarded them, except, Daniel thought, this time with more than tolerance. His expression said they were all from or around that same small town north of the Missouri; they had drilled together and not long ago had faced real bullets together. Standing there, he looked assured and trustworthy. He could be outside Rookwood's General Store, nodding, greeting, no face escaping his notice as he strolled toward the loafers on the porch to discuss politics.

Daniel hadn't mentioned Hooper's actions at the Boonville skirmish. Who could say who had straggled or held back when everyone had reason to be scared? During a prolonged charge against heavy musket or cannon fire, likely every man would have turned tail. Artillery. That was why the green Confederates had skedaddled. Still, the episode bothered Daniel in a vague way.

"I hope you'll consider me for your company captain," Hooper was saying. "It would be an honor." He left the barracks, and, in spite of his dislike, even his distrust, Daniel had to admit Hooper made a strong impression.

After a spell of silence, Jesse Nance spoke. "What's your notion about the election, boys? Stark's a good recruiter. We all know that. He's better educated than be any of us." He wore a forced concentration, an uncomfortable manner of searching out of loyalty for added qualifications that he couldn't name spontaneously.

Seth Coots stood. His blue fatigue blouse lent him a taller look. He was homely and lank-jawed, given to stormy impulses. "I got a notion, you betcha. I say let's all pledge our votes for Stark Hooper right here 'n' now."

"Hold on, Seth." Daniel was on his feet before he thought. "Let's all have our say 'fore we go whole hog." He could see by Coots's scowl that not all old scores had been settled, and he said: "Why don't we put up at least one more name for captain?"

He looked around. One recruit yawned. Another was admiring his new forage cap. Daniel, swallowing his impatience, began to understand. They were here for a frolic instead of a war. They sought none of an officer's responsibilities. If Hooper wanted captain, why let him have the chore.

"You . . . Jesse . . . you," Daniel said. "I'd vote for you. But I won't for Stark Hooper."

"What's wrong with Stark?" Coots demanded. A fuming resentment peppered his whangy voice the same as it had after the gang fight behind Rookwood's General Store. "What's your kick?"

Daniel barely stifled a quick retort. He could damage Hooper's standing by just questioning his bravery. The temptation slid into his mind, then he let it slip away, thinking: *No, we were all scared and it was only a skirmish, our first.* A moment of cowardice was the worst mark you could set against a man. And how could he prove it?

"I'd just rather vote for Jesse," he answered. "That's reason enough. I want him to run for captain."

Jesse Nance looked miserable, near fright. He was extremely well liked without being conscious of his popularity. That liking gleamed through on the faces turning his way. Coots was the lone exception.

"Come on, Jesse," Tim Forehand coaxed.

Daniel had never realized before the deep extent of Jesse's shyness. Its pain was stamped upon the slim face and behind the mild blue eyes.

"I'd die if I had to give orders out there in front of the whole regiment," he groaned. "I would!"

"You'll get used to it," Daniel said.

"No . . . ." Jesse's inflection was final. He, too, searched around for a receptive face, discovered none, and his attention returned to Daniel, contemplating him. "Dan . . . you run. We trust you."

"Even if he is from Indian Mound," Andy Green seconded.

And before Daniel could stop them, suddenly Tim Forehand slapped his thigh and brayed: "Perfessor, git yourself a big stump. 'Cause we're runnin' you for company cap'n."

Daniel's hasty impulse was to refuse, for he didn't covet it, either. But when he saw them crowding forward and heard their friendly voices, and felt them slapping his back, something seemed to lift him high. "All right," he said, wondering at himself. "I will."

While the company was larking outside after dinner, Daniel hurried to his bunk and began a letter:

Dear Laurel,

I couldn't meet you because I joined the Union company and the Army marched us plumb to the river that same night. I'm mighty sorry. We got in a little skirmish at Boonville. Some Confederate boys and a few on our side were killed and wounded, but nobody from Foley's Prairie. I don't think Justin's company had time to get there.

There was a reception when we marched off the boat at St. Louis. The bands played. Guess the folks thought we had won the "battle", when truly we didn't fire a shot. Well, they gave us cookies and beer and the girls kissed the boys that were willing, and some that weren't, and Tim Forehand kissed any girl that was handy. You should have seen Jesse Nance break his halter when a fat little Dutch girl tried to hug him. We are in training here at Jefferson barracks. We don't know a thing.

Laurel, I think of you always. You are truly a fine girl. "Your loveliness increases: it will never pass into nothingness." Now I know what Mr. Keats meant.

God bless you.
Love, Daniel Wade

Writing her excited a light mood in him. Near the bottom he penned an afterthought:

There seems to be a considerable lack of persimmons hereabouts.

Late in the afternoon, another batch of disorderly Missouri recruits took over the other end of the company barracks. Before they could struggle into new uniforms, Hooper, trailed by Seth Coots, was among them shaking hands. A calming judgment told Daniel to wait. Be ample time for electioneering between now and voting time at eleven o'clock tomorrow morning.

After supper, the company strayed toward its quarters through the humid twilight. The regiment's thousand voices created a constant humming.

A hand tapped Daniel's shoulder from behind. He stared at the slouched figure of Seth Coots. "Got a minute, Daniel?" His speech contained a relishing quality. "Fella over here wants to see you."

Walking beside him to an empty barracks building, Daniel wasn't surprised when he saw Hooper waiting out of sight around the corner. But he wasn't expecting the instant accusation: "So you're running for captain? I suggest you drop out. You haven't got a chance against me."

Contempt, superiority, jealousy, perhaps even hate—Daniel was seeing the Stark Hooper he recognized best. Erased entirely was the friendly tolerance he had suspected in camp at Foley's Prairie. That, Daniel saw now, had been nothing

160

more than a pose leading into the election.

He said: "If I didn't have a chance, you wouldn't be worried."

"Worried! Me!" Hooper's affront was enormous. He threw back his head in the high look. "I merely want to save your own self-respect. You forget you don't know the new men."

"I will by voting time."

"You . . . ." Scorn thickened the resonant, positive voice. But it seemed to lose strength when Daniel did not speak. Hooper pursed his broad lips. His shoulders bunched and fell. "You don't bluff. Therefore, we can get down to plain mule-barn politics, Missouri style. I'm prepared to make you a good proposition. Withdraw and I'll guarantee you a lieutenancy."

His assurance, the certainty with which he assumed Daniel would accept, hastened Daniel's reply: "I told the boys I'd run for captain. Not lieutenant."

"You're a fool. Besides, you've had no field experience."

"I was at Boonville, same as you," Daniel said, and the rest of it rushed out of him like a shot. "You didn't show up till we got to the woods. When General Lyon rode by, you were Johnny on the spot, though. Ready to salute."

Hooper was perfectly motionless. "So?"

"Where were you during the charge, Stark? Hiding somewhere?"

"If you think so, why don't you accuse me in front of the company?"

"Because every one of us was scared. I was. Tim Forehand said he was. Andy . . . Jesse. It's not that. It's later I'm thinkin' about. You're not man enough to lead us in a real battle."

Sweat glistened as grease on Hooper's clean-shaven face. "Seth," he said, "tell him where I was during the charge at Boonville."

"Glad to. I remember you gave the order to charge. Little bunches of us started off. Remember, Daniel? I was right alongside Stark all the way."

Daniel kept silent. He wanted to believe Coots. Somehow he couldn't.

"The lieutenancy is yours," he heard Hooper say.

"I won't horse trade."

"Then you'll get nothing. You'll see."

By ten o'clock the next morning the barracks had the sounds and smells of Rookwood's front porch on election day. Tobacco smoke floated in thick, blue clouds. Little knots of men held heated conversations. There was loud betting. An empty hardtack box had been placed on a table to hold the ballots. Hooper, again wearing his affable mien, passed from group to group. Coots was handing out stogies and doing a good deal of low talking. Now and again recruits left the barracks; they were slow returning. Back home Coots had never been the center of an event that Daniel could remember. A constant grumbler, he was the first to pile on in a fight, and in school he had been an uncaught thief. Today, for the first time, he was noticed and given consideration because he had something to give away for Hooper. It was a new rôle for him, marked by his overbearing manner.

"Listen," said Andy Green, hurrying in from outside to where Daniel paused between rounds of electioneering, "It's gonna take more than handshakes to win. Hooper's got him a barrel of bust-head whiskey across the road at the sutler's. You just go in the back door. Two drinks for ever' vote. Two more if he wins."

"I know. I've been smelling it."

"We could buy us a jug. There's a little time yet."

"If I have to get a man drunk 'fore he'll vote for me, I know he'll be sorry later. It won't do, Andy."

Andy's face was doleful. "Dan, you'll never make a politician."

"I know it."

Tim Forehand pressed through to them. A worried scowl puckered his rugged features. "Perfessor, you got to make a speech. That's all there are to it."

"I'm talked out, Tim. Had my say all around."

"I mean a stand-up speech."—as Tim spoke,

Daniel felt himself flinching. "Like old Major Vandiver give on the Fourth of July, or Brother Winn when he's hot after the devil. You know . . . give 'em hell. Tell 'em who laid the chunk."

Daniel wiped his jaw, still unwilling. But he hadn't time to refuse again. Tim was pushing through the capering recruits and standing on a table, shouting for attention and getting it.

"Boys . . . since the ee-lection starts in a few minutes, I want to interduce our mighty fine candeedate . . . the pride o' Foley's Prairie . . . and say a few words in his behalf. Rain or shine, you can count on Dan'l Wade. He's some punkins, he is. Reckon I know . . . 'cause I and Dan'l we been like fleas on a hound since we's just little warts." Someone guffawed. Tim spoke louder, drowning the interruption. "Dan'l Wade can spit a mile an' he can throw a bear by the tail. He's tough as a mule and twicet as smart." Tim smacked a mighty fist into his palm. "Why is he? I'll tell you why. 'Cause he's got sand in his craw an' he's read ever' book in forty mile o' Foley's Prairie. Now come on up here, perfessor! You-son-of-a-gun!"

Daniel felt both hot and cold. When he mounted the table and looked around and the din of whooping and stomping lessened, he told them that Boonville proved they weren't ready to fight. Therefore, they needed training for the war, which might last a long time. They were in for mud and rain, hunger and cold. . . .

So he gave them a short, sincere speech and promised to do his best for them if elected, and yet, when he finished, he could tell from the scattering applause that he had failed to impress many outside his Indian Mound and Coon Creek friends who were going to vote for him anyway. These young men wanted to hear about a war chuck-full of fun and glory, and new sights and experiences they could brag about to their girls. They wanted him to say everyone would come back. He studied the shiny toe of his new brogan, thinking of the Andy Jackson book and the hard lessons therein.

Coots bounded forth. Hooper wisely motioned him back and ascended the table. "Prepare yourselves well," he said, his convincing voice taking on a patriotic fervor, "and the war will be short. You'll be home with your sweethearts sooner than you think. All we need is one good victory . . . just one! . . . and the war'll be over. The enemy will know we're serious about keeping the old Union together. There's not a man here who can't whip two Confederates. Didn't they skedaddle at Boonville? I say hurrah for the Union and let me lead you!"

Applause for him filled the long room, whistles, stomps, cheers, hand clapping. He hurled Daniel a challenging look and leaned against a bunk, arms folded across his chest.

Daniel felt his jaws lock, and he was on the table and answering before he realized his action: "I just wish everything was true that my opponent claims, but it's not. For one thing, the war's just started. Who can say when it'll be finished? And the Confederates ran at Boonville because we had artillery and they didn't. If they'd fired round shot at us, we'd 'a' run, too. Maybe faster." He jumped down, his mouth taut, all too aware of the lukewarm applause, and he heard Andy groan: "Dan, that last one busted the churn."

Now Andy and Coots marched to the hardtack box, marked and dropped their ballots, and stood by to supervise the voting. When the last recruit had left his piece of folded paper, the two counters took the box to a corner to tally the votes.

Waiting, Daniel had mingled emotions. Truthfully he didn't want the commission as much as he wished to best Stark Hooper, and something warned him he might not.

He was unable to read the results on his friend's face as the counters came forward minutes after, for Andy could cover his feelings, but, when Coots leaped to the table, Daniel knew in advance of the crowing voice: "The count was fifty-four to thirty-three. Stark Hooper's your captain, boys!" A roar went up.

Unreasonably Daniel felt bitterly disappointed. He had to force himself to push through the noisy bluecoats and offer his hand. As he saw and felt the acid look play over him, he saw, also, the exulting face become entirely different, long remembering. Last, he saw Hooper stare down at his outstretched hand as though he had found something offensive there, before the man turned his back with his unforgotten malice.

Chapter Twelve

FOLEY'S PRAIRIE IS BEST

It was the Saturday afternoon following Hooper's victory that Seth Coots, now brandishing his sergeant's chevrons, brought a new recruit to the barracks. Daniel glanced up from his letter writing to see a stocky, wide-necked man, with dull but unwavering eyes that looked out over the pitted slopes of a broad face and the knob of a flattened nose. Gray streaked the thick hair bushing out under the forage cap; his ears were like pieces of gnarled rind.

Daniel saw the pair stop. For a moment longer the older man's eyes stayed on him. There was no particular feeling in them, just an embedded weariness.

167

They went by, and Daniel reflected on Coots's new stripes. Coots was the only Coon Creeker to receive a promotion. Hooper had chosen his lieutenants from those volunteers who had swung the election for him. While Jesse Nance remained a sergeant, he would probably go no higher. At any rate the company had become the "Coon Creek Cougars" thanks to Tim Forehand's brawn. Taking each man in turn, he had thrown and pinned the advocates of the "Invincibles", which Tim swore sounded like gentlemen instead of fighters, and the "Tigers" and "Roughs" and "Guards".

Daniel directed his attention back to the letter he had just finished:

Dear Folks,

There wasn't time to come home. We marched on to Boonville in a mighty big hurry. I reckon you heard about the little skirmish there. Nobody in our company was even wounded.

We get plenty of hardtack, beans, salt pork, and coffee. I draw thirteen dollars a month. I have signed papers for the government to send you ten dollars every pay day. I don't need much here. We either drill or sleep. Looks like we'll have to go on down the river if we find anybody to fight.

St. Louis is a mighty big place, sure enough. But Foley's Prairie smells a heap cleaner. The weather is hot and muggy and our wool uniforms are too heavy for summer.

Mama, I bought a pie at the sutler's. It couldn't get on the same plate with one of yours. I hope you are feeling tolerable well, Papa. Wish I could help you with the chores. Pat old Shep for me.

Your affectionate son,
Daniel

Also, he was becoming the correspondent for boys who could neither read nor write. With the regiment organized and the newness of Army life wearing off, they, like him, were thinking of home and bothered by twinges of neglect for not writing.

Tim Forehand came over to Daniel's bunk. "You know I'm not much of a hand at writin'," he said, embarrassed. "Would you fix me up a letter to my folks?" When Daniel had paper and pencil ready, Tim launched a halting account of Boonville, travel, the river, weather, and food. He soon ran out of words. "Reckon that's all, Dan'l."

"This is just a note. Can't you think of something else? Your folks'll think you're sick if you don't."

Tim dwelled on that, his rough features contorted in study. "Well, just tell 'em I been to Saint Louis an' looked around an' taken in all the sights thereabouts, and it can't hold a candle to Foley's Prairie," he said gravely. "No, by jinks, it can't! There's just no comparison."

Daniel had to smile. Everyone he'd written letters for had expressed the same general contempt. Home, no matter where, was superior in all respects.

Tim expelled a long sigh, relieved to have the letter-writing chore out of the way. A jew's-harp twanged down the barracks, striking faster and faster. His eyes lighted up.

"It's Saturday night," he said, leaning closer. "I been hearin' about an off-bounds place called the Bull of the Woods."

"I'm sick of new sergeants," Daniel said. "Let's go."

At full darkness, figures began quietly leaving the barracks. When Daniel came to the unlighted hulk of the regimental surgeon's office, Amos and Obadiah Swink and Tim stepped out. Moments later Jesse Nance and Andy Green showed up.

"Six is all," Tim said. "Reckon that's enough."

"Enough for what?" Obadiah questioned.

"Well, a body dasn't go by himself," Tim said innocently. "Just follow me, boys. Stay in the shadows. When the sentry walks to the other end of his post, we'll slip by."

Daniel thought he sensed more to the nose counting than Tim had let on. Tonight, however, nothing mattered except a frolic.

They followed a line of steady trees to the edge of the post, and halted. About five rods away a sentry hummed while he paced. He about-faced, stood in one spot looking off at the starry sky, never at the trees where the six waited, and resumed his humming and pacing toward the opposite end of his post.

"Now," Tim whispered, and they stole forward, across a road, and into another stand of trees. A beaten path grew dimly beyond, and Tim took it.

"That soldier couldn't be sentry for me," Jesse said, disapproving.

"What'd you expect of an Illinois clodhopper?" Tim said.

Obadiah Swink was quick. "Tim, how'd you know he's from Illinois?"

"Why, any jackass could tell by the way he stood guard. Careless like."

They passed through the timber, crossed a little patch of open pasture, and entered more woods, and the way, lighted by a rising moon, widened as another path converged.

Obadiah checked up suddenly and turned. "I think I hear somethin' behind us."

"Just the wind," Tim said. "Come on. I smell honey."

The worn path broadened to a lane beneath the trees. A slit of light cut the gloom ahead. They came to a long, log building. Within, Daniel could hear the muffled clash of voices. He had to duck through the low doorway into a dim room where a single lantern burned. Tim pushed open another door, and it was as if he had turned up a great many lamps at once. Light flooded the smoky room beyond. Its smell was like a substance, something Daniel could almost touch and feel. He blinked, seeing soldiers at the long bar and tables.

The Coon Creek boys marched to the bar, and the fleshy man behind it said: "Let's see the shine of your coin, boys."

"Since when?" Tim was indignant. The barkeep shrugged, turned away. Six hands whapped down silver.

"Beer," Daniel said.

More men entered the place. Obadiah looked first. "I told you somebody was behind us. It's Seth Coots and that new fella. What's his name?"

"I heard Seth call him Murphy," Jesse said. "He's no young buck, is he? Looks rough as a cob to me."

Coots nodded to them and slouched to a position down the bar with Murphy, and, when Murphy hitched around, Daniel saw the man turn his cold weariness upon him and keep it there.

An oddness began tapping inside Daniel, a watchfulness.

Additional soldiers pushed aside, led by a burly man who, searching the faces, looked once at Tim Forehand, and took his bunch in alongside the Coon Creekers, voicing sarcasm as he did: "Wondered if you'd show up."

"Who got here first?" Tim countered. "An' what time's the patrol?"

"Ten o'clock. Where you stump-jumpers from?"

"Foley's Prairie."

"Is it in a state?"

"Best in the Union . . . good ol' Miz-zoo-ree." Tim was enjoying himself. "Where might you fine gents be from?"

"Cairo."

"Cairo? Let's see. Can't seem to place it. Is it a town?"

"Best in Illinois."

"Well, 'scuse me. I had it mixed up with a little mud bank down south o' here."

The spontaneous muttering that followed brought the proprietor hurrying from the other end of the bar. "Take your damned fight outside. Nobody's paid for the tables you busted up last night. What I get for runnin' a gentleman's establishment."

"Don't look at me," Tim said, all innocence. "I just came in for ice cream."

173

Amused, the Illinois men relaxed and faced back, a patient foretaste on their faces. No particular rancor burned in them, Daniel could tell, only the ferment of brawny young men tired of farm work and now of drilling and the boredom of barracks life.

After a short time, Daniel felt someone pushing in between Jesse and himself and elbows digging into his ribs. "Hey . . . !" He turned, astonished, and glimpsed Murphy and Murphy's uplifted arm. The savage blow struck Daniel's cheek. It knocked him spinning, across the floor and against an empty table, which crashed over. He flung around, charged with angry bewilderment, to hear Murphy say: "Ye crowded me, boy."

Daniel's jaw hung. "You crowded me."

"Ye're a liar, boy. Yellow to boot."

Daniel stepped toward him then, feeling the sawdust slipping beneath his brogans.

"Watch out!" a voice yelled. "He's a pug."

Daniel hardly had his guard up when Murphy barged for him. The Irishman didn't look angry. Except for a glint of purposefulness, his eyes cast the same flat dullness. He held his left arm well extended, his right cocked like a hammer. His feet shuffled, and Daniel saw Murphy's right hand jerk. But it was Murphy's left that landed, and Daniel reeled backward. His head was booming.

He found Murphy coolly upon him, as methodical as a man chopping wood. Daniel missed two swings at the weaving head before his own cleared, and in that time he took brutal smashes to his body. He beat Murphy off when, in desperation, he bulled into him and punched the ample belly and suddenly pulled back.

"That's it . . . stay away from 'im!"

In all that continuous yelling, the shouted encouragement sounded remote, for Murphy gave him no rest. His powerful forearms were as handles for the sledges of his lump-knuckled fists. Many of Daniel's blows landed on Murphy's elbows. Murphy's body had the solidness of horseflesh when Daniel did hit him, except the belly. There, he sensed, lay a guarded softness.

Across to the bar they fought again, and back to the other side of the packed room, the ranks of watchers breaking and closing. Sometimes Daniel surrendered ground; sometimes he gained. He learned his reach was longer, he was hurting Murphy, and he was ciphering some of Murphy's fooling shifts. So, again, Daniel slugged the pillow-shaped belly.

Murphy hauled up. His color was crimson. He heaved like a winded work horse. Sweat fled down his battered face. His dull eyes looked beaten. He appeared to falter.

Daniel lunged for him. He drove a fist through

Murphy's guard that shook the pitted face. He battered Murphy's middle once more. Murphy backed up, the first time that he had really retreated, and the yelling of the soldiers urging Daniel on was a wild music in his ears.

He was rushing in too fast. An instinct warned him. But when he saw Murphy covering up, all dogged and his shoulders humping, Daniel couldn't hold himself back. Hence, he wasn't ready when Murphy shifted his feet, an odd shuffling motion that shunted him to Daniel's left at astonishing speed. Before Daniel could change fronts, Murphy's fist clubbed his jaw, and a brilliance crackled through his brain, and he knew only that he was reeling and falling.

When he opened his eyes, someone was pouring cold water over his face. Bit by bit the haze lifted and the indistinct features above him turned out to belong to the worried face of Andy Green.

"Time you came to!"

Arms pulled him to his feet, caught him when he toppled. Just when he steadied and had his head up, a pile-driving pain slammed him between the eyes. He dropped his head against blinding, thundering agony, both hands pressing. When he could stand without falling, hands guided him to a chair.

The first recognizable face around him was that of Murphy, at a nearby table. He stared gloomily toward the bar, an empty glass by his elbow. An extreme weariness engraved his puffy face. One hand cuddled his paunch. Coots sat near him. Murphy ignored him.

"He'll whip you next time," Tim Forehand said. His tone said it wasn't finished. "If he don't, I will. How about tomorrow night?"

Murphy's thick lips stirred, fashioning the contempt of a seasoned brawler. He tramped to the bar, came back, and set a small glass of whiskey on the table. Tim kept on—"I said he'll whip you next time."—and Murphy met the remark with calm silence. He owned the battered and indifferent dignity of a man who had weathered more fights than he could ever remember, who had won more than he had lost, and so was cognizant of his strength and limitations. He took his drink and sat a moment. Quite suddenly he faced Daniel.

"Boy, ye came in off balance, rushin' like a mad bull. When I slid into me pivot, yer jaw was wide open. I could 'a' hung me hat on it, or hit ye with a fairy's wand." His rough voice seemed loath to give credit. But when he leaned back, he said: "Ye're all right, boy. Made me earn every bit of it."

Daniel looked up from rubbing his jaw. "Earn what?"

He saw Coots lose his slouch and stare hard at Murphy, a silencing look. The fighter, his stolidness unaffected, said: "Just an expression, boy. Just an expression."

Daniel looked from him to Coots again. An insight was forming, an ugly one, surging, when a soldier flung open the door and yelled: "Patrol's comin' down the road!"

Everyone started up and rushed for the back door. Over the scrambling racket sailed the Illinois man's reminder: "Try you next week, Missouri."

Daniel shoved his way outside and hurried along the backside of the building and into the deep woods. He halted with the others when he heard the *stomp-stomp* of marching. A hoarse voice barked from the darkness of the road: "Close up! Close up! Step lively!" A voice that was needlessly loud. It sent a clarion warning ahead as the patrol passed the men in the woods and tramped on to the saloon. "Patrol . . . halt! Right . . . face! At ease! Dorgan . . . see what's goin' on inside!"

A soldier went laggardly in. He returned after a little run of time. "Nobody here, Sarge. Quiet as a church."

"Just as I thought. A long hike for nothin'." The hoarse voice picked up volume: "Just the same we'll look down the road a piece! Patrol . . . ten-shun! Left face! Forwarrrd . . . harch!"

Hurrying up the road from the Bull of the Woods, Daniel could find little grievance left in the humid night. Even if Murphy had well nigh broken his head. Even if Hooper had hired Murphy, that wasn't surprising, and Hooper was less a man for it. A perception both subtle and exalting enriched him as he strode along, felt in the good-natured voices and the shoulder rubbings. He had covered some distance before it was conveyed to him in whole.

He could hold his own among these boisterous men, some of them older than himself. And with them he would go down the brawling river to faraway wooded hills and green valleys steaming under the Southern sun, and together they would pass through darkness and light.

"Mail call!"

At the first whoop Daniel joined the headlong rush out of the barracks where Seth Coots stood posted, a lumpy gray bag on his shoulder. He always waited until every last man had assembled before he gave out the mail, even then he liked to delay and pretend to have to ponder the writing on each letter and package. He started to do so now, prompting Amos Swink's testy complaint. "Come on. Hand 'em out! They ain't yours."

"Everybody here?" Coots said, officious.

"How could that be? Ain't somebody always in the guardhouse or hospital?"

Coots began calling names. His voice carried

a recently acquired importance. Each name he spoke sounded like a command. Each letter he passed out seemed the result of his personal generosity.

Daniel waited, his hopes rising and ebbing. Around him his barrack mates were eagerly scanning letters and opening packages. The bag looked empty when Coots barked: "Wade . . . Daniel Lester Wade . . . front an' center!"

Coots took his time. He dallied so long over the letter, questioning whether it really was Daniel's after all, that Daniel snatched it free. One look told him—his mother's oval-shaped handwriting, his first letter from home. He tore it open and started reading: Dear Son: We hope this finds. . . . He looked up, drawn by Coots's attitude. The expression curling his thin mouth. It was belittling, imitative of Hooper.

"Don't you want the other 'un?" Coots mocked, and from behind him he drew a letter on which Daniel glimpsed delicate handwriting. Blood pounded to his face. He stepped toward Coots, who backed up and fluttered the letter to his long nose, sniffing. "Ah . . . now who'd be a-writin' you besides your folks? Mattie Hull, maybe?"

Everything reddened. Daniel took one long, reaching step and hit Seth Coots in the mouth. It was a looping blow that knocked Coots loose from mailbag and letter. He dropped on his side, astounded, and touched fingers to his bleeding lips.

"By dogs, stay clear o' me!" Daniel said, standing over him and yearning to punish him again. But Coots's face was drained of any will to rise. Daniel saw enough to turn him away, and disgust thinned his fury. He heard voices. He picked up his letter and was brushing it off when he saw Hooper coming on the double-quick. Daniel waited.

"Ten-shun!"

An air of authority braced Hooper as he stopped.

Amos Swink said: "Seth keeps foolin' with the mail. Time somebody learned him."

"What do you have to say?" Hooper demanded of Daniel.

"Amos just said it. Seth refused to give me my letter."

"You struck him over a letter? A mere letter?"

Daniel didn't speak. Hooper could see the letter he still held. Coots got up and wiped his mouth.

"You struck a non-commissioned officer," Hooper said gravely. "I saw it across the parade. For such disrespect I could have you tied up, bucked, or gagged." He chewed reflectively on his lower lip, a hesitation that suggested tolerance. "Maybe three days carrying a rifle and fifty pounds of stones in your knapsack will remind you that your conduct is prejudicial to good order. Your extra duty is effective immediately. Dismissed."

After supper, Daniel read his letters:

Dear Son:

We hope this finds you well and in good spirits. I pray this terrible bad war will soon be over and you can leave that place down there and come home. Maybe peas will come before thay's a big battle. Don't worry a bote us. We are fine. Your father does his chores if he is up to it or not.

Patty Russell's baby seems a mite stronger. Mattie Hull up and married the Simms boy last week. They say he had his front teeth pulled so he couldn't bite catrages and have to go off to war. More boys are going across the river to join the Confederates.

Shep caught a rabbit today. I mailed you a box of sugar cookies. Read your Bible every day. May the Lord watch over you and everybody from Foley's Prairie.

Love,
Mother

The even, labored handwriting, so clear when

he started reading, lost its vividness and suddenly blurred, obscured by the green mist falling across his eyes. He blinked and turned to the second letter, to the small, dainty letters, prettily formed. A magic clarity in them. His imagination, for a moment, took him to the great house, and he could see Laurel at a writing desk, sunbeams glimmering on her light brown hair. His fumbling fingers opened the letter.

Dear Daniel:

Your letter just arrived today. I'm so glad you are safe.

You are correct, Justin's company wasn't at Boonville. How terrible to have you on different sides. Of course, I understand why you weren't at the mound that afternoon. Yes, I went there. I waited for you. It didn't seem like the same place, alone.

All the women around Foley's Prairie are busy with one side or the other. The Confederate Ladies made a flag which we presented to Justin's company the day after the boys left.

My father says the lawless element may rise up while so many of our fine young men are away. However, nothing has happened and will not, I am positive. Our concern is not here at home, but away, in the camps and on the battlefields, and mine is devotedly with you and Justin.

Send me your picture. I am sending you a recent daguerreotype of myself which I hope you will not find too objectionable, and perhaps will cause you to remember me fondly.

My sincere love,
Laurel

That night he experienced the crush of homesickness for the first time. A yearning that drained the spirit and numbed the body, and in the darkness he wept.

Chapter Thirteen

THE UNION IS DISGRACED

As weeks passed and the Coon Creek Company seemed doomed to drill everlastingly on the dusty parade ground, the war took ominous turns. Out of Virginia in late July crashed the news of First Bull Run. Not only had the Union Army lost the battle, it had broken and fled back to Washington, disgraced. In August another Union reverse occurred, the defeat at Wilson's

Creek down in southwestern Missouri and the death of General Lyon.

Gloom swept the company. "If we don't git in this mighty soon, the Rebs'll win the war and we'll all be back on the farm," Tim Forehand predicted, wholly dejected. "Maybe it's already over." He had turned up with a cheap, round-faced watch the same day Daniel visited a St. Louis daguerreotypist's shop to have his picture taken. He fished out the enormous timepiece, dangling on a stout chain, and regarded it fondly and rubbed it against his shirt as a small boy would shine an apple. "Be time for drill in a little bit," he said, following his newly developed fondness for announcing the time of day. "By jinks, I'd druther be home behind a mule."

Daniel read the newspapers without enthusiasm. A deadening lull had settled over the entire nation, North and South. Nothing happened. He thought more and more of home and Laurel. Her promised daguerreotype hadn't arrived, nor further letters from her, although he was hearing from his folks. By the time the woods were turning crimson and gold and a delightful sunlit coolness blessed the countryside, he could bear the suspense no longer.

Captain Hooper's office showed the propriety of an old Army post. A stiff-backed orderly stood outside. Upon the closed door, polished to a dark, shiny gloss, were the prominent letters:

CAPT. STARK CHITTENDEN HOOPER
Company D

Daniel stated his name and business to the orderly, who rapped on the door.

"What is it?" Hooper sounded annoyed.

"Private Wade to see you, sir."

"What about?"

"A furlough, sir."

"Tell him to wait. I'm busy."

Daniel sat and weighed his slim chances, thinking how Hooper had avoided him since his fight with Murphy. Half an hour later, when finally he was told to enter and the orderly had closed the door behind him, he saw Hooper lay aside a copy of *Harper's Weekly*. Daniel saluted, his mouth hardening.

Hooper took a black cigar from his mouth and slowly tapped its white ash into the saucer of a coffee cup. Seated before his desk, Hooper looked heavier than when the company had left home. An atmosphere of self-satisfaction surrounded him. His face had the fullness and color of good living. Back were his mustache, trimmed to modish points that drooped at the ends, and his goatee, a neat, gold tuft under the full lip, and his fringed, gold epaulettes, on which rested twin captain's bars of silver. His handsome sword and its sling and black belt were draped over a chair by the desk.

Hooper's return salute was a twitch of fore and middle fingers. He was leaning back, his relaxation designed. He assumed the formal air of an officer about to listen to a subordinate's complaints.

"Well?"

"The orderly told you. I need a furlough home."

"Why?"

"My father's sick. He can't get all his work done."

"Any particular work?"

Hooper's deliberate questions were provoking. Daniel could feel the blood rising up his neck. "Plowing . . . for sowing fall wheat."

"You have neighbors."

"Their boys are gone, too."

Hooper leaned in, a motion that shook his fringed epaulettes. "Is that the real reason behind your request?"

"Isn't that enough?" Daniel's temper was jerking at him. His voice fluted up.

Hooper slid back his chair and stood, his military pretensions forgotten. He stepped around the desk and stopped an arm's length away. His lips stretched, slurring an expression of ridicule. "Don't you think you're being a little absurd? Even ridiculous . . . in your position . . . to think Laurel Vandiver might be interested in you? Even remotely so? A person of her genteel background? Refinement? Education? Family?"

"Stark, you're a poor loser."

Hooper's right hand flicked. His open palm smacked across Daniel's cheek. Daniel swayed backward, and, when he moved forward with knotted fists, he saw Hooper step away and wheel swiftly with drawn sword. Pointing the tip at Daniel's chest, he said: "Come on. I believe the Ninth Article of War covers insubordination by physical violence."

"Does it," Daniel said, almost against the jabbing point, "cover hiring thugs to beat up enlisted men?"

"One more step and I shall prefer charges against you."

"You won't because the boys know about Murphy. He same as told us."

Hooper's face switched. He struggled to regain a modicum of composure. He put on his mask of military propriety and pulled back his sword, but left the blade extended before him as though he didn't trust Daniel's impulses.

"Request for furlough denied, Private Wade. You are dismissed."

Leaving the office, Daniel seemed to be walking through a dense fog that shut out all sounds and obscured all objects. In him there beat a fury so powerful that he was trembling. Never had he known this destructive feeling toward another person. It frightened him in a way because it ran deeper than the surface violence of warring young men testing their brawn. For that reason it wasn't good, and yet he couldn't force it down, or the rebellion he felt.

When he entered the barracks, his comrades were sleeping, writing letters, loafing and talking, it being Saturday afternoon and no drill. He slumped on his bunk to contemplate the future.

Hooper would make him dance hereafter. Life would be miserable. He could take that, all of it. But he could not take his uncertainty over conditions at home and why Laurel's letters did not come. Not that his mother was one to complain. Rather, it was what she refrained from mentioning in her letters. Since summer, there had been a conspicuous lack of reference to his father. Last fall, he recalled, his father had been unable to follow a plow; now he would be less able. Neither could he believe that Laurel would stop writing him. His experience told him it was the major.

"What ails you, Dan?" It was Jesse Nance asking. "You look peaked."

Daniel limited his brief account to denial of the furlough.

"Don't tell me you expected him to give *you* one?" Amos Swink joked, and his curious look let fall that he and the others knew more than Daniel might suppose.

"Dan's father is sick," Jesse explained.

Daniel sat upright. "Sick?"

"Didn't you hear?"

Daniel shook his head. "When was this?"

An awkward silence heaped up between them. "Why," Jesse stammered, scowling his self-reproach, "my folks just wrote that your father was under the weather. I figured you knew. That's all I know. Maybe he's better now, Dan."

Daniel sank back, his surprise fading. So he was right. He'd felt it for some time. From far back in the passages of his mind rushed a half-formed thought that took on a wild resolve, butting at discipline and reason. It planted itself firmly, persisting, refusing to leave, and presently he knew what he was going to do.

Half an hour after Taps, Daniel threw off his blanket and began putting on his uniform. He glanced toward the empty bunks of his friends, gone to the Bull of the Woods, where he would be had he not said he felt the shakes coming on him. The boys were battling the Illinois company tonight, and Murphy was along for good measure. He shook himself free of regret and hurried dressing.

A chill clutched the clear night toward the dark blur of trees, yonder. He knew his surroundings well. It was the only logical way to go. Across the road ran the path leading to the Bull of the Woods, a path he intended to follow some distance before striking out on a round-about circle that would bring him to the Missouri River.

Since it was Saturday night, he could sense the furtive movements of other figures traversing the autumnal darkness under the cool yellow moon. He wore his infantry greatcoat and carried a knapsack of personal items and edibles purchased at the sutler's.

A sharpening sense of the action he was about to take came to him as he reached the end of the trees. He understood the consequences that would come, he understood fully, but his people needed him, and there all discipline broke, dashed on a race of feeling.

He concentrated on the sentry, who was making his turn at the other end of the post. When the man paced opposite him, about-faced, and started back, Daniel slipped out and passed quickly to the road and into the timber.

He was free now, outside the confines of the post, and on that recognition he slowed step and looked over his shoulder. At that moment he picked up a difference in the night's tone. A scuffle of sound that was out of place. A sense of presence nearby. He reacted instinctively, on guard.

Many hands grasped him from behind before he could look. One clapped over his mouth, and he was dragged, manhandled, toted, fetched, and carried, struggling and thrashing, for some rods under the trees.

A rough voice panted: "What're you tryin' to

do . . . go home and git yourself shot?" Tim Forehand's voice.

Daniel quit fighting, too surprised to resist further. They hauled him up, still holding onto him, however, and he saw the little ring of heaving shapes around him.

"Let me through," he said suddenly, and tried to push out.

They clutched him again and shook him roughly, making him helpless. Once more he stood clear, and once more the determined shapes surrounded him.

"You ain't goin' nowhere," Obadiah Swink swore.

"Not without us," said Amos.

There were other voices muttering at him that Daniel recognized. Jesse and Andy. Even Murphy. And he hung his head, beginning to feel the first sting of shame.

"How'd you know to be here?" he said. His let-down voice came piecemeal from the pit of his stomach. He shook his head, trying to clear away the haze that cluttered his mind.

"Mean how'd we not know," Tim rebuked him. "That sick look on your face all day about the furlough. If that wasn't a giveaway, it was when you begged off on our little ramble with the Illinois boys tonight. You never hung back before when we needed you." He swung his high shoulders. His voice changed to impatience.

"Cuss it, we're late. If we don't hitch along, they'll think we're afraid."

He stepped out, and then paused, a question hanging. No other word was said. The others shifted toward Tim, and, as Daniel saw that they were likewise waiting for him and even depending on him, the bitter fog lifted from his head. He belonged here.

Ever so slowly he said—"Let's go."—and stepped with them. As he lengthened his stride beside them, he knew at last that he was turning his back on home and a long time would pass before he might see it again.

Chapter Fourteen

FORT DONELSON, FEBRUARY, 1862

They tramped along the muddy Tennessee road in the false warmth of early February, two days' rations bulging their haversacks, jaunty young men singing "John Brown's Body" over and over, especially one verse about hanging Jeff Davis to a sour apple tree. Now and then a perspiring recruit would toss away his heavy overcoat and blanket. Amos Swink shed his despite his older brother's warning. Daniel kept his, although tempted to lighten the load on the pack straps cutting his shoulders, curbed by home's absolute dictum that nothing usable, food or clothing, was ever wasted.

As far as he could see, forward and rear, a dark blue worm of striding figures was wriggling four abreast between the oak-clad hills. Sunlight as soft as early spring bathed the bobbing column, glinted on long Springfield rifle barrels, and sparkled against the clear sky. One company would sing a while, pause for breath, and the lusty voices of another would carry on the song.

Everywhere about him Daniel could feel the heartbeat of the invading army. It was more than the stout singing. It was part laughter, tinny equipment tinkles and clanks. It was part grumbling and stumbling, and heavy-footed tramping, and the crunch of brogans on yellow gravel. A great forward stir reaching ahead through the still and leafless hills. A thousand men marched in his regiment, a thousand Missourians.

He noticed bunched horsemen observing the passing files. There was crusty, profane old General C.F. Smith, his long white mustache ends flowing past his ruddy cheeks like the folds of a flag. Beside him, on a cream-colored horse, watched a short, spare officer whose sandy, unkempt beard ran from ear to ear. The Cairo newspapers had said Grant was a brand new brigadier general, whether he looked it or not.

Slightly stooped, his unbuttoned uniform rumpled, and his boots gory with yellow mud, he reminded Daniel of a farmer who had just tramped across his barnyard to study a pen full of stock. For all his ordinary appearance, though, he struck Daniel as a steady man, calm of manner, and his blue eyes looked kind and thoughtful.

Early that afternoon the shaggy, yet pleasing, face of the landscape changed. It began to hump up more, as if possessing a surly disposition underneath, and the studded hills mounted higher and bolder, as if wishing to bar the way. The singing fell off, the marching became harder. Daniel watched the thick underbrush on his side. The steady tramping had a dogged rhythm. He grew sensitive to small sounds and movements. His canteen was bumping; he shifted it. He saw Tim Forehand take out his shiny watch and look at it, admiring, when he could have told time by the sun. A hot stillness hung over the head-bent marchers.

Daniel looked up when distant rattles shook the peaceful countryside. Everyone craned to see, causing an unevenness in the company's striding gait. And when the column swung along a level stretch, he saw the agitated shapes of horsemen before a wooded ridge that lay astride the narrow road and puffed small balls of smoke.

Down the long line came the barked halt orders. There was nothing to do but watch the

cavalrymen play their game of rushing forward
and back, joined by crouching figures of
skirmishers filing through the timber. The popping grew brisk. When it weakened and scattered
after ten minutes, Daniel could discern figures
where the road crossed the spine of the ridge.

"They're on the run," Andy Green muttered.
"Why'n thunderation don't we charge?"

So Daniel wondered. He had the unsatisfying
aloofness of a spectator.

Clear and alert, a bugle's brassy notes called
across the pleasant air. Captain Hooper rode forward. Daniel followed the erect figure. He didn't
begrudge Hooper a mount. It was *how* he rode,
his unmistakable superiority. Hooper soon
galloped back. "Advance to the foot of that
ridge"—Daniel heard him tell the lieutenants—
"and start deploying." Hooper sounded snappish.
He turned to go forward again, reconsidered, and
rode down column, his gaze searching. Daniel
saw the eyes find him, and he saw Hooper nod
toward the woods and order: "Go out there and
see that no one slips in our flank."

Daniel stared. Feeling scorched his face. The
order was unnecessary, for cavalry rode on both
flanks. If he hadn't known it, the puzzlement of
his friends did for him.

"Did you hear the order, Private Wade?"

Daniel gave him a slight nod.

"Then speak up. Execute it."

Deliberately Daniel shifted his pack and deliberately he walked off the road, liking the flash of temper he saw leaping to Hooper's eyes. Another step and Hooper's voice lashed him from behind: "I said speak up!"

Daniel had a rein on himself. He heeled about, said—"Yes, sir."—and turned back.

Underbrush and fallen timber made the footing rougher, and he knew this was Hooper's method of riding him again. The captain had to hate him to continue it.

He had been sweating on the hot march. Now pushing through brush and climbing over logs brought rivulets down his face. He covered a long mile before he saw the company reach the ridge and deploy along it. Tim Forehand shook his head and grinned when Daniel took his place.

"See any Johnnies?"

"Woods are full of 'em."

Hooper was constantly turning his horse. As the company drew out its length in column of fours, he raised his voice and gave the order to go up the hill on the double.

Panting up the rough slant, Andy on one side of him, Tim on the other, Daniel met a forested emptiness and heard not a shot. Not until he grunted to the top and flopped down and gazed off did he understand. The Johnnies weren't whipped; they had fallen back after holding up the Union advance.

The regimental colonel rode along where the winded Coon Creek Company lay. His eyes glinted displeasure. His voice was curt: "Captain, your men have just finished a twelve mile hike with full packs. You should know not to run them up a hill." He passed on before Hooper could summon a reply.

There was no end to the rough ridges. It was down one and up another into the afternoon, and then Daniel saw a spectacle that took his breath and hung his jaw. Dread and awe spilled over him as he gazed far and wide.

Before him rose Fort Donelson, a glowering hulk planted on a high bluff against the curving Cumberland. A sullen monster crouched over acres of broken, wooded humps and ravines, a sweeping half circle of yellow-clay breastworks, rifle pits, and sharp-angled trenches. On its north edge gleamed a moat-like creek, swollen with backwater from the river on his left where cannon boomed. In front felled trees formed dense tangles of branches that faced outward; on up the steep hill lay the first line of raw-earth trenches. Tiny shapes still toiled there. His mind flung up a comparison: Fort Henry, back on the muddy banks of the Tennessee. There wasn't much resemblance. Federal gunboats had soon pounded it into surrender. Henry was just a little pea-wadding molehill compared to the likes of this forbidding fortress.

" 'Pears like we'll have to smoke 'em out," Amos Swink observed, studying the entrenchments.

"Smoke 'em out?" his brother asked. "A body's got to tree 'em first."

"Can't one Yank whip three Rebs?"

"Not Missouri Rebs. They's some up there, I calculate."

The afternoon dwindled, and the Coon Creek Company was ordered forward as sharpshooters. Crawling ahead, Daniel couldn't see much beyond the thick woods studding the ridge. It sloped sharply to a deep ravine, and the ascent climbed as steeply for the first line of Confederate earthworks. That was the way they would have to go if they captured Fort Donelson, down and up.

He posted himself behind a stump and fired when he saw movement on the fresh-turned trench line, which wasn't often, unable as he was to determine the effect of his shots. He doubted that he was hitting anybody. An occasional Minié ball whistled and shrieked near him. Ravels of gray smoke began to writhe and drift in the leafless timber; now he saw less than before.

An overhead banging took his attention. He looked up. Cat-like, intent, Seth Coots crouched in the fork of a large oak. His canteen dangled from a branch. The long barrel of his rifle rested across a strong bough. His eyes never left the fort. Suddenly the muscles in his lean jaws went taut. He pressed off a shot, peered an ascertaining moment, dropped down in the fork to tear cartridge, pour powder, and drop bullet, ram it home, draw back hammer, and press on a percussion cap. His movements were fluid, swift, balanced, relishing. Ready again, he eased out to his perch and scanned the hill afresh. As Daniel was settling down, he heard Coots's rifle again.

Purple dusk darkened the hollows when they went back up the slope to wolf cold rations.

"Say, boys," Coots bragged, hardtack lumping his jaws, "got myself two Johnnies back there."

Daniel put down his supper. He didn't like the way Coots said it, the same as enjoying killing.

"I saw 'em flop, and they didn't git back up," Coots went on, positive. He turned challenging eyes on Daniel. "Ain't that what we're here for? To kill Rebs?"

Daniel let his silence stand. He understood little of the reality of war. His notions sprang from reading about frontier heroes who fought hand-to-hand. Seth Coots was a better soldier than he was when it came to killing. But he knew that he had no use for sharpshooting. It seemed cowardly, cruel, and unnecessary.

Fresh pickets filed out, and the Missourians stacked arms and rolled in their blankets.

Over on the river, to the north, Daniel heard a gunboat teasing the Confederate batteries. One by one, the tired voices around him dropped off. The bivouac was still. He turned his face to the cool night, and his mind wavered between home and Laurel, longing, and he could see himself hurrying up the railed lane to the old clapboarded house or waiting in the venerable hush of the Indian mound. As his weary body relaxed, the faces and scenes dissolved faster than they had formed, and he fell asleep to the spiteful popping of pickets' rifles across the ravine.

He opened his eyes to the dove-gray of dawn, when the woods were still peaceful. Everything was so quiet that, for a moment, he didn't know where he was. So he lay a while in his blanket, wanting to keep the stillness a little longer. But as light touched the treetops and uncovered the yellow trenches scarring the steep hill yonder, uglier and more formidable than yesterday afternoon because the Johnnies had been tearing all night at the clay ridges, the pickets opened up again and the regiment came awake.

Back a way, the Missourians made fires and cooked coffee and bacon to go with their hard bread, and afterward they returned to the woods on the ridge top to wait. Waiting, Daniel was finding, fretted a body and seemed harder than fighting.

Tim had just looked at his watch and announced the hour as ten o'clock when a sharp clatter commenced to the south, where General

McClernand's Illinois boys were. Musket volleys mixed with the boom and jar of artillery. Daniel heard, as scraps of sound loose on the wind, pieces of shouted Union hurrahs and the higher yelling of the Confederates. All the action was hidden. He could only imagine it.

But soon he could see hundreds of blue figures forming to his right and, shortly, going down the slope to be enveloped by the dark woods and blooms of rising rifle smoke. New roars crashed; that came from the Rebel trenches flashing and smoking. Later, he watched the blue shapes straggling back up the ridge, their movements slower. Some hobbled; some were carried and helped.

The long day closed on that discouraging note, for the attack wasn't renewed.

On the third morning the Coon Creek Company was up and stirring early, the continued suspense of waiting turning everyone restless. So far they had done nothing but snipe and look. Except for the killing, Daniel thought, it wasn't much different than sitting on a rail fence watching two bulls butt heads in a pasture. He examined his rifle again and again, yet to be fired in anger. He eyed the opposite yellow ridge, basking in the warm sun, and scanned the sky. It had grown a little darker since early morning. The light wasn't quite so blue-clear, intimating that clouds might be building up north of the river.

Later in the day, deep sounds shook the hills. For hours Union gunboats and Confederate batteries had a cussing match on the river, their throaty resonance echoing like the strokes of mighty tom-toms.

At dusk Daniel felt the first spat of drizzle on his face. A gentle pattering began overhead. The wind was shifting, a bite in it. Within minutes it rushed out of the north, gusty and angry, shouting its temper through the treetops. By dark, the soft rain had turned to pellets of sleet and swirling snow, leaving him chilled despite his overcoat and blanket. Under the next oak the Swink brothers huddled together, while Obadiah vented himself of comments about any jackass who would throw away his overcoat in February.

"Wade . . . Wade!"

Seth Coots was hollering through the wind as he came up from the rear. In close, he said: "Captain says you relieve Murphy on post number one down the ridge." When Daniel did not move, Coots slouched a step nearer. "If you don't believe me, go ask the captain."

Daniel, at last, turning to take his rifle from the stack, glanced over his shoulder. Coots continued to stand there. The failing light revealed his lank, sallow face, the overbearing curl of the mouth.

Daniel went downridge, his body bent against the flailing storm. He found Murphy a hunched shape using the shelter of a groaning oak. Daniel gestured toward the bivouac. Murphy showed him a thankful look and hurried away.

He could see nothing through the slanting gray screen of ice and snow and the blurred ranks of timber. If the Johnnies decided to cross the ravine and attack, he'd not know until they were within a few feet of him. It was getting colder. Swiftly the last portion of dim daylight retreated from his swirling world. Now he stood deep in raging darkness. To keep warm he paced back and forth, peering toward the ravine. He felt that a long time had passed. No one came to relieve him, and he alternated cradling the heavy rifle in one arm and swinging and thrashing the other against his body and stamping his feet. Even so, a creeping numbness invaded him. He leaned the rifle against a tree and paced faster, swinging arms and stamping.

Much later, he knew, he heard a call behind him and saw the outline of a broad, short soldier. Andy Green shouted in his face: "Go back! We got a fire goin'!" The anger of his voice got through to Daniel despite the roaring.

He started uphill at a stiff-legged trot. At the second fire in the first hollow, he recognized the huddled figures of his friends behind a wind-break of boughs and logs. Someone handed him a cup of steaming coffee that he held crab-like, content for the hot tin to roast his benumbed hands. He squatted to let his deadened body soak up the heat. When he had gulped the scalding brew and could look up, he met puzzled stares.

"You should 'a' been relieved an hour ago," Jesse said.

"Didn't Coots tell anybody?"

"Not us. We thought you'd stopped at Murphy's fire till he came to borrow coffee."

Daniel sipped faster. But the flashing heat he felt wasn't from the coffee, and the trembling of his hands wasn't from the bitter cold. He forced himself to sit another minute, to finish another cup of coffee. Then he stood up.

"Where you goin'?" Tim asked suspiciously.

Daniel withheld reply. He was looking uphollow, seeing the string of fires as ruddy eyes set against the windy darkness. He went stumbling over the rough ground, at once feeling the howling rush of piercing cold. Three fires onward he arrived upon a comfortable camp. A sturdy lean-to and men bunched around a cheerful fire. One figure was lying down, apparently sleeping.

Daniel bent down and took Coots by the shoulder. He watched Coots blink and open his eyes and stifle a yawn that wasn't a yawn.

"You," Coots said. "Reckon I dozed off. I was goin' . . . ."

Daniel seized his overcoat front and jerked him upright on his haunches. Only now did he find honest reaction in the hatchet features as Coots, surprised, tried to pull back.

"You're lying," Daniel said, and hauled him to his feet and shook him, hoping Coots would fight back. But he saw Coots divine that and he saw sarcasm twitch along the spongy mouth.

Daniel's loathing leaped. Against his will he threw Coots upon his blanket, instead of hitting him, and, as he saw Coots continue to mouth the mocking expression, Daniel stopped. A thought blazed. If he let Coots go now, this would happen again and again in some fashion. Therefore, he sprang forward and got hold of Coots, and they commenced rolling over and over, Daniel hampered by his heavy clothing, Coots protected by his. This time Coots was fighting back, swinging and scrambling. When they rolled close to the fire, he came up clutching an arm-thick chunk of wood flaring like a torch on one end. Daniel threw up a warding arm, and felt the crash of pain and smelled the stench of singed wool. In fury, he waded inside Coots's guard and chopped the swinging arm. Coots yelled sharply. The blazing wood chunk fell spinning.

Daniel grappled Coots down and was hitting him about the face and shoulders, hitting him blindly, when he was torn off and held. He failed to recognize the Coon Creek faces at first.

"That's enough, Dan," Andy Green said, and demonstrated his own contempt for Coots.

"Don't dirty your hands on the likes of him. Leave him for the Johnnies."

Daniel looked down, but Coots wouldn't meet his eyes. The violence in Daniel throbbed on, not ebbing. Andy took his arm, and he was glad when his other friends crowded around him, and he allowed them to start him toward camp, for he feared himself unless he left quickly.

Shivering, he woke to an icy wind coated with the down of a light snow, a wintry fairyland not intended for war. His trouser legs were frozen stiff, and he was hungry and miserable. Seeing the haggard faces around him, though, he understood it was no worse for him than for them, and he busied himself building up the fire.

Obadiah, bringing in wood, said—"A company says some wounded froze to death last night between the lines."—and blew on his hands.

Shortly after sunrise, while they were cooking breakfast, Daniel caught a crackle of musketry. It spread to an abrupt crescendo. Every man turned to the south. Off there, hidden from the eye, lay the Federal right wing and the little town of Dover that the Confederates held. A different pattern marked this morning's firing. Although the volleys would spatter off, they always regained their terse rattle, as heavy as before, if not heavier. The racket continued after breakfast, on and on, moving farther south. It meant,

Daniel recognized by now, the rolling roar of a savage, shifting battle.

Middle morning arrived before the Coon Creek Company heard any news: "The Johnnies started pitching into McClernand's boys at daybreak and driving them back."

Afterward, little wads of men waited around the fires and smoked and talked, dried out their blankets, or gathered more firewood. The weather was warming, turning the snow and ice to slush under the dripping oaks.

Around two o'clock Daniel noticed horsemen on the wooded ridge, and before long he saw General Smith, his face like a red apple, and his staff pass along the regiment's front and disappear.

The next interval was more burdensome than the long morning. Daniel saw no troops moving. He heard no commands. Yet he knew something was coming. Jesse was reading the Bible. Obadiah, cold fingers clamped around a pencil stub, labored over a letter home, using his canteen for a writing board. Amos and Tim and Andy were joking about the Cairo girls.

Daniel reflected on his own feelings. Was he supposed to be afraid? He was, and, although he thought of home and Laurel and her one letter between the leaves of his New Testament, the deep ravine and the yellow-soaked trenches and rifle pits occupied his mind as well.

An officer, his mount kicking up muddy snow and leaves, galloped back from the direction General Smith had gone, hard for the colonel's tent. The pranking Coon Creek voices stopped. Even as the rider was rushing away, the first command was barked, muffled down the line, and then clear as it was shouted along.

Hooper appeared suddenly, striding through the company bivouac. "Fall in . . . fall in," he said, irritable and scowling.

Daniel stepped to his rifle stack. In an incredibly brief time, it seemed to him, they were filing two abreast through the bare, black timber, north toward the swollen creek. Across the deep ravine the Confederates were as still as Indians. All Daniel could hear above the scuffing tramp was the savage rip of guns to the south.

Once they halted and Tim pondered: "Maybe the idea is to outflank 'em."

Nobody offered a better notion. They marched on, halted again, and right-faced. It was then that Daniel, looking across the ravine, understood where they were going. Along the brow of the ridge other blue companies were forming on both flanks of the Coon Creekers. Another wait. Another breathless pause. Daniel saw the company on his right go forward, a dark, uneven wave flowing downslope. Near the bottom he lost them in the trees. Moments and he saw them as oblique figures struggling up the opposite ridge.

At the same time the Confederate trenches flowered smoke puffs, crackled and roared as the drawing back of a wide curtain.

A command jarred Daniel's concentration there: "Forward . . . harch!"

There was a lurching and heaving forward, and he, too, started downhill. His throat felt dry. He kept opening and closing his mouth, and wetting his lips. All chill had fled his body; he began to feel warmly uncomfortable. A heavy rock seemed to ride his chest.

They advanced now over the flattened-out footing of the ravine's bottom, and, as they neared the last fringe of trees before the naked hill, Daniel heard a halt order and another—no firing until they passed the felled trees. He noticed Hooper, afoot today, his face like ashes. Now: "Fix bayonets."

The metallic grating of steel on steel clattered along the company's length. Old General Smith rode out in front and gestured uphill, his saber held high. A bugle was blowing *rat-a-tat-tat*.

When they ran forward, then, into the open, a rush of homebound thoughts darted swiftly through Daniel's mind. His brogans dug into the steep ridge, slippery with mud and melting snow, and, when he glanced upward, the breastworks beyond the tangled abatis were spouting flame and smoke, and the rifle balls came hissing.

The Coon Creek Company was yelling, and he

was yelling with them. The sound of his voice gave him a feeling of tremendous relief. He saw no enemy, only smoke. He dodged around a tree stump and slid backward and half around, a position that left him looking along the struggling line and behind it. He saw a wake of fallen bodies, some unmoving and others dragging themselves downhill. The sights appalled him, took his attention from the crashing din above.

He went scrambling upward again, hearing a cannon boom and feeling the shot rushing overhead like the crashing of a locomotive. He pulled up, surprised to see the mass of cut trees breast-high before him. With the others, he started tearing at the clawing branches and sliding over trunks. Through, he saw the yellow breastworks not a hundred feet away. Here the hissings and shriekings were loudest and the face of the hill tilted more steeply. He crouched behind a stump and fired at a face on the parapet, dropped down, and pulled a cartridge from his box, bit, charged, rammed, cocked, capped, and poked the rifle around the stump again. For the first time since the charge had begun, he sensed his slackening. On all sides of him Coon Creekers were firing and reloading, kneeling and prone. The assault, like himself, was halted.

Hurrahs soared above the tumultuous firing. Men were jerking to look behind them. Daniel saw a figure on horseback, lunging uphill. It was

General Smith, high in the saddle and really too old for fighting, the wind-blown banners of his white mustache-ends laid back against his ruddy cheeks.

Daniel found his voice again. All around men were shouting and stirring. He humped up and forward, toward the close *rap-rap* of the firearms on the hill. Running, sliding sometimes, he could see the clay parapet flaming and smoking. But it was not when he scrambled to the top. Figures were already struggling in the trench. He jumped down, dodging a gray shape making a bayonet stab for him, and, when the man whirled, jabbing again, Daniel shot him. The Minié ball drove the Confederate back against the raw-yellow wall. When he slid downward and his mouth fell open, Daniel saw that he wasn't a man but a boy.

Suddenly the stabbing, clubbing, and shooting ended. Higher on the hill Daniel saw a second line of breastworks toward which the enemy was retreating to fight again, for already the humming and hissing rifle balls were searching for the Missourians, who took cover on the outer side of the trench.

Hugging the muddy clay, Daniel felt the sag of an exhaustion unnoticed until now. Sweat fell down his forehead and trickled off the end of his nose. He had no breath. He saw himself in Tim Forehand's powder-blackened lips, Tim's black-ringed mouth and heaving chest. These sensations registered briefly, dulled by the cries of the wounded men down the hill and in the trenches. Their moaning, screaming, and cursing blotted out the relief he had felt over coming through the charge.

A lull settled just before dark. Across the short space between the trenches, a softly sardonic voice called down: "Why'n't you Yankee Doodle Dandies come up?"

"Why'n't you Johnnies git more sociable?" Tim answered back.

So the banter ran, to fade, to resume, to fade completely when darkness covered the cold ridge. As the bitter night advanced, the face of the Confederate Daniel had shot came to haunt his mind. He had no elation whatever. He could see him again, acutely defined. A boy near his own age. Fair hair that pouched below his rakish new cap. A slim face of open innocence, contorted and made savage by the same fear that had spurred Daniel.

Sudden remorse affected him. It turned him miserable during the raw night whenever he woke from a fitful doze, too cold to sleep, or a rifle's desultory *rap* jerked him awake. It remained with him early next morning when white flags fluttered along the Confederate lines, and even afterward when the hurrahing companies marched into the entrenchments behind old General Smith, and a body wondered if they had to fight another battle. Wasn't the capture of Fort Donelson enough? The greatest Union victory of the war?

Chapter Fifteen

SHILOH'S SPRINGTIME WOODS

They breasted the muddy lifeblood of the Tennessee, a strange river that flowed northward, victorious young bluecoats on transports scribbling plumes of angry black smoke across the southern springtime sky, to a steamboat landing below maize-colored bluffs and up them to haunting woodlands and pocket-size clearings where peach blossoms spread their pink webs.

A fine place to camp an army, to Daniel Wade's approving notion, welcome after the chilling ridges around Fort Donelson, and a fine place, too, for a picnic. Gray squirrels played under stalwart oak and hackberry trees, and magnolias, cedars, pines, and sour gums. Startled deer and rabbits fled as the noisy columns tramped away from the river to pitch tents. Off in the cool, bird-twittering woods, with the hot sun shuttered, everything became a pleasant confusion of trees, knolls, and glades, until a body wasn't certain of his directions. Marching out, Daniel noticed few signs of habitation: a log house above the landing, and onward, edging an overgrown field, an old wagon road, the tracings of its yellow ruts vanishing dimly into the hiding oaks.

A prankish, holiday air pervaded the camps. There was little drilling and no digging whatever of breastworks. Evidently the generals were waiting for more regiments to arrive before the Army struck deeper into the Southland. Boys in the Coon Creek Company, because they had fought at Donelson, assumed the swagger of bored amusement when green recruits asked eager questions. Practically every true Coon Creeker carried a captured Bowie knife at his belt; everyone had souvenirs to exhibit.

"He wants to know how we captured Fort Donelson," Tim Forehand said, hooking his thumb toward a bug-eyed Iowa farm boy visiting around camp one afternoon. "What a big battle's like. Well, I'm plumb tard of the subject myself. Why'n't you tell him, perfessor?"

"Not me." Daniel held off, equaling Tim's serious face. "It's only proper that you tell the story. Didn't you lead the charge?"

Tim squirmed and averted his eyes, observing a modest silence.

"Oh, he never will let on," Obadiah Swink confided in him. "But he sure did. Reckon I know, bein' as how I was right behind him goin' up the ridge."

Attesting to that were vigorous nods all around.

"Go ahead and tell him, Tim."

Showing obvious reluctance, Tim crossed his arms and commenced. "The thing about a battle is keepin' cool. Remember that. Always keep cool. A steady eye. That's what counts. Same as shootin' squirrels. That was how we took Fort Donelson there on the Cumberland in the mud an' snow, when we charged up the ridge that turrible afternoon. And Minner balls! You never saw the like. Why, it was like pecans a-showerin' down out of a tree, or bein' out in the middle of a hailstorm. Man had a big bucket he could 'a' caught it full in a second or two. Had he been fool enough to try, mind you. Minner balls make the dangdest fuss! *Snort-hiss-whistle-screech-hum-buzz.* Sometimes a body jes' swears there's a swarm of bees around his cap." Tim paused to gaze over the nodding faces. "Well, sir, I ain't much of a hand to take credit where credit ain't due. But us Coon Creek Boys . . . we're all from Miz-zoo-ree, you know . . . around Foley's Prairie . . . got to the top first. No time to reload."

Tim lowered his shoulders in a sudden lunge, his face quite fearsome. "She was hand-to-hand then, you betcha. Me and the boys right in the middle. Them Johnnies fightin' like treed cougars. Us yellin' the same . . . . That's our company name, you know . . . The Coon Creek Cougars . . . . She was all over in a cat's lick, though. Next morning, bright an' early, they had their white flags up, an' we all marched in. A mighty grand sight it was, too." He sighed, refolded his arms, and sat back on his log seat.

"Ain't you goin' to tell him about the cannons?" said Amos Swink, disappointed.

"You mean the battery we captured on the heights?" Tim, shrugging, stood, and fetched forth his round-faced watch on its chain. He blew on it fondly, and shined it against his shirt. "Not now, boys. My little keepsake here, which was give to me by a certain sweet-smellin' admirer in Saint Louis, says it's time for my chat with the colonel."

During the afternoons and evenings the regimental bands serenaded the camps with patriotic tunes, and green troops, fearing their gunpowder was damp after a shower, tested their muskets in the sleepy woods. Through these sounds ran the *r-r-rumping* drums and the wailing bugle signals. At night, rolling in his blanket, a recruit might discover a dead turtle or a snake or a frog. To amuse themselves further, the idling soldiers played cards, whittled, wrote letters, staged foot races, broad-jumping contests, and company wrestling matches and prize fights. Private

Murphy disposed of "A" Company's pride, a St. Louis Dutchman, but balked when urged to meet another company champion.

Morose and body sore, Murphy regarded his scarred fists and muttered: "To think that me poor father wanted me to play the fiddle and amount to somethin' in this dreary world. I've had enough, boys. I'm a peaceful man at heart. I am. Fightin' is a wasted way of life."

"But think of all the fun you'd 'a' missed," Andy Green said.

"With the lumps," Murphy philosophized, even gloomier.

"C Company's man says you're afraid to meet him."

"Afraid?" Murphy said, dumbfounded. "Nobody told me that. Afraid, am I? Afraid?" The word had an odd ring on his battered lips, and he appeared to struggle with himself. Presently Daniel saw a tiny gleam of interest behind his gloomy front. On the instant he looked much younger. He rubbed his hands and stood, light on his feet, shedding the years, and he asked: "What time now did y'say the frolic was?"

No personal effect was sacred. Amos posted himself in the company street and yelled: "Hey, listen to this!" He caressed his nose with a letter, inhaling deeply all the while, and, when an audience had gathered, he began reading in dulcet tones: "'Dear Obadiah. You are such a brave, sweet boy. Everybody on Coon Creek and in Foley's Prairie is talking about your gallant deeds at Fort Donelson. How you rallied your regiment when it was about to retreat. How you captured the Rebel flag on the crest. How you saved your wounded colonel from certain death, carrying him to shelter under terrible fire. I am so proud. . . .'"

Amos never finished. A figure tore around a tent. It was Obadiah, glaring, accusing. "Now I know who wrote her all that folderol. You did. Dang your hide!" He was raging forward as he spoke.

Amos, slim and quick, eluded his furious rush and took off for the woods, calling back derisive hoots of—"Bra-ave! . . . sweeet! . . . boy!"—as the heavier and slower Obadiah gave futile pursuit.

Once a debonair war correspondent sauntered into camp, dressed as Daniel supposed proper for a man of the world: wide-brimmed hat all a-tilt, knee-length boots of satiny gloss, checkered trousers, red shirt, and long-tailed coat. He leaned his ebony cane against an oak and from his portfolio drew sketching pad and pencil, meanwhile informing the Coon Creek Company that he had come "to portray the heroic veterans of Fort Donelson" for *Leslie's Illustrated Newspaper*.

Now this was something novel. It appealed to their naïve vanity, and at once they fell into poses of heroic indifference while he chatted about the war.

"Guess you boys will be marching on down to Corinth before long. That's where the Rebels are concentrating. Albert Sidney Johnston and P.G.T. Beauregard in command."

"Ain't that Boryreegard the general that fired on Fort Sumter?" Andy questioned.

"Indeed." The alert eyes over the sketching pad flicked here and there. The darting pencil skimmed faster. "Also had a hand in Bull Run. . . . Question is, of course, would the Rebels leave their base at Corinth and head this way? Perhaps not, else Grant would have you boys digging trenches." He smiled his approval of Tim's truculent stance, arms akimbo, Bowie knife prominently displayed, a fierce and reckless leer on his face. "At headquarters they say breastworks are bad for morale."

"Wouldn't hurt mine none," Jesse Nance said. "Can't see how they'd make a man cowardly. Should make him braver."

"I'll wager you sha'n't need any here."

"Not all the Johnnies are in Corinth," Daniel said. "We see some every day on our front, in the woods. They're watching us. But when we go looking for them, they seem to vanish."

"Probably just a few scouts."

The artist-correspondent tucked away his sketch pad and nodded his thanks.

"When's this comin' out?" Tim asked.

"I'll send you all a copy," the man said easily, and his voice acquired a gay quality. "Where'll it be, boys? Corinth? Vicksburg? Atlanta?" He left them with that, sauntering off toward an Illinois regiment.

Late in March, Daniel wrote home:

Dear Folks,
  We are camped in the woods by the Tennessee River. Other morning I saw General Grant riding by. Our position is between two creeks, with the river at our backs. I believe the timber is every bit as fine looking as we have in Missouri. The country around here is too pretty for war. Not far from our camp is a peach orchard in early bloom and a little log church called the Shiloh Methodist Meeting House. It reminds me of the one back home, except ours is a little bigger. Old Shep would like this place. I see rabbits every day beyond camp.
  Our little wad of boys from Foley's Prairie must lead charmed lives. We all came through the Fort Donelson fight without losing a man. Just five wounded. The Confederates fought like

devils. But it doesn't seem right to fight boys who look like us and speak the same language. *[He would never mention to anyone the fair-haired Rebel he had shot. That was like a secret between the two of them now, committed to his trust and shame forever.]*

We are all fine except for the same rations over and over. We joke about the malady we all seem to have. We call it the Tennessee Quickstep. At Jefferson Barracks it was the Missouri Quickstep. Papa, maybe you had a name for it in the Mexican War.

I hope this finds you both well. Have no fears for me. Don't try to do all your work by yourself, Papa. Call on our neighbors for help. You always helped them.

Your affectionate son,
Daniel

Home correspondence always brought him some bad moments. He hadn't stopped writing Laurel, even after his letters continued unanswered. And ever he returned to one saving conclusion: Major Vandiver was intercepting her letters and his. Too, he liked to think no other reason might exist. He still kept his one letter close, in the New Testament, carried in the breast pocket of his flannel shirt.

Why, he thought, it was nigh to a year since she had stolen off to meet him. No, it seemed more like an eternity. Laurel wasn't real. She was a dream or a vision he'd had. He had merely imagined her as he used to the make-believe games with his brother James. Never had he actually embraced her or felt her respond when he kissed her, around them the warm hush of the Indian mound. Thinking thus, he surrendered to sick despair.

On such a day early in April, he was looking off through the woods at nothing particular, dreaming. Abruptly he realized the dark-clothed, rake-handle figure had been approaching for several moments. He stared again to make certain, then called out: "Watch your language. Brother Winn's comin'!"

Brother Winn, indeed. In what looked like the identical dilapidated black hat, coat, and trousers he had worn the day of his doleful, yet true, prophecy, only shabbier, and himself leaner than Daniel ever remembered seeing him. The parson let out a whoop when he saw the boys assembling, and he waved and hurried faster, all feet and shank and wind-milling arms, as shaggy and gaunt and hungry-looking as a long-lost hound. But when he started pumping hands, Daniel found his distant impression contradicted.

The down-trodden Brother Winn was so only in appearance. Inside the caves of his bright blue eyes burned fierce lights. Warmly he spoke their names. His nasal voice had its usual strength, perhaps a greater feeling. He was, in a way, the company's all but forgotten conscience just now catching up.

"Boys," said Brother Winn heartily to all, "I've come to be with you. Figured you needed yourselves a chaplain. Somebody to lead the prayers and hymns. To show you the light. To be with you in time of mortal danger."

No one spoke an immediate welcome. For it had been good to leave home's restraints behind, to swear and fight and frolic when one took the notion. War was still a lark. Hadn't they captured Fort Donelson without losing one Coon Creek man? By jinks, they had! Dying was still remote, intended for someone else, for they were forever young, exempt from pain and destruction, actors in a conflict already legend and destined to change all America, maybe the world.

"We're mighty glad to see you, Brother Winn," Daniel said, when his turn came to shake hands. "How'd you get here, by steamboat?"

Levi Winn had to smile. "Walked. Walked down from Nashville."

"Nashville!"

"All the way. It's a right fur piece, I tell you. A farmer ferried me over. A good Methodist. They wouldn't let me on the boats at Cairo. Said I wasn't a regular Army chaplain, which I ain't, I had to admit. So I came ahead on my own."

"Then you're hungry?"

"Well . . . a mite."

Some doing was required to fill Brother Winn with hardtack, bacon, coffee, and mounds of flapjacks. Afterward, he visited from soldier to soldier, relating family and local news. Foley's Prairie was mighty quiet, even on Saturday. The crop outlook was good, plenty of rain. A company of Union militia was garrisoned in town, there to run down bushwhackers and not catching any.

Daniel thought Brother Winn showed a moment's hesitation when he faced him. "How is my father?" Daniel asked, feeling a start of shame as the tar-and-feathering crashed into his memory.

Brother Winn took another moment. His kind face seemed to grow a little kinder. "He's been sick, Daniel. Reckon you know that?" He was hesitating only because he was reluctant to bring bad news.

"I guessed he was, although my mother never came right out and said so. How is he now?"

"Your father's not well, Daniel. Yet I reckon he's tol'able for a sick man. Tol'able. Yes, he is. He gets about some. His neighbors help out . . . Tobe Russell, when he's sober, and Reuben

Nance, regular. I was by to see Sam before I left."

You, Daniel thought and winced inside. He said gratefully: "Thank you, Brother Winn. And my mother?"

"She's fine, Daniel. Just mighty fine."

Daniel's next thought sprang without warning: "And Miss Laurel Vandiver. Is she still home?"

"Was, when I left in February. Her and the major. Justin's in the Southern Army."

There. Still there. A flaming sensation seared him inside and burned steadily, climbing to his throat and face. He managed a calm voice: "Did my father give you a message for me?"

"I was comin' to that," said Brother Winn, somewhat too promptly. "He said to tell you to take care of yourself, Daniel. Do your duty to the Union. And uh . . . he hoped the war'd soon be over and you'd be home again." His wide mouth, surrounded by its thicket of reddish beard, relayed an encouraging smile, and he stepped on.

Daniel became unusually thoughtful. Brother Winn meant well. But there was one thing wrong. Sam Wade would never speak up for the Union.

Later that day, Daniel lay in the wilderness woods and watched the obscure flutter of movement on the other side of a clearing. Nothing big or sudden, and it wasn't always there. But to a country boy whose keen eyes had

226

searched for squirrels, rabbits, prairie chickens, and darting hawks, the blurs were as handwriting upon the green slate of the silent forest.

"Think I'll try me somethin'," Tim said, tired of the inactivity. He drew his ramrod and, placing his forage cap on the end, slowly hoisted it and waved it in little tantalizing circles. Nothing happened. Tim raised the ramrod higher and made larger, faster circles.

From across the clearing a Minié ball snarled. Daniel ducked, hearing the *pop* of a rifle. When he looked up, Tim's cap lay on the ground and he was grumbling. "By jinks, they got some shooters over there!" Chagrined, he crawled over and retrieved his perforated headpiece. "Jesse, why can't we sorta work around and . . . ?"

" . . . kick up a good fuss?" Jesse shook his head. "You know the orders. We're not to bring on a fight if we can help it."

"It don't make horse sense," Tim said.

"I reckon the idea is to wait for reinforcements 'fore we take on the whole dad-burned Confederate Army. That makes sense."

"They'd better hurry, then. These Johnnies are gittin' thicker'n fleas on a hound dog's belly."

Jesse rubbed one side of his lightly stubbled jaw and gazed off, thinking, frowning. "Dan, better ease back and ask the captain for new orders. Tell him this is the second batch of Johnnies on our front this afternoon."

Daniel prolonged his departure, tasting his bitter dislike of reporting to Hooper. Anyway, he crawled back a way, rose, and came to a road that shortly led him to company headquarters.

Hooper's striker was already preparing supper. A spit-and-polisher of airy manners who had shown up in Cairo, he looked up from his cooking and slung Daniel his contempt for common soldiery. Seeing that Daniel intended to go around him, he strutted to the tent's entrance and posted himself there, chest out.

"State name, rank, and business."

It galled Daniel to speak to him, even briefly, a haughty man in an army of informal farm boys who often called their officers by first names.

The expected delay followed. When Daniel entered, he saw only Hooper's broad back while the captain adjusted the front of his blouse before a small mirror and whisked at his sleeves with his fingers. Polished silverware shone on a white tablecloth covering a camp table. The neck of a dark wine bottle rose swan-like from a bucket.

Aware that Hooper would take no immediate note of him, Daniel stated his report without being asked.

"Oh, we've had scares for days now," Hooper said, yet in front of the mirror.

"And there are more Rebels out there every day."

Something seemed awry with the silver bars on his left shoulder, for Hooper fingered them. "Yesterday," he said, "General Sherman ordered pursuit of a so-called squadron of Confederate cavalry which turned out to be a mere squad." He still addressed the tent wall. "Hence, I can assure you, Wade, there is no respectable enemy force on our front. I repeat . . . no responsible enemy force. What you see are mere reconnoitering parties. Most of the Confederates are in Corinth."

"What about orders?"

"Obviously unchanged," Hooper replied, aloof and distant.

The blind conceit of him!

"Your platoon section," Hooper said, still adjusting, "must be rather frightened out there, crying wolf as often as you do."

Daniel's temper tugged; he hung on to it, knowing that Hooper, baiting him, wished him to lose it. "We report only what we see and hear. The Rebels can hide thousands of men in those thick woods. We expect to be attacked at any time."

"One thing more," Hooper said, disregarding the last entirely. He hadn't faced around, and Daniel sensed that he wasn't going to. "If you'd rather, I can detail you to digging sinks. It's far less dangerous . . . . Now you are dismissed, Wade."

Daniel walked back through the shadowed

woods to the road. When he grew old, he had hoped to say that in all his life he had never hated a fellow. Now he could not.

At deep dusk, while they waited for the relief pickets, he heard a rapping sound, quickening and vibratory, although he could see no motion through the curtain of thickening light. He strained to look. Hardly had he done so when the sound turned into a drumming roll, into a distinct rumble, approaching headlong, shaking the earth, and he could see horsemen bursting upon the picket post, *yee-haaaing!* as they came, their gun muzzles spouting flame.

He fired at a thundering shape. All about him the woods were roaring back. Before he could reload, the riders wheeled and cut, rumbling off, scattering defiant yells in their tracks.

As the yelling ceased and the clattering hoofs faded, Tim spat and made his mimicking voice aloofly superior: "Just a little reconnoiterin' party. Like Stark told Dan'l."

Rain drummed on Daniel's tent during the night, and the narrow road down which he filed next morning was slippery with yellow mud, and the dripping trees glittered under the bright sun. Somebody said it was Saturday, April 5th. Once again he observed the wall of trees across the clearing. Several times he spotted dim movements. Otherwise, the woods were fairly quiet today, a bit more mysterious than yesterday, when a body could tell the Johnnies were up to something.

Perhaps his senses misled him; perhaps, being restless, his imagination tricked him. Because he found himself wondering, as the uneasy afternoon stillness worked by, if he didn't hear distant stirrings. A remote hum. An awakening. The powerful writhings of some immense creature behind the masking woods, it might seem, and so unfathomable he was never quite certain what he heard. A feeling pressed. A vague foreknowledge. It did not leave him.

"Hear anything, Tim?"

"I ain't sure, perfessor. But I feel somethin'."

Late, late into the afternoon, Daniel started up. Disbelief froze him. Rabbits—scores, hundreds —were fleeing the mysterious woods and underbrush over yonder, and with them fled timorous deer that bounded ahead until, becoming aware of the Union soldiers in the opposite woods, they sprang away to the west. Many rabbits stopped and scurried here and there, confused, but many kept running into the Union lines. By their frightened eyes and scamperings, they seemed to have almost human qualities. The likeness vanished as he began to hear thumpings and the cries of soldiers knocking down their suppers. Then, as if seized by the same delayed suspicion, every man on the picket post watched the woods beyond the clearing.

"Now just who'd be chasin' *all* them rabbits?" Andy drawled, and he spoke for everyone.

As if to confound them, the veiled forest presented an even deeper, unnatural hush. Daniel saw not one flicker ahead. He heard not one foreign sound in the springtime distance. Even the quarrelsome Corinth road, where pickets had exchanged fire these past few days, was still. Everywhere he looked the silent woods seemed to nod.

Chapter Sixteen

THE RABBIT CHASERS

Daniel roused up to find the cellar blackness of his tent around him. Someone was shaking him gently. "Get up, Dan." Jesse Nance's soft voice. "Whole company's goin' out on scout."

"What time is it?"

"Three o'clock."

Stumbling into line, he puzzled dully over the order coming so early, because Hooper had never shown aggressiveness on his own as company commander. Later, down the road apiece, when they halted and he heard another column tramping up, he knew the Coon Creekers weren't marching out alone, and he wondered at the strength of the reconnaissance. A new general had taken command of the division. General Prentiss. A Missourian, too, the boys said, and he'd fight a cougar in his nightshirt.

Step by step, they left behind the pale tent rows of the sleeping regiments, and, two abreast, they took another faint road, not marching or tramping, instead, moving in the loose-legged stroll of skirmishers, rifles at the ready, like stalking bird hunters.

Rose light flushed the eastern sky as they prowled through the bird-song wilderness. Incongruously the breaking day, the keen smells, the twittering, and the sense of harmony combined to remind him that his father liked this hour best. Onward, still following the angling road, they groped past a picket post. After a little, he could see they were swinging parallel to the Union lines. The sky was shading off lighter. Back in the woods, he heard a Union bugler blowing a raucous Sunday Reveille. All ahead was still.

Their crunching feet carried them off the meandering road and down a slight dip into another huddle of woods, a closer caution upon them. For just yonder stretched an open field bordered on the other side by another broad tangle of dark woods.

Daniel, between Tim and Andy, walked with his eyes pinned on the blur of trees. Not far, and his steps lagged and he halted, struck by mistrust, by unreality, seeing dim figures gliding out of the murky woods. An entire line of stalking figures, and more figures behind them, moving forward as the Coon Creek Company stalked, weapons silent.

"There's our rabbit chasers," Tim muttered, and brought up his rifle.

Daniel heard no command. One wasn't needed. Everyone was firing moments before he saw blue flames leaping up along the line of advancing Confederate skirmishers and heard the wild, staccato yells. A pause as nervous fingers fumbled for paper cartridges and ramrods rattled, and the *rap-rap* of the firing was everywhere, the sweet air of morning gone on the hot acrid scents. Behind him, more men were piling into the woods.

After his first shot, he felt a strange kind of calmness and he took sharper notice. Millions of bumblebees seemed to be swarming among the trees, and hundreds of mocking voices were shouting—"Bull Run!"—and the Coon Creekers were jeering back: "Donelson! Fort Donelson!"

A Confederate officer dashed out of the woods on a magnificent black horse, halted, and pointed his saber toward the Union line. He sat his mount bravely, a statue in a town square, chivalric, immune to bullets. When Daniel happened to look again, the black horse was running away, riderless, stirrups flopping. A river's fog of smoke patches drifted through the woods. A Northern boy stumbled toward the rear, wide eyes beseeching, while he pressed hands to his wounded side. A comrade dropped his rifle to help and stared in curious horror.

The tremendous battle noises, the succession of wild-eyed, powder-blackened faces, the agonized shrieks and groans, the convulsive biting and ramming and firing—all seemed to be repeated everlastingly. Not many rods away the gray masses were building; their yelling sounded nearer. Daniel fought in fits and starts. He scented the wavering before he saw it take form, a let-up in the steady Union musketry.

Bold daylight had come when the reconnaissance companies gave ground toward their regiment. Some men took off running. One tried to jump a bush and landed astraddle, his feet churning for traction and barely skimming the ground, going nowhere. A howl of laughter erupted, and another when Murphy ran up and hoisted the stranded soldier over by the seat of his pants.

On a way, the Missourians turned to fight again. Twice they made counter charges over ground that they had given up, and once Daniel, crouching to reload, found a handsome little pistol under his knee that he stuck inside his belt. Forced back, back, as the morning wore on, the Coon Creek boys crossed a brambled field that sloped downward to more oak woods and found the tough, pebbly, yellowed ruts of the old wagon road lying athwart their retreat. They re-formed again, kneeling in the ruts and behind trees, their strongest position of the day.

During the ensuing lull, Tim Forehand, like a village watchman, sang out—"By jinks, it's ten o'clock sharp, boys!"—as cheerfully as had he been announcing drill at Jefferson Barracks.

A terrible thirst consumed Daniel. He drank sparingly from his canteen, willing himself not to gulp it all. Sweat streamed off his face. He dropped to the ground and hacked for wind, beaten down by the hardest day's work of his life. The grisly, red-eyed, black-mouthed creatures beside him were hardly recognizable. Murphy uttered a groan of exhaustion and slumped down next to him.

Watching the overgrown field, he forgot about water and weariness when he saw the bobbing heads of the Confederates top the long rise to the southwest. They came with banners flying, their line uneven but resolute. As he watched, the bumblebee sounds swarmed again. He brought himself ready.

The Missourians' fire appeared to have no effect during the first moments. But as the Southerners continued to advance, Daniel saw sudden gaps quickly filled, figures sprawling and dragging. Their line, surging nearer, swayed with each Union volley like a field of wind-blown wheat, while the survivors bowed their bodies as against a terrible storm.

Daniel's sensations were a confusion of sheets of flame, never-ending *yee-haaaing!* and whines and snarls, bits of flying bark and twigs, and of tearing, ramming, cocking, capping, firing.

When the Confederate charge broke, it did not happen at once. The gray line wobbled, hesitated. and halted, to falter and turn back and leave sheaves of strewn forms. The firing chopped off, also, although never finished. As the musketry dwindled, the shrieks of the wounded on the littered field and in the smoky woods reached a chorus of agony that tore at Daniel.

On his right Murphy lay prone, over his rifle. "Murph," Daniel said, hoarse-voiced. "You hurt bad?"

Murphy neither moved nor spoke. Daniel turned him over, and looked into sightless eyes staring straight ahead. Enraged, he flung up his rifle and fired at random toward the distant Rebels, wishing to kill as many of them as he could. He cursed them passionately, incoherently.

The breathing spell lasted but a pinch of minutes. In a sweeping tide the Confederates flowed against the woods again, and once more their wilted line drew off upslope. Daniel knew they were coming back, and they always did, young and green and brave, their voices as fierce as ever.

Now the Swink brothers fought on either side of him, and, when Amos clutched himself and collapsed, Daniel yelled to Obadiah, who scrambled over to him.

"Wake up, Amos!" He shook his brother's shoulder and screamed: "Amos . . . wake up! Wake up!" He slapped Amos's face; it rolled loosely. Amos was heaving. Crimson frothed on his lips. His eyes couldn't seem to find Obadiah.

Shouts in front grasped Daniel's attention. Some Confederates had reached the woods. When he could look again, Amos was still and Obadiah knelt beside him, loading and firing like a madman, mouthing cries, fiercely biting cartridges, ramming with ferocity, as if to plunge the ramrod through the chamber, capping and shooting in almost the same motion.

Daniel wasn't expecting Obadiah to stand up in that hail of bullets. He did suddenly. Daniel shouted at him. Obadiah, leaping on, ran out of the woods and onto the open field where the Confederates were firing as they fell back. Obadiah raced straight for them, head bare, screaming.

The last Daniel saw of him, Obadiah was gripping his rifle, two-handed, as a spear that he was going to thrust through the enemy. A moment later Obadiah disappeared, swallowed in the hanging smoke.

Daniel lost all track of time, although from what he could see of the sun beyond the trees and smoke, it must be well into the afternoon by now. He couldn't remember how many charges the Johnnies had made across the field and been driven off. He fought by rote. His ears were ringing. His throat burned for water. He shrank down when a new and shuddering violence began shrieking and sweeping through the trees, followed by the concentrated roar of artillery.

Not long afterward he realized his line was pulling back. "They're on our flank!" He heard that shout, heard it repeated and cried along the road, and he stumbled rearward with the others.

Rods past the sunken road, in a shallow ravine protected from the humming Minié balls and the screaming missiles, he nearly walked on a soldier behind a tree. The man looked dead. When Daniel saw arms and legs moving convulsively, he hesitated. Then, to his rising astonishment, he discovered that it was Stark Hooper, cowering and hugging the yellow earth. His face was like wax, without a smear of gunpowder. Into Hooper's eyes came a consciousness of his reproach. He heaved to his feet, his actions wild.

More on instinct than thought, Daniel headed him away from the battle's roar and toward the river. An acuteness made him glance around.

Everyone was hurrying. There was no order. No one but himself had stopped. It had all happened swiftly. He stumbled on to catch his friends.

He hurried up the other side of the ravine and saw the woods were thinning, and he strode faster. The uproar of the battle crashed on all sides of him, unseen. The Johnnies were on both flanks now. He could hear their shrill yells coming closer. He swerved at the sharp rip of musketry nearby.

That was when he spied the Confederate boy stepping from the underbrush, rifle lifting. Daniel wasn't quite ready. He was still swinging his weapon when he saw the gun muzzle flash and jump upward, and he felt something hot strike him, and he was going down, spun around. The soft floor of the forest seemed to float up to embrace him. As he hit and rolled, he was aware of feet pounding back, and he heard a savage flurry of shots and anxious voices calling his name.

At once Daniel was off in a world of shifting voices, now distinct, now dim, and of changing faces. Tim's, Jesse's, Andy's. Later Brother Winn's was there, eyes like burning hickory coals, and he was praying in a powerful, summoning voice—"Lord, help this poor boy. Please help him."—and the touch of Brother Winn's rough hand was like balm and it gave him strength and comfort. The roar of battle fell farther away.

Later still, he felt rain on his face, and afterward he heard raindrops pattering above him, which caused him to think of a squirrel scampering over his roof at home. But he did not feel the rain now, and by that he realized that he lay in a tent and other wounded lay there, also. Brother Winn seemed to come and go, come and go. A mighty restless man, as ever.

But he was there when orderlies placed Daniel on a stretcher, no one seeming to bother with the little pistol which was a joke, and fetched him through the dark woods where torches flickered about a long tent and dark figures milled like cattle and all he could hear was a dirge of shrieking, groaning, cursing, praying.

Brother Winn bent over him. "I'll go along with you, Daniel. You'll be all right, son."

Daniel bit his lip. He was more afraid now than during the battle. He raised up, his fear gathering faster, and his stare beheld what looked like a woodpile, until he saw that, instead, it was a heap of bloody arms and legs. Terror paralyzed him. He sank back, and, when they carried him inside, it was as if he had entered the very gates of everlasting hell and damnation.

A rotund figure came weaving across to flick a perfunctory appraisal on Daniel's bandaged thigh. A dimly familiar face above a blood-spattered surgeon's coat that would have been filthy without the battle gore. Seeing him under the sickly yellow lantern light, Daniel thought of some anticipating jovial fiend, and horror overwhelmed him when he recognized the regimental surgeon at Jefferson Barracks.

He saw the bleary eyes focus on him after effort, and he heard the blurred voice, mouthing geniality, saying to him—"Well, boy, let's be about our duties here."—and unsteadily then he indicated a rough table.

"No. . . ." That, Daniel found, was his own sudden refusal, high above the welter of cries.

"Wha's this?" The swaying figure gave an indignant jerk. "Leg's gotta come off, boy. Way 'bove the knee. Save your life." He wobbled back to the stretcher to rebuke Daniel, waggling a filthy forefinger. "Oughta be grateful. Y'll do fine, boy. Shh-ure."

Daniel could feel the little pistol nudging his arm. He drew it on impulse, in defense. "No . . . no, you won't."

"You'll die, boy," was the genial reminder. But the dreadful figure stepped no closer.

"Not by you!" Daniel pointed the pistol at him, and at a stretcher-bearer when the man leaned toward him.

Suddenly the foul shape swelled to fury. It gestured and shouted: "Take the young fool away! Let him rot. . . . Nex' man!"

Chapter Seventeen

HOMECOMING

Frightful scenes of smoke and fire tormented him. Through them sometimes, like grim actors, tramped the toilsome figures of the Swink boys and Murphy, alone or all together, recurrent images materializing and dissolving, until they lost identity in a sea of sad, pale faces. Strain as he might to catch them, they only retreated faster with each racing step he took. He remembered the cool April rain and the gliding ride on the rustling river. A knowledge absorbed him as he was swept gently along. He was no more a mere farm boy, brimming with innocence. He had grown old while helplessly seeing his friends perish. He, in turn, had shot the friends of other boys, and, in ironical turn, another boy had shot him. By some strange justice that seemed right. So in this short time he had become quite old and wise.

He remembered two full-bearded men standing like sentries at the foot of his cot. Doctors, except their white coats looked clean. Their puzzled manner said he was a strange one, indeed. He heard one remark about "the lack of

243

suppuration", and they shook their heads and went away.

An intuition talked to him. A fearful desperation. Someone had taken his pistol, so he was too weak to stop them a second time. Therefore, he set himself to waiting out his dread. Now and then he would pray. Every morning about the same time a doctor came to ponder over him, and Daniel contrived a little game of persuasion.

"I feel mighty fine," he would say. "Mighty fine." Once he was told: "Young man, I am thoroughly aware of your condition. A ball went clear through you. All I can say is that you have an abundance of native toughness." Something else bothered the doctor. He pulled on his beard. "Some of you boys do just as well without battlefield surgery. Even better."

"I feel just fine," Daniel insisted. He wasn't convincing, he saw that, and he spoke impulsively: "Will you have to take off my leg?"

Perhaps fatigue had dulled the doctor's hearing. He turned to the next bed.

When Daniel could sit up, he saw bearded faces on rows of cots and makeshift beds. The unrest of many voices was audible, an ever-present drone of pain. Militant women rushed about. He lost his fear of them when they tended him, when he discovered kindness behind their dutiful masks and gentleness in their fluttering hands.

Days passed and nothing happened to Daniel.

He never knew when he had escaped, but he sensed he had when orderlies helped him outside for the first time. He saw sunlight showering gold over the long porch, and he breathed air free of the ward's dreadful stench. He knew then, he knew.

Just as gradually he began to lose his elation, shaken by pity and horror even out here. Everywhere he looked he saw legless and armless men and boys sunning themselves. Everywhere. Shock ran through him, and he wanted to ask whether there were any whole people left anywhere.

Dear Folks:

I am here at Cairo in the hospital. We are all from Shiloh. I was hit late the first day. Preacher Winn stayed with me to the boat. He did all he could for me. We lost the Swink boys. Amos and Obadiah were brave as any soldiers we had. At Fort Donelson they laid out in the snow and rain and complained less than most of us.

A preacher from town asked me what the battle was like. All I could think of to say was thunder and lightning over and over. I was never scared worse. I figure the Confederates hurt us as much as we hurt them, even if they retreated to Corinth the second day and we took back our camps, like the newspapers say.

Folks from the Christian Commission see that we get plenty of reading material, but it is all mighty dull. Now the Cairo ladies do fine. Mama, a little lady whose son is in the bed next to mine gave me a big piece of white cake and it was nigh as good as yours. Yesterday she brought me some apple pie.

Papa, I keep wondering about you and Mama and how the old farm looks. I hope Shep is doing fine. Soon as I can walk good, the doctor says maybe I can come home a while.

Your affectionate son,
Daniel

The farmer's wagon inched and groaned its way north through a countryside that the October sunlight had turned indolent and still. Daniel sat with hungry eyes gulping the bright-leafed distance, beside him the small bag that the Cairo ladies had given him.

When Foley's Prairie grew yonder, a lump rose to his throat and his heart beat faster. As they drove into town, he feasted his sight on the neat houses, on the vined porches and white-washed fences, on the dusty, maple-shaded streets and the old stores. Strange, he thought, how all the buildings seemed shabby and smaller than he remembered, and in front of Rookwood's General Store, where the companies had marched that cock-strutting day, not one team of mules was tied. No one stirred behind the dingy windows of the *Citizen*. Four horses carrying McClellan saddles stood at the tavern's hitching rack. Otherwise, there was no stir.

Mr. Rookwood, round of girth, gray of beard, waddled out on the store's broad porch and looked up and down the listless street. Daniel waved vigorously. The storekeeper waved back, but his expression was blank. So Mr. Rookwood had no inkling who he was, and Daniel's anonymity gave him a secret pleasure.

"Milishy," the farmer nodded toward the tavern, his tone dripping scorn. "Ain't worth a durn. Supposed to protect the county. Catch bushwhackers. All they do is hang around town. Drink and play cards."

"Bushwhackers?" Daniel said a little vaguely.

"Bushwhackers or outlaws . . . both the same. We've got 'em now."

Daniel merely nodded. Any threat save war must stay remote on the day of his homecoming. At the edge of town he obeyed a sudden impulse and asked the farmer to stop, and he came down to walk the rest of the way.

"Figure you can make it on home? You look peaked."

"I'll take my time," Daniel said, and thanked him. After the wagon had creaked away, he stood motionless in the road, trembling, in a state of excitement. By dogs! He was truly standing on good Missouri loam. Not Shiloh's yellow mud. There wasn't any cold rain. No weeping woodlands. No death shrieks of boys. And he knew now that he had never expected to see home again, yet here he was. He felt humble and grateful.

He set a pace neither slow nor rapid, just steady, favoring his weakness. When the white mass of the Vandiver house loomed through the grove of proud trees, he stepped faster. When he saw the lane before him, he entered after the briefest indecision, a directness not in him a year and a half ago.

He walked through a dwelling silence, an unusual silence for this brightest of places. Coming to the lane's end, he was puzzled to find the black iron gate closed. He drew it open, starting at the shrill of the hinges, and went inside. Weeds grew along the curving line of the bricked drive. A muteness cloaked the massive, handsome house. The Great House, he liked to think of it. He walked slower, troubled. He stopped short of the steps, observing the coating of undisturbed dust on the wide verandah.

"Stan' right there, white man!"

Daniel whirled. By the corner of the house stood a determined, gray-haired darky aiming a shotgun at him.

"I hyeared you open de big gate. Reckon you is bushwhackin' aroun'."

"I'm a Union soldier. Can't you see? And I remember you . . . you're Mack. You used to drive the family carriage."

The doubting eyes behind the shotgun relaxed slightly, glowing momentarily, and settled, suspicious again. "Maybe you is . . . maybe you ain't."

"You don't see a gun, do you? I'm Daniel Wade. Before the war I came here a few times to see Miss Laurel."

Steadfastly the old Negro shook his head. "Maybe you come to spy aroun', anyhow. An' Miz' Laurel, she's done gone."

"Gone? Gone where?" Daniel was glaring, denying. But when he saw the persisting truth in Mack's face, he looked aside, stunned.

Mack, watching him, said softly after a little: "I reckon you is Mistuh Wade. I remembers you. When de stealin' an' killin' got so mighty bad las' spring, de major, he carried 'bout all de folks down below Nashville."

All Daniel's expectations had dulled. He slumped on the steps and dropped the bag between his feet. It didn't matter much now, but he asked: "Whereabouts below Nashville?"

"Little village dey call Franklin. Where de major first come from."

"So the major's there, too?"

"I ain't sayin'."

Daniel looked up. "Justin? Any word from him?"

"I ain't sayin'."

"You don't exactly trust me, do you, Mack?" Daniel said, expressing a faint smile.

"You is a Yankee soldier, Mistuh Wade. Truf is I don't trust nobody, way de country is now."

"I think that's best," Daniel said, and got up. He walked to the gate, and closed it behind him.

He believed Mack. Laurel *was* gone. If the major had returned, it was to protect his property interests. Justin, of course, was in the Southern Army, if he wasn't dead.

Although the day's sparkle had gone out, country most familiar to him lay ahead. He could not ignore it, and, while he went along, it seemed to beckon and comfort him. Every hill, every field, every patch of woods the winding road revealed, step by step, was like a friendly face waiting to greet him. An angle of rail fence, a stretch of meadow, a distant white farm house or red barn, a forgotten roadside oak in whose shade he had rested—all seemed to leap up and show themselves, now fresh again in his memory. Grasshoppers whirred in the tall grass, turning golden under the autumnal sun. A redbird whistled at him from its top-rail perch. He raised his head, hearing every flap of a crow's spying flight over the road. Even though he couldn't see it from here, he knew precisely when he passed the ancient Indian mound.

The unaccustomed exertion was tiring him. When he reached the turn-off to Swink's Spring, five miles distant, he stopped and looked down the road, thinking: *Just as soon as I see my folks.* He was wearing down, yet he had no wish to rest. He hurried on. He seemed to walk an unbearable time. The sun was lowering. But when he crossed the dry branch and turned into the lane for home, his step was light and all his toil was forgotten.

He heard an on-guard bark and saw a yellow-haired dog charging forth. Daniel called—"Shep . . . Shep!"—and held out his hand. The old dog halted, startled. He cocked his head and slowly flattened down, ears back, whining. Daniel stroked the muzzle, gray with age, and saw all doubt crumble as the piteous whimpering came, just before Shep, his deep brown eyes gleaming rapturous fire, gave a leaping, joyous bound of recognition that left Daniel's cheek licked wet. Down, bounding, Shep raced around and around faster, faster, uttering the sharp, foolish little yips of a puppy.

In that whirling confusion, striding on, trying to hurry, Daniel could see the old house lying in an Elysian sea of glittering sunshine, more serene than ever in his life. Over the low gate by the log barn he saw two mules' heads, watching. Zeke and Babe. They seemed to know him.

He took the porch in a single bound and stepped inside and set down his bag, seeing no one. The house was dead quiet and dim. He breathed a mixture of delightful smells, of fresh bread and soap, of hickory smoke and good side meat frying. He turned his head toward the kitchen, and there he saw his mother.

Emily Wade stood perfectly still, her even lips opening and closing. Her dark eyes kept enlarging on him, her belief in miracles secure. He went across to her in two strides. She kissed him so hard his head pushed back, and he could feel her strong hands gripping him. Afterward, when she let go of him to look at him, she started dabbing her eyes with her apron.

"Don't cry, Mama. I'm all right."

"Daniel," she said, still dabbing, "you're taller . . . and thinner. We got your letter from Cairo." At that, the tears started again.

"I'm all right," he said. "I walked all the way from town." He trailed his eyes around, hearing no sound except Shep whining outside the door, and he turned to her again, afraid to ask.

"Papa's resting," she said, calmly putting away all save cheerfulness.

Entering the bedroom, he met a deeper dimness, a deeper stillness. On the quilt-covered bed lay a slight shape, a man, shrunken, an old man fully clothed. It was his father, and his hair and beard were snow white. Daniel flinched, stopped. Going on, he forced a terrible discipline on himself to accept the eroded features he could scarcely recognize. Still, when he came around to the bedside and saw his father turn his face toward him, the blue eyes were as alert and indomitable as always.

"Papa, I'm home."

He saw feeling tremble on his father's lips, and go away after but a moment, and saw that his father's right hand, flat on the coverlet, did not lift to his own.

"Papa, do you understand? It's me . . . Daniel. I'm home . . . home!" He grasped his father's hand in both his; it felt as light as a cornhusk.

As of old, the harsh slit in the stubbly white beard parted. The hawk's eyes sized Daniel up and down, now marking the blue uniform. "Nothin' wrong with my hearin', Dan. Sight neither. . . . Well, I'm glad you're alive. Glad your own people didn't kill you the way they did the poor, misguided Swink boys."

Daniel didn't know when his father withdrew his hand—but he had. Whereupon, Sam Wade shifted his head back on the pillow and said straight to his wife: "I'll have my supper now, Em."

Chapter Eighteen

THE BUSHWHACKERS

After paying a visit next day to the Swinks and promising to return a week hence for dinner, Daniel plunged into a frenzy of work around the run-down farm. He cut and hauled wood and patched rail fences, meantime, trying to ration his limited strength, hitched the brown mules to the plow and commenced turning under the wheat and oat stubble for fall sowing. He tired quickly; he ate enormously. At night he sharpened tools and mended harness, until exhaustion drove him to bed.

Often his thoughts sheered southward to the little Tennessee village of Franklin, and to his friends. Down what dusty lane were they marching today? What wooded ambuscade awaited them? Reading in the *Citizen* of bloody battles at Iuka and Corinth prompted his feverish searching of the weekly for casualty lists. He found some. His mother pointed out that two months had passed after Shiloh before the Swink boys' names had appeared. A restless feeling began to gnaw him.

Around his father, Daniel evaded discussion

of the war, which could not be ignored at all times, and, when it was not, a certain sense reached deeper within him: his father would never forgive him for joining the Union Army. But there was another threat closer than the big war. Once he asked his father: "Bushwhackers ever come around?"

"Here?" Sam Wade mocked, and bitterness gathered like a cloud in his sharp eyes. "They wouldn't want anything we have."

"You've got a smokehouse that's not empty."

"I've hid out some meat."

"You've got mules."

"Old Zeke and Babe ain't much any more."

"All you've got, Papa," Daniel said patiently. "Who are these men?"

"They're not Southerners," Sam Wade averred, his gaze starting to smolder. "You can bet on that. They're"—he pounced on the word— "Abolitionists! . . . come to prey on us. That's what they are, by God!"

"I was told they're just outlaws. Not on either side."

"Whoever said that is ignorant as a loose hog."

Forthwith the sparks of a bitter quarrel were flying. Emily Wade's dark eyes showed a sudden pain.

"Papa," Daniel said, trying to circle more argument, "does anybody know where their camp is?"

"Tobe Russell does. So does Reuben Nance. It's around the old Indian mound. Good cover there. Plenty wood, water."

Daniel could understand why. Picturing the wooded mass of the mound and the silvery run of the cool spring, now usurped, brought before him the helplessness of his family and his neighbors whose sons had gone to war.

That held steady root in his mind when he saddled Zeke and rode to Swink's Spring for a dinner and visit with two old people whose pathetic hunger to learn more about their lost soldier sons kept him long after he had intended to leave. Henceforth, the afternoon was sliding toward early dusk when he started home.

He rode as he had coming over, following the edge of the road so he could cut into the woods if he saw horsemen. He met no one. In fact, the country looked deserted, swept empty, the daylight as still as night.

An hour's ride took him to the main road. Before turning onto it, he looked off where the Indian mound lay, hidden a mile or more away. Nothing grazed in the pastures or raised dust on the road bending southwest past the mound and on to Foley's Prairie. A reconnoitering hawk entered his vision. He watched it circle and dive, sail upward and circle again, hovering on the air drafts. Something else drew his attention farther beyond, almost invisible against the late sky. A plume. A smear. A cloud of dark smoke billowing high.

He scowled while trying to calculate the fire's location. It wasn't in the right place for Foley's Prairie. It was, he decided, this side of town, and whatever burned had to be a mighty big barn or house, maybe both. A sudden apprehension sprang to his mind, and he flailed his heels against Zeke's flanks.

Loping up a wooded rise and dropping down to a level stretch, he spied action across the broad pasture. Enough horsemen, he saw, for a company of cavalry. They rode heavily, encumbered by an awkward assortment of bulky burdens, yet too far away for him to tell what. By their course he thought they were going to ride straight upon him. He let out his breath when the head of the column turned and the trailing riders disappeared behind a tongue of timber, a march in line with Indian mound.

For some minutes before he saw it, Daniel knew that the great Vandiver house was burning. As he heeled the laboring Zeke down the lane, the magnitude of the destruction appalled him. Heat clutched him this far away. The whole house was a smoking, crackling hill of fire; through the lower windows he could see leaping cherry-red flames. Something once proud and beautiful, something he used to think of as indestructible, was being consumed and terribly wasted. And the treasured books. Their loss, everything, dismayed him.

Beyond the open iron gate ran the futile figures of darkies dashing puny buckets of water upon the runaway flames. Old Zeke balked and stiffened. Daniel swung down, running, seized an empty bucket, and hastened to the well behind the house. When he ran back, a Negro was pointing toward the front door, shouting for his attention. But the crackling roar smothered his meaning, and all Daniel could see was more smoke and fire.

Again the Negro shouted. This time Daniel saw movement, two figures, one supporting the other, weaving out of the smoke and across the verandah. Running forward, Daniel saw Mack straining mightily under the major's weighty body. The major's head lolled and his dull eyes and open mouth were oddly entreating, while his arms protected a large framed picture.

Daniel and the Negro helped carry the major over by the gate. When they eased him down on the grass, he groped spasmodically for the picture. Daniel recognized the portrait of Laurel's mother; in the flickering, smoky twilight, her face looked alive and calmly reassuring.

A heavy crash sounded inside the house. Everyone but the major looked. Sparks showered. Engulfing flames danced higher.

"De sweet ol' house is givin' up de ghos'," Mack groaned.

Daniel watched, resigned. The great house was doomed. He recoiled when the roof caved in, roaring, shooting a fusillade of fiery fragments above the treetops. He turned back to the major. Mack was bathing the pallid face. Daniel loosened the major's shirt and rubbed the slack hands.

Daniel, engrossed, watching the grayish features, did not look up when horses clattered down the lane. It was Mack's gasp of relief that caused him to glance away. He went rigid. Horsemen, Confederate horsemen, were crowding through the gate. One rider flung down and rushed over, eyes only for the old man in the grass. Daniel, rising, saw Justin Vandiver bend over his father.

Mack started to explain, saw now wasn't the time, and went back to bathing the major's face, gently, as if each stroke gave life. A little later young Vandiver carefully loosened his father's grip on the portrait and moved it aside, saying: "You can stop now, Mack. Thank you. He doesn't feel it any more." Suddenly he held both hands to his face. A low moan, between wail and chant, escaped Mack and spread among the other Negroes. Justin got up.

Daniel, taking an instinctive step toward him, felt a rough jab against his back. A voice said—

259

"Don't move, blue-belly."—and called: "Cap'n, you know we got a Yankee here?"

Justin's manner was dazed. "Yankee, you say?"

"Yes, sir. What'll we do with him? Maybe he knows who burned your house."

"Mistuh Justin," Mack protested. "That's Daniel Wade. He tried to help us."

Justin stepped toward Daniel, recognition struggling through his shock. "Daniel? Why, so it is. Let him be." He didn't sound like a soldier. As if he had forgotten himself, he turned curtly to Mack.

"What happened? How did it start?"

"White trash started it. White trash bush-whackers. De major he make me put away de shotgun. Say it's no use. Wish now I'd 'a' used it." Mack moaned and shook his head back and forth. "When dey rides up, de major he come out on de po'ch. Dey asks for money. De major say he ain't got none. So dey starts lootin' de house. Dey starts to steal yo' mother's picture. An' you know what de major do?" A powerful pride shone through his anguish like a steady flame. "Why, he stan' right up dare facin' all dem ugly guns, an' he tell dem white trash to leave dat picture alone. An' you know what? . . . dey do . . . yas, suh!" Mack's voice broke. "Den dey ties us up quick, sets far to de house an' leaves us inside to burn to death. . . . By an' by we gets loose an' comes outside. But de major he go back for yo' mother's picture. Dat's all."

"Except it was Mack who carried your father out," Daniel said. "I saw him."

Justin Vandiver, nodding, accepting, turned to watch the flaming house, settling tiredly between the bulwark stone chimneys on each end. After a long, long look, he went off by himself.

Daniel waited but a short time. He found Justin in the flower garden. "I'll be with you when you're ready to go after them," Daniel told him.

Justin's teeth clicked. "Tonight! There aren't many of us, but . . . ."

"We'll need more than the few or so you have here."

"Numbers didn't stop us at Shiloh." Justin's thrusting gesture swept away all patience.

"Justin, there's fifty bushwhackers, at least. I saw the whole bunch on my way here. They're camped at the old Indian mound. If we don't finish 'em good, they'll scatter like quail. Come again after we've gone."

"So?"

"We need help. I can start going around to the neighbors in the morning. We could meet here. Say about dark tomorrow?" He stopped short, remembering. "But I'm forgetting your father. We can wait."

"No," said Justin, surprisingly emphatic, "we can't wait. They may shift camp now. My father will be buried here in the morning." A differing note changed his voice. "I like your plan except for one thing, Daniel. I feel that only Southerners ought to take part in this. It's our duty alone."

"I don't see it that way. Everybody's suffering. Northern families as well." It was all he could do not to remark on high Vandiver pride.

"That's not all my reason," Justin said frankly after a moment. "I'm here recruiting. Lean as the pickings are. It isn't wise for everyone to know, and they will."

"You forget I'm on furlough. Now all you Johnnies know it, and you can take pot shots at a Union soldier."

A horse ran down the lane and into the yard. A man came up. "Cap'n, millishy's comin' cautious-like down the road."

Justin Vandiver held out his hand to Daniel. "Tomorrow evening then, here. We'll pass the word, too."

One by one, the neighbors gathered in the blistered grove. Some rode mules and heavy-footed work horses. A few walked over, a lively hike yet to their step; others hobbled. Among the early Union arrivals were Si Swink, Reuben Nance, Ed Green, and Rufus Forehand, the last even taller and broader than his brawny son Tim. Accompanying both sides was a trickle of mere boys not old enough for either army, but fascinated by prospects of a fight. The volunteers carried a variety of weapons which had one common standard, great vintage. Muzzleloaders, shotguns, pistols, knives. Daniel had his father's old Hawken.

His misgivings mounted when he saw the little band assembling. Last evening's plan, forged in the white heat of vengeance, now occurred to him as impulsive and ill-conceived, even ridiculous and foolhardy. For there was no in between; everyone looked either too old or too young for bloodshed. A few, he recalled from hearing his father reminisce, had served in the Mexican War. One was Larkin Sampson, a long-time neighbor of the Wades, who came bearing a percussion Kentucky rifle and a dented brass bugle riding on its rawhide strap. Daniel used to hold him in awe, because old man Sampson had scaled the heights of Chapultepec, by dogs!

As the oldsters arrived, they aligned themselves with their respective factions. They nodded around, spoke, and stared back at the other side and dipped their chins in measured recognition, thereafter to reflect about the major, now resting in the family plot, and to ponder the smoke-bubbling waste of the once magnificent house, these divided neighbors. For most of them, Daniel guessed, this was the first occasion to meet and speak since Missouri troops had entered the war.

The boys withdrew behind their elders, as watchful and restless as cubs. When one ventured to poke among the ruins, he was sharply ordered away. Obeying, they idled about, and, before the old men had quite realized it, the youngsters had drifted beyond the wilted flower garden and were sizing each other up and down.

Old Tobe Russell was the last to arrive, and not alone as Daniel had anticipated. A butternut figure rode alongside him on a mule. Going out to meet them, Daniel saw Sim Russell dismount. He looked as hot-eyed as ever but, like himself, more filled out and a good deal grown up. Without meaning to, Daniel hesitated. Sim did likewise. Then, of one accord, they shook hands.

"I hid out in the woods when I saw you comin' to the house," Sim said. "Papa says you never know who'll come callin' these times. I'm home on furlough."

"So am I."

At ease, they walked back together.

Just before dark, horsemen thudded down the lane, and Justin Vandiver led his little dab of Confederates in under the trees. When he dismounted, the old men collected around him, and disagreeable old Tobe started in immediately.

"By jinks, I want to know just who it is we're gettin' ready to fight," he demanded, swinging his arms. "A bunch of Union soldiers came to my place. Cleaned out my smokehouse. Left me what they claimed was a quartermaster's receipt. When I took it in town to the milishy, they just laughed at me. Dang their hides!"

"How'd you know it was Union soldiers?" Si Swink asked.

"Well, hell, they had on blue uniforms. Ain't that Union enough?"

"Could 'a' been deserters, Tobe."

"I don't figure so."

"Tobe, last week I saw Confederates . . . least-wise they wore Confederate uniforms . . . steal the last saddle horse I had. I sure as hell did, an' don't you deny it, an' don't you be forgettin' that I lost both my boys at bloody Shiloh." Swink's voice was shaking. His eyes were dangerous.

Tobe Russell shifted his eyes downward. He swiped at his tobacco-stained chin whiskers. He nodded once. From him, that stood for an expression of understanding, for sympathetic speech wasn't in him. But it passed with the moment. He concentrated his glare again on Si Swink, and Swink fired his on him, neither budging a hair.

"Si," old Tobe said tenaciously, "maybe you better hear what nigger Mack told me a minute ago. The dirty scoun'ls that burned down this fine house and caused the major's death . . . they wore blue, too."

Several men stationed themselves behind Swink. Others crowded behind old Tobe. Grumblings broke out.

In another minute, Daniel saw, both sides would be fighting each other, instead of together. He said: "We don't know who these men are, but we know what they've done and where they're camped. That's the thing."

The temperish grumbling abated, only to return.

"Atten-tion!"

Justin Vandiver's voice, like his father's, had an authoritative quality. The Confederate soldiers swung to attention. The old men who had served in the Mexican War hitched up stooped shoulders, and those who had not quit gabbling. Every person watched young Vandiver.

"What Daniel Wade just said is true," he began. "It's not important right now who those people are . . . deserters, outlaws, bushwhackers, guerrillas . . . or what uniforms they wear. We've got to clean them out while we can. In a few days I'll be leaving with the detail of men you see here, plus some recruits, I hope.

"Daniel is on furlough. So is Sim Russell. They'll have to go back soon, too. Militia won't protect you . . . you know that. About every available young man in the county is already in one army or the other. You can't wait." Angry disgust ground into his resonant voice. "On the other hand, if you'd rather squabble with our neighbors than fight your real enemies here at home . . . if you're afraid. . . ."

"Who's afeared?" old Tobe stormed. "By jinks, I'm ready. Come on, let's go!" He wasn't alone. Everybody crowded forward, talking at once.

"Not half cocked, you won't," Justin Vandiver swore. "No man marches away from here tonight unless he promises to follow orders. You understand?"

Chapter Nineteen

GLORY IN THE MORNING

A coon hunter's moon, brimful, glowing, hung in the eastern sky like an enormous vigilant eye when Justin Vandiver gave the order to form for the march to Indian mound. Cooking fires had been out hours ago, and the night was cool, nearly windless. Leather squeaks, clinks, thuds, curses, hoof-stampings, mufflings, and grunts multiplied during the confusion of cinching up and mounting.

All at once Vandiver said sharply: "Mack, what are you doing here?"

"I'se gwine with you, Mistuh Justin. Done got me a mule an' another shotgun."

"Miss Laurel would never forgive me if you as much as got a scratch. You being Father's favorite, too."

"Don' you fret none 'bout dat. Ev'thing's done happened to me that's gonna, except dyin', an' dat ain't impo'tant no mo'. They's some powerful settlin' up to do."

Vandiver did not answer immediately. "Just don't get any sudden notions."

When at last the column was under way, some of the animals carrying double, Daniel could count no more than thirty-odd men and boys, including the Confederate detail. The plan called for marching across fields and pastures to a point where the command would halt, while Daniel, young Russell, and Vandiver slipped ahead to reconnoiter. At daylight they would attack the camp.

The riders were noisy and disorganized in the beginning. But gradually the racket shook away to a muffled plodding and jangling, the line became a ragged file of twos, and by the time the blurred out-scatter of sheds and fences had dropped behind, there was a semblance of loose order.

Around three o'clock the little force halted, the youngest boys took charge of the horses and mules, and the three scouts went on afoot. Once, when they came to a standstill to take their bearings, Vandiver murmured to Daniel: "I notice you're limping. Were you at Shiloh?"

"I was, and I gather you were, too."

Sim Russell said: "We all were."

No more was said. They walked northeast across a sleeping land that was formless and blurred. Off in the clumps of woods, birds were starting to twitter. When a black hump materialized through the murk, Russell and Daniel stopped in recognition. "There she is," Sim said. "The old Injun mound."

"No sign of the camp," Vandiver said, "though it's late for a fire."

Daniel was recalling, visualizing. "Still some timber between us and the spring."

A keener chill seemed to slide across the night. They skirted the edge of the woods and turned northeast again. All Daniel could make out there was the indefinite black bulge of the persimmon ridge and the shaggy mound off by itself. His doubts massed. He'd been so certain the camp was here! They covered ten rods or so, treading lightly into further moon-washed emptiness. They took the sloping tail of the ridge, looked, and dropped immediately to their knees.

Over by the spring burned the spire of a fire. No one stirred around it, though. They watched a couple of minutes. They ducked lower when a man ambled to the fire, put down his rifle, and poured himself coffee. Little by little, Daniel began to find the vague limits of the camp, helped by the snuffle of picketed horses below him, and by others penned near the base of the mound. He could see the low Vs of scattered tents, the slant of lean-tos and sleeping shapes dimly visible on the ground.

Watching the cluttered encampment, he felt the flush of anger. There was a gap in the line of trees by the spring. Some of the fine old oaks there and down the spring's pretty course had been felled. So the beauty of this retreat, of this remembered place, undisturbed since olden Indian days, had been spoiled for years to come.

Vandiver tapped his shoulder, and Daniel saw Russell drifting down slope.

The sky was shedding its dark coat when Daniel heard the scuffing march of feet through the pasture grass. He tensed when someone stumbled. The scuffing ceased. A hush followed, deep and breathless. Afterward, he could hear among the figures old men puffing up the slope and filing along it, grunting and hauling themselves over dead timber. Sim Russell knelt next to him, and old Tobe grunted down on the other side of his son. Daniel hoped everybody knew what to do. No blundering charge. Not with old men and fuzzy-cheeked boys. The idea was to. . . .

Down the ridge someone coughed. An old man's raspy hack, uncontrollable, quickly smothered, but as audible as a shout in that still-ness, at a time when everyone wasn't yet in position.

Daniel, starting, looking, then eyeing the sentry by the fire, saw him stand and gaze around, rifle up, taking in the ridge, the camp, the mound, and back to the ridge again. The man stood stationary so long and the figures moving behind Daniel froze so still, that he thought the moment had passed. Instead, the next he knew the sentry was walking away from the fire, advancing deliberately on the ridge.

Old Tobe gabbled something. Off his guard, Daniel saw young Sim reach out to silence him, an instant late. Old Tobe, muttering to himself, rose suddenly and fired his rifle and let go a wildcat yell. He hit his mark. The sentry dropped. Figures scrambled faster on the ridge.

Through waves of muddy light, Daniel saw the sleeping camp rise almost as one and erupt to swirls of crouching, dodging, shouting shapes. Picketed horses were snorting and milling.

Ancient rifles clapped and shotguns boomed, blending with the stouter roar of the Confederates' Enfields. After the first volley, fire from the ridge was slow resuming. Trembling hands spilled powder and shot. Ramrods fell rattling; old hands searched for them in the darkness. Only the Enfields kept up a steady banging.

Below, the firing picked up, growing heavier. Blue flame flashes revealed where a stand was being made. Lead commenced pelting the trees on the slope.

"They don't surrender worth a tinker's damn!" squealed a high, peevish voice.

Down there a horseman dashed for the open pasture, broke clear. Another followed. A shotgun tried to reach him. The rider went on.

"Head them off!" Vandiver shouted.

More men were running for the corral, beyond shotgun range. Going that way at a low crouch, Daniel saw others having the same notion. One was old Tobe, puffing like a steam engine. "Stay down, Mister Russell," Daniel said.

Now, close by, inflexible old lips hissed into the bugle's cupped mouthpiece, as Larkin Sampson strained to find again the glory-dreaming notes of storied Chapultepec. All that came out was a frantic *phutting*. Ridiculous, farcical sounds, with bullets firing against the ridge. A ragged splutter, and the first clear note tore through, and on the heels of it, catching and lifting, Daniel heard the hot-blooded blast of Charge.

Old voices whooped, sounding young again. Boys screeched. Shapes rose, forming for the very foolhardy assault the young veterans had tried to avoid, the oldsters squalling like cougars.

Daniel felt it, too. He moved with them. Everyone, together, swept down the slope, and the racket they brought spooked the picketed horses, swung them slamming upon the camp, knocking down lean-tos, trampling tents, pots, and dodging men. Shotguns coughed in close. Daniel, rushing toward the penned horses, fired and saw the figures turn back. Thereafter, rapidly, he heard the shooting hang and drop off to scattered pops, and the dominant sound changed from gunfire to the running rumble of terrified horses still fleeing.

When he saw the bushwhackers raising their hands, he knew it was over. . . .

Daylight uncovered an unkempt lot of prisoners, well-fed from living off the countryside. They huddled in the guarded corral, glum and temperish, and glowered when they discovered that old men and extremely young boys had played active rôles in their capture. Old men, Daniel thought, whose steps were firmer this morning, whose voices sounded livelier, and who seemed to stand a notch straighter.

Not a bushwhacker was in uniform. When spleenful old Tobe saw that, he embarked on a poking search of the wrecked camp. Pretty soon he stopped for something and called in triumph: "What'd I tell you, Si Swink? Here's a blue uniform. By God, they're Yankees! Come over here 'n' see for yourself!"

Si Swink, as stout and uncomplaining as Obadiah had been, tramped across and looked. His voice hurled no rash denial, no set to passionate argument with his neighbor.

"That's exactly what it is, Tobe. You betcha. Where'd you find it?" Tobe, elated, jabbed an accusing forefinger toward a trampled blanket

273

roll, and Si's chin moved up and down in an agreeable nod. "A body can't deny that. Brand new, too. Now what do you make of this?" he asked, bringing a bundle from under his arm and shaking out a wadded gray blouse.

Old Tobe's eyes pushed outward. The rusty door of his tobacco-brown mouth gaped, then clamped shut. "By jinks," he said, "it's just like the one Sim's wearin'."

"Well, I wouldn't say it's as clean, Tobe. Not by considerable," Si Swink concluded, and gave a low laugh. Old Tobe laughed, too. Then, all of a sudden, the old men were laughing together.

Vandiver glared at the sullen prisoners. "Where you men from?"

One flung up a vague hand toward the west.

"You mean the Missouri-Kansas border?"

The man nodded.

"Thugs, robbers, murderers! You've come a long way to prey on country people! We have the right to shoot every one of you!"

At that they commenced to stir and assume pleading faces.

Then a boy rushed up. "Milishy's comin' down the road from town! A big ol' bunch."

"My detail and I will have to leave," Vandiver said reluctantly, looking around at his neighbors.

"Go on," Daniel urged. "We'll turn the prisoners over. They should be held for action by a military court."

"If they try to escape, we know what to do," Si Swink swore. "We're shore much obliged to you and your boys, Justin. Come on, men! Let's git 'em goin'!"

There was yet something unfinished as Daniel and Vandiver held up. Sim Russell walked over. They all shook hands and wished each other good luck.

Watching his friends go, Daniel felt a lump rise to his throat and wondered if he would ever see them again.

Chapter Twenty

THE HOLLY SPRINGS ROAD

Late autumn's smoky haze lay over the Southern hills and woods before Daniel caught up with the Coon Creek Company in Memphis. Thousands of stout-backed recruits from Indiana, Illinois, Missouri, and Iowa crammed the burgeoning camps, crowded the streets in off-duty hours, watched the writhing river slide by in ropy coils, stared at disgruntled cotton farmers, at the many wandering Negroes scattered like grain by the new wind that had freed them, their dusky faces abeam, not yet understanding what had happened to them.

He stared likewise when he saw his old friends. The boys he had left at Shiloh in early April had grown into men, veterans who had seen the elephant, as the saying went. All wore beards. Their hair was shaggy, and their cheek bones rode higher above lean jaws, their eyes wiser, their voices deeper and more assured. Being victors, they still displayed carefree attitudes, but the transparent innocence of Donelson and of Shiloh's larking camp days had disappeared; they would not to their regret possess it again, and neither would he.

Among other changes, Tim Forehand had blossomed into a burlesque performer, the only play actor in the entire company. This evening, on an outdoor stage lighted by lanterns and pitch-pine torches, the regiment was presenting an original satire on officers entitled: "Here's Your Mule" or "Home on Furlough".

Daniel sat between Jesse Nance and Andy Green. Appropriate to the play's theme, one Private Duff, an Illinois song teacher, to the accompaniment of a sad-faced banjo player, manfully rendered "The Old Folks at Home" quickly and enthusiastically, followed by "Who Will Care for Mother Now?". Before he could commence another lugubrious number, his restless comrades drove him cruelly to cover under a barrage of missiles and hoots.

A dramatic hush. A significant pounding of

hoofs, of boots clomping off stage. A bugle blared, and Tim Forehand, magnificent in glossy jackboots, plumed hat, gold braid that looped to the floor, clanking sword, clusters of stars on each shoulder, advanced to the center and bowed stiffly from the waist, an arrogant and hated martinet if one was ever seen.

A thunderstorm of jeering greeted him. Unruffled, he strutted toward a table, tripped on his saber, sat, and bellowed for wine.

Out tripped a burly young creature from C Company, with flour-powdered cheeks and a pouting, painted mouth, to plop on the general's lap and hug him hard.

"Easy there, girl," came the loud moan. "That's my old wound."

"Oh, I didn't know," cried the high, anguished voice, "I thought generals *always* stayed behind the firing line!"

"Not me," said the general, slapping his chest. "Where I lead others *always* follow."

A fusillade of jeers.

"You're so brave, General! Is that why the boys *always* go to the Memphis Belle on Saturday night?"

Ribald laughter, shrill whistles, whapping applause. The general and the barmaid stood and took deep reveling bows. . . .

The play was over and a damp chill climbed from the mighty river, its bite sharpening as the night advanced. Lights of the conquered city formed a dappling glow. All around the white blurs of the Army's tents spread on and on, endlessly.

Daniel Wade paced up and down, watching the murk beyond his post, watching the sky, listening to the hum of the encampment. In spite of its green thousands, more order and efficiency prevailed here than at Shiloh. Discipline had tightened a good deal. Time, he thought, and the demands of war. No longer were breastworks an indication of cowardice, but a sign of practical common sense. A bugle scattered Taps' somber notes across the night, and the camp seemed to murmur and yawn. A patrol tramped past him, on the prowl for late arrivals from town.

As he paced, he reflected that, except to make his folks more comfortable for the winter, he had accomplished little by going home. He had left behind him an inflexible stillness that had hardened whenever he tried to reach his father after that first day. At the last he had not tried again. Therefore, he had failed. Likely he would not see his father alive again.

Turning about, he noticed a lone, hurrying figure on the camp side. The man had a quick, stiff-legged walk. Daniel moved on while continuing to watch, and saw him come straight on.

"Hold up, Wade."

Feeling flashed through Daniel. A sudden

impulse bade him to pretend that he had not heard. In time he remembered where he was and halted properly. He faced Captain Stark Chittenden Hooper and saluted, disciplining himself to hide whatever he felt.

Hooper did not return the salute. He stopped, looked left and right nervously, and walked quickly toward Daniel. His strong voice, pitched low, threw out its accusing coldness ahead of him: "Why did you ever come back?"

"Why?" Daniel could find but one reply. "Mean you thought I was killed at Shiloh. Hoped I was. Well, it was mighty close." He grounded his rifle and stood at deliberate ease. Hooper was so near him that Daniel could see the shine of his eyes and smell the fragrance of his recent good cigar.

"Come to attention when an officer addresses you."

"You," Daniel said, holding his purposeful stance, "might act like an officer by returning my salute."

"I could prefer charges of insubordination against you."

Daniel shook his head wearily. "Reckon you said that at Jefferson Barracks. You had no cause then, and none now."

Hooper turned to listen for the patrol's return swing, then he said: "Listen! The war's going on and on. Vicksburg's next. You know what that means. You can walk off your post now. This instant. I won't stop you."

Daniel was dumbfounded, but only for a moment. "I believe desert is what you mean, isn't it? Desert . . . so the patrol could hunt me down." His disgust was also lighting up his mind. "Is it you're afraid I'll bring up Shiloh? When I found you? Helped you up? The boys say you're greasing for major. So it's not just Laurel this time. Maybe I ought to tell everyone how brave you are."

Hooper became rigidly erect. "Your word against mine . . . an officer's. Before I'm finished with you, you'll wish you'd gone over the hill tonight."

"You're rotten, Stark. You always were. Just a stump politician."

He fully expected Hooper to strike him, and so he was prepared when Hooper swung. He pulled his head back, and Hooper missed. Daniel's control snapped then. He was reaching for him with one hand when Hooper, swift of movement, confronted him with drawn revolver.

"Come right ahead," Hooper said. "I can say I caught you deserting and you attacked me."

Daniel held back, eyes lifting from the weapon to the wedge of Hooper's face. He could hear Hooper's ragged breathing. Off in the darkness he caught the cadenced tramp and jingle of the patrol returning. "I believe you would," he said.

Hooper cursed him, his voice low and wicked, then wheeled and struck for camp.

At five o'clock on a December morning, the regiment, double filed, flankers out, was striding southeast as escort for a train of wagons bound for General Grant's new base of supplies at Holly Springs. Overnight the weather had turned snappish, prompting remarks from the ranks derogatory to the "sunny South" and the land of honey and magnolias. But as the sun warmed up and the marchers found their rolling gait, the glum silence of early morning waned and the country put on its glittering face.

Daniel saw oak-studded hills that pitched away on a bright and swaying sea of gentle swells, holding the pleased eye until it lost the farthest tossing mast. Wood smoke scented the crisp air. Behind him, Andy Green and a glib, cocksure Irish replacement named Turley were matching story for story, in which each pictured himself as the paragon of bravery and the possessor of natural, winning ways with the fair sex. Since the day would be a long one, there was never a rush to reach the conclusion of a tale. The raconteurs squeezed each morsel to its essence. When one man lagged, the other would bait him into another ribald vein of discussion.

"Ye keep sayin' what a fine gentleman ye are, Mister Green, and how wild the ladies be after ye. Sure, thin, ye can tell us less fortunate boys what makes the likes of one?"

"A gentleman," said Andy, so readily it was evident he had anticipated the question, "is never an Irishman . . . that's gospel. A gentleman shaves every day. He takes a bath every Saturday, whether he needs it or not. He smells like a Frenchman and is always invited into the parlor."

"Thin ye're no gentleman, Mister Green."

"Leastwise, no girl's old man shot at me the other night in Memphis."

Guffaws descended upon Turley. He was soon ready with a countering story. "Oh, bedad, sir, thin it's time to relate me experience of the other day, when I was strollin' in the park after church . . . . Me eye happen to chance on a nice-lookin' girl so lonesome there. I tipped me hat as usual and sat down beside her, keepin' my proper distance, of course, thinkin' to inquire as to the health of her poor fawhter and mother. Pretty soon she raised her fine hand and drew back, sniffed the air, and says to me . . . 'I smell a very obnoxious odor.' I says . . . 'Ye know somethin', lady, I do, too. It must be that smelly horse soldier over yonder.'

"Right away she says back . . . 'Sir, I want you to know I did not come here to be insulted! I shall have to leave at once!' "

Turley let the story teeter there. The company paced on some distance. Finally a voice called:

"I'll bite, Paddy! What happened then?"

"I said . . . 'Ohhh . . . nayther did I, lady. If he comes any closer, we'll both git up an' go.' That, sir-r-r," said Turley through the laughter, "is the mark of a *true* gentleman."

They marched on another piece, and another voice spoke: "Say, Paddy, can you tell us innocent lads what a Cyprian is?"

Turley had to meditate on that one. Then: "Why, a Cyprian, ye poor, ignorant boys, is just a kind-hearted soul of a sweet girl who comforts her friends and has no enemies."

Far into the morning, a brief splatter of shots stilled the chattering voices. The marchers halted. Officers loped ahead. A wait, and Captain Hooper spurred back and ordered the Coon Creek Company out of line and along the road to the advance, where he signaled it into the woods. As best Daniel could tell, flankers had received fire from ambush. Now the Coon Creekers, coming up in support, were to prowl that flank and keep it clear while the command continued on.

Nothing happened here, and the deployed company scouted to the edge of a wide old cotton field thick with burrs. On its farther edge squatted a shanty, no sign of life around it. Hooper studied it through his glasses.

"Wade," he ordered, "scout ahead to that shack. See if it's occupied. Move fast. We've got to keep pace with the column."

Daniel walked off, a familiar inkling prickling his spine. Hooper's impatience smashed at him: "By God, I said move! Get going!"

He would not provide Hooper the relish of seeing him trot, and, therefore, Hooper be damned, he walked. An insight warned him. This wasn't the carefree road to Fort Donelson on that sunny February day, when they were all as green as young corn and Hooper had pulled him out of ranks on a hazing walk. A harmless walk. This went deeper. It was malicious. Daniel didn't know what lay ahead. Three-quarters across the field he went down the bank of a small branch and, following the dry course, came upon fresh horse tracks. Their cluttered pattern ran ahead, turned sharply, and, when he climbed out after them, the shanty stood close at hand. The place looked deserted long ago. Nothing moved. Nevertheless, he began circling it and peering inside, and afterward scouted past it. There was hardly cover around here for a squad of infantry, none for horses. Hooper, Daniel realized, could see all this through his glasses.

Rankling, Daniel returned to the yard and motioned his comrades to come ahead.

Hooper, riding up, ignored Daniel and ordered the company to advance. A hundred yards on he halted his men again. Raising his glasses, he scrutinized the terrain at length, at unusual length, Daniel thought, considering Hooper's announced haste. The next danger point was a hill. Oaks covered it, tall and straight in the sunlight, dark and unknown toward their close-growing center. Hooper telescoped his glasses with a snap, his actions urgent again.

"Now, Wade . . . scout out that wooded hill. On the double-quick."

It was a good half mile, perhaps farther, across broken ground. Daniel lashed him a look.

"Do I have to repeat the order?"

Daniel, expressionless, swung into a dog-trot, holding it until he reached the first dip in the land, when he eased off to his long-striding, limping walk. When the footing took him upward again, and he knew he was visible in Hooper's glasses, he returned to the dog-trot. So he had covered half the up-and-down distance, feeling a summer sweat, pack straps rubbing, before reason cooled his temper. He was, he saw, allowing his angry mortification to make him careless. After that, he gave the hill keener attention. Nothing changed there.

He was fifteen or more rods away and bobbing up a broken slope toward the silent woods, when his illusion of serenity burst. A ball whirred, plucking for the top of his cap, before he heard the rifle's *pop* and was diving headlong into a shallow wash. Three more balls *chuffed* the thin winter grass above his head.

He played 'possum, waiting, waiting, and

crawled along the wash, raised up, and eased his rifle over the top. There was nothing to shoot. All he saw was inscrutable woods. Not a shot came. By and by, a clattering behind the hill told him why: the rap of horses going off hard. Working his way to the top, he saw several riders fading into the countryside. Militia. Only militia would pot from afar when they could better kill a Yankee in close. Only a militia would run so fortuitously.

Looking back, he sighted the hurrying figures of the company. From here all objects stood out. The shanty on the little rise, and the draws and dips he had crossed. He turned, intending to sit and rest. Instead, something swung him around to his previous position. He raised his head and drew his eye on a line from the shanty to where Hooper had halted a second time to look through his glasses and on to the hill. Had Hooper seen the militiamen in his spyglass? Had he known they were there all the time?

Chapter Twenty-One

THE FORAGERS

After months of frustration, of fighting and wallowing through jungle growths beset by alligators, snakes, and sharpshooters, it was hard to believe the Union Army was marching for high ground on the east side of the river below Vicksburg. It was incredible, and the Confederate command seemed paralyzed, although one division hurried down from Grand Gulf. A sharp fight erupted around Port Gibson, in a setting of narrow ravines choked with underbrush and cane, before the Yankees turned a flank and went striding ahead.

Bivouacked that evening, Daniel Wade listened to a mockingbird's song swell through the lulling twilight of early May. All around him, he could hear the awakened chorus of his regiment, freed at last from the mucky lowlands. There was hardly a man whose hands weren't blistered from digging on Grant's canals and cutting levees and clearing bayous, projects doomed by underwater stumps, the cantankerous Mississippi, and masked Rebel batteries.

By the third day the total absence of supply wagons bringing rations still presented no problems. Grant's army was living off a bountiful land. Of a morning the Northerners started out with flat haversacks and filled them from smokehouses, cellars, and chicken roosts along the way. Roses and honeysuckles, blooming by the roadsides, smiled at the young barbarians, blanket rolls slung carelessly over shoulders, singing, shouting, bellowing, swinging down narrow roads ankle-deep in yellow dust. The Missourians were as loud as any regiment. After almost two years of death and disease, the company from Foley's Prairie had lost its share of men, and Stark Chittenden Hooper was now a major attached to brigade headquarters, but the boys still called themselves the Coon Creek Cougars, and so they told the world.

At night Daniel and Jesse buttoned their canvas shelter halves together to form a tent. Often they fixed bayonets on rifles and stuck them into the ground and strung a light rope between the trigger guards for support, then pegged down the tent corners.

By this time the non-essentials of Donelson and Shiloh had disappeared. On the march, Daniel tucked his spare clothing, personal items, shelter half, and rubber poncho inside his blanket roll which had replaced his bulky knapsack. Alongside his haversack, hanging down his left hip from a sling, clattered coffee pot, canteen, and tin cup. His pocket knife was the only cutlery needed; for a dish a solid hardtack cracker did as well as his tin plate. Any man worth his salt could have a meal ready thirty minutes after halting. A bayonet scabbard protruded from his infantry waist belt on the left; on his right hung a pouch of percussion caps and a leather cartridge box containing forty rounds. Suspenders held up his light blue woolen pants. He wore a gray flannel shirt under his dark blue blouse. A slanting red chicken feather decorated his tilted forage cap. He marched with the long, free-swinging stride of an infantryman in the Army of the Tennessee, unheeding the limp he would have the rest of his life.

Excitement crowded each day. The enemy was falling back. There was the feel of victory on the fragrant air. Uncomplaining droves of Negroes collected in the Army's devastated wake, afoot, in ancient wagons, on mules, come to see Father Lincum's liberators for themselves. In Daniel's ears the murmur of their soft voices was a moving chant heard above the tramp and rumble of the Army, as a rising sea beating upon the steps of the conquerors. *Glory! Glory! Hallelujah!* The warm eyes of their campfires burned long after the weary Coon Creek soldiers slept; their cheerful voices caressed the glittering darkness and greeted the pink dawn. *Judgment*

Day a-comin'. De chariot's a-comin'. De Jubilee yar. No mo' hoein'. No mo' pickin'.

One morning Daniel became aware of a slave singing and marching steadily on his flank. A slight old fellow, no larger than a sapling boy, hair like white wool, no shoes on his dusty feet. He toted nothing on his back or in his hands, but he had wonderful, happy, rolling eyes, and he was singing over and over:

Hit's de jubilee yar
Father Lincum's comin' in his chariot
Comin', comin', comin'

The patriarch seemed to take a shine to Daniel as the company marched, never straying far away. Whenever Daniel looked to his left, he found the warm eyes favoring him, the cottony head nodding to him.

During a halt, the old man approached and said shyly: "I'se Uncle Noah. I'se joined up."

"We got a long way to march, Uncle. You'll get mighty tired before we get there."

Uncle Noah smiled back, not at all discouraged, and squatted in the dust to wait. When the company swung off again, he took his place and began singing. Soon he marched closer to Daniel. After a little more, he was shoulder to shoulder with Daniel, keeping step. He said: "Lemme tote yo' gun."

Daniel handed the heavy Springfield to him. Uncle Noah placed it proudly on his shoulder. By and by, at his insistence, he was also carrying Daniel's cooking utensils.

That evening Uncle Noah cooked supper for the boys. He had a way with cornbread. Afterward, he sang songs for them in a voice that was still rich and full, swaying and clapping his hands all the while. He was adept at making up songs extolling President Lincoln, his favorite subject.

> Father Lincum's a mighty big man
> He's comin' down de road in his chariot
> I know, I know

Without pausing, he would commence another.

> Father Lincum's strong as a lion
> An' sweet as a dove
> Yo' bet, yo' bet

The soaring voice would go on.

> Father Lincum's got a crown on his head
> A light on his face
> He's comin' in his chariot
> Comin', comin', comin'

Daniel listened, fascinated, moved, feeling what

the old slave felt. As he listened, he thought he understood for the first time what the war was really about.

Uncle Noah danced for them, a shuffling, foot-slapping dance that brought soldiers from other mess fires, had them ringed around him, beating time to his skittering feet. Later, Daniel gave him a shirt, Tim a red bandanna, Andy a jew's-harp, and Jesse a clay pipe.

"Uncle," Daniel said on the second day, "how would you like to go home with me when the war's over? Be a free man and work for wages?"

"Wages?" The old man's face lit up like a pine torch.

"Yes. Get paid by the month. Work on my father's farm."

"An' whar be yo' home, Mistuh Dan?"

"Missouri."

"Miz-zouree?" the old man repeated softly, liking the sound of the unfamiliar word.

"That's north up the big river."

"Norf? Way up de big river?" Noah's anticipation waned. "Dat's a long ways off. But I'll think about hit."

On the third morning Daniel left the regiment with a party of foragers in charge of Sergeant Seth Coots. Uncle Noah trailed along ever near but never in the way. Daniel had grown fond of this child-like old fellow who smiled most of the time and owned an ungrudging cheerfulness.

His open pleasure over the smallest gift made Daniel feel over-blessed.

Spreading out, the foragers approached an old farmhouse. There was no indication of life. Not a sound. Not one hen's cackle. Other Union men, Daniel saw shortly, had already looted the smokehouse and granary, caught all the chickens, slaughtered all the hogs, and seized all the vehicles, cleaned the place bare. In addition, the pond near the barn had been cut and drained, obviously for the purpose of finding valuables.

"Looks like the cavalry got here first, as usual," Andy drawled. "You know what they say . . . the first to forage and the last to fight."

"I don't like to see the boys clean out poor folks this way," Jesse said, expressing a farmer's understanding. "Here's a whole season's work gone."

Inside, the house had been ransacked and smashed. Coots was like an ant, up and down stairs, peeping, searching, crawling in and out of dark places. He stayed inside after his comrades went to the yard to keep watch on the woods. Daniel heard him tapping and sounding on boards with his rifle butt, ripping planks, and tramping about.

When Coots left the house, he had a stack of clothing, a jug of molasses, and a pillowcase full of shoes. "How's that," he gloated, "for second time around." As he spoke, some shoes fell out.

Seeing Uncle Noah beside Daniel, he said: "Git over here. Pick up this stuff."

Old Noah swayed a little, but did not obey. If anything, his back stiffened a hitch.

"Leave him be," Daniel said. "He's not your man."

"I reckon he's your nigger?" Coots sneered. "Way he's been lookin' after you, follerin' you around."

"Not mine or anybody's. He's a free man."

Uncle Noah jogged his head vigorously to that. At the same time he sidled nearer Daniel.

Coots said: "You talk high and mighty."

"Just leave him be."

"Said he'd *jined up*, didn't he?" Coots replied, mimicking the Negro's drawl.

Tim Forehand, thinking of more urgent matters, took a departing step. "Hell, let's go. We ain't found the company's supper yet. They's bound to be Secesh cavalry up the road."

No more was said. Shrugging, Coots started shoving the shoes inside the pillowcase, and Daniel walked off. As long ago as Memphis, it returned to him, Coots had begun displaying the fruits of sudden wealth, unusual in a company of uniformly poor young men. He had money to lend at shackling rates of interest, and an assortment of articles to trade or sell, such as watches, knives, cheap jewelry, and sometimes whiskey.

By noon, a mule, found lame in the timber, was transporting Coots's mounting accumulation of loot. Accompanying each wobbly movement of the miserable beast was the metallic jostling of purloined silverware and cooking utensils. Little of worth had escaped the sergeant's eyes. While a woman stood by wringing her hands and moaning, Coots had drawn a shallow cistern nigh dry to uncover her cherished hoard of jewelry on the bottom. And from under a flower bed stepping stone he had moled out the family's cache of table silver.

"Trash!" she cried, her sweeping gesture including all the foragers. "White trash!"

"Lady," Andy Green answered solemnly, "we didn't start this dirty war. You folks did when you told that Boryreegard to fire on the grand old flag."

At another farm, Daniel, exploring a dark storm cellar, discovered some cobwebbed bottles of wine. While the young Unionists stood in the front yard and drew the corks with their teeth, a pretty girl pranced through the front door and, standing on the porch, sang "The Bonnie Blue Flag".

Instead of the angry response she expected and wanted, the soldiers accorded her noble applause. She tossed her head and whirled to go inside. At the door she turned and showed them an obscure look, more pleased than not.

"See that?" Tim Forehand called. "These Secesh gals are just like the ones back home."

As they walked along the road, Uncle Noah looked up at Daniel. "Have yo' ever seed Father Lincum?" he asked, his voice taking on a hushed reverence.

"No," said Daniel, yet not wanting to disappoint his friend. "But he's off yonder." Daniel pointed east. "He's there, all right. He's there."

"I reckon Father Lincum be ever'whar," Noah said, nodding to himself. "He walk de earth lak de Lord Almighty."

The drowsy afternoon ambled on. Just a few miles away on the foragers' left flank the Union Army marched through a countryside blooming under a canopy of flowers. Save for the brief stand at Fort Gibson followed by sporadic cavalry clashes, the invaders advanced unhindered to the northeast, while the Confederates bided for the moment when Grant would pivot toward the main prize of fortress Vicksburg.

Daniel stopped short, seeing a blur of riders up the side road. At the same instant Minié balls whizzed overhead. Calmly the foragers slipped into a grove of oaks. Old soldiers now, they stood their ground and trained their rifles on the turning shapes, squeezing off their shots, reloading expertly, at a rate of fire of three balls to the minute. Uncle Noah pressed against a tree, his wide eyes showing as much wonderment as fright.

All at once the enemy's fire sputtered out, dribbled, done. Nothing moved on the road. Daniel guessed the Rebels had faded out toward New Auburn, on the main road to Jackson, up which the Union Army was taking long strides.

The foragers moved on. Bird songs throbbed through the May-time woods. Daniel breathed the incense of flowers and magnolias, wild and sweet. The foragers turned a bend in the dusty road, and Daniel, looking beyond, was struck spellbound, unprepared for the house he saw. The wine still sang through his head, but it wasn't so much that. This was no mere country house. It was a white mansion. More magnificent even than the Great House back in Missouri. Framed against the dark woods, its two stories seemed to float, softly luminous, on a bed of swaying greenery. Eight huge columns supported the front gallery, as stately as sentinels before the entrance of a Greek temple. Not a person or animal could be seen anywhere. He heard not a sound. In the lulling springtime hush, nothing seemed real.

Spreading out, the foragers swept across the broad lawn, tramping through the yard and flower beds. Through the open front door, Daniel could see daylight down a wide central hall. A rushing noise caused the soldiers to look behind them. A carriage came careening down the road. An old plug of a horse and a bony mule struggled under the rein lashings of a woman.

"I thought everybody was gone," Daniel said. "Well, there's no need to bother a woman."

"If it was up to you, we wouldn't git a god-damned thing," Coots said, walking faster. "No Southern bitch is gonna stop us."

The woman, whipping her poor team harder, reached the gallery steps first and barred the foragers' way with the carriage. She faced them unhesitatingly, a proud, trembling woman, about the age of Daniel's mother. Her gray eyes looked smoky with rage. "Get off my property!" she commanded.

"We're Union soldiers, ma'am, an' mighty hungry," Tim spoke up.

"Soldiers! There's not a decent man among you! You're all Grant's thieves! Grant's vandals!"

On impulse, Daniel said: "Ma'am, we're foragers. We need food. We won't bother you or your place."

"Says you . . . I'm in charge," Coots growled. He roved his judging eyes over the mansion and started around the carriage like a lean hound.

Instantly the woman sprang down to the gallery. Her high voice flailed hatred at him: "Vultures! Cowards! Murderers! And you call yourselves soldiers!"

Coots ignored her and slouched inside, already

on the look-out for plunder. A bluecoat began digging in a flower bed, his spade going *snick, snick.*

She whirled on him, crying hysterically: "Go ahead . . . dig! But you won't find a thing. . . . I've just taken it all away! Everything's hidden!"

The soldier ceased digging to peer downward. He stooped, gave a whoop, and straightened up, clutching aloft a silver jewelry box.

Hands clasped, she bowed her head and turned her back. A pack of soldiers streamed past her. Resigned, she followed them into the house. There, above the ransacking noises, her clear, dignified voice reached Daniel: "I want you-all to remember this . . . I did not invite you into my house. You are no more than ordinary thieves."

Daniel and Andy darted around the house, past a little, white office building. Daniel's ears still rang with the bottomless hatred of the cool-voiced woman. A sensation of shame struck him. He saw an A Company man leave the doorway of the glass-topped greenhouse, a sprig of greenery atilt in his cap. These three ran on to the smoke-house, where soldiers were using fence rails to batter the locked door. It crashed inward.

"She's chuck full," the first man in shouted. "Let's load up the old lady's carriage." He dashed out.

Negroes drifted up from their quarters to watch, their faces serious and uncertain.

"Hello, folks," Daniel said. "Do you know who we are?"

An old man nodded, his eyes commencing to glow. "Yo' is Father Lincum's boys come to set us black folks free."

"That's right. And there's thousands more of us marching over there on the main road. If you listen right good this evening, you can hear 'em singing."

"Den Judgment Day hit's come," the old man said, his voice trembling.

"Say, Uncle, there any Confederate soldiers around here?"

"Dey is . . . an' yo' better look out."

Swaying, wheels spinning dust, the carriage arrived. Soldiers piled in cured hams, sausages, bacon, and pots of lard. Not far away, Daniel heard the squawking of captured chickens. When he and Andy returned to the front of the house, the gallery was in chaos. Soldiers were as pirates prying open chests, tearing through boxes, strewing clothes about, and discarding bric-a-brac. The woman wasn't there.

"Look-ee yonder at the soldier suit I and Jesse foraged!" Tim roared. A clownish figure was strutting on the bricked drive, hiking his arms up and down, wearing the cocked hat and cutaway blue coat of a Revolutionary soldier. It was Uncle

Noah and he was puffing away on his white clay pipe. Daniel and Andy laughed and flung Noah an extravagant salute. He, in turn, brought up his arm in a grandiose arc and saluted them.

Seth Coots slouched out on the gallery. He was gnawing a chicken leg that he then flipped, half eaten, on the drive. A rough scowl of irritation furrowed his greasy, lank-jawed face. After him came the woman, dignified and ashy pale. Her high manner made clear that she did not follow him in subservience.

"Hell, she's hid all the good stuff," Coots complained out loud.

"We've got plenty of rations," Daniel said. "Let's go."

Coots said nothing for a moment. His mouth worked. He scrubbed a hand across his chin and said: "We'll head back now. But, first, we're gonna burn this fancy shebang right down to the hocks."

A scream sliced across the last of his speech. The woman held a hand to her throat.

"Well, git started," Coots said, and looked around. No man moved. "You heard the order! Git started!"

"By dogs, I won't do it," Daniel said. "I'll see you in hell first."

Again Coots glanced around for support. As yet, no man stirred. The woman clenched her white hands and waited, seeming to sense that one shrill invective might destroy the favoring wind.

Someone was running hard. A Unionist rounded the house, brogans churning. He swung a bunch of chickens tied by the legs. He panted: "Reb cavalry . . . they're comin'!"

The driver of the carriage jumped in and whipped the startled team into motion. From old habit the handful of Coon Creek soldiers in the party drew together and ran down the drive for the woods. They had covered about seventy-five yards, when Daniel heard hoofs clattering behind the house. Over his shoulder, he saw horsemen whirl around the corner, their mounts lunging faster. There wasn't time to reach the woods. Sprawling into a weedy ditch, Daniel aimed the Springfield at the foremost rider. Rifles cracked along the ditch. Puffs of smoke rose. Two riderless horses broke stride, and the attackers, some fifteen or so, veered away. At that, the Northerners jumped up and scurried into the woods behind the shaking carriage.

Daniel was surprised to see the Confederates circling and drumming back for another charge. They drove straight in, firing, turned, and began to wheel past, leaving a forager screaming in pain. A horse tumbled and threw its rider, who lost his carbine and rolled and lay still, apparently stunned. Shaking his head, he pushed up on his arms. There was a pistol stuck in his belt. A beseeching look filled his face as he glanced back at the retreating horsemen, too far away to help him. Daniel saw that futility on the Confederate's face.

"Put up your hands and come ahead!" Daniel called to him. "You're our prisoner."

The cavalryman turned and hesitated, frozen there by distrust. Daniel saw fear run across the man's features and dissolve. He started to rise. A rifle banged, and dust puffed high on his butternut blouse. He jerked and fell backward, mouth open, a stunned surprise shocking his face.

Daniel whipped half about, to see Coots lowering his rifle. "What the hell's wrong with you?" Daniel shouted. "Didn't you see he was surrendered . . . *didn't you?*"

"You fool," Coots said, not turning his head, "he was going for his pistol."

Later, they filed westward through the languid woods, following the boot-burdened carriage, pushing it uphill when the old team weakened. Daniel trailed his comrades. The gall of revulsion and rage that had risen to his throat was still in him, lodged like a rock. What had happened to him? To them all?

As though he had waited long enough, Uncle Noah fell in step beside him. "Mistuh Dan," the old man said, wondering and softly, "sometimes yo' don't act lak no Yankee a-tall. Jest what is yo'?"

Chapter Twenty-Two

VICKSBURG

At dawn, next morning, trumpeters sounded Reveille along the miles of figures sleeping beside stacked muskets. A hush settled and held for a few moments, then Daniel heard the first awakening rustle of the Army magnify to a colossal undertone, murmurous and muttering, that grew to be a defined racket of axes thudding on fence rails, of mess kits banging, of hoarse commands, and horse-watering details jangling out. Forthwith, the orange-red eyes of countless fires began speckling the pallid darkness. Bacon and coffee smells scented the fragrant spring morning.

Uncle Noah did not show up for breakfast, or after. Daniel went looking and found him in the woods, sitting slumped, back against an oak. Unhappiness had routed his usual cheerful mien. Gone, Daniel saw, was yesterday's laughter-provoking cocked hat and cutaway coat. In place of them, Noah wore the same trousers and coat in which he had joined the company. There was a small bundle beside him.

"What's ailing you, Uncle?" Daniel asked.

304

"I ain't hongry."

"We'll be on the march in a minute."

"Mistuh Dan," said Noah, growing more dejected, "I don' know 'bout stayin' jined up wif you Yankee boys. I'se kinda poorly, too."

Daniel, reading the bundle's meaning, said sympathetically: "You're homesick. That's what."

"Yassuh. I reckon dat's hit."

"Well, we can't have a good man like you on the sick list, Uncle. You'd better go home."

Noah's relief was instantaneous. "Yo' is right," he said, his face altering. His gravity evaporated. He was happy again. He stood, and his mood changed once more. Dampening came over him, a remembering. "Reckon I'll go on thinkin' 'bout dem wages till my dyin' day. Mebbe, iffen de war's over, yo' kin come back dis way again."

"Maybe so, Uncle."

When the "Fall in!" order was shouted and the Coon Creek Boys lined up, they watched Uncle Noah leave. He was singing as he turned down the dusty road, going home. "Father Lincum's comin' in his chariot. Comin', comin', comin'." It seemed to Daniel that he could hear Noah's earthy voice long after he had passed from sight. But, no, that couldn't be just one voice. That was a murmur he heard. Like the wind moving through treetops. Or the drone of a restless multitude, chanting while it pressed on, its patience done. "Glory! Glory! Hallelujah! Blow ye the

305

trumpet, blow." In the eye of his mind, he pictured a tide breaking and lapping on all sides of the blue hosts. He carried that feeling forward when the regiment marched northeast, aching for battle, certain of its strength and destiny.

On a breathless June afternoon, Daniel Wade peered between the parapet logs of his rifle pit toward the maze of outlying Confederate trenches defending Vicksburg. Siege warfare was dull, indeed, after the exciting campaign of May, when in seventeen days the Union Army had marched 130 miles, won five battles in all, burned the city of Jackson, defeated the Rebels at Champion's Hill, and pursued them across the Big Black River into their fortress on the Mississippi. Nothing had happened since May 22nd, when the Rebels threw back Grant's last assault.

Daniel had learned how to construct a revetment of felled trees, to dig a hasty trench, and throw the dirt upon the logs, and to fix horizontal loopholes for rifle fire. At the revetment's top was a head log, resting on poles or skids placed across the ditch to prevent the log, when struck by a cannonball, from falling on the men below.

As the parallel lines crept closer, the pickets grew chummy. Nearly every afternoon at four o'clock, although contrary to orders, soldiers fraternized between the lines. After all, these young men spoke the same language, some knew each other and some were blood brothers, and before the war they had worshiped the same set of national heroes. They experienced the same fears of death and longings for home and their girls and suffered an identical boredom. Past that, their situations differed sharply, the Rebs being hungry and woefully short of medical supplies. Even mule meat was scarce.

Daniel heard that a barrel of flour cost $1,000 inside the besieged city, that enterprising Union soldiers were getting rich smuggling chloroform and ether across the lines, despite the vigilance of the provost guards. Rations on the Northern side, while plentiful, seldom varied from salt pork, hardtack, and coffee. . . . Blackberries are the best cure for the Quick-Step, don't you know? Dandelion greens will ward off the scurvy, you betcha. . . . Now these new brogans are something, wouldn't you say? One for the left foot, one for the right foot . . . made thataway.

Down the line Daniel heard an outpost call: "Say, Johnny, I need a haircut! 'Bout how far is it into town?"

"Farther'n you'll ever git, by God."

"I don't know 'bout that, Johnny. Us Yanks didn't come down here to pick peaches."

"Come right over. We'll part your hair for you . . . same as we did on the Twenty-Second."

Another voice asked: "How do you Johnnies

like your new general? What's his name? General Starvation?"

"An' how do you fat blue-bellies like your nigger wives?" a taunting voice replied. "Have they improved the breed any?"

Daniel, seeing a stir on the other side, called: "Hey, Johnny! Let's swap a little. Got any tobacco?"

"Hello, Yank. Allus got tobacco. Got any o' that Abe Lincoln coffee?"

"Plenty coffee. Meet you by that big stump."

"All right."

"Hold your fire now," Daniel said.

"You bet. Come ahead."

Daniel scouted first for officers. Seeing none, he picked up a little brown sack of coffee beans and crawled over the parapet. It was a steamy day, a smothery haze hanging over the distant river lowlands, and he heard not a shot anywhere as he walked toward the rendezvous. In the midst of all this latent destruction, birds were singing. The Confederates had yet to break one of these informal truces between common soldiers. Nevertheless, every time Daniel ventured between the lines he had a prickly uneasiness, which left him once the visiting and bartering began.

Across, he saw a butternut shape climb the ditch before the enemy trench and advance to meet him. Daniel came face to face with a black-haired young Rebel. They regarded each other curiously, shook hands, and sat on stumps, like country boys meeting on a Saturday afternoon.

"I'm from Alabama," the boy said, proud of it.

"I'm from Missouri," Daniel said, proud, too.

"Come a long ways to fight, didn't we?"

"You Johnnies don't make it easy."

"We-uns don't aim to. Say, Yank, have you got any late newspapers?"

"I'll look around camp tonight. Here's your coffee."

The Confederate held out three twists of tobacco. "Think that's fair enough?"

"Suits me. We don't get enough tobacco."

"We get plenty o' that. But that's all."

Daniel said—"I've got a pretty fair pocket knife here, too."—and he laid it in his hand to show. "I'll swap."

Nodding agreeably, the Rebel dug out his knife. Each passed his possession across, in turn opened the blades, ran thumb along the cutting edge, closed, and examined the handle.

"Fair enough," the Alabaman said. "Don't reckon nary one of us will git skinned." There was ease between them. They compared crops back home, narrow escapes, camp ailments and rations, generals good and middling, shoes, weather, horses and mules, and they talked about home and their people. "You ain't a bad fellow, Yank. If it was up to us, we'd settle this whole shebang right now and go back to farmin'."

"Wish we could, Johnny."

"Care to see a tintype of my girl, Yank?" The Rebel's tone was shy but also eager. Hardly waiting for Daniel's nod, he drew forth a handsome, leather-covered case, pressed its catch, and Daniel, taking it with care, saw brown curls around a small, bewitching face.

"You've got a right pretty girl, Johnny. You betcha."

"Glad you think so. Name's Harriet. Where's your picture?"

He hadn't realized it would be difficult to say, even to someone he didn't know. "I don't have one," Daniel said, "and I haven't seen her since 'Sixty-One."

"Two years . . . that's rough. I had a furlough home last April."

A look-out on the Union side whistled, the warning signal that officers approached.

"Good luck, Johnny."

"Good luck, Yank."

Half an hour before darkness, Daniel's platoon filed back to the regimental encampment, an orderly village of shelter tents and conical Sibleys set up behind a neck of woods. The new company captain and a detail of infantry looked on as Sergeant Jesse Nance prepared to dismiss the men.

"Hold up, Sergeant," the captain said, walking over. He looked grim. "Private Daniel Lester Wade. Step forward."

Daniel stiffened in surprise. He took one step out of ranks, taut with uneasiness.

"Sergeant," the captain said, "take the prisoner's rifle."

Jesse stepped in front. As Daniel gave up the rifle, he saw in his friend's eyes his own numb shock. He heard the captain say—"Forward march."—and, as he obeyed, the detail swung in behind him.

They marched to regimental headquarters, a farmhouse off the Jackson-Vicksburg road. Officers overran the smoky room. Daniel recognized the regimental commander, Colonel Pontius Orr, who looked troubled and distraught.

Daniel halted. A lean, saturnine captain, mustache and spade goatee bristling like a porcupine, came forward. He glowered menacingly and the contracting of his busy brows increased his threatening air.

"Private Wade," he said, when the foot shufflings ceased, "isn't it true that you come from Southern parentage?"

Daniel glanced in appeal to Colonel Orr, who said, not without sympathy: "At ease. Just answer the questions."

"Yes, sir," Daniel said. "But so do a lot of us Union boys from Missouri." And suddenly he thought he understood everything. He spoke in heat, his one purpose to defend the name of an irascible but brave old man who was dying years before his time because he had fought for his country. "My father was wounded in the Mexican War. He served with Doniphan's expedition. He was a good soldier, sir. He. . . ."

Like a knife, the captain's silencing gesture severed Daniel's speech. "Confine your remarks to the question, soldier. From what section of the South did your parents come?"

"My parents were born in the North, sir. My father's father lived in Virginia, then moved to Ohio where my father was born. My mother was born in Missouri after her folks moved there from North Carolina."

The captain began pacing back and forth, growling over his shoulder. "Private Wade, you have been observed conversing with enemy pickets between the lines. Not once, mind you, but on several occasions. You did so again this afternoon. Repeated violations in defiance of standing orders against fraternizing. Do you deny it?"

"Why, no, sir," Daniel replied, cooling off a little. "It's done all up and down the line."

Once more the chopping gesture fell. "That's the second time you've added extraneous remarks. Answer the questions yes or no."

Daniel heard the sudden scrape of a chair

being shoved back. "Captain," said Colonel Orr, rising stiffly, "I see no reason for the provost guard to browbeat this young soldier. His record is good, and I remind you that he comes from a regiment that's been fighting its way south since Fort Donelson." Orr was a gangling, kindly backwoods schoolteacher reluctant to admonish his brawny pupils. Now his black eyes snapped. When the provost captain opened his mouth to interrupt, the colonel put out a staying hand. "What Private Wade says is very true. Visiting and swapping go on just about every afternoon. We haven't been able to stop it. Judging by the number of Rebels entering our lines this week for a good meal, I'd say the practice is hurting the enemy's morale . . . not ours."

"Colonel," said the captain, somewhat appeased, "I am concerned only with the flow of Union medical supplies inside Vicksburg."

"We're all aware of that noble aim, Captain. I suggest that you get on with your investigation."

A high pink flushing his face, the captain confronted Daniel again. "Between four and four-thirty this afternoon you were observed passing something to a Rebel who you met between the lines. Do you deny that?"

"Not a-tall, sir."

"What happened?"

"We swapped pocket knives, for one thing."

Quickly: "Was that all?"

313

"No, sir. I was coming to the rest. I traded a little sack of coffee for three twists of tobacco."

"A little sack of *coffee,* you say?" Clicking his heels, the provost captain paced to a table behind him, picked up an object, and wheeled about. "Wasn't it something more precious to the Rebel cause than coffee?" he asked, advancing on Daniel. "Wasn't it now, soldier?" He held something in a brown sack.

"I don't understand."

"As if you didn't know," the captain said softly, bringing a dark-colored bottle from the sack and gripping it like a bomb. "The sticker reads c-h-l-o-r-o-f-o-r-m. That spells chloroform!" he was shouting and his face was purple. "This single bottle is worth a thousand dollars in Vicksburg . . . not Confederate money . . . but in gold. It was stolen only yesterday from your regimental field hospital!"

"But I didn't . . . ," Daniel choked and got out no more, for the pitiless voice shouted: "This afternoon it was found in your tent! You can't deny that!"

"But I do deny it!" Daniel shouted back. A fiery haze floated before his eyes into which he seemed to be sinking helplessly. All he saw was the bristly face. "And the gold," he said, groping, desperate. "I just came from the line. Search me! Wouldn't it be on me?"

"Not necessarily. You could hide it or pass it

on to a comrade. That's the way the little game works. I regret to inform you, Private Wade, that you are being held for general court-martial."

Chapter Twenty-Three
THE VOLUNTEERS

Some days Daniel wasn't certain whether he languished in the Union provost guard's stockade at Memphis or a Confederate prison. From sunup to sundown the prisoners labored over endless tasks that combined degradation and incessant toil. They chopped and sawed wood, and, when they ran out of logs, they dug ditches, cleaned stables and latrines, and sweated on road gangs and dug entrenchments, or carried balls and chains around the prison yard, or stood on barrels in the blazing sun until they dropped. News of Vicksburg's fall seemed remote and unimportant. Gettysburg meant less.

In official eyes no punishment could be undeserved for these base violators of military law, these thieves, cowards, murderers, deserters, rapists, bounty jumpers, malingerers, and general offenders. Sometimes the prison commandant paraded his charges past the city's garrison troops as examples of wrongdoing receiving just retribution. The prison, formerly used as a slave pen, was a mockery of overcrowded, louse-infested sheds and one shallow water well inside a brick wall surrounded by wire. New blockhouses buttressed the four corners. During that brutal summer of 1863, the sheds were like bake ovens; the following winter, icy winds howled between the unchinked logs and the sick froze to death in their sleep. Nearly every day men died and muffled drums beat beyond the stockade.

From the beginning of his trial Daniel had divined the preordained verdict. The war was growing heavier, officers' patience shorter. The fatherly attitude of the conflict's early months had changed. He felt no great surprise when convicted and sent to prison for an indefinite term at hard labor, plus eventual dishonorable discharge and forfeiture of all pay. He moved in a stupor of weariness. What had become of the first Daniel Wade? Plowboy, bare-knuckle fighter, wrestler, jumper, foot racer, muleskinner, wood chopper, dancer, rural scholar, worshiper of Old Hickory? Once lover of a face and form of joyous beauty beneath the bowered shade of an ancient Indian mound? Once a thirsty dreamer at the endless fountain? He had managed to save Laurel's letter, and once in a while he would read through the memorized lines and ponder whether they had been addressed to him. Was he that long-ago Daniel Wade? Was he anything at all?

When fog trailed in from the river and the creeping dampness laid mossy fingers over his chest, the whistling cries of the boats sounded like children adrift, lost as he was lost from all that he had known.

It was May, 1864, when the middle-aged prisoner joined the shaggy scarecrow rabble living in the stinking sheds and eating the wretched rations of mule meat and cornmeal gruel. Rather than drag step as most new men did, appalled at the miserable surroundings and smells, he proceeded to stroll around the prison yard as though on a tour of inspection. No mark of rank distinguished his buttonless, threadbare uniform, and yet he wore it with seemliness on his emaciated frame. And to his slouched hat he had imparted an air of dignity by slanting the left side of the brim. His black boots were cracked, but his step was springy, and his glittering black eyes kept darting here and there.

A raggedy, long-haired figure assumed a mockingly obsequious manner, bowing and murmuring: "Welcome, sir, to the Memphis House. We are known all up and down the river for our oysters on the half shell. Our green turtle *à l'Anglaise.* Our *consommé à la Royale.*"

The newcomer bowed back. A smile flickered on his lips. "Had I known of your unexcelled cuisine," he said graciously, "I should not have dined before my arrival."

Selecting a place on the straw under Daniel's shed, he pulled off his hat, and Daniel saw a dark and sensitive face, laced with heavy brows, crisp black hair penciled with white, and a closely cropped beard. Another prisoner, fawning, spoke to the stranger, who nodded and no more. The other man drew back, and the newcomer crossed his legs and seemed to wait, his face turned to the heat-glazed yard.

Two days afterward, Daniel and the older prisoner toiled side-by-side on the same work gang beyond town. The morning was still and vaporous, the sun merciless. Daniel's strength bled in driblets. His companion paused often for breath. His hands shook when he brushed sweat dripping off his chin. Up close his face revealed the ruin of a drunkard's cross-hatching of purple and reddish veins. His shovel slipped from his hands, and he fell to the ground on all fours. Daniel reached to help him.

The man pushed Daniel's hand aside and staggered up, strain shadowing his face. He spoke in precise gulps: "Poor judgment, soldier . . . helping another man, here. . . . Save your strength."

"Maybe that helps keep me alive."

A perceptive look narrowed in the black eyes. A guard shouted. The older prisoner picked up his shovel and Daniel his. They worked without let-up until noon, filling a wash across a wagon road.

During the brief rest, Daniel lay flat in the woods, eyes shuttered, forcing himself not to think, to let his mind drift suspended. The new man's conversational tone caught him off guard.

"I've been observing you, soldier. You don't complain."

"What good would it do?"

"None. I'm a little curious, though. Why are you here?" Daniel opened his eyes fully, but withheld his reply. The clear, even-pitched voice—that of a man accustomed to command —continued agreeably: "Don't if you'd rather not. I understand a soldier's wish for privacy. However, your story couldn't be as dastardly as mine. You've heard of Holly Springs, Mississippi? Of course . . . . Well, I was in command of the supply depot there when General Van Dorn burned it back in December of 'Sixty-Two."

Daniel sat up. "You . . . ?"

"No less, I am reluctant to admit. I am the infamous Colonel Isaac Boliver Steadman who, they say, allowed four million dollars worth of stores to go up. Who, they say, was caught napping. Who . . . they do not say . . . gave the order to his adjutant to double the guards that rainy night . . . an order that was never carried out."

"Why?"

"My adjutant merely decided to wait until morning, and morning was too late," Steadman said, half amused. "I see that you doubt me, soldier. Just as Grant did, just as the judges did at the court-martial. In addition to neglect of duty, which I denied, I was accused of the preposterous allegation of being drunk on duty, which I also denied . . . I see that you are even more skeptical. At any rate, thirty thousand men were left hungry and Grant's advance on Vicksburg was delayed for months." Steadman shook his head. "Poor, noble Van Dorn . . . we were friends before the war . . . that mighty deed brought him no good at all. Quite the hero, he went calling one evening up in Tennessee, overstayed his visit past two o'clock in the morning. At which time the lovely lady's inconsiderate husband returned and shot poor Van in the bedroom. Rather, I should say, in the head. So they say."

"You've been in prison a long time," Daniel said.

"I've had the comfort of variety, at least. First, the Nashville stockade. An outstandingly horrible hole in the winter. Then Jackson, Tennessee. That was even worse. They shipped me here, I suppose, because Memphis is the foulest pig's pen of all." Daniel saw the dark eyes quicken upon him. "Judging from the looks of you, you've spent quite a spell here yourself."

Daniel told him how long. Although it was not his intention, he began relating his story in detail. It was the first full accounting he had given anyone, for he had sought no close friends since his early days in prison, principally because the few men he had liked had departed with the muffled drums.

"Escape is the only way," Daniel concluded, a bitterness coming up in him. "That's one reason why they feed us so little, to keep us weak so we can't get away."

"Where would you go?"

"Join the Southern Army, maybe."

"I don't think you mean that. You've been a Union soldier too long. You'd be fighting your friends."

"I have friends and neighbors who are Confederates."

"It wouldn't be the way you think it is on the other side." Steadman let a thoughtful silence settle between them. "Wait a while. At least you're alive."

" 'Pears to me I've already waited too long," Daniel said. "I'd rather be dead than another year of this."

"Make one foolhardy move and you will be. Wait, soldier."

Summer's pestilential heat, which had clutched the prison yard for so long, began lifting as October approached. But still men died, and still more victims stumbled through the gate. Daniel figured some five hundred soldiers now crowded the stockade, backwater from the garrisons ruling Mississippi and southern Tennessee. The hard fighting had shifted to Georgia, where three armies under Sherman, including the Army of the Tennessee, had smashed southward to capture Atlanta.

"It never fails," former Colonel Steadman observed, watching fresh prisoners arrive. "Garrison duty breeds disciplinary problems. An army's health and conduct are always improved when it's marching and fighting."

One morning the guards posted a notice on a post by the gate. Daniel and Steadman went over to see. It read:

VOLUNTEERS ARE WANTED
FOR SPECIAL DUTY
A FORMATION WILL BE CALLED
AT 9 O'CLOCK

Steadman, seeing Daniel's interest, said: "Never volunteer until you know what it's all about. I know. I've sent out my share of damn' fool details. The deadbeats will be the first, because they're looking for something soft, and I can't say I blame them. It won't be. I assure you. They'll also be the first rejected. Better see what happens first."

"You mean *wait?*" Daniel asked, full of sarcasm.

"Be patient," Steadman said, sounding cheerful.

"Sherman's captured Atlanta. The war will be over in a few months."

"I can't put it off that long."

Promptly at nine o'clock a sergeant called the formation and a pell-mell rush followed. The miserable figures shuffled away, heavily guarded; within the hour most of them had returned.

"What did I tell you?" said Steadman.

"What if they don't call another formation?"

"Have to . . . as many men as they're sending back."

Daniel's mind was set. "I'm going with the next bunch," he said, and sought out some volunteers. None, he learned, had been told the nature of the special duty. Virtually all who had passed the cursory physical examination were rejected after questioning and a review of their records.

At eleven o'clock another formation was called. As Daniel started off, Steadman said: "We can go now, Wade."

"We?"

"Don't look so surprised. You knew all the time I was going."

After hasty physical examinations, the volunteers entered a long building jammed with clerks, who kept a careful distance from the malodorous prisoners. At the far end of the hall-like room, Daniel could see two officers questioning each volunteer.

Two hours later only a handful of men remained, among them Daniel and ex-Colonel Steadman. All sat on long benches against the wall, waiting to be interviewed.

"This has the distinct odor of dirty duty," Steadman groaned under his breath. "I can tell. Observe how they question. We are just fodder, my young friend."

Daniel watched and listened closely as the volunteer next in line, a thin, sallow man, faced a captain and major seated behind a desk. The prisoner saluted half-heartedly, shoulders slumped.

"By now you should know how to come to attention," the captain said. "Give your name, former rank, and regiment."

"Uriah Bates, sir . . . sergeant . . . Tenth Illinois Infantry."

The captain pawed through papers on the desk, hovered over a page, and studied it briefly. "Let's see," he said, "you were caught deserting during the siege of Vicksburg."

"There was nobody home to see after my sick wife and hungry young 'uns," Bates said, his voice bitter and steady. "I couldn't get a furlough, so I went anyway."

The captain glanced in inquiry to the major, who shrugged.

"Go back to the bench and wait," the captain said. When the prisoner pivoted to go, Daniel saw the letter D branded on his right cheek.

"That man," Steadman whispered, "is a good soldier."

Two more volunteers were eliminated and sent from the building before a blond, smooth-faced young man of careless manner idled across to the desk.

"Willie Oats, sir . . . private . . . Second Ohio Cavalry."

An interval held as the captain shuffled the papers. Then: "According to the record, you stole your colonel's watch."

"Not exactly, sir. You see . . . ."

Peremptorily the captain thumbed him to the bench, prompting Steadman's disgusted whisper: "This is ridiculous."

Now only three volunteers remained. A short, broad man, his wasted frame still showing the outline of massive strength, rose next, and he made no pretense of hiding his belligerent scowl.

"George Pogue, sir . . . corporal . . . First Iowa Cavalry. If I say so myself, I was the best damned farrier in the regiment."

After a bit of report reading, the captain said: "You were found guilty of murder . . . of bashing a fellow soldier over the head with a whiskey bottle."

"It was him or me, sir."

"Never mind the details."

"I caught him and my girl together. He came at me with a knife. . . ."

"That's enough! Wait over there."

While the two officers conversed in low tones, Steadman whispered frantically to Daniel: "For God's sake withdraw from this!"

Daniel shook his head no.

Steadman's turn followed. He stood at the captain's nod, marched across, and saluted, every move militarily correct.

"Isaac Boliver Steadman, sir, formerly a colonel of infantry."

At the sound of his name the Army clerks turned to stare and whisper among themselves. A stillness let down over the long room.

"And formerly commander of the Holly Springs supply depot," the captain said severely. "Aren't you a West Pointer?"

"Yes, sir. Class of 'Forty-Six."

"You have high family connections in Philadelphia, I see."

"That's totally in error, sir. I had only a wife there . . . long ago."

"I'm surprised you volunteered."

"Inactivity bores me, sir."

"Step over there."

Daniel found the captain no less abrupt and impatient. He said: "They seemed to have made an example of you in the Forty-Fourth Missouri at Vicksburg."

"I am innocent of the charge, Captain."

"You all are, to hear you tell it." Boredom

dulled the officious voice. "If you still want to volunteer, line up over there." With a sign of riddance, the captain rose and left the volunteers to the major.

Barking them to attention, the major marched the volunteers under guard to a forbidding stone building and halted them in a bare, high-ceilinged room. Some fifty or sixty prisoners were huddled there. Daniel, seeking Steadman's eye for an explanation, drew an uneasy frown of uncertainty. Everything, Daniel knew, was too off-handed, done too fast and slipshod, too indifferently.

"Steadman!" the major bellowed.

Steadman's mouth hung. He overcame his surprise and went forward to accompany the major out of the room.

In less than an hour they returned, flanking an old colonel whose drooping handlebar mustache ends formed a perfect oxbow and whose spindly legs, encased in glossy black boots, resembled pipe-stems beneath the enormous featherbed of his paunch. Just seeing him angered Daniel. Such greedy girth was hideous and inhuman in a room of hungry specters.

Steadman looked morose.

"At ease, boys, at ease!" the colonel boomed, and gazed over them, the hesitation of a practiced stump speaker. His voice projected a ponderous oratorical quality as he resumed. "You have volunteered for an undertaking which is of the greatest importance to the noble cause of our great Union." An ingratiating smile reflected the walrus face. "If your mission succeeds . . . and we are confident it will . . . you will be reinstated at your former rank, all charges will be wiped off your records, and your back pay will be restored in full."

A murmur of approval, yet also of suspicion, ran through the ragged figures.

"And, too," the monstrous form said, his promising tone like honey, "you will be issued all new clothing, uniforms, and shoes. Given a separate barracks for a period of rest, good food, and training."

Daniel held up his hand. "What if the mission fails?"

"Should that remote possibility occur," the colonel answered, as disarming as before, "you will be sent back here to finish out your sentences."

"You mean to rot, don't you?" a voice snarled.

Daniel raised his hand again. "Don't we have the right to know what the mission is?"

The well-nourished flesh on the colonel's cheeks flamed a sudden pink. "All I can tell you at this time is that there may be some fighting. Any volunteer who wants to go back to the stockade may do so now, but not later."

Immediately several men turned, muttering, to

the rear. Daniel felt the same pull of mistrust. Why was the colonel so vague? Why didn't the Army use troops, instead of prisoners? Turning his head, Daniel saw the ex-colonel's eyes on him like a bull prod. Daniel looked away, feeling the air of suspense spreading over the room.

"Mister Steadman," the colonel said, clearing his throat, "will be your acting lieutenant in charge."

The volunteers were shuffling outside when Daniel heard Steadman's whispering rasp in his ear: "Are you blind? I tried to warn you. We're going to fight a whole damned guerrilla army!"

Chapter Twenty-Four
MISSION WITHOUT HOPE

Acting Sergeant Wade and acting Lieutenant Steadman halted on the brow of an oak-shaded hill several miles outside Memphis, watched eight wagons—outwardly a small Union supply train lightly defended—file along the Corinth road. Inside each lumbering vehicle, hidden under the bowed hoods of white canvas, rode eight uniformed volunteers armed with shotguns, pistols, and new Spencer repeating rifles that held seven copper-cased .52-caliber cartridges in a tubular magazine in the butt stock and another shell in the chamber. In veteran hands, these could be fired at the rate of twenty-one a minute, seven times faster than the muzzle-loading Springfields, and could kill at up to 800 yards or more.

The battalions of mule-mounted infantry followed at an interval of two miles, ready to rush up should guerrillas attack the train. Scouts ranged ahead.

"I like the idea even less than I did in the beginning," Steadman said, turning his mule down the road. "We're no more than decoys. If the scouted infantry is slow coming up, we could be swarmed under. You can't expect much of bandbox garrison troops who've never smelled battle smoke."

Daniel couldn't share his superior's pessimism. The clean sky and the rolling wooded hills had a special vividness for him today, as though his eyes had been opened for the first time and he saw the world glorified.

"Colonel," Daniel said, "if the guerrillas. . . ."

Steadman interrupted him. "Even in the field remember to address an officer properly."

"Sorry, Lieutenant. Only I think of you as colonel . . . . If the guerrillas don't attack, we go back to prison."

"Oh, I think they'll come out," Steadman

prophesied. "Our first objective is to let them know we're around. Make ourselves as conspicuous as possible. Travel leisurely. Chunk up big campfires at night. It should be hard for our friends to resist such tempting bait. They haven't let a single wagon through in six weeks, and the Memphis-Corinth railroad, which they cut two months ago, is still out of operation."

Daniel learned more as the morning shortened, details told Steadman at headquarters. One self-styled Colonel Daggett, who rode a handsome white horse, led the guerrillas, composed of Union and Confederate deserters, conscription evaders, outlaws, horse thieves, robbers, and murderers. They also terrorized plantation families and small farmers. Union intelligence estimated the raiders' strength between three and four hundred men, possibly five hundred, mounted on splendid horseflesh stolen in Mississippi and Tennessee.

"The Union would go a long way toward soothing civilian tempers if we smashed Daggett," Steadman said. "About all the Army's been able to do for their protection is garrison a few blockhouses out a ways from Memphis on the main road."

Twilight was near when the train creaked up to the first blockhouse, a rough, two-story log affair manned by a detail of careless infantrymen. Steadman chose to bivouac nearby and corral his wagons pioneer style, keeping the mules under heavy picket guard.

The star-dappled night, the voices, the smells, and the supper fires gleaming and crackling, awakened in Daniel the larking Shiloh days and the spring-scented march from the river to Vicksburg, by far the best times of his life. These men, still prisoners, had lost in some degree their haunted looks of the stockade, although the new uniforms hung on their hard, kneaded bodies. These men had seen Iuka, Corinth, Chickasaw Bluffs, and Vicksburg. After their privations at Memphis, no man complained tonight, for they were soldiers again.

Of all the volunteers, Daniel thought, only Willie Oats appeared unmarked by imprisonment. His face was round and fair, indicating that he had contrived to eat well, and his hands looked soft and smooth. And Daniel knew why. Every company had one. The deadbeat, the shirker, one who courted the favor of officers.

While Daniel and the lieutenant cooked their suppers, Oats asked to share their fire. Steadman's reserved nod brought Oats in at once. In a short time he struck up a flattering tone of conversation: "Lieutenant, sir, could you use a good orderly?"

"It should be obvious that I don't require the services of even an incompetent orderly,"

Steadman replied, spinning him an old soldier's discernment.

"Reason I asked, Lieutenant, sir, is that one time I attended a cultivated gentleman like yourself, and it happened he was a colonel."

Steadman laughed outright. "By God, soldier, you should be in politics. But it will get you no favors from me." Next, as though relenting his short manner: "You have brass. I hope you fight as well."

Oats, who seemed to like the impression he had made, nursed his silence until after supper, when he made a trip to his blanket roll and back, his nimble hands hiding something. He glanced about, a model of discretion, and extended a bottle of whiskey toward the lieutenant. "Like a drink, sir?"

Steadman looked up, unprepared. He shut his lips together, and his eyes, focusing on the bottle, became fixed there. His mouth stirred; he wet his lips. Thirst leaked through into his steady concentration.

"Pour that out, soldier," he said sternly, rising. But the look of desire he fastened on the bottle seemed to counter his command. He appeared to grapple with himself before he turned deliberately away. Oats did not move.

"You heard the order," Daniel said. "Pour it out."

Winking, Oats lifted the bottle to slip it inside

his blouse. Daniel gripped his arm. "The lieutenant can't handle whiskey. That's why he's with us. Pour it out."

Oats, bearing a painful grimace, pulled the cork, upended the bottle, and let the contents gurgle out on the ground.

"That'd better be all of it," Daniel said.

"Every last drop," Oats swore, exhibiting a face of innocence. "Search my blanket roll."

While the wagon train continued its ambling advance next day, Daniel eyed the rolling land on all sides, his response a mixture of pleasure and distrust. Most of the cotton had been picked. Only now and then did he see darkies in the distance. The South was raising more corn than cotton since Daniel had tramped out of Memphis with the Coon Creek Company almost two years ago. Old fields lay brown with autumn. A mule-riding farmer passed, close-mouthed, uncommunicative, in a hurry to get on when Lieutenant Steadman tried to question him. For all the lack of activity on the road, Daniel could sense the movements of a soft-footed district, alive behind the rises and in the dark, tangled woods. Wood smoke scented the slight northern breeze. He liked that smell; it reminded him of fall, back home, and it went with this drowsy country, now aflame in scarlet and gold.

Fresh hoof tracks pitted the orange-colored road ahead. George Pogue, the burly farrier, dismounted to see. "They came out of the woods, here, and went back," he told Steadman. "About ten riders."

"When?"

"Hour or so ago. Rode shod horses."

"More civilians than we've seen in two days," Steadman observed, and turned to Daniel. "Perhaps I'd better send word back to our support. No . . . ," he said uncertainly, "that would serve no purpose." He took a deep breath and rubbed his mouth and chin, looking somewhat pale.

"You all right, Lieutenant?" Daniel asked.

"Oh, yes. I was thinking of the next blockhouse. I want to get there before dark."

At noon Daniel rode ahead with Uriah Bates to take the point. Dense stands of oaks hugged both sides of the road, too thick for flankers to penetrate. The few scattered farmhouses Daniel saw looked deserted, untouched by the war. Once a man on foot hurried across a distant meadow, looking over his shoulder at the Yankees. There wasn't a flicker of life on the road. Although no fighting had occurred through here, the region was evidently strangling in the coils of three years of raiding and suppression.

"Creepy country," Bates said. "Just the same, it beats rottin' in jail." Rest and food had scarcely improved his sallow coloring or put weight on his rake-thin body. From time to time he rubbed the raw-looking letter D branded on his right cheek. He was, Daniel thought, a calmly bitter man who went about his duties because they had to be done.

"I was in the room that day when the captain questioned you," Daniel said. "Is it any better back home?"

"Don't know. Been no word of any kind in a year."

Daniel jogged his head, understanding. Nor had he. He had been told that no regulations existed against the prisoners receiving letters, except they never got any.

"I'll tell you something, Wade. I'd do about anything to be a free man again. Just hope we get in one whale of a big fight."

That afternoon Daniel and Bates rumbled across a narrow bridge that spanned a deep ravine. Half a mile farther, the squatty shape of a blockhouse jutted up beside the road. Bates pulled in his mule. Daniel did likewise, seeing blue shapes scattered around the doorway like broken stick figures.

"I'll wait here," he said, his sick fury welling up. "Go back and tell the lieutenant."

In a minute Lieutenant Steadman charged up and dismounted, Bates whipping his mule to stay even. Inside the blockhouse lay the rest of the tiny garrison, amid a clutter of food and utensils. The attack, coming at breakfast time, had been executed efficiently to the last man. Steadman went outside, looking pale and distracted. Many hoofs had pitted the earth all around the blockhouse. He swept his gaze about, murmuring in irony: "More than ten, wouldn't you say?"

When the train arrived, he circled it around the blockhouse, ordered the men inside the wagons to stay out of sight, and hastened the drivers to form a burial detail. His agitation of the morning returned. He strode back and forth, gesturing and talking. "Did it ever occur to you, Wade, that there's something grotesque and bizarre about this hideous damned war? I've seen men stop and lift the hand of a dying Confederate to give him a sip of water, the thing he wanted most in the world. I've seen the same Good Samaritan rip open the belly of a helpless old farmer who'd stumbled over his sword, too weary to fight. . . . It's a farce . . . a pageant of cruel contradictions . . . . The Rebels send out a handsome young officer lofting a flag of truce. His voice is pleasantly soft to the ear and chivalric . . . 'Sir, I have the honor to convey a request from my commanding officer for a one hour truce so both sides may remove their wounded.' I've heard those exact words. Our charity toward one another is, indeed, touching . . . . Yet the South starves our men at Andersonville, and we return the compliment in pest holes like Camp Douglas,

in slave pens like the one we know at Memphis.
. . . Now this. Cold-blooded murder. These
poor fellows were obviously taken by surprise.
So why couldn't they have been made prisoners?"

For emphasis, Steadman faced Daniel at close
quarters, his black eyes glittering indignation, his
once handsome, tragic features inches away.
Daniel leaned back. Steadman reeked. He was
near drunk.

"Answer me, soldier," the lieutenant was saying, and he tugged at Daniel's sleeve. "Did that
ever occur to you?"

Motion across the field, beyond the blockhouse, attracted Daniel's eye. A horseman, it was,
waving a white flag as he loped toward the
wagon train.

Steadman swayed slightly. "My God," he
moaned, "even here!"

"It's no truce flag," Daniel said.

Steadman crossed his arms and struck an
exaggerated pose of dignity. "Escort him in."

"Wait, Lieutenant. You don't want him to see
inside our wagons. Let me meet him out a piece."
Daniel's mind raced. *Neither would it be wise
for the enemy to see Steadman in his condition.*

An amiable expression curved along the
lieutenant's mouth. "Very well, Wade. Hop to it."

Waiting outside the ring of wagons, Daniel
had plenty of time to study the flag-bearer's
variegated get-up—gray slouch hat, blue blouse,

red shirt, butternut jeans, and cavalry boots. He rode a high-stepping bay gelding that he set to prancing left and right. And, checking up in front of Daniel, he tight-reined his handsome mount so it would shake its fine head.

"Got a little message for you Yankee boys," he drawled.

"I'll take it."

"Be a mite quicker if I ride in. Time's short, young feller."

"This is as far as you go. Where is it?"

In annoyance, the messenger handed him a piece of paper.

Daniel scanned it rapidly

To the officer in charge—
   To avoid needless effusion of blood, I demand the immediate surrender of your wagon train. If you refuse, I will be forced to wipe out your command to the last man, as we did the garrison.
   You have ten minutes.
                                                Colonel Daggett

Turning, Daniel found Uriah Bates and George Pogue posted behind him, their rifles ready.

"Unnecessarily rhetorical, but to the point," Steadman commented after reading the ultimatum. "Tell him his request is refused." His outstretched hand restrained Daniel. "I fear I am not being proper," he said, back in his mocking vein. "Murder must be arranged in the chivalrous style of our noble times." He scribbled a reply on the backside of Daggett's message, murmuring in aside: "We can hold them off until the infantry comes up."

"I don't know about that, Lieutenant," Daniel said. "Look."

Coils of black smoke were rising on the road to the wagon train's rear, black against the sky, growing by the moment.

Steadman watched now, the ironic levity vanishing from his face. "Isn't that about where the bridge crosses the ravine?" he asked.

"Just about."

"We're cut off," the lieutenant said. "Very neatly."

Not even by primitive frontier standards was the blockhouse an acceptable model of defensive sturdiness. Small and hastily built, its notched logs ill-fitting, it had shelter and loopholes for only a dozen or so men below and in the loft. A well, fifty yards away in the open, provided the nearest water, and the pole stock pen, without shed or barn, afforded no protection for the mules. Yet the field of fire from the left was excellent. On that side of the road, where the little post stood, a stump-dotted clearing stretched for several hundred yards. Across the yellow-clay road sloped a broad cotton field.

Steadman's preparations for battle bore the briskness of a veteran field commander. He stationed sharpshooters in the loft at once, pulled his wagons in tighter, unhitched and drove the mules inside the pen, had water brought and canteens filled, all without shifting the men still under cover in the wagons and thus revealing the one real force he had.

The ten minutes passed. Half an hour. Nothing changed across the clearing, nothing disturbed the scarlet wall of oak thickets. About then Daniel missed the lieutenant. His apprehension redoubled when he failed to locate Steadman around the wagons. That left only one place he could be.

Afternoon gloom darkened the blockhouse inside. From above came the hum of the sharpshooters' voices. Daniel stopped dead. The reek of bust-head whiskey was like a smear in the air. In the farthest corner, a figure was slumped face down on a table. Steadman. In disgust, Daniel called the lieutenant's name. Steadman, mumbling, raised up and reached for the bottle before him.

Daniel wheeled to walk out, his gusty anger taking him to the door. Steadman, drunk, was squandering the last chance these men had. Hearing another mumble, more distinct, he flung around to see Steadman lurching to his feet, bewildered, blinking like a sleepy owl. "So's you, Wade . . . . Well, y'll have t' take over, soldier. I'm unfit f'duty." He was, Daniel perceived, actually waiting for Daniel to agree, an infuriating expectancy behind his eyes.

That did it. Daniel lunged across and smashed the bottle against the logs, and, even as Steadman was protesting, Daniel took his shoulders and shook him until his head rolled, then slapped his face back and forth repeatedly. Steadman started to keel backward. Daniel set him in the chair, and, seeing the blockhouse water bucket, he soused dipper after dipper over the lieutenant's head, leaving him spluttering and arm waving.

"Lieutenant," Daniel snarled into the bearded face "you're gonna fight this time. There's no adjutant to blame . . . like at Holly Springs. No other officer . . . . Nothin' to hide behind . . . no bottle to crawl into."

Steadman didn't speak. But his eyes were fully open, and that intolerable expression was gone. Daniel shoved him back in the chair and left him there, a dark, wretched shape.

There was a rustle at the top of the loft ladder. Pogue's square-cut face appeared. "What the hell's goin' on down there?"

"The lieutenant's taking a little nap. Leave him be."

Before long, Daniel, watching the clearing, saw the scarlet thickets open and release coveys of horsemen. Shortly that was all, and Daniel scowled. Instead of the fearsome numbers that Union intelligence had reported, he saw a mere fifty-some riders and a smattering of men afoot, who got behind stumps. The *rap-rap* of their muskets ripped the cool stillness, and the sharpshooters in the loft replied.

As the firing swelled, Daniel saw the lieutenant weave to the doorway. A miserable and irresolute figure, his left hand pressed to his stomach while he leaned against the door frame for support, his disheveled head cocked to the musketry that had aroused him.

A shout caused Daniel to turn back to the clearing. The guerrillas were still forming, although, to a soldier who had lived through these years of war, the horsemen seemed to be performing excessive, time-taking convolutions. Finally they were arrayed on a widely spaced front, and at last they stirred forward. Although in motion, they did not charge. They walked their horses forward.

That was when Daniel, glancing again around the wagon circle, observed the lieutenant yet standing in the doorway. This time he wobbled outside and flattened himself against the blockhouse wall and worked to the corner. The guerrillas, advancing slowly, opened the wagons and knocked bark from the blockhouse logs with their gunfire.

Steadman shrank against the wall, his eyes hawked on the clearing. Across and back, he trailed his gauging and intense concentration. His mouth was pursed. He stopped, and next Daniel saw him look toward him and shout and wave his arms, shouts that the booming volunteers' rifles deadened. With those frantic efforts he struck off his wretchedness. Suddenly he looked taller and straighter, in command of himself. He gestured at the road. Daniel looked. It and the cotton field were empty.

Steadman dropped his hands in frustration. It was almost that each man stood on a high bank and a river's violence separated them, for a lively hail of bullets peppered the open ground between blockhouse and wagons. The lieutenant drew back. Daniel saw him haul in a great gulp of air. A moment and he lurched out, ducking and flinging himself in Daniel's direction. He ran with a terrible determination, arms straining and pumping. He was scant rods away when Daniel saw him flinch. Steadman clutched his chest and, falling forward, stretched out his right hand in entreaty. Daniel and Bates ran forth and dragged him behind a wagon.

The cross-hatched tracery of Steadman's veined face looked pasted on over his ashen skin. His mouth hung. His head sagged to one side. His bloodshot eyes, straight on Daniel, relayed a pleading quality.

"Listen," he panted. "That's just a demonstration out there . . . watch behind. . . ."

Daniel opened the bloody blouse, looked, and gently cleaned the wound, hiding what he saw from his expression, not understanding how the lieutenant could talk.

" . . . soldier! . . . obey the order!" He was coughing blood as Daniel got up.

Across the stumpy clearing, the guerrillas had halted. They continued to raise a fuss, firing and yelling. Still, it was a funny way to fight if you meant business.

A glimmering swiftness struck Daniel. He passed an order. Within a little time, he had half the men on that side shifting to those wagons that faced the cotton field and the road. In the gaps between the vehicles, he stationed men with shotguns.

It seemed an unbearable wait. Yet only a brief time had gone by when Daniel saw the bobbing motions of hurrying riders. Not where he expected, across the cotton field, but to the rear, back down the road leading to the burned-out bridge. Its smoke, much fainter by now, still stained the western sky.

Four abreast, the guerrillas rushed through the first hazy makings of cool twilight, a long column of tough, bearded men. One rode a superb white horse. The volunteers, under the wagon sheets and crouched behind the wheels and in the blockhouse, all trained for this moment, battle-wise fighters who could fire seven times before reloading, waited until the mass of riders drummed within murderous range.

A shotgun bellowed. Instantly sheets of continuous flame spurted from the wagons, and the road changed into a twisting crush of toppling riders and thrashing, whinnying horses. The second and third volleys threw the column back upon itself, piled riders in the road, and sent others, in panic, spurring frantically away, only to smash into oncoming horsemen. By the fifth volley the attackers were breaking across the field, where the Spencers continued to search them out. The fine white horse had no rider.

It was done, and likewise on the clearing side where the other guerrillas had rushed into the repeaters' fire, in its wake the moaning and shrieking from the road. Daniel turned his back on the cries and hastened across to Steadman, who was coughing uncontrollably. Daniel ripped off his own shirt, stuffed it around the hole in the shattered chest. He then took hold of Steadman's heaving shoulders and held him, aching to lend his strength, wondering what was keeping him alive.

"Colonel . . . we licked 'em good. They did just what you said they'd do . . . came in behind. Hear me, Colonel?"

Steadman quieted a little. His black eyes were

enlarged, a distant stare in them. His crusted lips moved: "Address me properly, soldier. Properly."

"I did, Colonel. It's me . . . it's Wade . . . I'm right here with you. We licked 'em good. And we got that Colonel Daggett. We're all free men again! Free!"

Perhaps the meaning got through, perhaps not. Daniel couldn't tell.

There was nothing pleasant about the way the volunteers' commander fought out the last of his life there by the yellow-clay road to Corinth. Eyes open to the evening sky, chin upthrust, one arm out-flung, fingers clenched, toes turned out. Isaac Bolivar Steadman. Colonel of Infantry, sir. United States Army.

Chapter Twenty-Five

FRANKLIN, TENNESSEE, NOVEMBER, 1864

There were many new faces in the old Coon Creek Company when Daniel found it bivouacked at Pulaski, in middle Tennessee. He walked as a hesitant stranger between the rows of tents until he saw three familiar figures. Only then did his gnawing dread disappear. He said no greeting while he stood watching Tim Forehand, Andy Green, and Jesse Nance cooking their dinners, letting them feel his silent attention.

Andy glanced up first, followed by Jesse, and next Tim. Their sprung-eyed stares said he couldn't be real. Then Tim roared—"Holy Moses, look who's back!"—and the threesome charged Daniel, grabbing, mussing, scuffling, whacking him across the back, tickling him in the ribs. Panting, they felt of his new blouse, gawked over his new brogans, and remarked about the raw quality of recruits the regiment was getting these days.

"You're just in time," Andy said when the rumpus subsided. "We're havin' slow deer for dinner."

"Slow deer?" Daniel echoed, smiling.

"It's a new breed the Secesh farmers have hereabouts. It squeals and grunts. It's short-legged. It's got a curly-cue tail and a long snout. Back in Missouri, now, we'd call it a hog, which is what it tastes like."

Following dinner, Daniel related his story bit by bit, and listened to his old comrades. After fighting to Atlanta, the regiment had been detached to Major-General John M. Schofield's command to help keep an eye on General Hood's army, which was marching north since crossing the Tennessee River.

That evening Tim got to talking about how, at a Confederate picket's invitation, he had crossed the lines and attended a country dance during the Atlanta campaign.

"It beat anything I ever did see," he recalled. "The Johnnies dressed me up in civilian clothes, interduced me around as Cousin Tim from Big Shanty. We danced the flat rock and we did the reel. The fiddlin' was fine. A right purty little red-headed girl named Pearl took me in tow. She asked me how many Yankees I'd shot and wasn't the Yankees just awful, so I had to agree, didn't I? So I said . . . 'Reckon I've laid away a brigade or so, Miss Pearl. More or less. I never keep tab, mind you. It ain't genteel. It ain't Christian. Yankees! Why, they're the awfulest, most sorriest critters ever was. They stick bayonets through poor little pickaninnies, make a big fire, and roast 'em alive.' 'How cruel!' she said. 'How cruel! Let's dance, Cousin Tim.' "

"Well, Cousin Tim," Daniel asked, "did you think to tell Miss Pearl about your old wound."

"That's where I made my mistake. I let drop I'd been wounded serious at Vicksburg, and, after a sorrowful look, she said . . . 'I thought all our captured boys was paroled not to bear arms again, and here you have broke your word of honor?' I said . . . 'It just happened I made my escape before the surrender.' How's that for headwork, Dan'l? So we danced the flat rock some more. The fiddlin' was fine. I kinda hated to leave." The fire was down to glowing coals. Daniel felt a touch of chill. "You know," Tim said, deeply musing, "them Rebs are just like you an' me? Like any good ol' boy back home?"

"Tim's got gentle as a lamb," Andy said.

"It ain't that," Tim amended. "I'm just plumb wore out fightin'. I want to go home. Git myself a wife. Settle down. Farm again. Foller a jug-headed mule down the corn rows. I've been a roughneck all my life . . . always in trouble. Maybe God's done give up on me by now."

Daniel had never seen Tim so gloomy and sub-dued. A repentant earnestness enveloped his ruddy face, not unlike the look of a child asking forgiveness for some unintentional hurt he had caused.

"You boys have told me everything except what happened to Seth Coots," Daniel said after a while. "I don't see him around camp."

Andy feigned sorrow. "A sad story. Our own Sergeant Coots has boot-blacked himself into a soft job at headquarters. Carries messages around. Mighty uppity. Dan, we figure he's the one who put that chloroform in your tent."

"I've thought about it, too," Daniel admitted. "Maybe he did. Maybe he didn't. I don't know. There was a bunch in the same business. I met some of 'em in the stockade. Anyway, it's over, and I'm lucky to be back, thanks to one man."

"It will all come to a head in time," Jesse said calmly. "Such things always do."

Daniel's restful reunion was brief. The Army went hurrying off north, and the old sounds of the tramping marches surrounded him once more. On November 30th, in golden Indian summer weather, he was striding up the flinty Columbia pike, thinking of last night's rare fortune at Spring Hill. Johnny Reb, he decided, must be losing his dash. While Confederate campfires burned on their flank—near enough for Daniel to hear the sleepy voices of pickets— the Yankees had slipped through to continue their retreat toward Nashville, when one determined Rebel attack would have cut off Schofield's entire army with its miles of wagons.

Now, as if determined to make up for that unaccountable laxness, shamed and angry, Hood's muttering army crowded the Yankee rear.

"Franklin's up ahead," Jesse said.

Daniel knew. The name carried an almost imaginary meaning for him, a place he had supposed he would never see in wartime. It suggested something bittersweet from the frayed pages of the letter in his blouse, the misty fragrance about a slim, pale face. Major Vandiver had sent Laurel to Franklin in 1862, when the bushwhacker trouble worsened. An odd feeling strengthened in Daniel that maybe everything was changing for the better after the bad times he had undergone beginning at Shiloh. A caution restrained him, too. A soldier lived from day to day, which was why he had survived the ordeal of the stockade, that and because of Colonel Steadman. If a foot soldier found food and shelter, if he fought and yet lived, he ought not, by conscience, to expect more.

Nevertheless, when the regiment clattered to the crest of a hill and he sighted the fringes of the village about two miles away, he could not quiet his rising excitement. Onward he marched past open, rolling fields and pastures, and through the V of shallow forward breastworks, farther on, through a crescent of deep entrenchment, heavily manned, and a cotton gin, and a red brick farmhouse resting on a broad hill. Spread out below huddled the pleasant clutter of Franklin, bounded on the east and north by the looping Harpeth River. In the warm clear sunshine the houses looked neat and comfortable, and church steeples rose like provocative arms above the glistening rooftops.

Below the hill the regiment plodded half a mile into the village. Civilians hurried on the streets. Many peered from windows and gazed from porches and yards, proud, stiff Southern faces watching the Yankees march by. Every young woman's face seemed momentarily familiar to Daniel. But he didn't find her, and his disappointment deepened. Would he know her if he saw her? Well, soon he would be on the other side of the river, trudging north for Nashville. Once there, the regiment would march off somewhere else, to another far-off place, and after that to another.

A courier on horseback galloped past just as the head of the column approached the planked railway bridge over which supply and baggage trains were rumbling. The regiment halted, and the men stood at ease.

"It wasn't this way with Uncle Billy Sherman in Georgia," Andy confided in a tone of injured pride. "We never retreated down there, did we?"

Tim gave an indifferent shake of his head. He had been silent all morning, gloomy and preoccupied.

When the regiment turned about to retrace its march, Andy said: "Old Schofield figures he might need us, after all. Reckon he knows who captured Atlanta."

The plodding Tim smiled at that, but he seemed to be thinking of another thing.

Daniel was scanning the faces in the yards and houses. He'd only make a fool of himself and be turned away, a blue-bellied Yankee inquiring for a Southern girl. That was precisely what he was going to do, however, if there was no battle and the regiment bivouacked here for the night.

Tramping toward the hill south of town, he noticed a white frame house where a plump, middle-aged woman stood on the top porch step. With ostentatious defiance, she draped a Confederate banner across her broad bosom and folded her stout arms, glaring her contempt upon the passing blue files.

"Lady," Andy called, his left hand slanted to one side of his mouth, "you'd better look out. We got orders to charge all works where that flag flies."

Laughter rolled down the tramping ranks.

The militant figure on the porch step stiffened and swelled to more menacing proportions. "Black Republicans!" she hissed. "Black Republicans!"

"No, ma'am," Andy spoke back. "Just Missourians. We're from Foley's Prairie!"

As Andy's saucy reply died, another woman came out the front door. She crossed the porch quickly, her face partly in shadow as she took the flag-bearer's arm, a restraining gesture. No— Daniel saw—not a woman. A slim girl. Her eyes flecked inquiringly over the marchers; she went to the front step, and, as she faced them, sunlight fell across light brown hair and touched it with gold.

An explosive recognition burst in Daniel. He

waved violently and shouted Laurel's name. The capering marchers shouted, also, overriding his voice. Laurel—it *was* Laurel!—waved back. He could see her face, vivid and striking. She turned her head this way and that to distinguish the voices. Daniel shouted again, and again he could not be heard through the score of voices in front and behind him. By that time the company had passed the house.

Daniel's last glimpse was of the stout woman, her flag flaunting forgotten, like a fluttering mother hen, ushering Laurel toward the door. Daniel's mind beat fast. That woman—she must be an aunt. The major's sister. Her proud carriage and domineering manner reminded him of the major.

So the Coon Creek Company marched south on the pike and broke ranks below the hill where the red farmhouse stood, astir with couriers and officers. After mess, while his comrades dozed and lounged on the grass, smoking and waiting, Daniel watched the small white house the regiment had passed. No one stirred around it.

He watched, in a tension of joy and frustration. There Laurel was, no more than two hundred yards away, and he could not go there. Not now. Provost guards walked the pike to discourage deserters and stragglers, always a sign of approaching battle. Another was the presence of Illinois and Ohio regiments, also resting off the pike in reserve. He hoped fervently that the Johnnies wouldn't attack today. Once darkness fell, there was no provost guard alive who could stop him from going to that house.

The afternoon was still young when Daniel observed that, except for stragglers, a rider leading a lame horse, an infantryman hobbling in on swollen feet, the pike was empty. Once in a while the brassy *tom-tom* of cannon crashed convulsively to the south: the Union rear guard firing on the Confederate advance. Sounds that kept creeping closer.

Sergeant Seth Coots paused *en route* from the headquarters farmhouse, the first time Daniel had seen him since Vicksburg. He wasn't so slouchy as formerly, but he was still self-important. For a moment, it occurred to Daniel that Coots, always an outsider at Foley's Prairie, always avoided, delayed out of loneliness because he wanted to talk to someone from home. That perception rose and fell as Coots, his overbearing manner sliding back, hesitated in front of Andy.

"What's the guff from headquarters?" Andy asked, his dislike evident. "There gonna be a fight?"

"We," Coots answered, his air that of one in receipt of superior knowledge, "don't calculate Hood will attack us here."

"Oh, *we* don't!" Tim muttered peevishly. "Then

why've the Johnnies follered us all the way from Spring Hill?"

"They'd be fools to come across them open fields out yonder."

Tim raised up. "I don't recollect that open ground ever stopped 'em in Georgia. At Ezra Church or Peachtree Crick. Or when they charged across the briar patch at Shiloh, time after time."

"You smart alecks wanted my opinion," Coots retorted, his head lofty. "I told you." He swung to go, halting when he noticed Daniel. His eyes popped in surprise. An undetermined expression formed on his extremely narrow mouth.

"Hello, Seth," Daniel said.

"Hello," Coots said, low, and walked stiffly away, his course taking him toward the Illinois regiment.

Darkly Tim muttered after him: "It ain't right for the likes of him to strut around, when Amos an' Obadiah an' a heap more good boys are long gone." His lips squeezed together, and he studied the tip of one scuffed brogan, bitter and melancholy.

"I wonder," said Jesse, contradicting without meaning to, "I wonder if we can say who's got a right to live and who ought to die? Rightly, can any of us boys?"

Tim didn't reply. Neither did his expression change.

Although no wave of religious conversion had swept the regiment as the newspapers said it had in the Southern camps, the Coon Creek boys, victorious and from the self-reliant West, had grown more reverent since Shiloh and Vicksburg. So Daniel had noted upon his return. They spoke often of Brother Winn, invalided home with camp fever, of him and his fiery sayings and prophecies, as if he alone understood their tenuous relation to the Almighty.

It was middle afternoon when Daniel climbed the hill to look. Half a mile away the rear guard was entering the forward rifle pits. Tim, following to watch beside him, said: "The Johnnies are comin' sure as shootin'. You know it. I know it. Anybody with a lick of horse sense would know it." He released a laugh, humorless and dry. "Anybody but generals and Seth Coots, cuss his hide." His voice lost disdain, softened. "Remember Mattie Hull? I been thinkin' about her. How you an' me fought that night. That was all my doin'. I deserved to git licked." His ruddy, reminiscent face was warm. "Reckon that was the best fight I ever had, Dan'l. The best. I was mighty sweet on Mattie. Except she had her sights on better prospects. She's smart. Don't blame her. She knew I'd never 'mount to much. Just a stump-headed farmer . . . . An' to think she married a no-good coward . . . that Simms fella. Him that had his teeth pulled so he couldn't

358

bite catrages." Tim looked hurt and bewildered. Mattie Hull's decision, actually, was beyond his simple way of reasoning.

"Tim," Daniel said, narrowly eying his face, "are you ailing?"

"Naw. Never been sick a day in my life. Been mighty lucky. I know it. Recollect how the bullets flew like hailstones at Shiloh, an' the guns sounded like a thunderstorm comin' up?" He shook his head, wondering. "Me, I never got a scratch all these years. A body just can't git by on a rabbit's foot forever. It wears out. Dan'l, I don't mind tellin' you, I'm plumb scared." He was fumbling at his pocket. "Here . . . keep this for me."

Daniel looked down at Tim's polished watch, fat on its stout chain, and up into Tim's unashamed face, seeing its open uncertainty.

"Keep it? You don't need me to . . . Tim!" Daniel couldn't stop him.

Tim pressed his possession into Daniel's right hand and folded Daniel's fingers around it, and said: "Just keep it for me. You might want to know the time of day, perfesssor."

He was already striding away, and he hadn't called Daniel "perfessor" since the pranking Shiloh camp days.

The warm afternoon ebbed. Not a shot disturbed the golden distance. In the forward posts the riflemen and cannoneers crouched, watching south. No sign of life ruffled the pastoral scene beyond them.

Daniel cocked his head. *Was that the roll of drums on the mild November breeze? Mocking the autumn-yellow peace of harvest time?* The long, unbroken moments piled up. Minutes slipped by; the dim sound struck again. Heavier. Distinct. A roll. A *r-r-rump*. Unmistakable. So the Johnnies were coming as they always had. He knew. He'd fought them too long not to know.

At last, when the farthest hill sprang alive, it happened suddenly, bobbing with swells of cavalry and infantry. Daniel breathed through open lips, spellbound. He saw the ranking regiments come until they filled a broad front. He saw them writhe and halt, formed. Just a little longer they seemed to ready themselves, to dress their lines. Now, in perfect order, they stepped forward to shrilling bugles and throbbing drums. Somewhere bands were playing. Couriers galloped back and forth. That wasn't mere cavalry on the wings, but gallant men-at-arms. Those fluttering bright banners weren't mere battle flags, but the blood of brave men unfurled. The lowering sun was flashing on thousands of bayonets and rifle barrels. A two-mile tide of grandeur marching steadily down the heights to destruction.

Daniel Wade could not think of the Rebels as foes. He could feel no less than admiration and regret. Impulsively he wished they would turn back and save themselves. Their splendid sight lifted him up. Something was about to pass from the face of the earth that no man would see again. An age. A placid way of life. Pageantry, gentility—the last of high valor. In the next rushing minute that brave, precise magnificence would be shattered and mangled.

Still, one last precious pause was left them. The brilliant columns halted and deployed into two lines. A shell burst among them, raising a circle of dirty smoke. When Daniel heard the wild *yee-haas* and the spat of musketry from the Union outposts, he went down the hill to his company, a dense dread upon him.

After the Coon Creek boys fell in and stood at ease, it was the same as waiting for a storm to break. The musketry announcing the far-off rattles and rumbles, the artillery roaring out peals of thunder. Often men's voices told how a battle was going. Daniel listened. Deep *hurrahs* and shrill yells joined, one then the other dominating. He could feel the awful suspense, almost see the fighting. Voice by voice, the *hurrahs* fell more feeble, and the piercing Confederates' cries rose and kept rising.

Dead silent, the Coon Creek Company waited. Soon a courier spurred down the hill to the regiment's colonel.

"Ten-shun! For-waard! Harch!"

On the double-quick the regiment charged up the pike. Just rods ahead, Daniel saw the routed bluecoats, and behind them and mixed with them, climbing, shooting, thrusting, panted hundreds of wild-yelling demons in homespun yellow. He heard fleshy *thumps* and sudden cries as the vanguard of the panic-stricken men ran into the ranks ahead of him, and abruptly the Missourians were knocking headlong runners out of their path, striding over sprawled figures between them and the Rebels.

Daniel ripped out a yell. The entire Coon Creek outfit was screeching full voice, that high-wrought yell of the old Missouri frontier, ironically more Rebel-sounding than Union, and more wild Indian than Rebel.

Charging uphill to the farmhouse, the regiment loosed a volley and received a shuddering volley in return. Now each side, rifles empty, rushed forward, a seething mass of savage, cursing men, clubbing with rifles, thrusting with bayonets.

A shaggy butternut shape tried to run Daniel through. Steel grated as he turned the thrust and smashed his musket butt to the bearded face. Despite the continuous din, he could hear Tim Forehand squalling like a cougar. The two masses pulled apart some paces, reloading hurriedly. In seconds, sputtering volleys commenced, and the battle roared again. More rushing men filled the Union regiment's gaps. More blue ranks were charging up the other side of the pike.

Daniel fought in his own smoky hell. Through it now and then, like battle scenes from an old history book, he glimpsed snatches of what was happening. The Johnnies had breached the main line. Their inspired surge now halted, they were falling back, step by step, toward the trenches, strewing dead and wounded, flags and guns. Another fight was snarling east of the pike, by the cotton gin. Beyond the breastworks men charged whooping through the smoke.

He shifted right with the company, aware of its gapped ranks, and flushed graycoats around the farmhouse and a little brick kitchen. The Coon Creek boys charged deeper into the back yard and with clubbed muskets moved around parked supply wagons and outbuildings. They took back a battery, west of the smokehouse.

Sometime later Daniel crouched in the main line. Across the smoky field and through the waning light the Johnnies came again, always yelling. Some clambered over the littered ditch and reached the trench, fighting over the top. Some, hugging the outside, crawled to the breastworks and fired under the head logs upon the works. Daniel fought likewise, poking his rifle through and firing quickly, at random, exposing only his hands.

A lull. He lay panting against the gouged earth,

watching the head log above him. As the quiet continued, he turned his eyes past the still shapes beside him. One wore on his collar the single gold star of a Confederate major. Searching fearfully, Daniel looked on down the line. Recognition dented his dull exhaustion—he saw the black-grimed faces of Andy and Jesse. But he didn't see Tim.

There was a little stir during the respite as more Union men crawled into the breastworks. Daniel saw cooks, clerks, servants, orderlies. Headquarters was sending every man who could fire a musket. Seth Coots was one.

The Johnnies were yelping again, and Daniel fired under the head log above him, jerked down, and reloaded. He looked up to see a Confederate officer trying to force his red horse over the barricade. Daniel pointed his rifle. He felt paralyzed, unable to fire. It was murder, the Rebel a helpless target, waving a puny saber. While Daniel hesitated, bullets toppled the man into the trench, and his riddled charger sagged, its fore hoofs hanging over the logs.

Why do they keep coming? Again and again Daniel asked himself, while the afternoon shrieked and thundered itself out and the gray lines continued to charge and reel. He'd lost count of the separate assaults long ago, and he'd never seen the dead so thick. In windrows, in stacks, some upright in the ditch, no room to fall.

Maybe darkness would end it. Yet, when darkness lowered, they came still, stumbling over the dead and wounded, their gun flashes stabbing the murk, these fierce-yelling men and boys, brave a thousand times.

The night was well advanced when the firing sputtered out. Daniel lay exhausted against the front side of the trench. There was no rest for him even then; in the unreal stillness his deafened ears could not shut out the mounting cries and moans of the wounded. He had a sensation of suffocating, of sinking in a slough of eternal suffering. Men were calling for water, for aid, the whole ones for missing friends. He stirred, remembering, and started feeling his way over and around the dead and wounded filling the trench, calling Andy and Jesse and Tim, and was relieved when, close by, Andy answered: "Over here, Dan. We're lookin' for you and Tim."

A swaying lantern threw wavering yellow light. Daniel gave a start when a man almost under him mumbled for water. Daniel uncapped his canteen, raised it, and looked into the face of Seth Coots, grayish with shock. He looked badly hurt. His forehead was ridged. Seeing the suffering face and its imploring helplessness, Daniel felt only pity. Coots drank deeply, gratefully. "Ahh . . . ahh. . . . You, Daniel?" His voice said he did not believe himself.

Andy and Jesse looked down from the rear of

the trench. With their help, Daniel lifted Coots out. His voice pitched upward in a rending cry of pain as they laid him down behind the trench; it reached higher and higher. Daniel strained against the sound. Coots was gasping and struggling for breath. He called again for water. Daniel gave him a swallow while Jesse lifted his head. That was all they could do for him now. Daniel stood up, saying: "We'd better find Tim."

Coots reached out suddenly, a staying motion. Daniel saw, but his intention was to go. Jesse, who was watching Coots, spoke in a peculiar tone: "Dan . . . I think he wants to tell you something."

Coots moved his head up and down. Daniel had to kneel to hear him as Coots murmured— "I wasn't the only one in on it."—and ran out of breath. "Vicksburg . . . tradin' with the Johnnies." Coots sounded calmer. He had to reach deep within himself for his next breath. "Provost guards got hot after us. So I put that bottle in your tent." Andy and Jesse were bent down, listening, too. "Changed my mind a little later," Coots said, his voice trailing off. In the poor light his face showed a fixed concentration. Suddenly he gasped out: "Honest to God, I did! When I went back, it was too late. Th' truth, Dan."

Daniel got to his feet, too dulled by weariness to know what he felt. Gradually a thought trickled through: *It's not important any more.*

Two stretcher-bearers, the front man swinging a lantern, hurried up to the trench. Andy called to them, and they placed Coots on the stretcher and took him away.

A myriad of glowworms seemed to be milling over the fields where Hood's men had charged. Torches and lanterns bobbed as well behind the Union lines. The farmhouse was alight; men dashed in and out. At last Daniel could believe that the fighting was finished.

The three Coon Creek boys began searching for Tim. Trying to retrace the company's advance was tedious and, at best, half blind. When a soldier grumbled that a retreat order was imminent, Andy and Jesse decided to hurry to the pike, where the regiment was first engaged. Daniel was to work toward them.

Grievous horror wrung him as he scanned the ghastly faces, set in terrible expressions. One moment the light would be sallow, then dim, then gone as the torch or lantern holder passed. When a man put down his lantern to assist stretcher-bearers, Daniel snared the light.

He could look faster now. He scouted past the recaptured battery, past the smokehouse, and around the brick kitchen. Every few moments he would call Tim's name. Sometimes the moaning cries muffled his voice. Despairing, he thought of the wagons and commenced searching back and forth between them. All through here the

Coon Creek boys had fought furiously, taking and giving. And some lay there, still.

On the north side of the wagon park, he came upon another blue corpse, that of a major, hatless, disheveled, fallen forward, face turned to one side—tawny mustache and clipped goatee. Daniel needed a moment to convince himself, even when he knew that Stark Hooper lay there. It was Hooper. Yes, it was. Hooper faced north, no weapon in his hands or close by. He had, Daniel discerned, simply quit the roaring fight as he had at Shiloh, except that a bullet had taken him in the back.

Across the night, Daniel heard his name being called. Andy was shouting for him. Daniel opened and closed his mouth, silenced by an instinctive protest. On impulse he put down the lantern and tugged Hooper's body about so that he faced south, in the direction of the battle, and not understanding why he did it. Andy shouted again.

Daniel, standing, sensed that something was lacking. His hurried eye catching Hooper's sword in its steel scabbard, he drew the saber and fixed it in Hooper's right hand. Why? Daniel didn't know. His honest regret wasn't much. Nothing like the Swink boys. For them it had been grief.

Now, swinging the lantern back and forth, he called Andy and heard his answering shout. Andy's walk was slack and heavy when he tramped into the light. He said: "We found him.

Daniel stood quite still.

"Over on the pike . . . he's dead."

Looking straight into Andy's eyes, Daniel knew that neither had expected to find Tim alive. Daniel hung his head. His gaze fell on Hooper's body. After a moment, he gestured downward.

Andy stared. "Him? I never figured he'd get it. Us, maybe. Never him."

"Looks like he was going forward."

Andy continued to stare, a longer look that might be suspending judgment. But when he turned, he said—"Guess so."—in a voice that brushed indifference, moving as he spoke.

Tim Forehand lay on the edge of the pike, not far from the front door of the farmhouse. His forage cap was gone, his sandy hair was tousled in the lantern's glow, which gave him a boyish look, still, and his face was upturned in that dreadful sleep that Daniel had seen so many times.

He knelt. A cruel acceptance smote him. A resignation. All at once his throat caught, and, when he rose, his cheeks were wet.

The three carried Tim's body out of the way to the front yard and assembled his few personal effects. Afterward, they stood near the pike, drenched in the after-battle stupor of extreme exhaustion and indecision. No one spoke. Only at the farmhouse did some aspect of order prevail. Regiments were hopelessly mixed this night. The walking wounded of both sides mingled on the road and straggled downhill toward the village, alive with lights.

Andy and Jesse, presently, went looking for the company. Daniel sat slumped on the grass, having neither the spirit nor inclination to follow them. He wished, almost, that he were dead, too. Piteous wailings pierced the soul. As often as he had heard those suffering sounds, he could never make himself insensible to them.

A strange and unusual light flushed the night, unsteady, somber, unearthly, depressing. In his utter stupefaction, it puzzled him until he saw that the light came from more torches and lanterns around the headquarters farmhouse and the trenches as the Union Army struggled to locate its whole parts and to succor its wounded.

Other lights were bobbing up the pike. Villagers, Daniel saw, shrinking from the terrible sights and sounds, coming on, nevertheless. Women wearing shawls and kerchiefs against the night's chill. A particularly large woman held up a lantern while she peered into the faces of the dead and wounded on the pike. Another woman searched beside her. They went on to another shape, looked down, and shook their heads, and Daniel saw then the face he knew. He was standing at the same time, drawn irresistibly toward them. Across, he heard a firm, older voice say: "Never mind. We will keep on looking."

He stood by them a moment before they were

aware of him. "I guess you're looking for Justin," he said. "I'll help you."

"We want none of your Yankee help, whoever you are," the stout woman sang out, training her belligerency upon him.

Daniel disregarded her. He was intent on Laurel's face, watching it change, her incredulity lessening, her eyes narrowing and now widening in recognition.

"Aunt Cordelia," she objected. "I know him . . . he's from home . . . he's Daniel Wade. If he can help us find Justin!"

"Hood's army has pulled back," Daniel said.

She took his arm. "A wounded soldier from Justin's company told us he fell along here this afternoon."

"Come on," Daniel said. When he reached for the lantern, Aunt Cordelia stiffened and would have drawn away had he not taken hold of the wire handle. She let go reluctantly.

He tracked his mind back over those fiery moments of the afternoon, and led off southward, past the farmhouse. At every step the thicker lay the Confederates and the greater the night's confusion. Commands rang, in them the urgency of a battered army trying to rise from its death grapple and reform. Here and there looters worked swiftly.

Daniel saw a man in blue—unaware of their approach—rise, dangling a watch. At the same moment Laurel, uttering a small cry of discovery, ran forward. The looter whirled. Daniel shouted and rushed him. Like a cat, the man fled across the pike. After several strides, Daniel gave up the futile chase.

"You Yankees kill us, then you rob our dead," Aunt Cordelia intoned.

Laurel had dropped to her knees. She was crying. Not an arm's stretch away lay Justin Vandiver, whose watch the looter had stolen. Captain Vandiver . . . three gold bars on the collar of his blood-soaked blouse. Daniel feared he was dead. However, when Laurel touched her brother's face, he groaned and stirred.

Daniel slid his arms under Justin, rose, and started down the pike, surprised at his own strength. Laurel tried to hold up Justin's head, while Aunt Cordelia barged briskly along on the other side, trailing advice: "Now, Laurel, we must get the kettle on first thing . . . tear up some sheets. . . . Find Doctor Buford. . . . Young man, I don't mind saying that I would prefer anyone but a Yankee carried my only nephew to his bed."

"Ma'am," Daniel said coldly, "you'd better think about Justin, instead of yourself." He was of a mind to tell her the worst—that Justin was nearly dead.

"Young man . . . ," she persisted.

"Aunt Cordelia," Laurel's voice fluted up, all

patience gone, "will you please be still? He *is* helping us."

Below the hill, Daniel saw a line of torches across the pike, where provost guards blocked a milling crowd of wounded and stragglers from going on to the village. He halted.

"Why in the world are you stopping?" Laurel's aunt demanded.

"Guards are blocking off the pike. If they see me, they won't let you through. Turn out the lantern, Laurel." She did, and he took them off the pike through the afternoon bivouac of his regiment, a circling detour that brought them in not far from the woman's lighted house.

Aunt Cordelia seized command at once. She directed Daniel to lay Justin on a low couch in the parlor. He had no more than done so, when she turned on him like a surly bear. "Now get out!" she ordered.

His amazement yielded to flashing anger. "Not yet," he said, and bent down to assist Laurel, who was struggling to remove her brother's blouse.

"Young man," the loathing voice said, "I have ordered you out of my house. Now leave!"

Laurel's high-pitched dismay lifted across the room. "Aunt Cordelia, bring something . . . he's bleeding." Her aunt stood graven with determination. The great mounds of her breasts heaved. "Aunt Cordelia!" At Laurel's cry, she busied herself by scurrying across the hall to the bedroom.

When Daniel saw the wound, he didn't say anything to the women. He used the next minutes doing what he could. Justin's shattered chest and faint breathing held an irrevocable ending. Parts of the early afternoon fighting pieced together in Daniel's mind, and he was depressed by what he knew now. His regiment had fought Justin's on the pike; very likely the Coon Creek Company had even fought Justin's company of local Confederates. Missourians against Missourians. Foley's Prairie against Foley's Prairie. It all left him sickened anew.

After some time, new sounds found their way into the still room. Men tramping past on the pike. Hoarse voices. The *clop* of teams and rumbling wagons, their wheel rims grinding on the hard Tennessee road, shaking their cargoes of moaning wounded. Sounds that meant he would have to leave soon.

"Young man," Aunt Cordelia said, "get another bucket of water." She seemed to have forgotten her earlier aversion of him.

He hurried through the kitchen and out to the well. Here, in the open night, he could hear the marching columns distinctly. Fumbling in the darkness, he released the bucket on its rope, let it *plop* and sink, pulled up, and filled his bucket.

He heard the sobbing the instant he entered the kitchen. It was a young woman's unbroken, convulsive grief, and terrible to hear. Hurrying to the parlor, he saw Cordelia with her arms around Laurel while they gazed down at the bloodless face on the couch. Daniel was at a loss what to do. How could they understand how he felt? And just how would he tell them? As he hesitated, boots stomped the porch. Abruptly the door was shoved open. It banged the wall, and he saw three provost guards crowding inside.

"Clear out, soldier," the first guard ordered, and he waved a pistol to underscore his command. "We're pulling back across the river. What're you doin' here, anyway?"

Daniel inclined his head at the couch. "I brought him here. He just died." Delaying, Daniel spoke to Laurel: "I'm mighty sorry." In his ears the words fell back on him as chaff.

Laurel didn't seem to hear him or to be aware of him. She was looking past him toward the guards. A resistless force was beginning to materialize behind her grief.

"Come on," the guard bellowed, motioning with the pistol.

Something in Laurel's manner caused him to break off. She stood straight and unafraid. *Beautiful, too,* Daniel thought. The other guards grew still, also. They all did an unexpected thing. They snatched off their forage caps, and, in that moment they looked not like soldiers, but the awkward farm boys they used to be.

"*Yankees*," Laurel breathed, giving the term a peculiar emphasis, quite low, heard just above the steady *crunch* of feet outside on the pike. "*Yankees*. . . . You dare come here, after what you have done to my brother? Break into our home? But you will never beat us. I hate you . . . I hate you *all!*"

The pure hatred her voice sent was real and encompassing. Daniel was feeling and thinking that as he stepped through the doorway, ahead of the guards.

At eleven o'clock that night, by Tim Forehand's round-faced watch, General Schofield had withdrawn his punished army across the Harpeth River behind his baggage and supply trains, and Daniel Wade had rejoined the remnant Coon Creek Company. A chill dawn was approaching before they bivouacked on the stony Nashville road, made fires, and boiled coffee. No one said a word until the coffee was steaming in the tin cups.

"Dan," Andy asked, "you still figure Seth Coots went back for that bottle of chloroform?"

Daniel blew on his coffee and sipped it at thoughtful length, holding the cup between his hands for warmth. In Jesse's eyes he saw the same questioning skepticism.

"Seth didn't have to tell us anything," Daniel said. "But he did. He knew I couldn't prove he did it. Yes, I reckon he told the truth."

Jesse looked surprised. "Why? Why?"

"I don't know exactly," Daniel said. "Maybe because he didn't try to blame it on somebody else. On a dead man, say."

Chapter Twenty-Six

MISSOURI, 1865

Missouri stood warm and bright, deep and rich with spring. April breezes rustled the bluegrassed pastures. The three young Union men hurried without seeming to or saying so, just eye-feasting soldiers coming home. Gone were their bravado, their innocence. Each had experienced a lifetime, compressed in camps, on marches and mangled fields, tramping humid Southern valleys, stony hills, and wilderness woods. Each had left a great deal of his being in field hospitals and in long, shallow trenches.

After Franklin and Nashville, Hood's broken army had retreated and the war in the West was over, save for skirmishes and garrison duty and the waiting, and now that was finished, too.

They strode through Foley's Prairie with hardly

a pause, up the wooded slopes north of town, and followed the dusty road by the Vandiver farm. They stared at the chimneys standing forlornly above the ruins of the Great House, and asked Daniel to tell them again how it had happened back in 1862. Activity hummed behind the rampart of giant trees, hammering and sawing. Daniel walked faster, the hurry gnawing at him again.

Andy Green's turn-off came first. He stopped and swung his bag a time or two. They had been together too long and experienced too much to make parting speeches. Yet something lived powerfully behind Andy's black eyes, a going back.

"Come over," he said. When Jesse and Daniel nodded and said the same to him, he took sturdy strides down the road to Coon Creek, headed home.

Jesse Nance's fork was next. This side of the turn-off to Swink's Spring, he broke stride and paused. "Well, Dan," he said, facing around, "we made it back home."

"That's something, all right," Daniel said. Both nodded to that and to other things that needed no voice.

"Come over, now," Jesse said.

"I will. Same to you."

"Hope you're in time." After Jesse Nance said that, he turned toward home.

Daniel's haste whipped faster, on a sense of lateness. His father was dying or he was already dead. Brother Winn's letter, which had reached Daniel in camp at Cairo after Lee's surrender, had said that Sam Wade was worse. Come home soon as you can, Daniel . . . . He stretched out, his long-limping, marching stride taking him steadily on. *My*, he thought, *everything's mighty still!* And he realized that was normal. Always his home had been quiet. It had a blessed calm he used to mock, mistaking tranquility for dullness, for weakness, when there was strength all around. He could feel it, and it made him stronger.

By the time he had gone a few rods, he was dog-trotting, a pace he held grimly to the lane. There he turned in, listening for a bark and hoping to see a charging yellow blur and dreading he would not. Clear to the lane's end he hastened, and he had heard no sound and detected no movement.

But as he turned toward the house, he spied the old yellow dog guarding the border of his domain, by the yard's flowering edge, and he heard the strengthless bark of defiance. Daniel ran over to Shep and wooled him, rubbed the gray muzzle for a moment, and hurried ahead.

A woman stepped to the doorway. A stranger wearing rusty black. He had to stare long and hard before he would accept who she was. Miss Josie, it was, the neighborhood's efficient maiden lady, a large, comforting soul, who made it her bounden duty to stay with the grieving.

All momentum forsook him. He took another dragging step, and then stood still, watching the plump face don its calm pretension of well-being.

And so, then, with the old dog whining at his heels, he went on to the house, home too late.

There wasn't a fence corner or shed niche or piece of frayed harness or worn tool that did not bear his father's vivid stamp. Not a pole, gate, or cow path or glade-like pasture, not an animal, and the brown mules most of all, that did not suggest something his dour father had said or done.

Andy and Jesse came the next day. Their steady, familiar voices warmed the empty house. There was laughter, also, and it was good to hear.

On his third night home, after a day spent walking over the neglected farm, marching, marching, it seemed, for comfort, he undressed for bed. Tim Forehand's watch lay on the rough hardwood table. He did not remember leaving it here by his books, but there it was, its round, simple face turned up to him like a gentle reminder.

Next morning he took the watch and tramped over to the Forehand farm on Coon Creek, and stayed for dinner. Two o'clock passed before he limped out on the road to Foley's Prairie and stopped, feeling his refusal deepen. He kicked a clod. He buried his hands in his pockets and turned his eyes over the lush springtime, not seeing much, thinking this was the last duty he wanted to perform, ever. And duty was what it was, no more.

It angered him that the *Citizen*, in a rambling, rhetorical account of Union boys killed at the Battle of Franklin, had accorded Stark Hooper an excess of attention in contrast to that paid Tim and the others:

> . . . Missouri's undaunted 44th regiment had more casualties than all other regiments in Colonel Upydyck's valiant brigade. One half of our courageous company from Foley's Prairie lay dead on the field after an heroic struggle against the hordes of Secession.
>
> Major Stark Chittenden Hooper, the son of Judge and Mrs. W. T. Hooper, was a regimental aide at the time of his gallant death. Major Hooper was a credit to the highest Christian ideals. He will long be remembered as one of Missouri's most promising young men, known for his soldierly courage, for his utter forgetfulness of self in his zeal for state and Union.
>
> As the first captain of our brave volunteer Union company, which also

distinguished itself so nobly at Fort Donalsen, Shiloh, and Vicksburg, in the Atlanta campaign, and on other bloody fields, he was soon called to a higher rank of honor and responsibility, the duties of which he discharged with promptness and fidelity. He cultivated and cherished friendship. . . .

One voice kept reminding Daniel that the war was over and all that had happened to him was past; another played on old loyalties and raked up old injustices. He did not know how long he lagged there, fighting himself, before he overcame his rankling. He would go. If he didn't do so now, he never would.

Going by the Vandiver farm, he heard the busy hammering and sawing again. The sun was dropping, and he hurried past, the unwillingness dogging every step.

The Hoopers resided in a white, lordly, two-story house that frowned from behind a fence of equally white palings and a flower garden of touch-me-nots, roses, and marigolds. On the brick sidewalk wooden boxing protected fragrant locust trees.

Judge Hooper, formal and polite, answered Daniel's knock. His side-whiskers had turned white and the dignified carriage that Daniel remembered was stooped. The gray, reserved

eyes wavered toward recognition, while courte-
ously beholding Daniel's uniform.

"Judge Hooper, I'm Daniel Wade. I was in your
son's company."

The unsmiling countenance altered at once.
"Come in! My apologies, Daniel. I remember you
as a boy, not as a man. I'm afraid the war has
changed us all." He showed the way into the
parlor, and, when Daniel was seated, he said: "I
regret to hear of your father's death . . . and I
hope you are well. I could not but notice your
limp."

"Thank you, sir. Guess I'm like my father in
many ways."

A light step sounded in the hallway, and a
tremulous, weary voice called: "Will, who is it?"
A fragile-looking woman of transparent pale-
ness and unsteady balance came to the parlor
entrance.

"This is Daniel Wade," her husband said, rising
quickly to assist her. "He was"—Judge Hooper
hesitated—"in Stark's company."

Her chin lifted slightly; her eyes took on a
sudden intensity. As she and the judge stood
side-by-side, Daniel could see in each a marked
resemblance to Stark Hooper—the correctness,
the proud bearing, the well-molded looks, and
perhaps a trace of aloofness. But not Stark's cruel
arrogance, not his contempt for humanity. From
these two persons, aged by sorrow, there sprang

an unsuspected kindness that he felt like a hand touch.

"It's most thoughtful of you to come," she said, walking slowly on her husband's arm and holding out her white hand to Daniel. Sitting, she gave Daniel her gracious attention. "I believe you're some years younger then Stark."

"Yes, ma'am."

They passed general pleasantries for a while, without the strain that Daniel had dreaded. He began telling them about the regiment at Fort Donelson and Shiloh, and described the long marches, the heat and the cold, the rain and the mud, and Memphis, Vicksburg, and middle Tennessee, and the Southern rivers and crops he'd seen, and the lost bewilderment of the child-like slaves when freed. He stopped upon realizing that he had been talking for considerable time, as he might have told his own folks, and as yet he had not broached his reason for coming here. In truth, he didn't know how to say it.

There was a waiting on their absorbed faces, an incompleteness he had not filled. Judge Hooper hadn't moved. His wife kept wadding and smoothing a little handkerchief. Their courteous attention, although inward and far away, never left his face.

"I've really come to tell you about Stark," Daniel heard himself saying at last. Their faces stilled, waiting. "I was going to tell you that I was the one who found him," he tried again, directing his voice between them, his eyes on the rose-patterned carpet.

"We've had no details," Judge Hooper said. He turned an oblique look of concern on his wife. "There's been nothing additional in the newspapers."

"Sir," Daniel said, "all I can tell you is that I found Stark where the fighting was thickest. It looked like he was going forward when hit. I remember . . . his saber was in his hand."

Mrs. Hooper was dabbing with the handkerchief and thanking him with her eyes. They were misty and large and remembering, but she wasn't crying. The judge pulled erect, looking grateful. He said: "We're very proud and thankful to learn that. I can't tell you what this means to us, Daniel. Your coming here to tell us. Otherwise, we would never have known."

"Yes, sir. I understand."

"We want to go to Franklin when travel is easier," she said.

"It's pretty country," Daniel said. "The hills. . . ." He stood, finished. He felt much better, enormously lifted up. *It was right. It was.* Only now did he understand himself that night at Franklin.

Judge Hooper excused himself, and left the parlor. Daniel was bidding Mrs. Hooper good bye when the judge returned to stand in the hallway. He followed Daniel out onto the porch, closing the door behind him, and Daniel felt a packet being placed in his hands.

"These," Judge Hooper said, "were among Stark's belongings found in his baggage and returned to us." All formality sank from the courteous voice. "I think you'd better have them, late as it is . . . . We're dreadfully sorry. You've been generous, which is more than I could say for my own son." Daniel, dumb-founded, saw the pained eyes close and open. "Perhaps you'd better see for yourself, Daniel. Open it."

Daniel slid the loose string and unwrapped the brown paper. There were letters. All opened. All in Laurel's pretty handwriting, addressed to him. He shuffled them, his eyes swallowing the dates. Some the first year of the war. Some for every year. Some bearing Franklin postmarks. Last of all, he found a daguerreotype of Laurel.

"She's home now, Daniel. Old Mack is building a little cottage for her. Haven't you been out there?"

"No . . . sir. There's been no time, and a lot has happened since these letters were written."

"It is my conservative opinion," Judge Hooper said, "that mere assumptions are generally unreliable."

Daniel felt incapable of effort. It must have

been several moments later when he heard the door open and close softly. He was alone on the cool porch. Abruptly he went down the steps to the shaded street and struck out in the long-swinging walk of a rifleman in the Army of the Tennessee. When he reached the edge of town, he was trotting.

The hammering and sawing behind the grove of trees was still going on when Daniel turned into the lane. Beyond the ruins of the house a much smaller one was nearing completion. It was already roofed and sided, with a tidy front porch. Daniel could hear a rackety banging inside. In the front yard a Negro was cutting boards laid across two sawhorses. He glanced up, put down his saw, and smiled broadly. It was old Mack.

"Well, I know Miss Laurel's here this time," Daniel said.

Mack shook his head, amused. "She ain't ag'in. Took herself a ride out to dat spooky ol' Indian mound."

"Indian mound?" Daniel repeated, looking in that direction.

"Hit's shorter across de pasture," Mack said. "A heap shorter, if you is in a hurry."

"Reckon I am, Mack."

The way seemed endless because of the open country and the lateness of the warm afternoon.

When the forested persimmon ridge and the rounded hump of Indian mound stood out and he did not see her, he decided that she had taken the road home.

Walking slower, he rounded the sloping end of the ridge and saw the mound on his right. Time and spring foliage had healed in some degree the slashed stretch by the little brook where the bushwhackers had felled the handsome oaks; by this time the stumps did not look so rawly yellow. But the destructive gap was still a kindling sore to remembering eyes. He turned to look at the spring. No one was there.

Scowling impatience, he tramped over to the spring. It was the same, as clear and unspoiled as ever. He could hear its tiny voice laughing over rounded stones where it became a stream, and he could see whorls of golden sand and nests of small pebbles on the bottom, turned gem-like by the slanting sunlight. Picking up a nugget of stone, he flipped it into the water and watched its languid descent.

An acute thirst seized him. He knelt on hands and knees, drinking deeply, and the water tasted cool and sweet. He raised up and wiped his dripping face with his sleeve, his senses lulled. And then, crouched there, he saw the surface of the spring change, suddenly transformed. He was seeing a face. It was wavering and illusive and strange, shimmering and yet not strange as it smiled at him. He whirled to his feet, too astonished to speak.

"I saw you from the ridge," Laurel said.

"You . . . you come out here alone?"

"Often. There's nothing to be afraid of here."

He took off his forage cap. His straight black hair, uncut for weeks, hung long down his neck. "How are you?" he asked.

"Fine," she said, and it reached him in a wild crashing of thoughts that he remembered her dark-green riding habit and the feathered hat from long ago. Somehow she looked subtly changed, more even than he had glimpsed at Franklin, and he began to see why. Laurel wasn't a girl any more. She had grown into a woman.

"I want to thank you," he said, "for going over to see my mother."

"I was glad to."

So far he had spoken the obvious things. Now he gestured about, a wrought-up motion. "See what the bushwhackers did? Where they cut down those great old trees? Do you know what happened here, Laurel?"

"Mack told me."

"Justin helped whip them," he said. "We all did. Neighbors from both sides." He shook his head in bewilderment, partly in bitterness, too. "Then we had to go on and finish the war."

"That was necessary, too," she said gently.

He continued, more harshly than before. "Do

you know that my regiment, the Forty-Fourth Missouri, fought Justin's regiment at Franklin? Do you know that the local Union company was engaged on the pike, right there in front of the farmhouse where Justin fell? Tim Forehand as well?" His sense of guilt pressed so mightily that it was all he could do to meet her eyes.

"What are you trying to tell me, Daniel?" she asked. "I know all that." As she spoke the years rolled back, when they were quite young, and she was striving to reassure him while they sat back there on the ridge and Justin strolled in the distance.

He said: "I want to get every bit of this out of me, once and forever, before I. . . ." He broke off.

"Before what, Daniel?"

He had moved nearer without knowing he had. Laurel said nothing. She came to him, instead, and lifted her face for him, and he kissed her and held her with his rough hands. "I was afraid you wouldn't come back," she said.

All around them, Daniel seemed to see a wonderful light shining over the springtime land, glowing and peculiar to the eye, making everything mysterious and, he knew also, real.